Maria Louise Pool

Against Human Nature

A Novel

Maria Louise Pool

Against Human Nature
A Novel

ISBN/EAN: 9783337032081

Printed in Europe, USA, Canada, Australia, Japan

Cover: Foto ©Andreas Hilbeck / pixelio.de

More available books at **www.hansebooks.com**

A Novel

BY

MARIA LOUISE POOL

AUTHOR OF

"DALLY" "OUT OF STEP" "THE TWO SALOMES"
"MRS. KEATS BRADFORD" ETC.

NEW YORK

HARPER & BROTHERS PUBLISHERS

1895

CONTENTS

AGAINST HUMAN NATURE

I

A LETTER

SHE was hurrying along the road with her shawl wrapped so closely about her that her thin shoulders, with their sharp bones, were defined so plainly that one could not help being sorry for her.

Her shawl was striped blue and white, the blue having gone into the white and the white into the blue on that occasion, long ago, when its owner tried the experiment of washing the garment.

She always said she "guessed she made a mistake in puttin' sody into the water, but she shouldn't make the same mistake again ; there was that much about it."

She wore a black straw hat with what was called a "dish brim." This brim made an excellent shade now over the upper half of her face. Only the narrow chin and small mouth were in the sunlight. This light revealed relentlessly the two long wrinkles, one on each side of the mouth, and the sagging of the cheeks which begins to come soon after middle age. Where is the patent-medicine man who will take away that last dreadful sign of the years from the aging woman? In doing that he will seem to annihilate time, and will also become fabulously rich.

Not that Almina Drowdy would have employed any such

means. She would have said that the Lord had seemed to make women on purpose to grow old, 'n' she didn't reckon she was so foolish as to try to stop the Lord's work. She'd had her time of being young and not being exactly a fright either, and what were you to expect?—that you'd have more'n one chance in this world? And now Miss Drowdy had come to a dish hat and a faded shawl, and to a sublime unconcern as to how her dress "hung."

The road stretched out white and dusty before her; it looked as if it would never end. But Miss Drowdy knew that just beyond the farther clump of white birches there was a turn, and beyond the turn there was a house. It was to this place that she was going.

She glanced up at the sun. Then she walked faster still.

"I hadn't ought to have come out," she thought; "'n' my bread a-rising. Well, if I have to eat sour bread it's my own lookout. I ain't got no men folks, thank the Lord, to find fault!"

Before she reached the corner she put her hand down suddenly to her skirt, and then stooped still lower till she touched the bottom of her deep pocket. She pulled out a letter and looked at it.

"It'd been a great joke if I'd got the wrong one," she said, "I have so many," with a laugh that softened the lines in her face wonderfully, and gave some hint of what the face had been fifteen or twenty years ago.

Five minutes later she had opened the outer back door of a little house which had so long an "L" that it was a great deal more L than house. But by this time the visitor had carefully dropped all appearance of hurry; she entered leisurely.

"That you, Alminy?"

The question was put by a woman who sat in a low rocker by the north window.

This woman was sewing buttons on the vamps of shoes with a rapidity that made the very air twinkle about her. Her needle and thread hesitated for the briefest space as she spoke, then they went on again.

"Yes," said the caller, "it's me — I should think, Livy, you'd about perish with them buttons. How many has the baby swallered this morning?"

The hand of the woman addressed flashed out to the length of a long, new needleful. She held the hand suspended as she answered :

"I do hope and believe it ain't got to any of um so far to-day. But they ain't seemed to hurt him a mite."

"No," said Alminy, "they agree with him first - rate. I d'know but shoe-buttons are better'n milk for children of his age."

"You always make fun of everything, Alminy," said the other, reproachfully.

"Do I? Well, I'm thankful I can make fun," was the response. "The land knows there's no need of trying to be solemn in this world."

After this there was a silence for several minutes, during which the new-comer watched her sister intently. For the two women were sisters, though there was not even a "family look" in common between them.

"I s'pose there ain't any news, is there?" at last asked Olivia.

Almina hesitated slightly before she replied, but her companion did not notice the hesitation.

"I had a letter yesterday," she said, finally, "and I didn't sleep a wink last night."

"Mercy sake!" exclaimed Olivia, "I didn't know as you was correspondin' with anybody."

"No more I ain't."

Olivia waited ; but she kept on working as she waited. She knew that her sister would tell her news when she was ready to tell it, and that she would not tell it before. She had learned long ago that "it was no use to waste breath questioning Alminy."

At last she glanced at her companion. She saw that her sister's gaze was fixed in an unseeing way upon the window. She saw also that the hard, rough hands were clasped tightly on the gingham apron which Almina had neglected to take off before she started from the house. In her anxiety Olivia could not sew fast enough. Her thimble presently caught in her thread; she gave the thread a twitch and broke it. She began to be afraid that the man would come for the case of shoes before they were finished. She wished that Almina would speak; or else she wished she had stayed at home.

Finally Olivia's patience gave out. She tried to thread her needle and could not.

"I'll bet a dollar I've broken the eye to this needle!" she exclaimed. "That last paper wasn't worth a cent."

"I wouldn't let Freddy git to the needles," said Almina, rousing, "they might not be as good for him as buttons. I s'pose some things are really better for a baby's inside than others."

The speaker laughed nervously.

Olivia's eyes flashed with annoyance. She wanted to ask her sister to stop being so provoking, but she shut her lips tightly and did not speak.

In a moment Almina rose from her chair and began walking about the room. She took off her hat and threw it on the table. There were wrinkles of excitement upon her forehead, which was still delicate and almost handsome, with its soft hair, which would "ring up," lying loosely about it. She would have scoffed at the idea, but she was still an interesting woman; that is, many a stranger would have been likely to think so, but here in her native village no one thought anything about her, save that she was an old maid and lived by herself, with money enough to support her in that small way which called for a very little sum per week.

Almina paused at length by her sister's chair.

"I s'pose you remember Roger Crawford, don't you, Livy?"

Olivia put down her shoe, and looked up with wide-open eyes.

"Oh, Alminy!" she cried, "of course I remember him.

But I didn't know but you'd forgotten him. I hoped you had."

"Forgotten him!" repeated Almina. "That ain't likely. But I must own I ain't thought of him so much late years. God does let time, as it goes on, do something for us. If He didn't I d'know what we should do."

The speaker's hands were hanging beside her; they were shut fast as hands involuntarily shut at some intolerable memory.

Olivia reached forward and took one of those hands in both of her own. The buttons fell rattling on the floor from her lap as she did so.

"More buttons for Freddy," Almina said, a flash of fun coming to her gray eyes; but the fun subsided instantly.

"You don't mean you've heard from him?" asked Olivia, keeping hold of her sister's hand.

"Oh no; no indeed. But I've heard from his daughter."

"Then he's dead?"

"I don't know. Read that, then tell me what you think. I'm sure I don't know what to think myself."

Miss Drowdy drew the letter from her pocket and tossed it into her sister's lap. Then she began walking about the room again. Her lips were pressed tightly together; the lines on her forehead were still more marked; the darkness under her eyes was heavier.

But still there was a curious kind of triumph in her aspect—a triumph as of one who has again wakened from half a life into a life containing more than the sordid every-day cares. Suffering might be life, but torpor was not, even though it might be mistaken for peace.

Olivia was not, as she would have said, much used to reading writing. She held the sheet in both hands, and held it far from her, though she had not come to spectacles, and could see perfectly well. Somehow she could not quite bring her mind to the written words. She was thinking of Roger Crawford. The thought of him had not crossed her mind for years. Now it seemed to her that she recalled everything about him "in a flash."

Roger and Almina had certainly been what is called "in love" with each other, and see how it all turned out! Olivia did not understand anything about being in love, and therefore she did not in the least believe in any such state. It was unnatural and really quite indelicate for a woman to feel anything more than respect and a moderate liking for a man.

If it had not been for that affair with Roger, and for the fact that Almina had a silly streak of sentimentality in her somewhere, she might have married Dr. Newcomb ten years ago, and been living now in that brick-ended two-story house right in the middle of the village.

Dr. Newcomb had lost his wife, and Almina Drowdy was his first choice for his second partner.

Olivia, comfortably married and settled, had argued and pleaded with her sister to become Mrs. Newcomb.

"There ain't a thing against the doctor," she said. "You can't say, Alminy, as there's a thing against him ; now, can you ?"

"Why, no, of course I can't. Who said there was ?" had been the response.

Olivia had gazed despairingly at her sister.

"And you like him, don't you ?"

"Yes, indeed."

"Then why don't you marry him ?"

At this point in every conversation Almina had laughed in the most irritating way as she answered,

"I don't know as it's any reason why I should marry a man because there isn't anything against him, and because I like him. I know half a dozen men in this village whom there isn't anything against, and whom I like."

"But they don't want to marry you," said her sister.

"No, they don't, and that's a fact. So that puts them out of the question."

And then Almina had laughed again, and her sister had

sighed and said that there wa'n't no use ; Alminy was jest as odd as she could be.   And she had added, warningly,

"You know you're growin' older every day. The men 'll be lookin' for younger women. You can't expect many more chances."

"I know it," was the reckless response.

In her secret heart Olivia had wondered if Roger Crawford, or rather the memory of him, had had anything to do with making Almina so odd.   But Almina had been a little odd always, and of course she would grow more and more so, since she refused "to settle."   What could you expect of a woman who deliberately refused to settle?   And there was but one way made known whereby a woman could settle.

All these thoughts and memories were in a jumble in Olivia's mind as she sat there with the shoe vamps about her, trying to read the letter her sister had given her.

She turned over the sheets and looked at the name signed.   She read it aloud.

"Temple—Temple Crawford.   What's that mean? That ain't no kind of a name.   Is it a girl?   What makes you think it's a girl?"

" I think so from the letter," answered Almina.

She stopped her walk in front of her sister.

" Temple was Roger's mother's maiden name.   I s'pose that's why he named his daughter so.   He thought a lot of his mother."

The tones of the speaker were so different from her ordinary voice that Olivia looked up at her in a kind of fright.

"Here," she said, extending the paper, " I wish you'd read it.   'Taint very plain writing.   I s'pose you've made it out once, 'n' you can agin.   Jest read it to me, will you?"

Almina took the letter, and, still standing, read it aloud.

" *To the one who was Almina K. Drowdy, of Hoyt, Massachusetts.*

"DEAR MADAME,—I had a letter from father last night. He said he thought he should be dead by the time I got it.   He went to Manitoba for his health almost a year ago, and I haven't seen him since.

You see, I don't know which to tell first, for I'm not used to writing, and my pen won't say anything I want it to. I'll write just as things come into my head. I'm a girl, though folks don't seem to think so when they just hear my name without seeing me. My grandmother was a Temple ; my father always said that there wasn't any better name under the canopy. So he named me that. It doesn't make any difference to me. My father was a queer kind of man. I reckon I love him, because he's my father ; but I get along mighty well without him. And I do as I please now, and I make Sally do as I please, and Bartholomew. You ought to see Sally ; but then you will see her, of course, when you come down. Here is the check that father sent for you to come down with. You see your name is on it. He wrote he was sure you'd come just the same without the check if you had means ; but he didn't know whether you had means or not. He wanted me to be sure and tell you that I needed you. He said that would be enough for you. But he's just plumb mistaken about one thing ; I don't need you one bit. I'm getting along splendid. I ride horseback most of the time. Some days I ride for hours without meeting up with a single solitary soul. I like it. I always have some of my dogs with me, and Little Bull would just as lief take a piece out of the calf of a man's leg as swallow the liver wing of a roast chicken. So, you see, I needn't be afraid as long as Little Bull is with me. He's a common yellow dog, but I know you'll like him when you get acquainted with him. That is, if you ain't one of the fool kind of folks who are afraid of dogs anyway. If you are afraid you'll be bowdaciously sorry you came here, for there are more dogs than people here, and I'm glad of that. Bowdacious is one of Sally's words, and I think it's excellent. It's so expressive. I like words that mean something. But father's always tried to have me talk what he calls English. If he's really dead I reckon I ought to try more than ever to talk English. I can talk it well enough if I want to. How my pen does go on ! But I knew it was just no use at all for me to try to write as the Complete Letter-writer instructs. I wouldn't write that a-way if I died for not doing it.

"I want you to address me like this : Miss Temple Crawford, Busbee, North Carolina. That's three miles away, and part of it on the State road, and the State road isn't much fun ; but I ride to Busbee two or three times a week, and I shall go every day when it's time to begin to expect to hear from you. You must tell me when you think you'll arrive. You are to stop at Asheville Junction, and not go on to Asheville, you know. I'll be there with the wagon. If you are afraid of dogs I wouldn't advise you to think of coming at all. If you do come, and turn out to be the kind I like, I shall be powerful glad to have you here.   With great respect,

"I remain your obedient servant,

"TEMPLE CRAWFORD."

"Postscriptum.—I wrote this letter three days ago, and now, when I come to read it over, I'm afraid I haven't said enough about your coming. And I've read father's letter over again, and there are these sentences in it. It seems to me somehow you ought to know these sentences: 'Tell Almina Drowdy that if she has not forgotten the old days —if she really cared as she thought she cared, and as I, too late, found that I cared—she will come to my daughter. That is all I ask. When she knows Temple she will decide whether to take her home to New England. But first, she must see the child in her own home. She will not be likely to understand the girl otherwise. And she must understand her before she judges her.'

"I don't know what this means, but perhaps you do. It sounds sentimental to me, and if there was ever anything that father was not it was that. Don't forget to let me know, so I can be at the Junction with the wagon and the mules."

Almina stopped reading. Her hand dropped, with the sheets held tightly.

It is impossible to tell how very strangely this epistle had sounded in that prim, decorous little New-England room.

Olivia pushed the remaining vamps from her lap in her helpless astonishment.

"Mercy, Alminy!" she exclaimed in a half-whisper. Then, as her sister did not speak, she added, in the same voice: "You ain't thinkin'—it ain't crossed your mind to think of such a thing as—as goin', has it?"

The two sisters stared at each other. But in truth Almina did not see her companion in the least, though her eyes were fixed upon her. She was thinking with that vague intentness which is, after all, but a phase of memory. She was seeing herself at twenty years. She was wondering why she did not feel older now.

"Say," began Olivia, "you ain't goin' to tell me that you have got the slightest idea—why, it's out of all sense! It's jest outrageous! I sh'd like to know what Roger Crawford was thinkin' about. I declare I should!"

The other woman tried to rouse herself.

"What?" she asked.

"You ain't been listenin' a natom," remarked Olivia, with some resentment mingled with her alarm.

"Well, no, I haven't.   But you needn't be mad about it," was the answer.

Almina looked down at the letter, which she now carefully folded.

"I'm all worked up," remarked Olivia, "and it's so sudden, too."   She tried to speak calmly.

"Most things that we don't know anything about are kind of sudden," said Almina.

She turned and sat down in a chair near.   She bent forward, and rested her chin on her two hands.   She was never conventional about anything, even her attitudes, and this lack of conventionality had always worried her sister.   What could be expected of a woman who had refused to marry a man when she had nothing against him ?

In her secret heart Olivia was convinced that such a woman was liable to do almost any strange and monstrous thing.

Olivia glanced at her sister.   She tried to speak meekly as she said that "she s'posed when the time come that Alminy would tell what she thought of a letter like that.   As for her, Olivia Wilson, she was free to say it was the strangest thing she ever seen.   How old was that girl, that Temple Crawford, anyway ?"

"I don't know."

"Ain't you any idea ?"

"No, of course not."

Almina sat up straight.   Her face had such an unusual expression upon it that her sister was really frightened.   She rose and moved to the door.   With her hand on the latch, she said she would get a few drops of red lavender and some water.   It didn't make much matter what kind of a spell was coming on ; red lavender was good for all spells, whatever their nature.

Almina burst into a laugh, rose, and went to her sister's side.   She put one hand on Olivia's shoulder.

"I do wish I believed in red lavender as much as you do, Livy," she exclaimed. "But I don't need any now."

"Can't you relieve my mind, Alminy?" wistfully asked the other.

"If I could relieve my own mind I'd relieve yours," was the answer.

"I shouldn't think you'd give such a matter a thought."

"Well, I do. I laid awake all last night givin' it thoughts."

"Oh, Alminy!"

Olivia's comely, unwrinkled face began to pucker as if its owner were about to cry.

"But how can you go?" she asked, despairingly. "You can't leave your hens or your pig; 'n' you live so far off 'taint handy for my husband to do your chores."

"You could take my hens, 'n' you could eat my pig," replied Almina.

Olivia now began really to weep.

"So you are goin'!" she cried. "'N' North Caroliny's a dretful place. 'N' Freddy'll grow up, 'n' you won't know any of his cunnin' ways."

"Oh dear!" responded Almina. "I told you I ain't made up my mind. I guess I'll go home now 'n' p'raps I shall have some light."

The speaker walked to the door and opened it. She passed through it, and Mrs. Wilson returned to her chair, gathering up the scattered vamps in a confused way. She was "all upset in her mind," as she told herself, and she began to fear seriously that the man would come for the case before they were all buttoned.

She was trying to thread her needle, and failing on account of the blur over her eyes, when she heard a sound in the next room, and in a moment her sister entered again.

She had a child in her arms. This child was rubbing its eyes with its fists, and yawning till one saw the red roof of its mouth and its few milky-white upper teeth.

"What do you think he was doing now?" asked his aunt. "He was off the bed, and had got as far 's the suller door."

The mother sprang up and held out her arms.

"Who left that suller door open?" she exclaimed. "That door 'll be the death of me yet. Somebody's always leavin' of it open. Give him to me. It's no use for me to try to git that case of shoes done, for I can't do it."

Almina put Freddy in his mother's lap, and now really started for home. She turned when she was in the yard to look back. She saw Olivia rocking back and forth with her boy's head on her shoulder. Olivia did not see her sister at all. It was as if she had forgotten her.

"Why should not I go?" was the question in the woman's mind. "Livy has Freddy. I'm glad she's got him. And I—why," with a smile, "I've got my hens and my pig. I ought to have had a dog. Yes," beginning to walk very fast, "there wa'n't only one reason why I shouldn't have had a dog—and that was 'cause I should have got to lovin' it so. It's such a foolish thing to git to lovin'—now," with another smile, "there ain't no such danger 'bout hens and a pig; though I did hear of a woman that set an awful store by a hen. But, as for me, the way a hen 'll pull up one leg out of sight, look at you with one eye, and wink upward, 's enough for me. I can't love a hen."

Nevertheless, when Almina Drowdy reached her own home she went to the barn and took some corn in her apron. She flung this corn about in the yard, calling in a high voice as she did so, "Cut, cut, cut!" and the white Brahma hens began to gather, picking up the corn so fast that their bills on the gravel made a noise like falling hail.

Almina's face settled into a deep gravity as she watched them.

"Livy's got enough," she said aloud. "I could give 'em to old Widder George. Yes, I could do that. But I'd give the pig to Freddy, 'n' he could call it his."

The woman turned from the flock of eager fowls. She looked over the fields upon which the early spring sun was shining. The meadow opposite was beginning to show green places; the clumps of young willows—which ought to be rooted out—were revealing in their slender stems that the sun had come again to the north. There was a smell of warm, wet earth in the air. Almina sniffed that odor. She didn't believe the ground smelled like that anywhere else in the world.

She shook the last kernel of corn from her apron. She felt the letter from Carolina in her pocket. She knew that she longed to see Temple Crawford.

"She ain't had no bringin' up," she said, as if to the hens. And then:

"I s'pose I could let my house, somehow."

A fever seemed to have entered into her blood. She did not know that she had already decided to go to Carolina. She did not know it even the next day, when her sister came over early in the morning to inquire. She told Olivia that she couldn't seem to make up her mind. Sometimes she was drawn one way and sometimes another. She couldn't see her path clear.

"Can't see it clear?" cried Livy. Then she stopped. What was the use? It was incredible to her that her sister could give a thought to a letter like that.

She looked around the room, as if in search of some means by which she could impress upon Almina the strangeness of her even considering such a request from Roger Crawford's daughter.

She had never quite understood about Crawford. She was three years younger than her sister, and had been not quite eighteen when the affair happened. It had not been considered necessary to inform her in regard to any of the particulars. She only knew that Almina had been ready to be married, and that she did not marry. Crawford did not come. Instead there came a letter from him somewhere in the South where he had to go on business. Almina had received the letter the day before the date set for the wedding. She had gone up-stairs to her own room to read it. After a while she had come down to the kitchen, where her mother and Olivia were. No one had been surprised that a letter should arrive; there had been one nearly every day since Roger had gone, six weeks before.

Olivia remembered to the minutest detail all concerning that time. But no one told her anything. When she had asked her mother what was the matter, she had been answered that "things have turned out so's there 'ain't goin' to be any wedding. Other arrangements have been made."

And that was all. Naturally she had almost forgotten Roger Crawford in all these years. But now she recalled him, and hated him with renewed freshness, as with the thought of him came the memory of what her sister's face had been then, and for long after.

But Almina had borne up bravely. She had informed her friends that the engagement was broken, and when asked where Mr. Crawford was she had replied that he was obliged to stay in the South. She did not even specify that he was in North Carolina. But every one knew he was there, for the woman who kept the post-office saw that his letters of late had been postmarked at Asheville, and as she knew, therefore a great many others knew, for what post-mistress is going to keep to herself a knowledge so valuable?

But no one was aware of one fact which Almina communicated to her mother that night. Mrs. Drowdy was a woman not given to the expression of affection. But she loved her children, though she never caressed them, and seemed to think that caresses were an infallible sign of what she would have called "flatness."

It was in the middle of the night that she had risen noiselessly and gone into her daughter's room. She found the girl lying perfectly still upon her bed. Mrs. Drowdy extinguished the light she carried, and laid herself silently down by her child. She put out her hand and groped for her daughter's hand, and, having found it, she lay motionless.

It was a long time before Almina spoke. At first she felt something like resentment that any one, even her mother, should intrude upon the solitude which just then was the only thing she wished for.

But at last she spoke.

"Mother," she said in a whisper, "I did not tell you all the letter said."

A pause, during which Mrs. Drowdy did not speak. She only held the hand more closely.

"He is married already."

"What!"

Mrs. Drowdy started up to a sitting posture. In the darkness her face grew purple with the anger that surged up to her brain. This was even worse than she had thought. It had even come to her mind that perhaps things might be explained, and the marriage take place, though she felt that she, herself, could never forgive Roger Crawford, and never wanted to see him. But she had decided that she would appear to forgive him for her child's sake.

"Yes," said the girl, "he was married four days ago. He wrote to me right away after—after—"

Almina's voice stopped.

Mrs. Drowdy waited a moment before she said, in a dry, even voice:

"He is a scamp, and you are well red of him. You'll live to see the day when you'll despise him, 'n' thank the Lord you ain't his wife."

"I wish I could despise him now," said the girl.

The next moment she cried out in a passionate voice: "Oh, how can I stop loving him! It will kill me to go on loving him like this!"

"No," said the mother, sternly, "it won't kill you, either. I know 'bout human nature. Things don't kill. I'm goin' to try to think of something to take up your mind."

"Neither mother nor daughter slept that night; but they did not talk any more, save for a single word now and then.

When Mrs. Drowdy, in the early dawn of a summer morning, went back to the room where her husband was now dressing, she was met by the anxious question,

"How's Alminy?"

"I guess she's as well's she can be. That vile wretch is married to somebody else. He told her so in his letter."

Benjamin Drowdy did not speak, but he looked murderous. His wife went on.

"I hope you c'n spare the money to let her go to her Aunt Johnson's for a few months. It 'll be a great change ; and Cordelia Johnson is a good woman, and a wise woman, if she is my sister. Everything 'll be new. Alminy 'll begin to git interested after a while."

Mr. Drowdy did spare the money. The Johnsons lived in Boston, and they had money enough to travel a little when they chose. Almina spent nearly a year with them. When she came home she looked so well that everybody said that Alminy Drowdy was gittin' over her disappointment first-rate. They guessed she hadn't much deep feelin' after all.

Olivia Wilson felt her hatred for Roger Crawford revive as she gazed at her sister in consternation that Almina could feel anything but repulsion at the thought of Crawford's daughter. And what a letter that girl had written.

"I'm supprised," said Olivia, "that you don't dislike even the thought of Temple Crawford."

"Why should I dislike her?" Almina fixed her clear gray eyes on her sister's face.

"Why? Because—because — why, I never seen nothin' so outrageous. And the way that man treated you! Of course he never loved you !"

"I know he didn't treat me well," was the response, "but I think he loved me ; and "—here the woman's voice changed greatly—"I've decided that I've loved him all these years."

"Oh, Alminy !"

This was what Olivia always said when other words failed her. She made up her mind then and there that she would not speak another word on the subject of her sister's going to Carolina. But she broke her resolve so far as to say in a melancholy manner a few days later that she didn't see how Alminy could go away when Freddy hadn't half got through having such cunnin' ways.

But Almina did go. She gave the hens to the Widow George and the pig to Freddy. She found a woman to live in her house until it could be let, and in one week from the time she had received Temple Crawford's letter she was in Mr. Wilson's open wagon, and he was driving her to the station to take the cars that connected with the Fall River boat to New York.

Her sister, having left Freddy in charge of a neighbor, was sitting on the back seat with her, and was crying gently and exasperatingly all the way.

Once Mr. Wilson looked back over his shoulder and asked with an impatience which he could not restrain:

"Livy, ain't you 'bout cried 'nough? This ain't Alminy's funeral—nor mine, neither."

Olivia tried to speak steadily as she answered that it might's well be a funeral fur's her feelin's were concerned.

Almina herself was not gay, but she cheerfully prophesied that Freddy would take up his mother's mind.

"And you know I sh'll write real often," she added. "Besides, I may come back any time."

But Almina could not help crying when she hugged her sister at the station before the cars came.

"If I should happen to stay a good while," she said, brokenly, "don't let Freddy forget me."

"No, no, I won't," sobbed Olivia, and the train rolled along, and seemed to sweep up Almina Drowdy into itself, and then dash off again.

"I can't seem to make it seem real," said Olivia, as she and her husband drove back along the familiar country road.

"Then if you can't I do wish you'd stop cryin'," said Mr. Wilson. "I'm awful sorry myself she's gone, 'n' I think it's a fool's errand. But Alminy's old enough to do what she pleases. Now, do cheer up, Livy."

So Olivia gradually cheered up, and by the time she was back again with Freddy she had begun to be reconciled.

And the neighborhood, after it had raked up that affair

2

about Roger Crawford and talked it all over again, subsided with perfect calmness into the habit of seeing some one else in Almina's house and in her pew at church.

Almina herself could hardly have had a more strange feeling if she had suddenly cut adrift from this planet and had taken passage for Mars.

But she did not regret. With every hour that passed her mind turned more and more strongly from the place she had left, and towards the place to which she was journeying.

She believed that she was a hard-hearted wretch, because she did not think more of her sister and of Freddy. Here she smiled.

"Is it possible," she asked herself, "that I'm going where I sha'n't know how many shoe-buttons Freddy swallers, nor how many times the cat scratches him?"

Almina had never been out of Massachusetts, therefore even the houses of Fall River, as seen in the spring twilight, had a foreign look, and she already felt as if she were in a strange land.

When she walked over the planking that led to the steamer she could hardly believe she was in America. Without really having given any thought to the matter, she now knew that she had expected this craft to be a kind of ferry.

There was a crowd of people. Somehow she was pushed along into a dim, electric-lighted place where women were sitting on magnificently upholstered couches, and where negro men in blue uniforms occasionally walked through, their feet making no noise on the thick carpet. There was a gentle motion ; there was the sound of wheels outside hurrying along the wharf, the cries of drivers, the ringing of engine-bells, and presently a voice somewhere shouted :

"All ashore 't's goin' ashore !" and then the enormous bulk that was the steamboat became possessed of a little more motion.

Almina all at once was conscious of a choking sensation. Hardly knowing what she did, she rose and hurried out through the large doors by which she had entered the ladies' cabin. She was possessed by a longing to see her country again.

She stepped outside, not minding who pushed against her.

There were the shores of Massachusetts sliding away from her. Her hands held tightly the package of lunch which her sister had carefully put up for her. It was not yet dark. The sun had gone down, but there was a cool, apple-green tinge over the west. The air from the land blew in a steady, chill breath.

Almina shivered. She did not know that there were tears on her face.

But when she turned to go back to the cabin it was curious that she was not thinking about leaving home. The words in her mind were:

"I do wonder why I always think of Roger as a young man," and her thought added, coldly, "Mebby he's dead; yes, I s'pose he's dead."

But no tears came. Strangest of all was the fact that from the moment she had contemplated this journey she had felt as if she were young again. She scoffed at this thought, but she could not quite put it away from her. Going by a large mirror she accidentally looked at herself.

"Oh, goodness me!" she exclaimed in a whisper, as she saw the middle-aged face. "I guess I ain't so young that everybody 'll be fallin' in love with me on this journey."

She sat down on one of the gorgeous chairs and forced herself to eat a doughnut, although swallowing a morsel seemed wellnigh impossible.

The stewardess came and asked her if she had a stateroom.

"I don't think I have," she answered.

The black woman replied that she would probably know it if she did have one.

"Yes," said Almina, with a nervous laugh, "just the same 's I'd know if I had a bandbox or an umbrella, I s'pose."

The attendant moved away, and presently Almina saw her

talking and laughing with a yellow man in a blue coat, and nodding towards her.

The night passed somehow. She spent it lying motionless on a mattress on the floor of the cabin, in a row of other mattresses and other women. Two or three times in the dim light she saw a black man stepping along between the beds. But no one seemed to mind him.

And in the morning there was New York. She was out on deck before the sun was up. She did not feel like crying now. The new day, the magnificent picture of the city that lay, calm and still, under the crimsoning sky, held her gaze. The glitter of the water, the white paths left by the ferry-boats and tugs, the whole effect of superb life not yet awakened for the morning, thrilled and stirred the woman with an emotion she had never felt before.

She wondered how any one could ever think of criticising that figure standing with commanding pose and torch upheld. She remembered having read in a newspaper something derogatory. She supposed there were folks just made to find fault with everything.

When she left the boat which transferred her to Jersey City her mind was strained to the utmost to assure itself that she was actually in the right city and really in the right car. She knew that cars were always being detached and sent off on other tracks, for no other purpose, apparently, than to take people to places where they did not want to go, and to cause them to buy new tickets that they might get back again.

In recalling the remainder of the journey it seemed to Miss Drowdy that she did nothing but ask conductors if it were really true that she was in the right car.

Nothing would convince her that she could ever reach Asheville Junction. She could not give her mind to the strange sights which hour by hour glided by her. Afterwards she remembered them.

She would not take a sleeping-car. Why should she do so, when it was an impossibility for her to sleep a wink?

But she must have been dozing when a woman in a

deep scoop bonnet came and sat down beside her and asked, "Where be yo' from?"

"Massachusetts," said Almina, proudly.

"What township's that?" was the next inquiry; and Almina's pride gave place to pity for one who had never heard of Massachusetts.   Could it be possible?"

The woman had a grimy face with sharp cheek-bones and sunken eyes.   She had a calico bundle which she kept from rolling off her lap with two hands which ended in long, black nails.

. "Gwine fur?" she asked, pleasantly.

"To Asheville Junction."

"So'm I.   It's thur nex' place."

"Is it?" eagerly.   "I must have dropped asleep."

Almina grasped her satchel and sat up rigidly, ready to jump off at an instant's notice.

"Do you know anybody by the name of Crawford?" she asked, after a silence.

The woman ruminated.

"Naw.   Reckon they don't live on thur State road?"

"Oh, I don't know," helplessly.   After this there was silence.

Presently the train began to slow.   Almina stood up in her place.   She forgot her fatigue in her excitement.

It was certainly at Asheville Junction that Temple Crawford had said she would be " with the mules."

II

A HORSEBACK RIDE

ALMINA DROWDY was left standing on the platform at the junction with the woman in the scoop bonnet. There seemed to be nobody else there. A roped and battered trunk had been thrown off. This trunk had just come from New England.

Almina, weary and faint and dazed, looked about her. The great hills standing here and there almost frightened her at this moment. In the distance were blue or cloudy peaks — Almina had lived in a flat country. She could hardly breathe as she looked at these mountains. For an instant she forgot that any one was to meet her.

"Don't you know whar yo' gwine?" asked the other woman, hesitatingly. "'Cos if yo' don't, come 'long of me, an' I'll fry ye some meat an' cakes. You'll be welcome."

The last words with an indescribable drawl.

There was no mistaking the genuineness of this hospitable offer.

Almina turned. She felt so desolate that she tried to draw herself up with pride.

"My friends will come," she answered. Then she choked with sheer homesickness. "You're dretful kind," she added, "but I guess I better wait right here."

She watched the wearer of the scoop as she walked down the yellow road. She went with a slouching, long stride.

Almina turned away and felt more forlorn than ever. She went and sat down on her trunk. She tried not to see the mountains. Nothing should make her remain in such a country as this. Olivia had been right. She ought to have known enough to stay at home.

A long-bearded man followed by two hound dogs came shambling from the other end of the platform. He fixed a contemplative gaze upon the woman sitting on her trunk.

"Waitin'?" he said at last.

"Yes."

Having received this answer, the man shambled into the station. The dogs came up, and carefully and exhaustively sniffed at Almina, then they also went into the station.

Almina gazed feverishly up and down the road which crossed the track and seemed to lead eventually into dreadful mountainous wild spaces.

Within fifteen minutes' time two small loads of wood passed. They were not at all like New England loads.

Almina wished that she had never accustomed herself to drinking coffee, because if she had not done so she would not now suffer so for the want of it.

No mules visible anywhere. There was a white pony with a woman on its back coming at a furious rate along the road at the left hand.

But this pony did not interest Almina in the least. She watched it, however, and very soon it became plain that it was coming to the station.

The animal kept up its headlong speed until the very instant it stopped, and then its rider was apparently discharged from its back, instead of dismounting, as is the custom. She landed on her feet, fortunately, and Almina now saw that she was a girl of twenty, perhaps, though her dress gave a younger appearance. Her skirt was short, of some kind of faded red stuff; she wore a black velvet garment which did not fit, and had the appearance of being really a man's sack-coat. The sleeves were very long and turned up at the wrist, so that the wearer's hands might be unfettered.

These hands were bare, and tanned to the very last degree of brownness. It was a startling thing to see on the left hand a quite magnificent diamond ring. A soft felt hat was on her head.

Brown leather leggings were on this girl's ankles, and

dilapidated congress boots covered her feet. There was a spur attached to one of these boots.

This person advanced straight to the woman sitting on the trunk and stopped before her.

"Almina K. Drowdy?" she said, in an interrogative manner.

Almina jumped up.

"That's my name," she answered.

"I thought you couldn't be anybody else," said the girl; and she added, with the utmost frankness, "I made sure when I was coming down the road there that nobody but a Yankee could sit like that on a trunk."

The Yankee's tired face flushed a little, and the Yankee's eyes darted an unpleasant fire.

"Oh, please don't look that way!" exclaimed the girl. "You'll have to make up your mind not to get mad with me, for if you do you'll be mad most of the time. And really, I'm powerful good at heart."

Here the speaker laughed. She stopped laughing immediately, and looked intently at her companion. She advanced a step nearer.

"I'm going to like you, I do believe," she said, "I'm mighty thankful for that. I was getting along well enough without anybody, though. I reckon you know who I am?"

Almina replied that she could guess, but that she didn't feel called upon to guess.

"Temple Crawford," was the answer. "I'm not much to look at, but there's a most awful lot to me when you come to know me," another laugh.

"I was lookin' for mules," now remarked Almina.

She had entirely forgotten her hunger and her fatigue in her interest in what she privately called "the specimen" before her. She wondered what the people of Hoyt, Mass., would say to this girl.

"For muels?" repeated the girl. "Oh, I know it. I was coming with the muels and the wagon; only when I went to harness I couldn't find the gears—that is, only part of the gears. I got one mule hitched to the wagon, and I had to give it up. Sally was gone, and Bartholomew was gone ; and so there was an end to it, for the gears were gone, too. But Thimble was left. That's my pony. So I saddled and bridled, and I picked up my needles and flew ; and here I am."

It would be quite impossible to imagine any one more free from shyness or embarrassment of any kind than this girl. And yet she did not strike Miss Drowdy as being bold ; only as utterly without self-consciousness. The woman hardly knew whether to be shocked or not.

"You see," remarked Temple, "I didn't put Buncombe County on it."

"What ?"

"Why, Buncombe County on my direction to you when you wrote. But I got your letter all the same. You look about fainted away. I'll make 'em give you some breakfast over yonder. It's a boarding-house. They say the coffee there's enough to make you wish you'd never been born. Come. Your trunk 'll be just as safe if you don't sit on it every minute."

The girl took hold of Miss Drowdy's arm gently and began to walk her across the track towards a two-story house that stood at a little distance.

This house the two entered at the rear door ; and immediately you entered here you felt as if you were in a log-cabin. There was an enormous fire on an enormous hearth, and a general black, dingy look diffused over everything. A bed was in one corner—a bed which still remained as its occupant had left it.

A thin woman in a dark, flapping calico gown came forward from somewhere where there was the sound of frying. She creased her cheeks in the form of a smile as she saw her guests.

"It's yo', is it, Miss Temple?" she said. "Howdy this mawnin'? Set by, won't yo'?"

Almina could not help feeling that she was having a thrilling and unusual experience. In her inmost soul she had never believed that anybody ever said "howdy." She had seen that word in books, and had always considered it a made-up term. Now she had actually heard it.

"I want you to give this lady a breakfast," said Temple. "Give it to her right soon, for she's starving. She's just from Massachusetts."

The woman turned her cadaverous face towards Almina for an instant.

"I've hearn there was such a place," she said, as if she still doubted the fact.

Then she left the room, her petticoats flapping about her ankles.

Almina sat staring into the fire. She did not think now that it made much difference whether she ever had anything to eat or not. She might as well die first as last. And she should never know any more of Freddy's cunning ways.

At this thought she could not help smiling. She looked up and found Temple Crawford's eyes fixed upon her. They were rather unusual eyes, of a golden black, and they were set wide apart, under heavy, straight brows. But the brows were not dark, they were light brown, as was her hair, which was shingled like a boy's.

This close-clipped hair revealed plainly the shape of her head, which was high above the ears, and markedly full also in those regions where phrenologists used to locate the affections and passions. But phrenology is now an exploded science, and this girl's head, perhaps, was no index to her character. It was, nevertheless, somehow a notable head, and now that the drooping felt hat was removed, Almina could not help gazing at it.

"I reckon you're thinkin' about your home?" said Temple, as she caught her companion's glance.

"Yes," was the answer, "and about you, too. You don't look like your father one bit."

The girl advanced and sat down in a chair near Almina,

contemplating her closely. Instead of replying, after a silence she said:

"I think you have awfully good eyes." She sighed heavily. "Too good. And if you stay with me you'll be miserable if I'm not a respectable sort of a girl." Another sigh. "And I'm not. I'm a wild animal, and I like to be. That's the very worst part of it, Miss Drowdy; I like to be a wild animal. I reckon I may get to be kind of a Nebuchadnezzar. He ate grass, didn't he? I sha'n't eat grass. But I don't like folks, and civilization, and smiling when you want to swear, and making believe, and all that kind of thing. Do you, Miss Drowdy?"

"I don't like makin' believe."

"Then you don't like civilization?"

Temple pushed back her chair.

"I smell your fried chicken going to the table, and here comes Mrs. Frady to tell you to go out there and eat."

The girl accompanied the new-comer into the next room, where there was a long table on which were a great many unwashed dishes and an enormous quantity of apple-butter in a big cracked dish. There were denuded chicken-bones here and there among the dishes.

A troop of five dogs came from somewhere unseen, and accompanied the women into this apartment. They were smooth-haired hounds, and they walked about the room with the solemnity of aspect which is peculiar to hounds, raising long, melancholy noses into the air in the direction of the clothless table.

The mistress of the house pointed to a chair, and advised Almina to "dror right urp" in front of a fresh plate of chicken and biscuit.

Almina obeyed. She had no more than drawn up before one of the hounds did the same. He sat down close to her and pushed his nose against her. Another hound immediately stationed himself on the other side. Almina was not afraid, but she did feel somewhat hampered, and found it difficult to bend forward far enough to reach the biscuit.

The mistress hustled a few bones into a soiled plate, then pushed the plate towards her guest. The dish slid along the table and paused near Miss Drowdy.

"Them thur dawgs," said Mrs. Frady, "are everlastin'ly hongry. Jest toss um thur hind-laig of a rooster now an' then, will yo'?" with a laugh, and directing her request to Almina, who immediately seized one bone and then another, which she administered alternately to the hound nearest her. There were two or three crunching movements, and then, as Temple expressed it, they were just as ready for roosters' hind-laigs as they ever were.

"You eat your breakfast and I'll feed the dogs," said the girl.

Meanwhile Mrs. Frady, having dumped the biscuit and chicken and the coffee-pot on the table, had disappeared in some back region, where her flat drawl could be heard in one continuous stream, uninterrupted by the sound of any other voice.

"She's talking to herself," remarked Temple. "She does it all the time, unless she's at her eatin's or her sleepin's."

Almina drank some of the black drink which was called coffee. She choked a little over it. She swallowed some chicken. She had long since passed the stage of hunger, and was now in that state of faintness and fatigue when it seemed to her that she could never eat again.

The five dogs were grouped in a partial circle in front of Temple, who tried to distribute bones impartially, and who administered reproof and reproach when there was too much snatching.

"Now don't you be as greedy as human beings," Almina heard her saying. "Jim, you let Short Tail have this. Stop! You villun, you! I'll pull it out of your mouth! You've had three to Devil's one. Devil, why don't you pitch in 'n' get your share? Jim, you sha'n't have the whole skeleton of that rooster!"

There was a scuffle; growls and yaps, dogs leaping high with front paws extended eagerly; and the girl standing with flushed face and sparkling eyes in the midst, with her hands held up, and a bone in each hand.

Almina hastily pushed back her chair. She felt as if she were in the midst of a dog-fight. There seemed a hundred hounds, all standing on their hind-legs and pawing in the air. They were whining and growling and slobbering. They were making frantic leaps up at the bones, and falling back, sometimes rolling over on their spines with their legs in the air.

"I ain't afraid of dorgs," said Miss Drowdy, "not as a general thing; but I should think that if there was any such thing as ketchin' hydrophoby, why, then, you'd ketch it."

The girl tried to push the animals away from her. She bustled and stamped and drove until she had forced the troop out at the open door.

She came back to Almina's side. There was the sparkle of sheer, soulless animal spirits in her eyes.

"They haven't got hydrophobia, so I can't catch it," she answered. "I suppose they've spoiled your breakfast."

"I found I wasn't hungry, after all," answered Almina. "I guess I'll pay that woman, and then what shall we do? I c'n go 'n' set on my trunk over there to the deepo a spell longer, though 'tain't any great fun."

Temple picked up her hat from the floor. She stood swinging it in her hand and gazing at her guest.

"Do you mean you're going to pay Mrs. Frady? No, indeed. She'd be mad to think of taking pay for any one I brought here. We'll start right away for home. I'm powerful sorry I couldn't come with the muels. You see, Bartholomew's been aiming to have the gears fixed for ages; and I s'pose he has taken them to-day, of all days, and he knew I was coming to meet you. Sometimes I think the whole poor white race might just as well be in Tophet, and be done with them."

Almina felt her face flush and then pale with amazement as she heard the fresh young voice calmly make this remark.

"What?" she asked, with some sternness.

"In Tophet, I said," was the answer.

"Do you think that's pretty talk?"

"Oh, I don't know about that," returned the girl, easily; "it's most mighty true talk, anyway. But there's Sally. You just wait till you've seen Sally."

As Temple ceased speaking she put on her hat with an entire absence of girlish manner, as if she had been a boy.

"Come on," she said. She led the way out of the house by a different door from the one by which the two had entered. Almina hurriedly put on her bonnet as best she could. She caught up her satchel and her umbrella, and hastened after her guide. She found Temple waiting outside. The girl was looking at a river which ran at the very end of the sloping yard. It ran broadly and yet swiftly, under drooping tree branches.

"That's the Swanannoa," said Temple, in a different tone from any her companion had yet heard from her, and which made Almina take a step towards her with a sudden desire to touch the girl caressingly. "I wouldn't give a cent for my life if I had to live it away from a river and from those hills."

As she said the last word Temple snatched off her hat and swung it towards the hills, towering everywhere in the distance; some of them so near, however, that their outlines showed with no veiling and beautifying haze.

She turned towards the woman, who was gazing steadily at her.

"My father used to say," she began, "that everybody was a fool about at least one thing, and ever so many people were fools about everything. He said I was a fool about rivers and mountains. What do you think, Miss Drowdy? What are you a fool about?"

"Everything, I guess."

Almina gave a short, hard laugh, that she might not sob.

What with her fatigue and her coming into such a strange country, and the excitement of meeting Roger Crawford's daughter, and finding her so much different from anything she could possibly have imagined, the Yankee woman found it difficult not to become hysterical. She had often said that if there was one thing she hated it was a "hystericky woman."

"Yes, indeed, everything," she repeated, with an apparently uncalled-for emphasis.

She glanced up to meet Temple's eyes.

"I shouldn't have said that," responded the girl. "But if you stay with me I shall find out." She turned towards the river again, as she continued: "I brought you out at this side of the house so that you could see the Swanannoa. I didn't know but it might sort of rest you to look at it. Running water washes away hate and sorrow and all bad things, you know."

"Does it?"

Almina was sure that she should burst into a violent fit of crying if this thing continued another moment, and she wished that she could stop trying to find some resemblance in Roger's daughter to Roger himself.

"Oh, yes, it does. You'll find it out fast enough. Now let's come."

Temple turned and walked rapidly to the front of the house. The white pony was standing there, its bridle pulled down over its head and twisted about the trunk of a tree.

"Get right on," said Temple; "it's only about four miles, and I can walk well enough."

"Get on where?" asked Almina, desperately.

She was thinking that she would ask when the next train started for Massachusetts, and that she would take that train.

"On Thimble, of course. He's most always gentle. And I shall walk beside you."

"But I can't get on him, and I couldn't ride him if I did."

Almina spoke with such decision that she seemed angry.

The girl faced about and gazed at her. Every woman, old and young, rode among the mountains. What did this mean?

"Anybody can ride Thimble," she said, with some contempt. "He doesn't trot at all."

"What does he do, then?" was the helpless question.

"Why, he paces, and single-steps, and gallops. He's a regular angel of light for a pony. I could go through fire and water on him."

"Well, I can't, and that's the end of that."

Almina turned about and looked for a spot where she might sit down. She again thought of the train for Massachusetts, and calculated how long it would take to get back home. She found the stump of a tree, and placed herself on it.

Temple stood a moment with her hand resting on the hogged mane of her pony. She was gazing at the woman sitting there.

"Your face looks somehow as if you had some will-power," she said, suddenly. "Besides, there isn't a wagon, and horses to go with it, short of about as far as 'twill be to get home. The two that belong here have gone to Asheville; the ones I could get, I mean. I'm going to lead Thimble up to that stump."

Almina could never tell why she rose and clambered on to the stump without another word of remonstrance. She got herself into the saddle in some way. The pony immediately walked across the railroad. Temple walked beside him. The girl contemplated her mounted companion with unaffected solicitude. She had hung the satchel on the pommel. The umbrella Almina still retained in her own hand, and with the same hand she somehow managed to clutch at something—in her confusion she hardly knew what.

"If you'd sit up straight you'd be much more comfortable, besides looking better," remarked Temple, with great frankness.

"Don't talk to me 'bout sitting up straight," was the reply. "I feel 's if I moved a grain I should fall off."

"Now, that's curious," said Temple, seriously. "I didn't know any one could feel that way on a horse's back. It must be a dreadful way to feel."

"Yes, 'tis a dretful way. How fur is it?"

"About four miles. When you let the pony canter a little it 'll be a great relief to you."

Almina held fast to the pommel with one hand, and the horn with the other. Her attendant adroitly caught the falling umbrella.

"I never sh'll canter," said Almina, feebly.

"Why not?" in great astonishment.

"'Cause I'm afraid."

Miss Drowdy did not know herself. She had always believed that she was rather a strong-minded woman. Now she was ready to sob violently, and to plead with this dreadful, tyrannical girl to let her get down to the ground.

"How can you be afraid? What are you afraid of?" asked Temple, who seemed to be actually unable to imagine Almina's state of feeling.

"I d' know," was the answer. "I can't tell whether it's the hoss, or what 'tis."

The girl came nearer and put one hand over the woman's cotton - gloved fingers that were clasped tightly over the horn.

"I reckon you're plum tired," she said, in a low voice.

Almina could not help being moved by that voice. She had never heard one like it; it was fresh and young and clear. But it was not those attributes that moved her. Some one who was more accustomed to the analysis of what puzzled her had decided in her own mind that, young as Temple was, there was a compelling power in her voice that made it more effectual than any mere sweetness.

"I guess I never was much tireder," was the answer; "'n' I'm all bewildered. I ain't used to travellin', and I should think I'd been travellin' for a month."

As Almina spoke in a desolate, dry way, her eyes were fixed on the ring upon the hand which was still pressed tightly over her own.

"Is that a real di'mond?" she asked, presently, in some awe.

Temple raised her hand and turned it so that the jewel sent out sparks of light in the sunshine.

"Real?" she repeated. Then, with a flush all over her face: "Yes, it's as real as the magnificent woman who gave it to me."

"I don't think I ever seen a genuine di'mond before," said Almina. "They be bright, ain't they? So 'twas a present?"

The speaker was really interested in what she was saying; but she was making a great effort to try to detach her mind from the fact that she was on horseback.

"Yes, 'twas a present," replied Temple. "The first time I saw her I happened to be of service to her. I'll tell you about it some time if you care to have me. She took the ring from her finger and gave it to me. I told her I didn't want to be paid. But she said she wasn't paying me; she only wanted me to remember that I had met her. As if I shouldn't remember! Miss Drowdy," with a sudden change of manner, "are you suffering a good deal?"

"Yes, I be!" in an ungovernable outburst, " 'n' I'm goin' to git off of this pony this minute. I won't stand it, 'n' that's a fact! Whoa! Stop! Whoa!"

The pony stopped and turned its head in an inquiring surprise.

Almina slipped off to the ground. She did not find the distance nearly so great as she had expected. When she felt the firm earth under her feet she began to think once more, as she told Temple, that she had a mind of her own, and wasn't quite an idiot. She seized her umbrella and appeared ready to take up a line of march in any direction.

"If anybody uses that pony it 'll be you," she said. "When I know I'm makin' a fool of myself, why it's my own fault if I don't stop it."

Temple took the umbrella from her companion; she strapped that and the satchel on to the saddle. Then she gave the pony a little push as she said: "You'd better go along home, Thimble, before the muels get all the roughness."

The pony tossed up its head, looked around at his mistress, then broke into a little amble up the hill they had commenced to mount.

"I s'pose he knows his way home?" interrogatively remarked Almina.

The girl glanced at her and then laughed. She made no other reply.

The two walked on side by side. In a quarter of an hour they left the public highway and entered upon a mountain wagon-path that curved this way and that constantly, sometimes rising steeply, sometimes almost level.

Temple walked with a free, easy step, her movements unimpeded by the short skirt she wore. She glanced from time to time with a kind of pitying inquiry at the woman near her. She had never seen such a woman before — one who could neither ride horseback nor walk up mountains. That must be a very strange condition of life where one did not ride and did not go up mountains; a very tame condition, indeed, and life could be hardly worth living.

"There seem to be pretty views all round here," said Almina, in a breathless way.

The girl turned again and looked at her. She smiled, but made no attempt at a reply.

Presently she asked Miss Drowdy to sit down on a fallen tree. Miss Drowdy obeyed. She watched the girl step here and there, and finally pause before a small tree, from which she began to cut a slender shoot. She handled her jack-knife with skill, and in a few minutes she had trimmed a staff which she brought to Almina.

"You can use that," she said. "I reckon it's a flat country where you come from. It must be dreadful to live in a flat country. I would rather die."

The two started on again. Almina began to feel that there was no end to these mountain roads, which were only tracks made by the trees having been cut down and carts and horses passing round the stumps until a sort of path had been made. Sometimes they crossed acres of ground where were standing like ghosts groves of dead trees stretching naked branches out into the air. The wind made a strange sound in these branches—a sort of scraping, guttural noise. The ground under the trees was green with springing grain.

With every rod she went Almina made a fresh vow that she wouldn't give in ; that nothing should make her give in. Her back and legs ached, there was a white circle about her mouth, a red spot on each cheek. She put her stick resolutely and fiercely on the ground and endeavored to pull herself along by it.

There were to be four miles of this. Well, she would be dead long before the end of the four miles was reached. It would be a good thing to be dead. She had been a fool to leave her home for the sake of Roger Crawford's daughter. She almost began to doubt if this were his daughter.

She paused, leaning on her stick and panting. Her companion paused also, and gazed at her.

"I s'pose you be really his child, ain't you?" she asked when she could command her voice.

The girl's eyes opened still wider.

"His, you know," went on the woman, nervously—"Roger's. It all seems so strange ; 'n' I'm kinder turned round in my mind. Bein' in them cars so long, 'n' then meetin' you, 'n' findin' you so—so sort of dif'runt."

"So different?"

"Yes, indeed. I guess you'd think so if you could see yourself in that red skirt, 'n' that velvet co't, 'n' that hat, 'n' them leggin's, 'n' that sharp thing on your heel "—here a pause and a quick-drawn breath before Almina continued in a sharp whisper—"'n' that hat that ain't like any hat I ever seen under the canopy. Folks wouldn't think you was a good girl if you wore that hat up in Hoyt."

Temple put her hand up to her head ; she glanced down at her feet and her skirt; then she flung back her shoulders.

"But I'm not up in Hoyt," she answered.

The woman still leaned on her stick ; her prim dress looked very strange by the side of her guide, and somehow out of place among these trees.

"And you be really Roger's daughter ?" repeated Almina. There was a wistful tremor all over her tired, thin face.

She felt that, in some mysterious way, she was losing something of the fair romance that for so many years had hung about the thought of her lover.

"Yes," said Temple, "I'm his daughter, the only child he ever had.   I don't see why it seems such a wonderful thing that he should be my father.   There was nothing wonderful about him, anyway.   He was just as selfish as he could be. I reckon that was because he was a man, wasn't it?"

"Why, Temple Crawford !"

"What?"

"To speak so of your father !"

Almina's face became quite firm again in her reproof.

"Well, that's the truth, anyway, and why shouldn't I say it? I know he's my father. If everything went exactly right there never could be any human being more agreeable than he was. But things didn't go exactly right very often. You'd better sit down again, Miss Drowdy. Here's another fallen tree. I s'pose I don't realize that a person can get tired walking among these mountains. We'd better have kept Thimble. Perhaps I can whistle him back. He'll be sure to stop and eat somewhere on the way home."

Almina sat down. She was now in that state of fatigue when she could not hold herself steady, when she was sure she should never be rested again, and never "see things straight."

The girl turned her face up the mountain. She thrust her hands into the pockets of her coat, tipped back her head, and immediately Almina heard a strong, penetrating whistle that sounded along the solitary spaces, carrying far up the acclivity.

Temple wheeled around, still with her hands in her pockets.

"It was wrong for us to let him go," she said again. "But he's almost sure to come back. He's a good fellow, and we understand each other." She sprang forward. "Why, Miss Drowdy, are you as tired as that?"

She knelt down by the woman's side and put her arms about her. Almina smiled feebly and made a great effort. She felt herself in a horrible nightmare from which she could not escape. And Massachusetts so far away!

"I'm kinder used up," she said, faintly.

In spite of herself she let her head drop on the young shoulder near her. But she made a fierce effort to retain her consciousness. She had a feeling that she should never be able to respect herself again if she should faint or do anything like that. "Almina Drowdy faint!"

The sting of this fear roused her a little. But she could not yet lift her head from the shoulder which was held perfectly still.

After a few moments she was able to say in a half-whisper :

"You see, I ain't slep', 'n' I' ain't et ; 'n' I guess I was some excited."

After a pause she added, with a slight and whimsical smile at her own folly :

"They used to call me nervous when I was a girl ; mebby I ain't outgrown it."

Here she tried to raise her head, but a firm hand prevented her. Temple did not speak immediately.

She looked strong and dominant as she knelt there on one knee by her guest.

"I'm afraid I didn't realize that folks could get so tired," she said at last, as if she were making an apology. "Don't move yet. I wish somebody would come along in a wagon. But it isn't in the least likely. There! Don't you hear a horse's step? No? But I do; and it's Thimble's step, light and quick.   There he is!   Dear old fellow!   Sweetest fellow in the world!   Come to your own true-love!"

As she made these exclamations Temple did not rise. She still continued to support Almina.   But she extended one hand.   The pony paused a few paces away, gazing at the group with neck raised and ears pointed sharply forward. After a brief examination he came nearer and fumbled with his lips upon Temple's outstretched hand.

Almina's umbrella and satchel were still strapped to the saddle.   The pony's mouth was green.

"You've been at somebody's new wheat," cried his mistress.

"You must mount again, now," she said, turning to her companion.   "You never can walk the two miles more; and it's up the mountain, too."

Almina did not reply.   She rose, much as if she were about to have a tooth extracted.   She had made up her mind.   And she was ashamed of the weakness she had displayed.   She could not walk.   Therefore she must ride.

The pony was brought up accurately alongside of the tree. Again Almina got into the saddle, and again she did not know how she did it.

The girl walked close by the pony.   So they started. Sometimes the path was very steep.   Once, in a depression, they crossed a hurrying stream of water which Temple spoke of as "the branch."   She walked calmly through this water, which was up to the tops of her shabby congress boots.

"Now your feet are wet," exclaimed Almina, "'n' you'll ketch cold."

"No, I sha'n't.   I don't think I ever had a cold in my life."

On they went.   Once the woman ventured to say tentatively that she supposed they should get there some time.

"Oh, yes," was the cheerful reply.

Going at a foot pace it takes a good while to travel nearly four miles along the side of a mountain.   And often these travellers found that a tree had fallen across the road and a circuit had to be made.

Almina was so far roused that she asked why the folks didn't take away those trees, and the reply was :

" They're aiming to."

A clear, ringing bark was heard a short distance away where the light was greater, as if there were an opening.

" That's Little Bull," said Temple ; he's heard us."

More barking in different keys.

" They've all heard us," continued Temple, "and they're coming to meet us. I'm glad you're not afraid of dogs, because you'd have a truly devilish time here if you were."

She spoke quite as if devilish were the word she wanted, and as if she were not afraid to use it.

One more slight turn in the road.

" There's the place," said the girl, "and here are the dogs. Brace up, for they'll go all over us. You'll think you're going to be eaten up. But you'll come out alive."

III

AN INTERRUPTED MEAL

A TROOP of five dogs rushed pell-mell, with open throats, down a clear slope towards the two figures that had just left the woods. They came from a building standing half way up the space, or rather from a group of buildings. One of these was a comparatively large log-house ; somewhat in its rear was a smaller one.

From the open door of this latter dwelling there stepped a tall woman. She put one hand to her hip and the other above her eyes. She was easily erect, with head thrown back. She was not large because she was fat, but by reason of a stalwart, strong frame. She did not know in the least what a magnificent pose she took. Almina Drowdy, looking up with weary eyes, had only a dim sense of something unusual. She was not conscious of much save the hope and belief that she was nearing a place where she could get off that little horse, shut herself up in a room, take off her gown and lie down. She had not taken off her gown since she left Hoyt. She had a conviction that if she could divest herself of that garment her mind would immediately begin to clear.

The dogs leaped upon Temple. They had the appearance of devouring her. They drew back and crouched down on their front paws, barking furiously. They sprang into the air, whining sharply. They smelled exhaustively at Almina's skirts.

"Don't any of um bite?" she asked, feebly.

"Oh, yes, indeed," was the reply ; "but they generally are sure to bite the right person."

Almina tried to smile as she expressed the hope that she was not the right person.

"Oh, you're safe enough," said Temple.

In a moment more they had come within a few yards of the woman. She advanced a step, now, with a hand on each hip.

Miss Drowdy's dazed eyes saw that she was a "yellow woman."

"It's Sally," said Temple, by way of introduction.

Sally now threw up one hand with an unconsciously dramatic movement. Her eyes were fixed on the thin, elderly face from which nearly every vestige of life and expression had been squeezed by fatigue and excitement.

Sally made a stride forward.

"Master King!" she exclaimed. She extended her arms, took Almina from the saddle, and carried her into the house.

Temple lingered a moment to get the satchel and the umbrella ; then she hastily unbuckled the girths and the throat-lash, and slipped off saddle and bridle, dropping them on the floor at the end of the wide stoop that ran along in front of the house.

The pony gave a little snort and cantered away at his own will.

The girl stood an instant on the porch, and looked off to Mt. Pisgah in the distance in front and at her right; her glance swept over the different peaks, blue or black. She turned and gazed at Busbee Mountain, which was so close that it almost seemed to lean forward towards her ; it revealed the seams and gullies on its surface. There were hills and mountains everywhere ; there were no level spaces. Sometimes there were hollows, and these hollows were usually green with springing grain.

The sun was shining straight down into Temple's face, for she had thrown off her hat.

She did not seem to mind the sun.

As she looked abroad she suddenly pressed the palms of

her hands tightly together and extended them, her face radiant.

Very soon she turned and went into the house. This house was of logs, and it was all ground-floor.

The girl walked through three rooms until she came to the door of the fourth. This she had selected for her visitor.

Almina was lying on the gay-covered bed in this apartment. There was a patch of sunlight from the one small window, and this patch was in the middle of the floor.

"The idea!" cried Almina, as soon as she saw the girl.

"What is it?" asked Temple.

"Why, didn't you see that woman pick me up 's if I'd been an infant babe? Yes, an infant babe. And she put me on this bed, 'n' she wanted to undress me. The idea! I jest wish the folks in Hoyt could have seen me. But it's jest as well they didn't. Who is that woman, anyway?"

The speaker rose on her elbow and looked with blinking eyes at her companion.

"Why, that's Sally," was the answer.

"But she's a—well, she's a negro, a colored person, ain't she?" with some hesitation.

Miss Drowdy did not know exactly how these people were mentioned in the South.

"She's not exactly a negro," replied Temple. "She's what we call a bright woman here."

"A bright woman?"

Almina was helplessly confused before such a remark as this.

"Yes, bright-colored, you know. An octoroon, or quadroon, or something like that."

"Oh."

The Yankee stranger closed her eyes for a moment.

Temple searched about and found a shawl, which she pinned up at the curtainless window so that the light should not be so glaring. It had never occurred to her before that there were no curtains anywhere in the house.

By a great effort Almina kept her smarting eyes shut.

She heard the girl moving quietly about the room. She felt the blanket which Sally had thrown over her drawn up more about her shoulders. She continued thinking about Sally. It was very curious that she had been conscious of a sensation of relief and comfort the moment the " bright woman " had lifted her from the pony. It was true that Sally had smelled strongly of tobacco, and of something indefinable which might be what Almina in a general way called "dirt." And she was a colored person. She had heard Sally whisper,

" Pore critter, yo' ! Pore critter !" as she bore her burden into the bedroom.

And somehow it had been a comfort at that time to be called a pore critter.

Sally had told her that she would bring some tea and toast " right soon." This she said as she laid Miss Drowdy on the bed.

"Oh, don't! don't!" Almina had cried. " Le' me be, now! Only jest le' me lay here and sense that I ain't in the cars. I want to sense that I ain't in the cars."

" Oh, laws !" had been the response. " I'll let yo' be fas' 'nough. Stay hyar a week ef yo' wan' to. But ain't yo' hongry ?"

" No, no. I ain't got over that cawfy I had to the deepo. I d' know when I shall git over that cawfy. It stan's by 's if I'd et a biled dinner. I jest want to be let alone."

When Temple had shut out the sun and had covered her guest she stood hesitating ; but she soon left the room. She went out of the house and across a space of a few yards to the small log-house which was Sally's kitchen and sleeping and smoking place.

It was now a smoking-place. Sally was sitting on her heels in front of an open fire. She had just picked up a live coal with her bare fingers, and was putting it skilfully on top of the tobacco in her pipe, sucking hard at the stem as she did so.

She flirted her fingers in the air, looked at the figure in the always-open doorway, and gave a short laugh. Then she bent forward and stirred something that was in a skillet that stood over a heap of coals drawn out on the stones of the hearth.

Having stirred this she looked once more at Temple, laughed again, and now exclaimed:

"Laws-a-mercy me! Oh, law me!" As Temple made no response to these exclamations Sally asked:

"Is she gwine ter stay?"

"I don't know. I expect so."

Sally pulled strongly and thoughtfully on her pipe. She turned her face so that she might gaze at her companion more conveniently.

"She seems sorter delikit," she said at last, but not as if that were what she had been thinking of saying.

"I don't think she's delicate at all," said Temple, decisively.

"Oh."

A short silence, broken by Sally, who said:

"She ain't what yo' might call much of er horsebacker, is she, now?"

"No," said Temple, with such solemnity that Sally restrained her laugh.

She rose to her feet. She threw back her chest and put her hands on her hips, clinching the pipe tightly between her white, strong teeth.

The young girl was somewhat more than the average height of women, but Sally looked down upon her.

The colored woman now gazed at her companion inquiringly, something as an animal might gaze, with a questioning that was not acute or well discriminated, but that was strong.

Temple met the glance of the yellowish, dusky eyes. She always was conscious of a peculiar sensation when she looked into Sally's eyes. It was as if she had a glimpse of wild, uncivilized days, of furious loves and hates, of some tiger life whose passions were like fire, tempest fury, and with the curious, undisciplined, unreliable warmth of heart and nature which often goes with such a make-up.

For Sally's unrestrained experiences were mostly behind her. She was not a young woman. To Temple she seemed old. She was, perhaps, forty. She was entirely uneducated; she could not read nor write. But she had lived much with educated people, and she did not use the real negro dialect. She had times of trying not to use it. But she was very far from talking English.

She spoke in a sort of throaty voice that may almost be said to belong to her race, and it had in a marked degree the indescribable, thick, honey sweetness and mellowness of the African tone. The white face and the dark, marked-featured face were turned towards each other for a moment.

"Wull, honey," said Sally, at last, "be yo' glad or be yo' sorry?"

Temple took a few steps about the room. She had thrust her hands into her coat-pockets. Her cropped head was bent. She was used to talking confidentially, in a measure, with Sally.

"I don't know," she said at last. "I had to send for her, because of father. But I think," lifting her head, "we were getting along mighty well as things were. I reckon," with a slight laugh, "that she's going to be the thing they call a chaperon."

"What's that?"

"Oh, I can't tell you so you'll know. It's something that young girls need to keep them from going straight to destruction."

Here Temple burst into a louder laugh.

Sally took her pipe from her mouth and smiled broadly.

"Laws, Miss Temple, you ain't gwine ter distruction; no sich er thing. An' if yo' war, ain't I hyar, I sh'd like to know? I swar I'd holp you frum gwine. Yo' carn't git nowhars nigh distruction while Sally's roun'. No, yo' carn't do hit."

Temple smiled intimately and gratefully at her companion.

"Sometimes," she said, "I have an idea that it must be great fun to go to destruction ; just while you're going, you know. But when you really get there, I suppose the fun stops."

"Oh, yes," said Sally, as one who knew, "it stops right thar. But what makes yo' talk that-a-way, chile ? Thar ain't no 'casion. Yo' jes' as safe hyar's when your par was hyar. Eggsac'ly."

Sally did not put her pipe back in her mouth. She held it in her hand. She did not look at the girl, but gazed into the fire as she asked :

"Reckon she'll try ter boss us roun' any ?"

Temple seemed to think the question was a joke, for she laughed and made no attempt at replying.

"What 'll Mrs. Ammidown think ?" now asked Sally. She looked suddenly at the girl as she put this question.

But Temple did not answer this question either. She walked up to the fireplace, carefully pushed a log back with the toe of her wet boot, then stooped to peer into the skillet.

As she lifted her head she asked :

"Chicken ?"

"No, rabbit. Bart, he foun' a couple in them snares," was the answer.

Temple walked to the door. She stepped without, paused, and glanced back to say, impressively :

"Remember, Sally, lots of sweet 'tater."

Temple sauntered back to her own house. The largest of the dogs that had come to meet her rose from a recumbent position near Sally's door-step and accompanied his mistress. He was a white Newfoundland—white, save for one black ear, and a splotch of black down his neck on the same side. That is, he would have been white if he had ever been clean. There were moments in his life when, having just come up from a prolonged swim in the French Broad, Yucatan was of a beautiful fluffy white. But those moments were rare and very brief. He was usually tinged with the yellow soil of the roads, and dingy with the dark loam of the cultivated places of the farms. Still, clean or dingy, it was a pleasure to look in this dog's face and meet the glance of his well-opened brown eyes. Yucatan had a great deal of dignity; so much, in fact, that it was not on first acquaintance usually known that he had a great love of fun also.

Having reached the middle room, where the largest fire-place was, Temple picked up a couple of "cord-wood" sticks that were lying on the hearth and flung them on the fire. She lifted them with tolerable ease, but they were too heavy for her to put down as gradually as she ought to have done. The coals flew out over the uncarpeted, untidy floor. This floor showed plainly that this was not the first time that coals had done thus. Temple seized a broom from a corner and swept the fiery pieces back again. Then she drew up a chair, and, after considerable pulling and coaxing, she succeeded in removing her sodden shoes. The feet that she thrust out towards the huge fire were covered with black stockings. It is dreadful to relate that these stockings had various holes in them through which the white flesh showed plainly.

Yucatan established himself gravely on his haunches at the other side of the hearth from his mistress. He also gazed contemplatively at the blaze. He did not reveal in the least by his manner that he had seen the holes in those stockings. And yet it was plainly evident that he must have seen them.

Occasionally the dog turned his eyes slowly upon his companion.

Temple's head was leaned against the back of her chair, which was a very comfortable rattan lounging-chair. Indeed, the chairs and the beds in this log-house were the chairs and beds of an extreme civilization. Roger Craw-ford had not intended to be uncomfortable.

The girl had her hands clasped on top of her head. Her wet stockings began to steam in the heat.

Yucatan stretched forward and sniffed at the feet. Then he looked at the owner of them.

Temple smiled in lazy content. She held out her hand, and the dog came and sat down close to her, leaning his big head on her lap.

"You needn't pretend to be shocked at my stockings, old fellow," said the girl; "you are a sight to behold yourself. I can see some of the loam from the Bucknor farm on your flanks; there's soil from the north side of Busbee on your chest; and the State road is daubed all over you. When were you on the State road last, dear one?"

Yucatan thumped the floor slowly with his enormous tail. But he made no other reply.

Temple gazed with indolent intentness down at the face on her knee.

"I do believe," she exclaimed, "that there's a place between your eyes that is clean enough to kiss."

She bent down and kissed the place. The tail thumped again, more decidedly than before.

Temple resumed her position with her head against the chair-back. She became very quiet. After a few moments the dog settled down on the floor with his nose between his paws. There was no sound in the room save the occasional falling of an ember in the fire.

Sometimes one of these burning embers would roll out on the hearth; but fortunately none rolled as far as the planking.

Temple was fast asleep. Of course the door was open; it was rarely closed in the daytime. But the fire was so large, and the girl was so thoroughly used to having a room this way that she did not feel cold.

After an hour Sally appeared in the doorway. She stood looking in. Her figure had a distant background of mountains. This background seemed fitting.

She made no noise, and presently disappeared.

Yucatan had raised his head and gazed at her, but had put it down again, not thinking it necessary to move.

Another hour passed, and the girl still slept. She had been restless the night before, for she had been secretly excited about Miss Drowdy's coming. She had resented being commanded to invite her. Things were going on excellently exactly as they were. Temple was out of doors all day, either on foot or on horseback, and that suited her. Sometimes she put on her best frock, and, instead of the slouch hat, a little stiff turban with a feather in it, and, having previously brushed Thimble and tied a ribbon to his bridle between his ears, she rode him into Asheville. She went to the stores and bought candies and writing-paper. Candies to eat, and paper upon which to write wild poems and rhapsodies—things as wild as, and more incoherent than, the scenes among which the girl lived.

She knew very well that these things were not worth anything at all as literature.

But she said to herself that, absolutely, she could not live if she did not at least try to express something of the ineffable glory that was in a mere life among these mountains. Just life and mountains and rivers. Why should any one ask for anything else?

That woman from Massachusetts had said that there seemed to be " pretty views about here."

Temple thought that she herself had behaved very well indeed when she refrained from an outburst of contemptuous fury as she heard those words.

But somehow, in spite of all, the girl had no contempt for the woman who had said that, and who could not ride horseback. She was aware that not much could be expected from one who could not ride and who had not lived among mountains. Great allowances should be made for such people. Temple was fully resolved to make those allowances. And she did not dislike this new-comer, who had evidently had so few advantages.

The girl supposed that Miss Drowdy must at one time in her life, years ago, have been in love with her father, Roger Crawford. It must be so ; although it seemed quite impossible when you came to think of it. But then people's fathers, when you came to think of that, also, had been young, and had been lovers.

Temple, in the time which had elapsed between writing to Miss Drowdy and that lady's arrival, had had long and serious seasons of thinking of her father. She did not care very much for him, and she was quite positive that he did not care very much for her. Still, she felt for him some of the attachment of custom and habitual companionship.

Now, as she sat in the chair at the fire, before she went to sleep, it seemed to her that the next moment he would enter at the open door and come forward—a tall, thin man, moving gracefully, always having his grizzled beard and hair trimmed carefully; though he was not very particular about his dress, generally lounging about in a somewhat rubbed velvet coat. His pointed beard and long mustache, the latter scrupulously and persistently pulled out and turned up at the ends, made a rather picturesque effect under a mountaineer's hat. Mr. Crawford had not yet given up glancing frequently at mirrors, though he lived on a mountain side in Limestone Township, North Carolina. He still had handsome teeth, which gleamed pleasantly under his mustache when he smiled.

Sometimes, when looking at him, Temple used to put the inquiry to her own mind:

" I wonder if he is the kind of man whom women would love ?"

When Mr. Crawford had gone to Manitoba for his health, and when the letter had come about Almina K. Drowdy, then Temple had said to herself:

" There's one of the women who loved him."

And she had been very curious. She supposed it was Yankee dialect which Miss Drowdy spoke. Her father did not use dialect of any kind.

Of her mother the girl remembered a few things which made the memory something always vivid and powerful.

Mrs. Crawford had been a Louisiana woman. Sally, who

had been her servant since both were children, always asserted that her mistress had married Mr. Crawford "fur lurv." She had remarked at the same time that, in her estimation, love was the last reason on the "yarth" for marrying.

In answer to Temple's insistent questions as to why she thought thus, the yellow woman had said that "a pusson war jes' likely's not ter lurv ten or twenty times; but natcherly a pusson couldn't expect ter marry that away."

And Temple had fully agreed with the latter part of this assertion.

From dark hints and darker looks the yellow woman had given the girl to understand that love was a passion of a short and tempestuous life, and likely to recur again and again.

Therefore the selection of a husband could have nothing to do with love.

To Temple Crawford the selection of a husband had not yet become of any interest. Her life was full. Had she not her horse, her dogs, and the whole world of mountain, tree, and rushing river?

In her momentary snatches of thought on this subject Temple acknowledged to herself that it must be that the ordinary woman was much absorbed in the thought of a husband. That was surely the way of the ordinary woman. But then that kind of feminine human being was so very— well, so excessively ordinary that she could not continue to think of her.

The second time that Sally appeared at the door of the cabin she walked in and began to pile up the coals with the tongs. As she was lifting a log to put on the fire Temple moved, opened her eyes, then yawned and stretched her arms high over her head.

"Oh, how hungry I am!" she exclaimed. "Oceans of sweet 'taters, Sally?"

"Oceans," answered Sally.

"Stewed in brown sugar and butter, Sally?"

"Shore, dey be," was the reply.

"Then let's eat. Put the dinner right on the table."

Temple rose. Yucatan also rose. He sniffed in the air towards the yellow woman who had brought in with her an aroma of rabbit and other good things.

But Sally made no immediate movement to go.

"Youse done forgot one thing," she said.

Temple looked about the room.

"De shapron pusson what's come fum de Norf," said Sally, in her most throaty voice, "ter keep yo' from destruction." Then she giggled deep down in her chest.

Temple threw out her hand in a gesture she had unconsciously learned from her companion. A look of dismay passed over her face.

"So I had," she cried. "She must be starved."

The girl darted out of the room. Sally walked deliberately into the apartment at the right where a table stood with some plates, tumblers, and knives and forks on it. She moved these tumblers and plates about in a casual manner. It was not worth while to hurry, save upon rare occasions, and on those occasions this woman could work like a lion— supposing lions were given to working.

This dining-room seemed also to be a little log cabin in itself. It had its own outer door, open of course ; its own fireplace, where was a pile of ashes, from which thin streams of smoke went up into the chimney.

Temple paused outside of Miss Drowdy's door.

It was now almost five hours since Almina had stepped from the cars at the junction.

She had taken off her gown the moment she had been left alone in her room. Let it be said in parenthesis that this room also had its outside door, and its own chimney and hearth. Almina had wrapped a shawl about her, shut her outside door, and carefully pulled an old trunk against it, not finding any lock. The other door she had let remain simply closed.

She had looked at herself in the glass ; had declared

forcibly that she was a "reg'lar fright," and had then laid herself down again on the bed, and drawn quilt and blanket up over her head, and down to her nose. She had announced to herself that she was "jest as wide-awake as a fish," and then immediately she had fallen into a deep sleep.

She was in this sleep when she heard a knock on the inner door, and instantly began to dream that it was Freddy who had grown tall enough to knock.

But on the second sound she started up with an infinitesimal kind of a scream, followed by the cry, "Where be I?" as she looked frantically round upon the log-walls, where the spaces were stuffed with what looked like mud.

"Aren't you hungry?" asked a voice outside.

Then Almina knew that, wherever she was, she had never been so nearly famished in her life.

"Yes," she answered. She was going to ask if it were dinner-time; then, knowing that it must be long after noon, she inquired if "there was a meal goin' on?"

"There's a meal going to go on the minute you come out," was the response. "And please, please don't stay to prink; there's nobody here but us, and I am starving. I feel as if I should swear blue blazes if you stop to put on a dinner-gown, or any such."

Refreshed by her sleep, Almina was able to answer glibly that all her dinner-rigs were in her trunk, and her trunk was to that station.

It then came home to the girl standing in the next room that she had entirely forgotten to make any arrangement for the bringing of the trunk. She found comfort in remembering that Bartholomew had not yet come back from Asheville. When Bartholomew did come back—

At this stage in her remorseful thoughts the door in front of her was opened a crack, and Almina asked, deprecatingly, "Could I have about a pint of water? I think mebby I could git 'long with a pint. I s'pose you have water in these mountains?"

Temple turned to fly, but before she took wing her guest detained her by saying :

" And some kind of a dish sootable to dab my fingers in, 'n' to wet a rag so's I can wipe off my face.   I hate to trouble ye."

Temple did not stay to listen any longer.   She ran to her own room, which was at the farther side of this group of connecting log-houses.

Uncivilized as her manner of life might be considered, she was quite up to the enlightened standard in regard to ablutions.

She took her own bowl and pitcher.   Her face was red with vexation at herself that she should have treated her guest in this way.   She ran back again with soap and towels.

She was waiting before the fire when Almina appeared with face pink from having been rubbed with a towel, and with hair carefully done on crimping-pins to be taken out "before tea-time."

Sally came striding in with the dish of rabbit in one hand and the sweet potatoes in the other.

Almina tried not to show how hungry she was.   She made a pretence of being deliberate.   And Sally's presence embarrassed her.   And they had not much more than begun to eat before the white Newfoundland stalked in through the open door and sat down solemnly by his mistress.   He was immediately given the leg of a rabbit, which was a mere nothing.

He was hardly seated before there entered a medium-sized mongrel, smooth of hair and yellow of color.   He sat down on the other side of Temple, and he also received the leg of a rabbit.   This last arrival was Little Bull.   He had a square jaw, with under - teeth protruding.   One eye had been gouged out, but had healed in a scientific manner, so that, according to Temple, Little Bull really had quite a distinguished appearance, as if he were a retired general. Perhaps this distinguished appearance was increased by the fact that one ear had remaining only a shred, the major part having been torn off in some forgotten battle. The eye of Little Bull which had not been gouged out had a red light in it which accorded perfectly with his jaw.

Temple laid down a morsel of hot biscuit that she might put her hand on the round, smooth head. Then she hastened to caress Yucatan lest he should suffer from jealousy.

"If either of these dogs is within a mile of the house you needn't be one bit afraid," remarked Temple to her guest.

Almina was reviving with great rapidity. She was not thinking so continuously of Massachusetts and home.

"You mean that they'll be so far off they can't hurt me?" she asked.

"No; I mean that they won't let anybody else hurt you."

"Oh!"

Almina had given up pretending not to be hungry. She was eating in that steady, business-like way that gives no sign of possible cessation. As she allowed her hostess to help her a third time to the stewed sweet potato she remarked that she was afraid she was turning into a mere animal. She asked the girl if she didn't think one ought to keep the spiritual part uppermost.

Temple replied that she had never thought much about the spiritual part; she considered that—

Having proceeded thus far, she paused and looked at the doorway, for some one had appeared there.

"Oh, Bart," exclaimed the girl, "I hope you've got the gears mended. I want you to take the mules and go right down to the junction for—"

Here Temple stopped again and pushed back from the table. She asked, in a moment,

"What's the matter, anyway?"

Almina now turned squarely round and saw a tall, grimy boy of seventeen or eighteen standing louting just within the room.

The boy hitched a little as he stood. He kept his gaze on the floor.

"It's that there Thimble," he began, and then stopped.

The girl rose; on each side of her a dog rose also, and stood.

"Is anything the matter with Thimble?"

When she put this question each dog glanced up at her with an indescribable air of putting himself fully on her side of the affair, whatever the affair might turn out to be.

The boy shuffled with his big, muddy feet. But he made no answer.

"Is anything the matter with Thimble?" repeated the girl, her voice taking on a tone which made Miss Drowdy's heart begin to beat in her throat.

Bartholomew this time did not dare to hesitate in his reply. But before he could speak Little Bull growled distinctly. Still he continued to stand by his mistress.

"He's be'n an' curt hisef," said the boy.

"Cut himself! Oh, you've done it! Where is he? Where is he? Speak, if you don't want me to kill you!"

Temple seemed to her guest to leap across the space which separated her from the figure at the door. And the dogs leaped with her. They sprang upon the boy; he fought them off with his fists.

Temple caught hold of his collar.

"Where is Thimble?" she cried again.

The girl's face was white. And yet her face, as well as her eyes, seemed in some strange way to be on fire.

Almina had risen also. She was carried away by the force of the girl's passion. All her education had taught her to believe in restraint, but her heart went out in spontaneous sympathy with the vigor and abandon of Temple's emotion.

"By thur lower shed," gurgled the boy.

He was down on his knees now with the dogs at him.

Temple turned and ran down the slope.

After a slight hesitation the dogs ran after her. But Bull came back once to smell at Bart, who had staggered up to his feet.

Bart kicked out at him, and muttered, "Cuss yo'!"

This remark Bull took with calmness. He finally decided that, since his mistress did not consider it necessary to remain and punish this creature, and since she had not requested him to do so, he also would go down to the lower shed and see what it was all about.

Sally had not been in the room, and now Almina was left alone. She stood undecided. She was wondering if this kind of scene was of frequent occurrence, and was it customary for ponies to cut themselves among these mountains? and if there was a cut there would have to be bandages and —she wished that she had brought some Arabian balsam with her.

She did not hesitate any longer. She hastened to find Sally. She told the yellow woman to get an old sheet and hurry down to the lower shed as fast as she could.

Sally was standing in the middle of her house. At the moment of Miss Drowdy's appearance she had a fragment of the frame of a rabbit in one hand, and a thick piece of corn pone in the other. She was alternately gnawing at the skeleton and biting into the corn bread.

"What's up?" she asked, after having heard Almina's request, and suspecting instantly that this Yankee woman was, as she phrased it to herself, "running mad."

"That person you call Bart said the pony had cut himself," was the answer.

Sally dropped her rabbit and her bread.

"Oh, Lord!" she cried, "then Bart's be'n a doin' sumpin' with him. Miss Temple she won't stan' it if nawthin' happen ter dat pony. Go 'long an' be er helpin'. I'll bring everything."

So Almina began to run down the slope. But she ran in a stiff, middle-aged way, and not as Temple had gone, "like a raging wild animal."

IV

DR. AMMIDOWN

As Miss Drowdy went down the hill she gathered impetus from the going until it seemed to her that her legs were moving on their own account and were running away with her. And she was confused and could not recognize her identity. Was it really herself, Almina K. Drowdy, spinster, of Hoyt, Mass., who was going at this unseemly pace down a North Carolina mountain? And why did she feel that unusual exhilaration of spirit? Was it what she had heard spoken of as the "mountain air"? She had never breathed mountain air before, and she did not know of what it was capable.

And where was the lower shed? And when she came to the lower shed should she be able to stop herself? She was almost afraid that something had developed in her legs that would make them keep on going after the owner of them wished to halt.

She followed a curve in the path. A few rods before her she saw a dilapidated building, with a roof slightly slanting, and with boards and shingles held in place on the roof by some stones and two or three small pieces of planking. Even at such a moment Miss Drowdy's thrifty eye took in the condition of that structure.

In front of it stood the pony. A stream of blood was trickling down its white fore-leg. He was standing quite still, with his head bent downward towards his mistress, who was kneeling on one knee and clasping her hands tightly about the upper part of the slender limb.

She had evidently been in this position for some minutes,

for there was a strained and painful look in her face. Her
mouth was shut so tight that her lips were white.

As Almina drew near, the big, white Newfoundland walked
up and snuffed anxiously at the blood on the ground. Little Bull, who had had time to arrive since leaving Bart, was
sitting on his haunches close to the group; he now turned
his nose heavenward and howled.

"Oh, do lemme help you!" exclaimed Almina, breathlessly. "What is it? I told Sally to bring a sheet."

"Thimble bleeds horribly if I let go," said Temple in a
low voice. "I couldn't find a cord in the shed here. There
never's anything anywhere. Oh," with a quick breath,
"somehow my hands get stiff so soon!"

She looked up at the long, intelligent pony face drooping
towards her. Then she sobbed heavily. But she did not
relax her hold.

"You want to tie something above the cut?" asked Almina, quickly.

"Oh, yes, yes!"

The woman had not even a handkerchief about her. But
she remembered her home-knit yarn garters. She threw up
her skirt and unwound one of these garters.

"Here," she said, "lemme bind it on."

Temple lifted her head, which had drooped again.

"Be quick! Be quick!" she whispered.

She watched her guest as she deftly and thoroughly bound
the garter above the wound.

"Hold on a minute longer," said Almina. "I want a
stick, or something. I know how to do it. I saw the doctor
up to home when Jimmy Bean cut his leg."

"There's the handle of a whip in the shed," said Temple.

Almina found the handle. In another moment she had
in effect a tourniquet arranged.

The girl watched her. From that moment the Yankee
woman held a different place in Temple's mind. Miss
Drowdy could not ride, and found it difficult to walk up
mountains, but—

The girl's heart glowed.

She took her hands from their hold. She remained on her knee a moment watching the slow trickle of blood ; the flow had nearly ceased. Then she rose and turned towards her companion. She sobbed again, this time more heavily. But her eyes were dry.

"I'm going to love you, Miss Drowdy ; yes, I do believe I'm going to love you," she said.

The woman felt a sudden melting of her heart as the voice, curiously sweet with an abandonment of gratitude, came to her ears.

"I hope so ; I hope so," she answered. She wondered why she whispered as she spoke.

Temple turned back almost instantly to the pony. She put a hand on each side of his face and looked at him for an instant, her lips quivering as she did so. But she did not speak until she had released the animal's face.

She glanced up the hill.

"There's Sally !" she exclaimed. The yellow woman was running towards them. She had a large white roll under one arm and what seemed to be a clothes-line in her hand.

She drew herself up with an abruptness and a strength that reminded one of a sinewy and supple horse.

"Fo' de Lord Gawd !" she cried out ; "whose blood's dat ?"

Temple did not reply. She snatched the white cloth from the woman and began tearing off broad strips of it.

Presently the cut was securely bound, and the girl was leading the pony slowly up the hill.

Almina and Sally walked behind. Yucatan and Little Bull and three other dogs walked still farther behind.

It was late in the afternoon. The sun was almost to the fringe of trees on the top of one of the distant western mountains. The shadows were very deep in the hollows below. The air was so still that the sound of the full-flowing French Broad came up from the valley off to the left of the little procession. One of the cows that Bart was driving up the mountain lowed in a mellow, prolonged tone.

In another moment the sun dropped out of sight. Then the marvellous flush began to spread over the top and sides of Busbee.

Almina's eyes distended painfully as she looked about her. Peak after peak stood against the growing violet of the sky. Almina felt as if she must pray.

Involuntarily, and with a gesture hitherto unknown to her, she clasped her hands together. She wanted to raise them thus clasped to the heavens. But she did not. She felt somehow that it would be theatrical if she should yield to the impulse upon her.

Temple turned into the yard of a little building not far from the house. To Almina's judgment there seemed to be a great many worthless, shiftless little structures here and there.

"I'll bed down de pony, Miss Temple," said Sally.

"No," was the reply. "Go on. I'll take care of him. Put some water on to heat. He shall have a warm mash."

Miss Drowdy lingered. She saw Temple fork out some straw and make a bed of it. Then the girl examined the bandage. Then she put her arms around Thimble's neck.

"They sha'n't hurt my own true love," Miss Drowdy heard her say.

The pony seemed quite comfortable; perhaps a little languid. He put his head down and fumbled with his lips for some bits of "roughness."

When Temple emerged from the hut where she had put the horse, the boy Bartholomew was coming down from the house, swinging a milkpail in one hand. He was shuffling along by the two women when Temple said,

"Stop!"

The boy stood still.

Without meaning to do so, Almina also stood still. She saw that Temple's face was thunderous.

"You were riding Thimble?" said the girl.

The boy moved his feet. His under-lip hung out.

The girl's voice deepened.

"You were riding Thimble?" she repeated.

"Ya'sm," was the answer. Bart edged away a little as he spoke, but Temple followed him.

"I told you never to mount him."

Miss Drowdy's face began to grow red with excitement as she heard Temple's words and voice.

"I rode him to thur branch for water," said Bart.

"I told you to lead him."

Silence on the boy's part. He was digging the toe of his broken shoe into the black soil.

"You made him fall!"

"Naw. He fell hisself—'gainst er billy-hook what war 'gainst er lawg."

Bart raised a surly, frightened face. He saw his infuriated mistress coming at him. He lifted one arm and bent it before his head. But it did not seem to defend him. Temple struck out like a young Fury, and Bart fell—but only to his knee. He scrambled up again. Temple walked on, with Miss Drowdy, horrified, by her side.

It seemed to the woman as if she must speak. She glanced at her companion. The girl's eyes were full of fire.

"Miss Crawford—Temple," began Almina.

The girl turned to her. The woman found that she could not say another word.

The two entered the house by the door of the largest room. Almina sat confusedly down in a chair in front of the hearth. She bent forward and spread out her hands, though she was not cold.

Temple passed on into the next room. Impelled by an acute interest, Almina rose and went to the outer door.

The purple was now deepened on all the mountains to the east. Almina had heard of an "amethyst light," but she had never quite believed in any such thing—it was just poetry. But here was the amethyst color—a miraculous tint so beautiful that Almina's pulses swelled again.

She saw Temple come out of Sally's cabin with a pail of

hot water in her hand. She went down towards Thimble's stable.

"Can't I help you?" asked Miss Drowdy.

"Thanks; there is no need." But Almina did not go in. She stood there looking about her. Already the color was fading. A wind swept up from the river. It seemed to have the scent of arbutus blossoms in it. Could it be that it was time for those flowers, and that they grew here?

After a while Almina went and got a shawl. She put it on her head and sat in the open doorway. She saw Sally go to a shed near by, lead out a mule and saddle it. Then Temple came from one of the numerous outer doors and mounted the mule. But first she went to Thimble's stable again. Miss Drowdy supposed it was Temple; but the girl was dressed now in something that seemed in the dusk like a close, plain skirt and dark jacket, with a little stiff hat on her head. It was almost like a disguise. She mounted the mule and rode down the mountain in the direction of the State road. From some place unseen, Yucatan rose, and Almina saw his white shape loping along the path. Then Little Bull trotted briskly after. But he was called sharply back by Sally, who walked out from her hut with a pipe clinched between her teeth, her hands on her hips, a small shawl twisted about her head.

Almina asked if Miss Temple were going away.

"Gwine ter Asheville fur de doctor," was the answer.

"The doctor?" in surprise.

"Fur de pony. She ain't gwine ter run no resks 'bout dat pony. She was dat pernicketty she wouldn't let me go."

Sally walked slowly back and forth before the door where Almina sat. She smoked and gazed about her.

The Massachusetts woman began to feel utterly desolate. The black shapes of the mountains frightened her. That large yellow woman might suddenly turn into a fiend. Who could tell what yellow women might do?

Almina rose. She asked timidly if the door couldn't be shut.

Sally said, "Laws, yas," and good-naturedly closed the door.

Almina hovered over the fire on the hearth. She wondered what her sister was doing in Hoyt. And had Freddy gone to bed? It was difficult to keep from crying.

Temple, riding in the sombre darkness under the trees and letting her mule pick its way, not only felt like crying, but yielded to that feeling.

She was thinking of how Thimble had looked at her when she was kneeling by him, gripping him so tightly that the blood might not come in that dreadful way.

The tears dropped on her cheeks and rolled off on the little jacket that she had outgrown. Thimble? Why, he had been part of herself for five years. Her father had bought him almost before the pony had been broken. She had risked her life in training him. If anything should happen to that pony—here the girl drew a deep breath and set her teeth. She set her teeth because she thought of Bartholomew. Perhaps she should kill that boy some time. If he ever mounted Thimble again she should certainly feel like killing him. It was just as well to rid the world of such vermin. And no one, absolutely no one, should mount Thimble without her express permission.

What a dull old brute this mule was! In her mind she said "muel." She had taken up some words that the negroes or poor whites employed, and the use of them had become second nature to her.

She pressed her spurred foot against the beast's side. He broke into a clumsy trot. She was now on the public road. There were the lights of the junction shining in the valley. Four miles away she saw the brilliance in the sky above Asheville. She continued to urge her beast, which did not want to trot, and was continually floundering back into a walk.

Frequently the girl met carts coming from the city. In these carts, slouching forward with elbows on knees, oftentimes were neighbors of hers. They peered at her, and then said:

5

"Howdy, Miss Temple?" and she nodded in return. Sometimes she said "Hullo" in response.

"I knowed ye by yer white dawg," said one, with a laugh.

Yucatan loped along soberly by the mule's side. Once in a while he stopped and smelled for a few minutes at something by the highway, then came racing on, overtook his mistress, and settled into his lope again.

At last there were the houses of Asheville; there were the scores of twinkling lights at Battery Park Hotel; there were the now solemn, dark shapes of mountains round about the town.

Temple did not hesitate. She went straight along a certain street and halted at a gate over which burned a lamp, on which was the name "Dr. Sublitt."

The girl slipped quickly out of her saddle and tied the bridle to a post. She went into the house. But in a moment she came back. The corners of her mouth drooped in disappointment. She hesitated but an instant. She put her arm through the mule's bridle and led him around past the court-house. Occasionally she met a man who doffed his hat to her and at whom she smiled in absent recognition. She went in at the grounds of Battery Park.

A black boy came out and took charge of the mule. The girl walked in. She did not ask any question of any servant. She went up one flight of stairs and knocked at a door.

There was a slight rustle, the frou-frou of silk skirts, and the door opened.

A tall woman, in a light-colored silk gown which trailed behind her, and which had a big bunch of sweet-smelling roses in the corsage, uttered an exclamation and then seized Temple's arm and drew her into the room. She smiled down at the girl an instant; then she said:

"Well?" interrogatively.

"I came in after Dr. Sublitt," said Temple, "but he isn't at home; the man told me he had gone over beyond Beaucatcher, and would be gone all night."

"Who's ill?" asked the young woman, quickly. And she added, "But, since you are here, there's nobody but Sally left."

"It isn't Sally; it's Thimble," was the answer.

"Thimble? But how did you come, then?"

"I came on a muel—a mule, I mean. But oh, Mrs. Ammidown, don't ask questions! I want a doctor so as to be sure we've taken care of Thimble all right. I could have relied on Dr. Sublitt. Now please tell me where to go for one, and don't hesitate. I can't bear it if you hesitate. I thought I never should get in here, anyway. A muel's no good."

Mrs. Ammidown was standing with her hands clasped behind her, looking at her unexpected guest. She was still smiling a little, though at mention of the pony she tried to look more grave.

"I must hesitate until I can think," she answered. "You might find all the doctors out. There's an epidemic of influenza, or something of the sort."

She took a turn across the room, still with her hands behind her. The girl stood near the door, gazing intently at her companion. The long silk trail swished softly behind the lady as she moved. She came back to Temple.

"If you wouldn't mock I'd offer Dr. Laura Ammidown," she said.

"What, you yourself?" exclaimed Temple, trying not to show too much impatience.

"Yes, I myself. You must remember that I am a regular, full-fledged physician, with five years' practice somewhere in the past."

"I do remember that you told me," was the answer, "but you never say anything about it, and I never think of it."

"Naturally. Will you trust me?" In spite of her effort not to hesitate, Temple did hesitate before she said:

"But the pony isn't sick; he's been cut; he bled. Do you think—" Here she stopped.

"I paid special attention to surgery," said Mrs. Ammi-down. "I could cut off your head, Temple Crawford, and take up the veins and arteries so that you should not bleed to death."

As she spoke the lady held out her right hand and looked at it with a glance of admiration for what it could do, perhaps for what it had done.

"Then I wish you'd come," responded the girl, hastily. "But that gown—you'll be ever so long taking it off, and if Thimble should begin to bleed again—"

Temple's face set in a resolution to contain herself in some way.

"Ever so long, shall I? Let the event decide."

Mrs. Ammidown laughed slightly, the laugh showing that her mouth was large and that her teeth overlapped each other, though very white. It was an agreeable mouth, nevertheless. This was the kind of woman who would make any feature almost, however ugly, agreeable. Who was that woman of the French court who was fascinating and apparently beautiful in her old age when she drooled, and as she sat playing cards was obliged to have her chin bound up with a handkerchief?

"Go down and give the order for Mrs. Ammidown's horse to be saddled instantly—instantly. I could ring and order it myself, but if you go it will give you occupation."

Temple left the room without replying. She was used to doing exactly what she pleased, and she was in no mood now to run the risk of a servant's delay. She gave the order, and she made her way to the stables and saw it obeyed.

She was surprised to find Mrs. Ammidown in cap and riding-habit waiting at the door when she came round with the groom and the horse.

"I didn't believe it," she explained, in a relieved voice.

"I know that," was the reply. Mrs. Ammidown sprang from the groom's hand. Temple got into her saddle by herself at the same moment. Yucatan darted on ahead as if for a reconnoitre.

The two kept together down the street from Battery Park. Just as they turned the corner on to the road that stretched out towards the junction, a man on a large black horse came cantering up the hill.   The light of a lamp fell upon him, and Mrs. Ammidown involuntarily pulled her horse in.

"Is that you, Richard?" she asked.

She spoke eagerly and gladly.   The man, who had not been noticing anybody apparently, turned and mechanically lifted his hat.

"Oh," he said, "it's Laura, is it?   Well, you see I've got here."

His glance wandered to Temple, then back again to the one who had addressed him.

"Go and have your dinner, then wait in my sitting-room at the Battery," was Mrs. Ammidown's next remark.   "I don't know when I shall be back."

The man looked again at Temple ; he said nothing, but continued to look at her for the space of the fraction of a moment, when the two women went on.   Then he half turned his horse as if to follow them.   But he did not follow.   He made his horse canter on to the hotel.   There he partook of an extremely abstemious meal for a man who had ridden horseback in mountain air all day.

Then he informed the clerk that he wished to be shown to Mrs. Ammidown's room, that he was her brother, and would wait there for her return.

He wrote in the register the name Richard Mercer.

Meanwhile Temple tried in vain to make her mule keep up with the steady, fast gallop of her companion's horse. But when the city was well behind them she gave up this attempt.

"You go on, please," she said, "and I'll come as fast as I can.   Sally will take you to Thimble.   I almost think he's doing well, but I couldn't rest without knowing positively."

So Mrs. Ammidown let her horse go still faster.   It was by reason of this arrangement that Almina Drowdy, during a restless walk about the log-house, with rubbers on her feet and a shawl on her head, saw in the semi-darkness what seemed a horsewoman coming up from the trees into the clearing far down the slope.

Sally was asleep by her own hearth. The dogs were the only live things that shared Almina's watch. And now, led by Little Bull, these animals scrambled down in full cry at the new-comer.

Almina knew that this was not Temple, for Temple was on a dark mule, and this was a light horse that was easily climbing the path at a swift walk.

Almina, to use her own words, "felt just as skittish as could be" when she saw this person approaching. At first the dusk prevented her from knowing certainly whether it were a man or a woman. If a man, of course he was capable of anything in the way of horrible crime. Miss Drowdy had a vague belief that men in these mountains lived but to do evil deeds.

She wondered if Little Bull would be of any account as a protector, and could she set Little Bull at that person's throat.

She drew her shawl closer about her head, and resolved to stand her ground in the doorway of the house.

Mrs. Ammidown came directly to her. When within comfortable speaking distance she asked, quickly:

"Where's the pony?" Almina sighed with relief. She advanced a step.

"Oh!" she exclaimed, "you're a woman, ain't you?"

"Of course I am. Where's the pony? And have you got a lantern?"

"And you ain't a moonshiner?" confusedly questioned the other.

Mrs. Ammidown laughed. She urged her horse yet nearer. She thrust the too demonstrative yellow dog down with her hand.

"No, I'm not a moonshiner. I'm the doctor come to see Miss Crawford's pony."

This also was confusing, for Almina was not used to women doctors; she didn't know whether she believed in them or not. But she roused herself. She tried to shake off the sense of bewilderment that had been upon her ever since her arrival. She did not know anything about a lantern, but she knew where Thimble was. She took a lamp and matches, and led this unusual doctor to the wretched little hut where the pony spent his nights.

When within its shelter, with the lamp lighted, she was conscious of the swift, comprehensive glance that swept over her.

It took Mrs. Ammidown but a short time to learn that everything proper had been done, and that Thimble was as right as he could be under the circumstances.

The two women went back to the house. They sat down on opposite sides of the hearth and looked at each other. Almina shrank a little as she encountered the keen eyes.

"Have you come to stay with Temple Crawford?" asked Mrs. Ammidown, so gently that her question lost some of its abruptness.

"I—I don't know," was the hesitating answer. "I guess I have. She sent for me."

"Sent for you? Ah!" The lady leaned forward towards her companion and into the firelight.

"What do you think of Temple?" she asked, this time using a more incisive tone.

"Think of her?" repeated Almina. Then she added, weakly: "I can't tell. I ain't much acquainted with her yet. I only came this morning."

Then she asked herself if it were only this morning, really. Her change of surroundings had somewhat obscured her natural sense and shrewdness. She felt that she was dull, and she also felt that she could not help being dull. She "hadn't got her bearings yet" she told herself, and things were so extremely different. She had always known theoretically, and had always said that she supposed "that there were places in the world where they did do things different from what they did in Hoyt, Mass." Still she had not been prepared to find so great an unlikeness.

She stared at the face opposite in the firelight; and she did not know whether she liked that face or not.

" Surely you cannot see a girl like Temple and not instantly have some strong opinion concerning her," said Mrs. Ammidown.

" I don't think I've come to my senses yet," returned Almina, helplessly. " I was struck down there to the deepo this morning when she come to me as I was settin' on my trunk. I was struck by her face; 'n' her jacket; 'n' her way of talkin'; 'n' that spur thing on her foot. I wouldn't have said that I should like any such kind of a girl, but I declare "—pausing to gather emphasis—" I do like her already."

Mrs. Ammidown nodded. She held up one large well-shaped hand between her and the fire.

" What do you think of her yourself?" inquired Almina, with increased courage and clearness of mind. This woman doctor did not put her down, after all, as she had expected her to do.

" I?" said Mrs. Ammidown. She rose suddenly and stood with her hands behind her, as it was a habit with her to stand. " I don't know what I think of her. I think a thousand things—strong, intense, delightful, dreadful. Every time I see her I ask myself what she is going to take from life for her own. Look at her eyes—' spirit, fire, and dew.' Look at her chin—strong, matter-of-fact, common-sense. If she hadn't that chin she would drift into purposeless emotion; having it, I've not the least idea what she'll do. Now she loves the mountains, her pony, and her dogs. I never saw any one love mountains, a pony, or dogs as she does. She saved my life the first time I saw her: swam into the French Broad and took me to the bank, after I had tipped myself over in a ridiculous little shallop which I would use on the river. That was a year ago, down here, not far away. I naturally thanked her rather warmly. But she laughed at me, and said that she could swim almost as well as she could ride or walk. She tried to conceal her contempt for a person who could not swim. There's a lot of common-sense in your face," looking suddenly and penetratingly at Almina, who was particularly pleased with this compliment, as she had begun to fear that she had never had any common-sense, after all, " so I wanted to know what you thought of Temple. But here she is now."

The sound of hoofs was heard. In a moment Temple opened the door and walked in. She looked eagerly at Mrs. Ammidown, but before she could speak that lady said :

" He's all right."

" And I needn't worry?"

" Not the least. You arranged a famous tourniquet, didn't you?"

" Oh, I didn't do that; it was Miss Drowdy who did that."

The girl looked warmly at Almina, who tried not to return the glance. Temple walked impetuously to her side and took her hand, holding it closely an instant.

" I saw what the doctor did when Jimmy Bean's leg was cut," she said, modestly.

" That was lucky for Thimble," said Mrs. Ammidown.

Temple sat down Turk fashion on the floor in front of the fire, and between the two women.

" I hate a mule," she remarked, with force and with seeming irrelevance. " This one fell lame, so that I was a good while getting home."

There was a scratching at the door.

" There's Yucatan. He was as disgusted with that beast as I was."

She rose and let in the Newfoundland, who immediately selected a good place by the fire and sat down. He rolled his eyes round upon the assembled company, seemed to consider them worthy of his presence, and then began carefully to lick his paw, which he had cut slightly on a broken bottle in Asheville Street.

Temple stood a moment in silence. Then she exclaimed that there must be something hospitable that she could attempt, and what was it? Eating and drinking were generally considered the things for guests to do. Was anybody hungry? She was, for one. She would have Sally fry a chicken and make some tea. Mrs. Ammidown would stay?

Certainly Mrs. Ammidown would stay. She said that her brother had arrived from Tennessee that evening, but that he could not find a more comfortable place than her room.

It was nine o'clock before the fried chicken and the rice curry were on the table, and the three women were eating as those eat who are out-of-doors among Carolina mountains.

Almina was sure that it was very strange to eat at this hour, and she would probably begin to have dyspepsia immediately. She did not believe there had ever before been a Drowdy who had eaten chicken and that hot kind of rice at that time of night. She dared not think what these things might do to her. And the talk began to be so strange that she was fascinated and frightened. She didn't know as people could talk in that manner. She began to watch Temple in a bewitched kind of way.

After supper, and while Sally was going to and fro between her cabin and the larger cabin, the girl went to her own room, and came back with a violin. She walked with it held in position up to her shoulder. She flourished the bow over it, but did not yet touch the strings.

Sally had just placed a large waiter covered with dishes on her head, and she had a pile of plates in her hands. She paused and gazed.

" Fo' Gawd's sake, Miss Temple, yo' ain't gwine ter play, air yo' ?" she asked.

" Perhaps," said Temple, who had now begun to tune the instrument as she stood at one end of the room.

Almina was afraid that this would be too much for her. She had never seen a woman with a violin before; she had never believed that a fiddle was a woman's instrument. A melodeon now—

She drew herself up in her chair, and prepared to endure whatever might happen. And it was her bedtime, too. Everything was all turned round here compared with the way she was used to having things.

Mrs. Ammidown—ought she to be called Dr. Ammidown?—was in one of the large chairs near the fire. Almina saw with distrust and reproof that this lady was not sitting; she was lolling. She had sunk down in her rocker, and her feet were stretched far out in front of her. She was gazing with half-closed eyes at Temple, whose head was bent slightly to catch the sounds as she screwed up the strings and picked at them.

"Why don't you want her to play, Sally?" asked Mrs. Ammidown, without turning her head.

"'Cause," was the reply. The yellow woman had not left the room; she was still standing in a fine pose with the tray on her head. After a moment she added, "It gits into my blood somehow, an' it gits into my spine. She don't play as the niggers play, she don't."

"Oh, your blood and your spine?" repeated Mrs. Ammidown.

She turned and looked at Sally.

"If I were only a sculptor," she exclaimed, with animation, "instead of a woman who was once a doctor, and who is now a rich widow—"

"Go about your work," said Temple, peremptorily, showing that she could be Sally's mistress as well as her companion.

The yellow woman left the room.

Temple lifted her fiddle to her shoulder, and drew the bow in one long sweep across all the strings. It was in tune.

"Play 'Dissembling Love,'" said Mrs. Ammidown.

For the life of her, Miss Drowdy could not explain why she should feel so excited. She confessed to herself that she was "all creepy, crawly."

That had been green tea that she had taken with her supper. And green tea always did make her drunk. And what was "Dissembling Love," anyway?

She didn't like the sound of that name. It couldn't be any proper kind of a piece to play, and for a young woman, and on a fiddle! Her whole life at home rose before her in strong reproach. If this were really Roger Crawford's daughter she would probably never be able to do a thing with her. It was a mysterious dispensation of Providence that she had been allowed to come down here to North Caro- lina. She almost began to believe that perhaps it had been an all-wise arrangement that had prevented her from mar- rying Roger.

Temple played a few bars. Then she stopped abruptly. She looked at Mrs. Ammidown, who was gazing beneath lowered lids at her.

"I suppose you think there is such a thing as love?" said the girl, suddenly.

"Oh yes, I think so," was the answer.

Almina stirred uneasily, but she said nothing.

"What makes you think so?" now inquired Temple.

She had laid her violin across her knees.

Mrs. Ammidown drew herself up a little in her chair.

"I think there is such a thing as love because I have felt it," she answered.

Almina wondered why the speaker did not blush, and she blushed for her.

Temple's lip curled up expressively.

"Then I suppose you married for love?" she said.

"Yes."

"How disgusting that must be!" said Temple, in a voice to suit her scornful lip.

Almina's blush deepened. This was not the way they talked of love in Hoyt. This girl must have been brought

up even more strangely than had at first appeared.   Almina
wondered if Temple could be reformed.

"What do you mean ?" asked Mrs. Ammidown.

"Why, I mean what I say—disgusting," was the answer.
" Men don't really care.   Men are the only kind of animals
that I could not possibly love."

" You haven't seen many men," remarked Mrs. Ammidown.

"No ; but I know them, I know them," with increased
emphasis.   " Animals !" in an exclamatory whisper.

"Temple, you really hadn't ought to talk that way," said
Almina, anxiously.   " It ain't exactly modest."

"Besides," said Mrs. Ammidown, " girls often talk like
that ; but women are going to love and marry to the end of
time."

" I wasn't speaking about marrying," said Temple, very
unexpectedly.

" I thought you were," was the response.

"No, only of love.   If I should think I loved some one
—only I could never think so—and then should be married
and get over loving—and everybody does get over it—then
I should hate myself and be utterly wretched.   I've decided that it would be better to marry, only I sha'n't marry,
just because I felt real friendly to some man.   And then
we should be comfortable, and never have any great happiness to—to fall from, you know.   Yes, I've decided that."

" Oh, you've decided that ?"

" Yes, I have.   And somehow I never thought about men
as girls in novels do.   They always seem to think men are
so attractive and wonderful and fine.   They're not.   They're
just brutes—selfish, coarse, repulsive.   I am sure the most
refined of them are repulsive when you come to know their
natures.   I know them better than you think, Mrs. Ammidown."

" Merciful Heaven !" cried that lady.

" Temple," said Almina, remonstrantly, " you forget your
father."

"No, I don't forget him, either. He was as selfish and as coarse at heart as he could be, and my mother knew it too. My mother—why, what have I said? You needn't look so shocked, Miss Drowdy. But, then, perhaps you were in love yourself with father. I should think you must have been. But, you see, you didn't have to live with him, so I suppose you never found him out, and he never got sick of you and let you see him just as he was. Oh, I know what men are."

Temple put her violin to her shoulder and again began "Dissembling Love," which she now played through with a sort of wild, untutored skill which made her hearers feel as if she were playing on their hearts.

V

WHEN she had finished the piece Temple put the fiddle on her knee again.

Almina wanted to cry, and she did not know whether it was the music or the green tea that affected her. And how dreadfully that girl had just talked!

"I suppose," said Temple, earnestly, looking first at one of her guests and then at the other—"I suppose that religion is a good thing."

"Capital," said Mrs. Ammidown, with a smile.

"Yes," said Temple, "that's what folks say. I've tried several times to get it. I've been to ever so many camp-meetings. I reckon my heart must be as hard as the nether millstone they tell about. There's Sally, she gets religion almost as often as she goes to preachin'. Don't you think there's something mighty queer about religion, Mrs. Ammidown? Now you think you've got it, and now you think you haven't. It must be a lot better than love, anyway."

"Temple!" from Almina.

"Ma'am?"

"Don't you think that mebby 'twould be just as well not to—not to—"

Poor Miss Drowdy paused, unable to find the word she wanted. For the short time she had been in North Carolina words seemed to her unusually incapable of expressing what she felt.

"Not to make light of cereous things," quoted Mrs. Ammidown, with a great appearance of soberness.

Temple again gazed from one to the other of the two women with an expression of great surprise.

"But I'm not making light," she responded. "I've tried awfully hard to get religion. I reckon it's the one thing needful; and that's the thing I'm after. Sometimes" —here the girl bent forward to Mrs. Ammidown with a sort of beseeching look in her face and attitude—" when I'm out riding alone among the mountains, and they're so grand, so beautiful, I feel as if I should die just because they are so wonderful, and my heart can't take it all in, and yet it keeps trying to take it in, you know. And I've often thought that if I could have religion, somehow I could bear to have the mountains and the sky so beautiful; and I could bear to love Thimble and Yucatan as I do now—"

Temple hesitated; she clasped her hands over her violin, and the strings gave out a low, melodious sound.

"If the world keeps on being so magnificent," she continued, " I don't see but that I shall have to be religious, or I shall go wild with it all. It's when I'm alone with my pony and my dog that I—that I suffer most with my heart feeling as if it would burst, you know. Now, don't you think that religion would make a difference?"

Mrs. Ammidown did not respond at first. She was looking with a gentle intentness at the speaker.

As for Almina, she also was watching the girl; and she was thrilled in some unusual way. She wished that she might cross over to where Temple sat and put her arms about her. But she did not dare to do that. And there was a dreadful flavor of heathendom in the girl's words. Miss Drowdy had never before heard of any one who wished for religion for such a purpose. It wasn't proper. Almina was quite sure it wasn't proper. She must say something.

"Temple," she began, in a rather unsteady voice, "I do hope you ain't got into the wrong track. I never knew in all my life of anybody's wanting religion for such a reason. It don't sound right. Why don't you ask your minister about it ?   Mebby he c'n throw a little light.   It's a minister's business to throw light."

"I haven't got any minister," replied Temple.   "I keep going to preachin'.   Sally says if you run kind of short of religion the thing to do is to go to preachin'.   And I've shouted with 'em, and I've gone forward for prayers."

As the girl paused Mrs. Ammidown smiled at her ; then she put out her hand and patted Temple's fingers, which were still clasped above her fiddle.

"I s'pose," said Almina, with painful earnestness—" I s'pose there are ministers to Asheville."

"Lots," replied Temple.   She lifted the violin to her shoulder again, and drew a little wail from its strings.   She leaned her head back on the wall, against which she had tipped her chair.

"I reckon I'm a devilish hard case," she remarked, "but if I don't change my mind I'm bound to get religion sooner or later.   I pray every night.   I really don't see how a fellow could live among these mountains and not have to pray."

Miss Drowdy sank back in her chair.   She was shocked at herself because she was not really more shocked at Temple.

"That ain't the way to talk," she said, feebly.

The girl was making a sort of whispering noise with her bow on the strings, and her head was bent as if listening. But she replied,

"That's the way I feel, and why shouldn't I talk so ?"

"But you must pray not to feel so," responded Miss Drowdy.

"I ain't aiming to pray in that line," was the answer ; and now Mrs. Ammidown laughed.   She glanced deprecatingly at the other woman and began to speak, but she stopped immediately, for her words were lost in the sound that suddenly burst forth.

It was the dogs dashing away from the house, barking as

they went. Yucatan, lying near his mistress, growled in a deep bass, but he did not think it worth while to lift his head.

Temple rose, and laid her violin on the table.

"Somebody is coming," she said. And no one climbed this part of the mountain who was not coming to the Temple residence.

Mrs. Ammidown sat upright and looked at her watch.

"I had actually forgotten to go back to Asheville!" she exclaimed.

A knock as if from a whip-handle came on the door. The dogs had stopped barking, but the Newfoundland now raised his head and growled again.

A man's voice outside asked,

. "Is this where the Crawfords live?"

And directly Sally was heard saying,

"Yes-ir; right hyar, suh. Won't ye 'light an' warm?"

"Don't you open the door!" cried Almina, hurriedly. "'Tain't no time for decent folks to be round."

Mrs. Ammidown looked surprised and annoyed. She walked to the door herself, as if she knew who had come. But Sally ushered in the new-comer, who entered with a certain assurance that yet was not unpleasant.

"Richard!" exclaimed Mrs. Ammidown, "why did you come?"

Mercer stood just within the room, with his hat and whip in his hand. He glanced all about him. He was dressed in a thick, short coat, corduroy riding-trousers, and brown leather leggings. He had very long gauntlet gloves on his hands.

"I came because I thought it would be better for you to have me ride back with you than for you to ride alone," he answered.

"But how did you know where to find me?"

"Oh, easy enough. The groom who saddled your horse told me that Miss Crawford had come for you. After that, of course, I could find where Miss Crawford lived on these mountains. Now, perhaps, you will present me to the ladies, Laura."

Mrs. Ammidown presented him. Temple bowed distantly; Miss Dowdy rose and shook hands.

"We were just wishing for a minister," said Mrs. Ammidown, with a hint of mischief in her smile, "and lo! here comes one."

Upon this Temple gazed intently at the man now sitting at her hearth.

"Is it true?" she asked. "Are you a minister?"

Mercer turned, and met the simple, direct glance.

"Yes," he answered.

Temple pulled her chair somewhat nearer. She was not in the full light of the fire, which was flaring with pine knots; but Mercer was in the full light.

"I am surprised," said the girl.

"But why?" asked Mercer. His mind was already stirring with a piercing kind of interest.

"I don't know why," replied the girl; "but" (hesitating) "I reckon it's on account of your looking so much like a gentleman."

Miss Drowdy flushed, but there was no added color on Temple's face.

"But don't you think a minister can be a gentleman?" asked Mercer.

"Maybe it's possible," was the reply, "but it isn't usual 'round here."

Temple really said "hyar." Before any response could be made to this remark, the girl went on,

"And you give preachin's?"

"Yes."

Temple's face showed a still deeper interest.

"I've been trying to get religion for some time," she said.

"I hope you will keep on trying until you do get it."

Mercer spoke with the utmost earnestness. A glow, other than that from the fire, came to his smoothly shaven, strong-featured face.

"Oh," said Temple, "I'm bound to have it, somehow or other. Sally seems to get it easy enough. She says it comes from shouting, and sometimes from spasms. She's had spasms so that she's bounded round on the floor, and only her head and her heels touched the planks. I suppose that's the power, isn't it, Mr. Mercer?"

Mercer knew that his sister was looking at him, but he did not show that he knew.

"That's what I call nervous excitement," he answered.

"But isn't it religion?" in surprise.

Mercer's eyes were upon the young girl, and his eyes alone showed the unusual interest he felt. The glow had faded from his face. He sat perfectly still, one leg crossed on the other, his gauntleted hands clasped over his knee. His somewhat narrow face was so calm that his sister could not restrain a secret feeling of admiration, for she knew him well enough to know that he was not calm.

She used to say to herself, in thinking of her brother Richard, that she supposed it was not in human nature to be both broad and deep. She privately believed that there never was any one whose outlook was clearer, and at the same time more limited, than was Richard's. She considered that her brother was a specimen of a human being who had actually "experienced religion," though personally Mrs. Ammidown was as far away as possible from understanding what that phrase meant.

Temple repeated her question. She could not see that the young man was obliged to make an effort to answer.

"No," he replied, "though it may be the path to it."

Mrs. Ammidown did not restrain a movement of impatience.

"Oh, don't," she exclaimed—"don't spoil this evening by that kind of talk! Be kind and reasonable, Richard, and leave revivals to some more appropriate season."

"Any season is appropriate for the saving of souls," was the answer.

Mercer's tone now had a kind of vibration in it that was

a hint of what the voice might be when he addressed a company. This tone thrilled Temple. Her eyes dilated.

"I should think," said the girl, speaking slowly, "that you might be the kind of man who could scare the devil away."

No one spoke and no one smiled. Temple was so deeply in earnest that it was impossible to smile.

In the silence that followed she spoke again.

"I'm very glad you've come, Mr. Mercer," she said, "for the devil makes great craps hereabouts. Sally says she believes the whole of Limestone Township's given up to the evil one." She said "craps."

Mrs. Ammidown rose suddenly. She walked to the chair where she had thrown her jacket and hat. As she went she caught sight of Miss Drowdy's face, and she began to laugh nervously.

"Let us go home!" she exclaimed. She put on her hat. Temple had not apparently heard her; she was standing, and still had her eyes fixed upon Mercer.

Mrs. Ammidown drew on her jacket. With a movement as if she had changed her intention she walked quickly over to Temple and placed her arm lightly but caressingly about her.

"I'm going now," she said. "Please stop thinking about your soul for a minute, and play some little thing for me."

Temple moved, glanced at her friend, and smiled. The smile so changed her face that the man sitting by the hearth had a curious notion that an entirely new pulse had stirred somewhere within him.

The girl took her violin again. The instant she had it in her hands her whole aspect changed—just as if, Miss Drowdy thought, she had flung away religion, and was never going to think of it again.

She threw back her head, and as she drew the bow across the strings she half closed her eyes. She began to play, and at the same time to sing in a half-voice:

> "A little bird in the air
> Is singing of Thyri the Fair,

> The sister of Svend the Dane;
> And the song of the garrulous bird
> In the streets of the town is heard,
> And repeated again and again."

With the last two or three bars she made a few sliding motions across the room, keeping time to the peculiar lilt of the music.

"Oh, thank you! thank you!" cried Mrs. Ammidown. "Now we are going. Good-night, Miss Drowdy. Good-night, Temple. I shall come and see about Thimble," and the woman hurried from the room.

Mercer shook hands formally with the two whom he was leaving. He had a way of closely holding the hand and bending over it. When he raised his head and looked at Temple as he thus bade her good-night, the fact that impressed him most was that he could not formulate a distinct opinion about her. And it was his habit to formulate distinct opinions concerning people and things.

As the brother and sister rode slowly down the mountain towards the highway they did not speak for a long time. When they had started Mrs. Ammidown had said, questioningly,

"Well, Richard?"

And Mercer had turned to her and responded,

"Well, Laura?"

After that the woman resolved to keep silence.

Up in the log-house Almina had risen to her feet. She said she had noticed that there was no lock on the door of her room, the door that led right outside.

Temple recommended that her guest have Yucatan with her. Miss Drowdy replied that she didn't know which she'd rather have in her room, a burglar or that great dog.

Temple made no reply. She was playing her fiddle again, and dancing slowly with its strains. So Almina retired, with the feeling that the world was a much more remarkable place than she had thought it to be; and also with a conviction that Temple Crawford was going to fiddle and dance all night. Perhaps that was the way girls did in this outlandish country.

Though she went to bed late, it was impossible for Almina to sleep late in the morning. Soon after sunrise she was peering out of the little windows. Wreaths of mist were curling slowly along the sides of the distant mountains, and the tops were hidden. There was no live thing in sight. But presently a rift of fog opened for a moment and disclosed a mule, with a girl on its back, walking down the slope to the west. It was Temple, in her slouch hat, her old red skirt, and the velvet coat that had once been her father's.

Almina thought she would go and help get breakfast. She was resolved to make herself useful. She started forth strong in this resolve. She went through the rooms until she came to the one where the supper had been eaten the night before.

There was the table, half cleared; even the chairs had not been set back. There was a fire on the hearth, because the logs put there had not burned out. There was no appearance that betokened that there would ever be a breakfast.

Almina stepped from the door, which was open, towards Sally's cabin. She found that person squatting on her heels in front of an immense fire, smoking, and contemplating the blaze.

"Mawnin'," said Sally, affably; "gwine fur a walk?"

"No," replied Almina. Then she stood silent and helpless.

The yellow woman smoked, and looked into the fire. She did not wish this intruder to enter, so she did not ask her to do so.

Miss Drowdy was startled to find that she was fast becoming ravenously hungry; she was startled, because she feared that it might be all day before Sally would decide to get breakfast. And in Hoyt one had breakfast at six, dinner at twelve, and supper at half-past five.

"Where's Miss Temple?" she asked.

"Dunno.   Reckon she's gone down ter de Broad ter meet urp with her young man."

"What?"

Almina's hair began to rise.

Sally repeated her words, with the added information that Miss Temple's young man was in the habit of coming down the river from Asheville two or three times a week "'bout dis time in de mawnin'."

Miss Drowdy could not mistake her duty now.   She must follow Temple.   Already she had an interest in the child. And what had she come to North Carolina for if not to watch over the girl?

"Which way is the river?"

Sally rose from her heels, came to the door, and pointed.

"That-a-way," she said.

Almina hurried into the house, and almost immediately emerged from it with a shawl and her best bonnet on.   Her trunk had not come, and she was obliged to put on her best bonnet.

Sally, now standing at her door and still smoking, saw Almina going towards the river, holding up her skirts with both hands, and carefully picking her way over the rough, wet ground.

"Laws, miss, you ain't gwine to follow her, be yo'?" she asked, in extremest surprise.

Almina turned.

"Yes, I be," she answered.   Then she went on.

She was thinking that if Temple had a "beau," and he was a decent, respectable sort of a man, there was no reason why he shouldn't come to the house in a decent, respectable way.

As she walked Almina found herself thinking that a girl with that kind of eyes would probably go to the bad—unless, indeed, that kind of chin might save her.

The sun was coming out; that dense line of mist over the river was lifting, wavering lightly here and there.   Between these lines the water sparkled a quarter of a mile away. And beyond all, framing in this little spot in the universe, were the mountains, with Pisgah, king of them all.

In spite of her anxiety, the scene had its effect upon the woman who had passed nearly all her life on a level bit of ground in Massachusetts. She was under the influence of a kind of exhilaration which she did not understand came from the air and the scenery. She recalled Temple's words of the evening before: that she needed religion to help her bear this love and delight and awe.

Once, as the mists gave a wide upward sweep and the sun poured light on the peaks of the Twin Brothers, Almina involuntarily paused. What was it that she used to read about " the strength of the hills "? And why did she have that strange desire to recite some lofty, wonderful poetry? But she knew no poetry of any kind. She was only a poor finite in the presence of infinite. Only there must be a spark of glory in her somewhere, a spark that was akin to all this outward glory.

Almina put her hand over her eyes as if to shield them, though the sun was behind her. A space on the river suddenly shone and smote her gaze. Into that space there came a small white boat, with one figure in it.

This was the figure of a man, who was rowing with long strokes, and who was at the same time gazing hard at the banks on the eastern side.

Suddenly he drew in his oars and, pulling off his cap, waved it eagerly. Then he immediately began rowing again.

Miss Drowdy had now forgotten the scenery, and was as resolved as any rigorous old duenna could be to know what was happening.

She grasped her skirts again in her hands, and went trembling down the decline.

Presently a wandering brier branch grasped her by the ankle and made her sit down quickly.

There was the boat, and there was Temple calmly stepping into it, just as if she were doing the most proper thing in the world.   And now Almina saw that the girl carried a green bag, which she held carefully.

Almina could never tell why, all at once, her intention to step between Temple and her beau died out of her mind.

Perhaps it was because the brier was very firm and very grasping; perhaps it was because of something else.   As she sat there, still held tightly, the mule, which had on a bridle but no saddle, came leisurely up from the river shore, cropping the new springing grass as he walked.

In the boat the young man carefully put his guest in the stern.

"You're awfully late," he said; "I've been rowing up and down here no end."

"I reckon you were in despair," remarked the girl.

"Yes, I was."

"Have you been swearing like a fiend?" asked Temple, looking smilingly up at her companion.

"Like a dozen fiends," was the prompt answer; "the air has been blue."

The young fellow was leaning on one oar and gazing down delightedly at the face below him.

"That's right," responded Temple.   "I don't care if you have been impatient.   I'm glad of it.   The last time you made me wait an hour.   Did you bring anything to eat?"

The young man knelt down and pulled a basket from under the seat and handed it to Temple, who opened it quickly, selected a thick piece of cold roast beef and a bis-cuit, and began to eat hungrily.

"If you had brought chicken I should have sworn my-self," she said, in an indistinct voice.   And she added, "You are just as good as you can be."

The young man frowned at this.   He felt that he would rather be called wicked.

"There's a pickle in the bottom of the basket," he said, gloomily—"a large, long, fat one.   You are just like any other girl, Temple Crawford; you love pickles."

Temple drew forth the preserved cucumber and bit off a piece.

"Have all your girls been fond of pickles?" she inquired. Then, with a haste that had some confusion in it, she continued, "But I ain't one of your girls."

"No," was the emphatic response, "you are not one of 'em; you are my only one."

"I understand," was the rather enigmatic rejoinder.

After a few moments of what might be called concentrated eating, Temple said,

"I wish you'd be tuning my fiddle."

The young man frowned again, but he took the green bag and carefully drew out the instrument.

He sat down and snapped the strings. The boat was rocking softly on the water where the sunlight was lying.

It was a mild morning, like some balmy May when May is particularly kind.

This young fellow felt that it was spring, indeed, in his veins; and he showed this fact in his countenance, for he had one of those interesting faces which can facilely reveal what is in the owner's heart. He could look love and admiration in the most charming way. His chin was a bit too much underhung, but eventually, no doubt, a beard would conceal that defect. He had full red lips, and very white teeth, and a hint of a mustache. His front head also receded somewhat, but his dark hair was curly and his forehead went up in a peak each side, much like the brow in some portraits of Lord Byron. He was dressed in rough, suitable clothes, and the picturesque way he had with his necktie was also apparent in his whole appearance.

Temple finished her breakfast, and brushed the crumbs from her lap with a decisive movement.

She extended her hand. "Give me the fiddle," she said, "and get your own. I'm going to learn a lot this morning."

"Are you? Well, you can't learn if I don't teach you," was the reply.

Instead of giving her the instrument, the young man took the hand and held it closely. Then he bent down and kissed it.

"It's odd how you like to do that," said Temple.

"Odd?" was the sharp response, and the hand was dropped.

"Yes," went on Temple, unmoved, "it's a curious thing. I've noticed that you take my hand rather often, and seem to want to hold it. What makes you?"

Mr. Yale Boynton looked for an instant as if he would swear, as he said he had been swearing before the girl came. But he thought better of that inclination.

"Don't you want to be near any one you—you care for?" he asked. His face was red, and his eyes sparkled with anger.

"Well," reflectively. Temple was going on with the tuning of her violin, but she paused in her employment. "Yes, I do," she went on; "there are two persons whom I can't hug enough."

"Two? Oh, the—" Boynton pulled himself up in time.

"You were going to say the devil," said Temple.

"Yes, I was."

"You may say it," kindly.

Boynton's face showed his confusion and indignation. This was not the first time he had longed to be sentimental with his companion.

"Temple Crawford, I do wish you were a little more like other girls!" he cried.

"I thought you approved of me because I wasn't like other girls."

The young man groaned. Temple's brown hand, with the ring on it, was gently stroking the dark wood of her violin as though she were caressing it.

"I never said I approved of you," began Boynton, hotly. "I said you drew me, you bewitched me, you—you—"

The quick-coming words were interrupted by Temple's laugh.

The young man's voice sank to a low tone. He gazed at his companion. He was already beginning to learn that he had a very effective way of looking when he chose.

"You are cruel, cruel!" he murmured. "Who are those two whom you hug?"

"Those two? Oh, my horse and my dog."

The young man uttered an exclamation of thanks.

Temple was contemplating him with great interest.

"You did that so well," she said, in something like his own murmur, "when you said 'cruel, cruel,' you know. It made things seem so interesting, some way; though I can't understand why it should be interesting or agreeable for a girl to hear herself called cruel—cruel to a man, I mean. Can you explain that, Mr. Boynton?"

The young man was dumb for a moment. He thought that he would have known well enough how to reply, if this girl had been talking mockingly, with that airy persiflage with which he was even now becoming acquainted in society. But Temple was speaking in earnest. There was not the least doubt about that. And this fact bewildered Boynton, and charmed him indescribably at the same time.

She never seemed to be moved in the least by the eyes he made at her. He was almost ready to believe that she supposed it was the habit of young men to make eyes, as it was their habit to smoke cigarettes.

"Can you explain that?" she insisted.

"No, I can't," he answered.

"All right, then," was the instant response, "and now let's drop it and go at 'The Kerry Dancing.' I want to learn that. And I wish you'd sing it. Your voice is very small, but it is sweet, what there is of it."

So it happened that Miss Drowdy, still sitting on the bank in her best bonnet, was aware of the fact that two violins were being played upon in that boat, and that a tenor voice was singing with great expression. She caught herself listening intently.

"O the days of the Kerry dancing!
  O the ring of the piper's tune!
O for one of those hours of gladness,
  Gone, alas! like youth, too soon.
When the boys began to gather in the glen of a summer night,
And the Kerry piper's tuning made us long with wild delight.
O to think of it, O to dream of it, fills my heart with tears."

Suddenly Temple dropped her bow and let her violin slide down from her shoulder to her lap. She turned her face, now pale and resplendent, towards her companion. Her lips quivered; her eyes were full of tears.

"Don't let's play it any more," she whispered. "It makes me so happy—and so unhappy!"

She clasped her hands. Young Boynton laid aside his fiddle so quickly that it clanged as if hurt.

He flung himself down on his knees by the girl, and put one hand over her clasped fingers. His eyes were glowing. At that moment he was a magnificent picture of a youth in love.

But Temple drew away as much as she could in that small space.

"Don't shrink from me! Don't shrink from me!" cried Boynton, under his breath. Then he whispered, ardently, "Oh, how I love you! There never was any one like you!"

Temple remained motionless, looking down at him for an instant.

"You take advantage of me," she exclaimed at last. "It was the music and—and—oh, I don't know what it was! Sometimes I wish I didn't feel anything. Now get up and let us play 'Money Musk.'"

"I should think you might smile at me the least little bit in the world," pleaded Boynton, "just enough to keep me alive."

He tried to speak lightly in his chagrin, but his voice trembled. And perhaps it was this tremor that changed the girl's aspect.

Her eyes softened as she looked at him now. But, then,

if he had only known it, they did so also for Yucatan and for Thimble.

"I want to keep you alive," she said.

She touched with the tip of one forefinger the curl that fell farthest forward on the young man's forehead, for his hat was off. Then, as she saw that he was about to press nearer, she said, quickly, in the most matter-of-fact voice,

"It's 'Money Musk' now, Mr. Boynton, and you just remember that I'm a cold-blooded creature who doesn't know anything about love. In all the books that I've read, everybody who loves is unhappy. Now!"

She drew her bow, and dashed into the twinkling time of the old tune she had mentioned.

Meantime on the bank, among a cluster of large, glassyleaved rhododendrons, sat the lady from Massachusetts.

She had ridden herself of the brier. But several ticks had now taken possession of her ankles, and were boring actively into this new flesh.

"I'm goin' to wait," said Almina, emphatically—"I'm goin' to wait till she comes back ; 'n' then I'll jest see what she has to say for herself."

VI

COMING TO PREACHING

MISS DROWDY was a woman of resolution and persistence, or she could not have held out during the two interminable hours which followed. But even interminable hours come to an end.

The two in that boat did not row any; the craft just drifted slowly, very slowly, down the stream, and they played their violins almost every moment.

The woman left her place among the rhododendrons, and followed a few rods along the shore. But she was right in her conclusion that they would come back, that Temple might land at the long trunk of a tree which, fallen into the river, made a sort of wharf.

When the girl did step upon the tree Miss Drowdy walked firmly down to meet her. She felt very firm, indeed; in fact, quite rigid. She did not smile in the least when Temple came close to her and held out her hand, saying, in her melodious, slightly drawling voice,

"Good-mawnin'. Ain't it lurvly out-doors to-day?"

"If that young man wants to see you, Temple Crawford, why don't he come to the house?" asked Almina.

"Oh, he does come," was the answer.

"Do you know," went on the elder woman—"do you know you've been out with him more than two mortal hours, alone?"

"Yes, ma'am."

The girl looked in surprise at her companion. Then she smiled brightly as she said,

"I was feared you'd get most bawdaciously tired."

" You seen me, then?"

" Oh yes, of course. And finally I begun to think you must be going to stay till I come back. Queer about it. What did you do it for? For a long time I thought you'd just come to look at the mountains."

" I knew your father, Temple Crawford, and I wanted to take care of his child."

The girl laughed as if greatly amused.

" My father?" she exclaimed. " I've been wondering if you were in love with him. He never took the slightest care of me in his life. I've always done what I pleased every hour of the twenty-four. Were you in love with him?"

She said "lurv" instead of love. She seemed greatly interested in this question. But she saw that her companion hesitated about replying.

" You needn't be afraid to tell me," she continued, " but, as for father, I don't believe he ever loved anything in his life."

Miss Drowdy was trying to discover how she had so suddenly and completely lost control of the situation. She wondered if it were because she had had no breakfast and was so faint.

" I—I was interested in your father," she began.

Temple suddenly put her arms about the woman who walked by her side, and whom in her young vigor she had an impulse to protect.

" Then I'm sorry for you," said the youthful, attractive voice.

Bewildered, invincibly drawn to this girl, Miss Drowdy tried to get herself in hand. If it had only been so that she could have had a cup of coffee it seemed to her that she could have done better.

" You ain't respectful," she began.

" Oh, don't bother about that," said Temple. " I respect you, anyway. Anybody's got to respect you."

Almina drew a long breath.

" I want to speak to you about that young man," she said.

7

"I've got to; it's my duty, you see. Be you engaged to him?"

"Oh no," with a laugh.

"Are you goin' to be engaged to him?"

"I reckon not. I reckon I'm not the kind of girl to be in love. And I s'pose a girl's got to be in love to be engaged, hasn't she?"

"She ought to be."

Miss Drowdy was very positive on this subject. Like most old maids, she believed in love, and could not reconcile herself to thinking of marriage as a bargain.

"Two or three times I've kind of had a notion," said Temple, "that I was in love with Yale Boynton; but, generally speaking, I'm plumb sure I ain't."

"Oh, dear," said Miss Drowdy, "then I wish you'd stop goin' out in a boat like that with him. Is he a likely young man?"

"I don't know. Likely?"

"Yes; respectable 'n'—'n' scrabblin'. Can he git a good livin'? 'n' would he be a good provider, do you think?"

"I don't know."

"Has he got religion? Is he pious?"

"I don't know."

"What do you know about him?"

"Not a thing," was the frank answer.

"Merciful sakes! How'd you git acquainted with him?"

"Why, I had my violin down by the Broad one day last summer, and this fellow came along in his boat; and he had a violin and was playing it. And he stopped and spoke to me. After we had talked a little he came ashore. I found he could play a lot better than I could, so I asked him to teach me. He came to the house sometimes. But it's ever so much nicer to be on the river. Of course I didn't see him in the winter. He went away somewhere."

Here the girl paused.

Again Almina was shocked because she was not more shocked.

" And he makes love to you ?"

"Sometimes — at least, that is what you'd call it, I reckon."

" Then the end of it 'll be that you'll love him—if he don't give up."

Temple paused in her walk ; her companion stopped also.

" Love him ?" repeated the girl, with just a perceptible emphasis on the pronoun.

She gazed off at the mountains, her face becoming softly illuminated ; her lips closed with an almost passionate curve.

Looking at her now, Almina was dimly conscious, woman though she was, of that strange and subtle attraction of mere sex which is in some women so greatly developed.

It is a mistake to assume that only men are aware of this attraction, this mystery for which there seems no explanation. That woman child who is born into the world possessing this power draws to her unconsciously. If she be good we yield unresistingly ; if she be bad we make a fight, but we generally yield all the same in the end — unless we run away.

Temple turned suddenly towards her friend ; she put her arm again about Almina's waist.

" It seems so ridiculous to talk of love," she said. "Didn't I tell you I am cold - blooded? I can imagine friendship and affection, but I don't understand anything else."

Miss Drowdy's look expressed her astonishment.

" I guess you ain't in earnest," she said.

" I am."

" Then I guess you ain't ever seen your face in the glass," was the impressive response.

Temple laughed ; she passed one hand quickly from her forehead down to her chin.

" I don't know what you mean," she said.

" Mebby you'll find out some time," answered the other.

The two had reached a path that led from the Frady farm through the Crawford estate. There were no real roads hereabouts; but these trodden ways went here and there over the mountains. And frequently they were obstructed by trees which had fallen and were hardly ever removed. People jumped these trees or climbed over them, or went around them.

At this moment, a little ways down the path, a horse was just jumping over a fallen black oak. The horse bore a man on his back, and this man swung off his cap, cantered up, and dismounted.

It was Mrs. Ammidown's brother, and, seen now in the daylight, he bore that resemblance to his sister that a face carved in marble might bear to one painted in rich colors.

It was a curious thing that when Mercer spoke his voice might make you think he possessed a warm opulence of nature which did not betray itself in his face—at least, not ordinarily.

The man had seen these two while he was at some distance along the path, and he had hurried his horse, making him leap as he would have made him leap had the barrier been twice as high.

He now walked by Miss Drowdy's side, and his horse followed him as a dog follows. This animal had not belonged to Mercer for five years and been his daily companion without learning many things.

Mercer glanced across the elder woman and said to Temple,

"I was going to call on you this morning. My sister thinks there's a building used as a school-house on your farm, Miss Crawford. If there is, I shall preach in it as soon as I can let the people know."

"Oh, shall you?"

Temple's eyes grew bright with her interest.

Mercer looked at her longer than was necessary. She met his eyes with a fearless expression of asking and longing.

"Perhaps you, at least, can tell us something," she said, in a fervent voice.

She had the effect of bending towards him as she went on, though in reality she maintained her upright position.

"You know we are told to seek and we shall find, Mr. Mercer. Now it seems to me that I have been seeking all my life. Only I have never found—never. Shall I find, Mr. Mercer? It isn't that I'm not happy—don't think that. That would be a lie. It's just that I'm too happy. Yes, too happy. You see, just to be alive here with these mountains all the time—to sleep with them—to wake with them—to have my horse and my dog—to be alive—to be alive!"

The girl had paused in her walk, and the others had paused with her. Almina had a vague fear that this was not the way any one ought to talk. Particularly was it somehow wrong for a woman to talk thus. And how could one be too happy? If this happiness came on account of having a lover—but, notwithstanding the interview on the river, Almina, romantic as she was, did not ascribe Temple's words to that cause.

Mercer's thin, ascetic face was turned towards the girl. In spite of the priest and the monk in him, the man in him—the unregenerate man, he would have said—thrilled strongly.

Temple, after her pause, suddenly added,

"It's because I want to learn how to bear it."

"I've often been appealed to for help in unhappiness," returned Mercer, "but never in happiness. The poor wretches among these mountains don't come to me with your grievance."

Temple's big soft hat was pushed back from her forehead. She had the baize bag holding the fiddle in one hand; the other hand was thrust into the pocket of the old velvet coat.

She was gazing with unfaltering intentness at the man before her. Just behind Mercer his horse had stopped. The animal had taken a mouthful of leaves from an oak shrub and was chewing them, a leaf or two protruding from his loosely moving lips as his benevolent, equine face showed above his master's shoulder.

Mercer felt a sort of undefined emotion, something that he was quite sure he must fight.

"The poor wretches," said Temple; "yes, I know that's what they are. They are like vermin among my great mountains. They don't care for the hills, nor for the sky, nor for anything but whiskey and bacon."

Mercer stepped forward as if with an uncontrollable movement; and it was with an uncontrollable movement that he put his hand lightly on Temple's arm. His eyes burned, but his pale features were quiet.

"It's my work to teach them to care for something besides whiskey and bacon," he said, his impressive voice seeming to make the still, sweet air quiver in response to an unconquerable purpose.

The two looked at each other for an instant.

Then Temple said, her eyes shining and her voice unsteady,

"That's a noble work! But you never can teach them. You see, I know them; I live here."

Mercer drew himself up. He made a slight movement as one might who is settling armor upon himself for a contest.

"I know them, too," he answered, "and they are men and women; therefore to be moved in some way."

He did not linger. He drew back a step for the two women to pass, taking off his hat as he did so.

He mounted his horse, and rode along the path and out of sight among the trees.

That afternoon he knocked at the door of his sister's room at Battery Park.

Mrs. Ammidown was half lying in a long chair. She was holding a book in her hand.

"Well," she said, "I knew your step, so I knew I needn't rise. What's the matter? If you wouldn't think me irreverent I should say you look as if you had found the Holy Grail."

"No, no," said Mercer, who was standing in front of his sister and looking down at her as if trying to bring his thoughts to her exclusively.

Mrs. Ammidown shut her book. She touched the spring which changed her couch into a chair.

"It is impossible to lounge near anything so upright as you, Richard," she said. "If I could change my backbone into a steel column, I suppose you'd approve."

"You are as nature made you," said Mercer, absently.

"Therefore, let me pass for a woman," was the response. "Did you get your school-house?"

"Yes."

"Then now you'll canvass for the Lord in Buncombe County."

There was more pity than mockery in the woman's voice. There was affection in the way she leaned forward now and took her brother's hand.

He bent over her and smoothed her hair with his other hand, but he did it absently. As he did not speak, his sister went on,

"It's a pity you don't belong in this century, Richard. One of those old flesh-mortifying, sin-tormented monks must be occupying your body. Oh, it's a great pity!"

"What do you mean, Laura? You don't know what you're talking about. I'm doing the Lord's work. Is there anything greater than to save souls? What is all the world compared with one poor sinner saved?"

Mrs. Ammidown made a little sound like an expostulatory moan.

"Oh, I know you are in earnest," she exclaimed. "And it's dreadful to be really in earnest. You ought to be able to move the foundations of the world. Perhaps you will move them."

Mercer made no reply to this remark. He went and stood beside the window, looking out. He was accustomed to his sister's worldliness. He deplored it, but he was too much used to it to be really shocked. He often told himself that he sinned much in not being more moved by her sin.   He knew he tolerated sin in her, and he never meant to cease fighting evil in himself and in everybody else.   He often wished that wickedness was visible, incarnate, and he could attack it with a scourge.   He had many times been conscious that he longed to take a handful of cords and flay himself for his sinfulness.   He wished that he could believe in the efficacy of such flaying, and of hair shirts, and of peas in one's shoes.   If he had been born a few centuries earlier he could have had faith in such measures.

"I suppose that the Miss Crawford out there is the one you wrote me about—the one who saved you from drowning?" at last said Mercer, without turning from the window.

"Yes."

Mrs. Ammidown was too wise to make any remark or to ask a question.   She knew her brother very well.

"She seems an unusual sort of girl," he said.

"Yes," said Mrs. Ammidown, once more.

"I saw her to-day again."

"Oh, did you?   Did she say how the pony is getting on?"

"No."

"I'm going to see the pony before dark."

The speaker drew out her watch and looked at it.   There was a smile on her face as she glanced at her brother's back.   And there was a little wonder and surprise also.   For this was the first time she had ever heard Richard say even as much as this about a woman.

"It appeals to one to see a girl like that in such a place," now remarked Mercer.

"I think it does," was the response.   "I'd like to take her with me."

Mercer turned with a quick gesture of dissent.

"You would make her a worldling," he said.

"Oh, dear!" exclaimed the woman.   "Does it never strike you that you are ridiculous, Richard?   Who talks of worldlings in these days?"

"I talk of them," was the severe answer.   "It's my mission to try to save them. These poor creatures in the country here are just as much worldlings as—"

"As I am, Richard," interrupted his sister. " But how do you classify Temple Crawford ?"

"I don't know—I don't know. She says she longs for religion because—just think of it—because she's so happy. It's only the miserable usually who want God to comfort them."

> "'That soul is dumb
> Who, woe being come—'"

"Don't !" cried Mercer, breaking in upon his sister's quotation. "Religion is nothing but poetry or literature to you. I pray it may be something more to that girl."

There came that peculiar note into the man's voice.

"I suppose," said Mrs. Ammidown, "that the soul of that girl isn't worth any more than the soul of a poor white, is it ?"

Mercer's brow contracted somewhat.

"No," he answered ; "a soul is a soul in God's sight."

The woman flung out her hand in a gesture of contempt. She evidently restrained a desire to say some stinging thing. When she did speak a moment later she seemed perfectly good-natured.

"You'll find strange soil to work on in Temple's character. She is the most emotional and the most unconventional being I ever met. She is very ignorant. She learned to read somehow—she never exactly knew how. She has told me about it. Her father didn't care. She went to school a few months in that little hut where you're going to preach. You can imagine what curious kind of teaching there was there. Her whole heart has been given to her horse and her dogs, and the mountains and rivers. Seriously, Richard, I sometimes think it's a wise thing to give one's heart in that way ; human beings, you know, are not worthy to receive much."

"But her father ?" questioned Mercer.

He seemed too interested to sit. He had moved away from the window, and was walking here and there about the room. His face, however, was set in that resolute calm in which he had drilled it.

"Oh, her father," said Mrs. Ammidown, with another gesture—"he was an indolent, intellectual, unworthy scamp. I call him a scamp, though I don't suppose he ever committed a crime. He used to read, and smoke, and stroll about the mountains in a broad hat and velvet coat, with a mustache like a musketeer's. He had the peculiar, misty, cloudy, absent look of an opium eater. I'm sure he was an opium eater. Possibly that was why he cared not in the least that his daughter should be educated. He did get her food to eat, because he got himself food, I suppose, and allowed her to share it. But he hardly provided her with clothes. If she had been a boy she would have had only his cast-off garments. As it is, she wears his coats now. And she is actually picturesque in them, too—which speaks volumes for her capabilities in that line."

"But what supports her? She must be obliged to have some money, if ever so little, living there. We all have to have some money."

"Well, I fancy you'd be surprised if you knew how little," was the reply. "But there were two or three hundred dollars left in a bank here in Asheville when Mr. Crawford went to Montana, where he died. Temple thinks that sum a fortune. But she never has had money to use, so she very rarely gets any of this. Sally runs the farm. Sally's no 'triflin'' yellow woman, I assure you. She is energy in the flesh when she pleases. She follows the plough, she makes that evil lout of a Bartholomew work. She hasn't any system—she's a sort of wild woman, in a way ; but she brings things to pass. You should see her walking up the mountain with a basket of picked-up wood on her head. I envy her. Why, she might be Boadicea or Semiramis, only I suppose neither of those women carried wood on the head. And Sally is a mine of old, strange stories that thrill and rouse one. Temple is actually intimate with her. They talk for hours together. Temple knows that wonderful, savage, generous nature, and loves it. I've had glimpses into Sally's soul, glimpses lurid and stirring and tempestuous. It's really Sally who has brought up the child. And she has told her curious tales ; she has imbued her with something mysterious and Oriental. My dear brother," looking up with a smile into the man's face, " if you begin a study of Temple Crawford I don't know whether to congratulate you or commiserate you. She says she wants religion. She has been with Sally to many preachings. She has seen Sally converted several times. The process is attended with groanings and shoutings and contortions, and it is a process which seems to have to be repeated ; it doesn't last even the seven years that vaccination is said to hold good."

" You know very well that I don't consider that groanings and contortions make religion," said Mercer, " though sometimes the coming of salvation may be accompanied by much mental and consequently physical disturbance. I'm sure of this, Laura."

Again the woman said, " Oh, dear !" as if she had no words, and would not try for any.

" But this woman, this Miss Drowdy ?" asked Mercer. " How came she here ?"

" Oh, that's one of Mr. Crawford's moves which shows how wise he was, and what a shirk. He knew that Miss Drowdy, once she was here with Temple, would never forsake the child again ; that Temple would always have a conscientious friend. I suspect that he was once a lover of the Yankee woman ; very likely he jilted her ; but she cherishes and adores his memory, you may be sure. And she'll cherish his daughter. Yes, it takes the thoroughly selfish man to make such a move as that."

Mrs. Ammidown now rose from her chair. She went to the glass and passed her hands over her face, as if to rub off the impress of thought.

" If you'll excuse me, Richard," she said, " I'll get ready to ride out there now.   Temple will never forgive me if I neglect her pony."

Mercer walked to the door.   " I wish," he said, looking back, " that you would not talk in your mocking way before the girl.   It's—it's really horrible of you."

" But I won't—I won't ; I give you my word," was the quick reply.   " When do you have a meeting in that school-house ?"

" To-morrow night.   I've been riding about among those people, talking with them and giving notice.   And I shall take in the other side of the mountain and towards Busbee to-morrow.   It's moonlight now, and they're always glad to go to preaching, you know.   It's a kind of excitement and pastime to them.   I know that as well as you can tell me, Laura.   But I want to get their attention ; I want to make them understand that religion means a good many things : that they shall stop drinking whiskey ; stop beating their wives and putting them to the plough ; stop swearing ; stop their brutish — no, not brutish, but human licentiousness. I'm going to help them.   I affirm to you, before God, Laura, that I'm going to help them."

The man's voice vibrated with the man's earnest soul. His eyes flamed.

Laura Ammidown, " caviller," as he would have called her, vibrated in response.   Her face flushed a little. She walked across the room and caught her brother's hand.

" Dear Richard," she said, just above a whisper, " at least you are sincere, and sincerity goes a great way.   I shall be at the preaching to-morrow night."

" No," said Mercer, " why should you go ?"

" Don't fear," she returned, " I sha'n't scoff.   Indeed, I can't scoff when you really get under way."

The next evening by eight o'clock, though Mercer him-self had not yet arrived, the meeting might be said to be " under way " most decidedly, in one sense.   The little log

school-house was crowded; nearly all the men had long, yellow beards and rough, uncut locks.   Their eager, demanding eyes were fixed on the door, through which the preacher was to enter; for the preacher was late.   They wore wool
shirts, and their rough trousers sagged from the hips.   They
had not taken their seats, but were lounging, in more or
less striking attitudes, about the room.   Every few moments
some one would take a big piece of light-wood from the
heap by the hearth and throw it upon the fire.   This fire
filled the cabin with a glowing, yellow flare.   The men spat
into the coals.   They did not talk much.   There were more
women than men, but these were seated; they were too
weary to spend any energy in moving about.   And they were
not good-looking, like so many of the men; they were wrin-
kled and sallow and toothless.   Their eyes were dull.   They
passed their lives in bearing children; in cooking " hog and
hominy "; in plodding along mountain furrows behind the
plough; in smoking in some rare moment of rest by the
chimney; in rolling a lump of snuff lovingly beneath a
loose under-lip; in drinking illicitly made whiskey.   These
also wanted religion.   Religion to them was like a sort of
whiskey that was not so common as what they kept in a jug
in some corner.

And black men and women were there, too.   There
was a kind of scintillating animation in their faces; a
sort of a shine, as of light glancing on polished black
wood.

Of course, the cabin door was open.   The brilliance of
the burning fat wood mingled with the cold, bright moonlight that was lying in long bars wherever it found an opening among the trees.

The smell of spring was filling the night with fragrance.
There was all about among the woods the odor of the arbutus, which was now past its prime.   Frogs were peeping
in hollow places where water stood.   There was no wind.
The trees barely moved their leafing twigs.

Two or three times a big negro sitting behind had struck

the first notes of a hymn and had been joined by the others.

They were now rolling out the words:

> " Be my themer I shall last,
> Jesus, Jesus crucified !"

The syllables went roaring outward into the night, and then died away.

What had those words meant?   Impossible to tell.   Did the singers know?

Presently from outside, and coming constantly nearer, was heard a contralto voice singing strongly:

> " De little chillen's feet so weary !"

Instantly the whole company joined in.   The very world appeared to be filled with the melody.

> "So weary, so weary, Lord !
> De little chillen's feet so weary, Lord !
>   Call de little chillen, Lord !
> Come ! Come ! Little chillen, come to me !"

Before the last line was reached Temple Crawford appeared in the doorway.   She had on the big hat and the velvet coat.   Her hands were in the coat pockets ; her head was thrown back ; her eyes shone.   She stood still, just within the door, and finished singing.   She repeated the phrase " Come to me " with an abandon of fervor that made the two women behind her shiver with a sort of fearsome ecstasy.   One of these women, Laura Ammidown, ascribed this ecstasy merely to her own susceptibility to certain phases of emotion.   The other woman, Almina Drowdy, believed this emotion to be part of religion.

" Somebody 'll be sure to experience to-night," she thought with exultation.

She looked with wonder at Temple.   She hoped that some time she should know what to make of that girl.   She watched her as she shook hands here and there with those horrible‑looking mountain people. Almina felt that she couldn't shake hands in that way. The long-legged, brawny men clustered around Temple. They asked her about her pony; they inquired what kind of craps she was "gwine to make this year." They recommended turning over "that there bit er land ter thur west." One of these men, young, with hair which appeared to have been combed, and which lay, sleek and yellow, back from his temples and behind his ears, pressed bashfully, but resolutely, up near to the girl.

Mrs. Ammidown, standing by the fire with her elegant wrap now held negligently on her arm, watched this young man with instant interest. She had never seen him before, but she was aware that she liked him directly. It was a distinction to be clean and well groomed among this "herd"; herd was the term the lady mentally used.

This young fellow's forehead was very white, his eyes clearly blue and transparent, his cheeks tanned. A straw-colored mustache swept away in a fine curve on either side of his upper-lip.

"You plumb promised me, Miss Temple," Mrs. Ammidown heard him say, "that you'd let me plough the west slope with my new oxen. You did, Miss Temple. Sally an' Bart carn't make no headway ploughin' of that slope. They carn't. Say I may curm ter-morrer, Miss Temple; say I may!"

Temple looked at him and smiled.

"When will she learn not to smile like that?" Mrs. Ammidown asked of herself.

The young man flushed with delight.

"Now, Lincoln," said Temple, "that's just what I was wanting—your oxen for that slope, you know. Our muel can't do hit. Sally was saying yesterday that if she could get Lincoln Dalvecker's oxen to turn urp that sod, she 'n' Bart could make a mighty fine crap. I do wish you would come. We c'n swop work somehow, I reckon."

The young man gave a little delighted laugh which made his face charming.

"I ain't aimin' to swop work," he answered. "I'll be shore to be there by sun-up ter-morrer."

"Link Dalvecker's allers in luck," exclaimed one man. "But yo' may jes' know, Miss Temple, as thur ain't a man nowhars on the mountings in Car'liny but 'd jump at thur chance to plough that slope. Now, be thur?"

The speaker turned towards the group of men as he put the question.

There was a laugh and a shout of " Naw! naw! That's thur gospel trewth—'tis!"

Even the women joined in this, though they did it more languidly, having no spare strength to put into anything.

Temple thanked them with a simple sincerity. She turned and glanced at Mrs. Ammidown and Almina as if to say,

"These be my mountaineers." In another moment a voice asked,

"Whar's thur preacher? Ain't we gwine ter have no preachin'? I'll be dad-burned if I warnt no preacher ter be foolin' of me. I curm to preachin'; I curm fur three mile t'other side Busbee to git religion. My 'oman tole me not ter darst to curm back 'thout I brung religion. Say, now!"

There was a darky snicker at this in the rear of the room. But it was hushed instantly, as Mercer appeared in the doorway.

He was dripping wet, and his face was flushed almost to a purple hue.

VII

YOUNG DALVECKER

MRS. AMMIDOWN advanced a step towards him, but Mercer motioned her back.

He walked into the room and up to the fire, standing back to it.

"I'm sorry I'm late," he said. "I started early enough, but I was detained."

He glanced down at his wet garments, hesitated a moment, as if in doubt whether to make any explanation, then he went on as if speaking of the most commonplace affair.

"There was a drunken fellow trying to cross the Broad in a boat. Of course he capsized, and he was too drunk to swim. I had to go in after him, and then I had to take him home. Has any one got a hymn-book? But it's no matter. Enough of you will know this."

And standing before the fire, with the water trickling off him and making a little pool at his feet, Mercer began to sing,

> " Hail to the brightness of Zion's glad morning !
>   Joy to the lands that in darkness have lain !
>   Hushed be the accents of sorrow and mourning,
>   Zion in triumph begins her mild reign."

For the whole of the first verse no one joined him. His resonant and triumphant voice went on by itself. All those dull, ignorant, besotted faces were turned towards him, and the firelight shone on them.

From the moment he had stepped into the room Mercer had control of the people within it. That he had just pulled a man out of the river, and had come to them without going back to change his clothes, had a decided weight with every one there.

Laura Ammidown was angry with her brother, and anxious about him, but she was conscious of that stirring of admiration which a recklessness of self, however absurd, is likely to excite.

When Mercer began the second verse, voice after voice joined in with fervor, and with strange pronunciation.

> " Hail to the brightness of Zion's glad morning,
>   Long by the prophets of Israel foretold ;
>   Hail to the millions from bondage returning ;
>   Gentiles and Jews the blest vision behold."

Mercer did not go on with the hymn.

He had heard his sister's thin but sweet soprano ; but he did not so much hear as feel the contralto notes that filled the cabin with magnificent sound.

He knew that Temple's gaze was upon him in that intense and hoping way which might almost inspire a block of wood to be eloquent.

" Are you returning from bondage ?" he asked, suddenly, his eyes gazing over the whole assembly.

Not one among that company was so stupid as not to know that " the power " would be displayed this evening. Dimly, but eagerly, they felt the stirring of the coming excitement.   It was going to be a good meetin'.

A strange, and what they thought holy, intoxication would get them—that was it.   It is a singular fact that man is an animal that longs to be intoxicated in some way—to be stirred beyond his normal condition.

Mercer's tall, broad-shouldered figure stood erect and dominant before the fire.   There was something compelling in him.   Even his sister felt it, and could not throw it off, though mentally she scoffed at herself for her weakness.

As for Almina, she yielded without a struggle to the force

which she called the spirit of God. It had come down to make men flee from eternal wrath.

Mercer gazed about him. His glance took in every person. Each person felt that it was to him, to his very soul, that this evangelist had come.

"Are you returning from bondage?"

The preacher repeated his words, his voice knocking at every heart. "From the bondage of sin to the freedom of the Lord Jesus Christ." Then he paused. Almina sat with terrible yet delicious chills chasing each other over her. She glanced at Temple, wondering if the girl would get religion.

Temple was looking straight at the speaker.

In the pause there was a movement at the door. Without glancing that way, Temple was aware that Sally was in the doorway, and she saw beside her the great white bulk of the Newfoundland Yucatan.

The girl made a slight motion with her hand, and the yellow woman and the dog came to her side. There was no room on the benches. Without any hesitation the woman sat down on the floor in front of her mistress. She drew up her legs and clasped her hands over her knees. The dog seated himself on his haunches, gazed at Temple, and slowly thumped the floor with his tail.

In the silence of this slight interruption Almina was looking forward with mingled misery and happiness to a powerful delineation of the eternal anger from which mortals must some way escape.

Mercer's eyes wandered over his little congregation; they came to the girl directly in front of him. Temple's eyes were still upon him absorbedly.

A sudden change of intention came to the preacher. He had intended to talk of the awful consequences of sin, the terrors of everlasting damnation. He had meant to exhort his hearers to flee—flee from the wrath to come.

His penetrating voice suddenly asked in its softest accents,

"Is there a man here who remembers that he loved his mother—or his father—or his wife—or any one in the whole world? Is there? Is there?"

Mercer's glance, now inexpressibly gentle and sweet, went again from one to the other of those stolid, ignorant, unthinking faces. His words may have had some effect, but there was that in the man's presence, the mysterious something which is given to some human beings, and which makes them leaders, which had far more effect.

A faint, tremulous voice, that yet came from a bearded man, behind the others, was heard saying,

"Yes, yes—fur shore—fur shore."

Then there was a movement through the whole company, and murmurs of assent.

Sally rocked herself to and fro, and groaned deep down in her chest. Temple sat perfectly still, her hand on Yucatan's head. Mercer was aware that her face was towards him. He was so intensely aware of it that he passed his hand involuntarily over his eyes that he might more fully give himself up to those others—those animals in the guise of men and women who were so in need of the salvation of love and peace which Jesus Christ had brought into the world.

A man near the door sprang to his feet. He had one hand on his hip; he flung the other out fiercely.

"There's my little gal—my little Tressy"—he cried, "lurv her! I'll be damned if I don't lurv her!"

Mercer turned like a flash upon this man.

"Yes, yes!" he exclaimed, "now you know what I mean. You love her, and you like to do what will please her. She likes to do what will please you. You'd do anything for her, because you love her. You'd die for her. There's something in every heart here to-night that knows what I'm talking about."

There was another movement. A light came upon dull faces, and grew, and grew. Sordid life of "crap making" and drinking and licentiousness seemed to drop away, piece by piece, like old rags from a beggar's body. It was not a God thundering curses at them, but a God loving them.

At the end of one of the sentences Mrs. Ammidown suddenly began to sing,

> "Oh, love divine, that stooped to share
>   Our sharpest pang, our bitterest tear !
> On Thee we cast each earthborn care ;
>   We smile at pain while Thou art near."

No one seemed to know this hymn among the natives, but at the third line Temple's strong, rich contralto joined in, and supported and bore up the other voice ; and thus the two sang to the end of the hymn.

The instant the words ceased Mercer broke forth into something quite different. He had no platitudes about the sentiment of religion then. He talked about drunkenness and laziness and wife-beating and adultery.

He lashed the people, and they took his lashing ; nay, they crouched to it. They writhed, they groaned, they swore with occasional outburst that it was God's truth he was speaking. They gazed at each other.

One great fellow with a beard down to his waistband, and big boots caked with yellow mud, sprang up and shouted,

"By thur devil ! I tell you-uns what 'tis, this man is a-tellin' thur trewth ! I'm gwine ter reform, I be ! I knocked my 'oman down yisterday. She war damned pervokin'." He glanced round the company. " You-uns know jes' how damn pervokin' my 'oman c'n be. But I ain't gwine ter knock her down ergin. Never onc't. I sw'ar hit. 'Tain't no work fur a man — to be knockin' down women —'tain't. Other preachers don't talk religion that makes er man do dif'runt. This is thur religion fur me. I'm gwine ter do dif'runt. Some of you-uns jes' spout er prayer as 'll fit my case."

The man threw himself down on his knees, and covered his face with a pair of grimy, hairy hands.

Even Mrs. Ammidown could not smile at the grotesque speech or the grotesque speaker. Her face was set in a more earnest look than was often seen on it. Genuine emotion is such a power, such a contagious power.

Temple was leaning forward as if she were listening for something more and something different from anything she had heard—or rather as if she were even now hearing the beginning of that something. Her eyes were still on the preacher. Mrs. Ammidown, glancing at her, saw that the intent eyes of the girl did not really see Mercer himself, but that they were gazing beyond him, through him ; they were searching.

As for Mercer himself, he was glorified, exultant. He had never before been so conscious of doing the Lord's work, of being in deed and in truth a laborer in the vineyard. He did not know why it was. But this evening a greater glory had been vouchsafed to him. It was as if he had been sealed by the Almighty as one who was worthy to work and to be blessed in his work.

His eyes sought Temple's. " Who is going to pray for our brother ?" he asked.

Temple slid down to her knees. Without knowing that she did so, she leaned heavily against Sally's stalwart frame as she had often leaned when she was a child.

She began to pray. Afterwards she could never remember anything she said at that time. She could only remember the ecstatic state of her mind in the conviction that God had at last given to her that she should "experience religion," that she should have a new heart with which to serve him all the years of her life, and for an eternity in heaven. This she remembered, and that she longed so fervently that God would help that man who had asked for prayers that the very fervor would insure the answer.

Sally shouted fiery words of triumph now and then in her mellow African voice. There were continuous exclamations all about in the room.

It was Mrs. Ammidown alone who could discriminate enough to know how wonderful the girl's prayer had really been.

Miss Drowdy burst out in a quivering, excited treble,
"Glory to God most high!"

And now the negroes were rocking to and fro, and moaning and shouting. Some of them were openly watching Sally, who was famous among them as one who could have the power beyond them all. She could contort her strong, big frame; she could writhe and undulate like a snake; her face would be set, her lips foaming.

Temple, the moment she had ceased praying, rose to her feet. She pushed Sally aside and moved towards the door, the men crowding back to let her pass. Behind her walked the white dog.

The girl and the dog made their way to where the heavens looked down on them. Temple had left her hat, but she did not know it.

She walked blindly down the mountain, the dog following close at her heels, his head and tail drooped.

Suddenly the girl stopped. She turned her face up towards the sky. She stretched out her clasped hands.

"This must be religion," she said, aloud. " I've wanted it for so long. It was that man who brought it. It was that man, because he is God's ambassador — God's ambassador."

The stars glittered down upon her. She remembered a phrase she had read the day before,

" In the night only Friedland's stars may shine."

She thought she knew now what those words meant. She had a feeling that all mysteries might be revealed to her now. And the ineffable glory of the night, of the dark shapes of the mountains, of the moist odors, of life and youth, did not at this moment make her heart ache so. That was because she had religion; she would now be able to bear the wonderful happiness which came from just being alive.

" Temple! Temple Crawford! Where are you ?"

Some one called from up the slope.

The girl stood silent, loath at first to answer. Yucatan

turned and looked up, then glanced at his mistress, as if questioning her. In the stillness that followed the call, a horse hitched at the school-house neighed shrilly; then another neighed and pawed, sending some stones rattling down.

"Where are you?" repeated the voice.

Then Temple saw a figure detach itself from the darkness under a tree, and come across the patches of light towards her. It was Mrs. Ammidown, and she was huddling her shawl up about her head and shoulders.

There was shouting, and a snatch of a hymn from the house; then the preacher's voice, strong and persuasive.

Mrs. Ammidown came swiftly to Temple, threw a fold of her wrap over the girl, and drew her close within her arm.

"Really," she said, "I was afraid to have you out here alone. In your exalted state you might unfold wings and fly away. And then, when the reaction came, your wings would suddenly fail and you would fall. My dear, I wanted to be near, that I might catch you when you fell."

Temple turned towards her friend.

"When I fell?" she questioned. "But I shall not fall."

"Oh, my dear little girl!" exclaimed Mrs. Ammidown, in a tender whisper.

Temple moved uneasily.

"You need not pity me," she said. And then, ardently, "No, don't pity! Any one might envy me to-night. You see," with a confiding motion towards the woman, "I've got religion—at last—at last." She clasped her hands again, and threw them outward. "I never thought I had it before. But to-night, when the preacher talked like that, something in my heart yielded—the Holy Ghost came in— I wanted to help people—to help these wretches around here. And you, Mrs. Ammidown—can't I help you?"

But the woman could not at first reply. She was very near to tears.

She was asking herself if there were, indeed, something

real in this state of mind which controlled Temple ; something which would not pass away, and which would affect life itself.

Her brother believed so ; there had been a time when she would have believed it. But now ?

She gazed wistfully at the girl's glorified face.

" It is a condition of the nerves," was what the woman was saying. And forlornly to herself she added, " Everything is a condition of the nerves—everything. And when our nerves are dead, where is the soul ?"

The physician in her, the materialist physician, became awake to the danger of the excitement which ruled Temple.

At that moment Dr. Ammidown wished that she knew positively whether religion, love itself, were all a mere matter of magnetism and neurosis. What particular nerves might be called the nerves of religion? Had they been discovered and labelled? A phrase of a famous doctor came into her mind, " The nerves that make us alive to music spread out in the most sensitive region of the marrow, just where it is widening to run upward into the hemispheres."

It was with a womanish shudder that Mrs. Ammidown recalled the hour in the dissecting-room when those nerves had been laid bare in that body—that body which had once been as alive as she was now, but that was then lying dead—dead, on the marble.

" Oh, the mystery that we call living ! And the mystery that we call death ! The knife of the dissecter could find neither the one mystery nor the other. The informing fire —what was that? Where was that?

All these things rushed through the woman's mind as she stood there with her arm around this girl who had within her such powers of sensation. And again the insatiable spirit asked, Was it all nerve sensation ? And what would be left if all sensation were taken away ? Only death ?

" Can't I help you ?"

Temple pressed still nearer her companion as she repeated this question. She was eager to begin to do something.

"Yes," said Mrs. Ammidown, promptly, "you can do something for me."

She was all physician now. The dilated eyes and brilliantly pale face of the girl alarmed her.

"Oh, what is it?"

"Come up the slope with me."

"What, and leave the preaching? I was going back."

"Never mind the preaching. You have had enough."

"But those people — they will listen and sing for an hour longer. They may have another blessing."

Mrs. Ammidown restrained the words that rose to her lips.

"They are blocks, stolid blocks," she said, imperatively; "they can bear any kind of dissipation. But you—child, you have no idea of your own face at this moment. Come, let us go and see the pony."

She took Temple's hand, and led her up the path. Temple yielded.

"I thought you said the pony was all right," she said.

"So I did. You can soon ride him. But let us see him, nevertheless—and the ox. I want to see the ox."

Temple glanced in wonder at the speaker.

"I don't know what you mean," she said.

"Never mind, but come."

They went on in silence until they were opposite the shed which held Thimble.

"This is the place," said Temple.

"But, come," responded the woman.

She was fearing every moment that the girl would assert herself, and that there would come into Temple's manner that authority and power to be obeyed which belonged to her. But she allowed herself to be led. They stopped at the rickety old shanty where Juba, the ox, lived. Juba ploughed when Bart or Sally chose to plough with him.

Most times, however, he was mildly browsing in far pastures, and sometimes coming home for " roughness " when pastures failed him.

The door, which had fallen down and had not been put up, allowed the moonlight to stream in upon Juba, who was meditatively chewing as he gazed over the bar which kept him from going out into the wide world.

" I suppose he is kind?" asked Mrs. Ammidown, as the two stopped in front of him.

" Kind? Oh yes. Besides, I shouldn't be afraid of him if he were not kind," was the answer.

" Go in there and lean against him; put your arms around his neck and hug him."

" What ?"

The girl stared through the moonlight at her companion. Already there was a trifle less of stress in the young face.

Mrs. Ammidown laughed a little.

" It is your doctor who speaks," she said. " People with your sensitive nerves are generally afraid, and, being afraid, they can't avail themselves of a thousand things good for them. But you are not afraid. These dumb animals carry comfort for such as can take it."

Temple's face relaxed so that she could smile slightly.

" Oh, I know what you mean," she exclaimed, " I know very well. Often when I've been out and seen such wonders of glory and beauty—the mountains, you know, and the sky—I have found that I was better able to bear it—to bear life, you see—"

Temple seemed to leave her sentence unfinished.

She stooped beneath the bar and went to the side of the ox, putting her arm over his neck and resting heavily upon him.

The animal turned slow eyes towards her, ceased his chewing for a moment, then, with a movement of throat and mouth, recalled the " cud " and began again upon it.

Mrs. Ammidown leaned her arms on the bar, and extended a dried cornstalk towards Juba, who calmly appropriated it.

Temple put her forehead down on Juba's shoulder. The shining pallor was leaving her face.

" How calm he is !" she said. " I fancy I feel his calmness and his strength coming into me. But then, I, myself, am strong."

The doctor looked at her admiringly.

" Yes," she responded, " you have not only nerve, but muscle and brawn. But, you see, nerves are things which, give them rein, wear through muscle and brawn."

" I'm not afraid."

" In truth, neither am I—much. But this getting religion—"

Mrs. Ammidown stopped. She was conscious that she was on uncertain ground. She had not yet decided in her own mind just how much there was in "getting religion." If there were in reality anything, then, in Heaven's name, let it give all it could. She would not wish to deprive poor human nature of any comfort it could get.

Temple did not ask her to finish her sentence. She was still leaning against Juba, and absently passing her hand over the ridge between his horns. She began to hum,

> " Oh, love divine, that stooped to share
>   Our sharpest pang, our bitterest tear."

" It was Dr. Holmes who wrote that ; and it was Dr. Holmes who told just what part of marrow and little scraps of our body make us feel music."

Mrs. Ammidown spoke with a trifle of impatience.

Temple was not impatient. She looked calmly at the woman on the other side of the bar.

" I don't see why you care so much to find out what makes us feel," she said. " It's enough that we do feel. My father used to say that any one was a fool who was always analyzing. Please give Juba that bit of roughness at your feet.   See, he thanks you.   Do you think I am what you call nervous now ?"

Temple extended her hand, and Mrs. Ammidown took it, holding it a moment, and gazing at the face before her.

The elder woman was not able to divest herself of a feeling that this hour was in some way a turning-point with the girl ; she could not have told why, however, and she disliked to have an emotion which she could not understand.   And she was conscious of some anger towards her brother.   Now she was away from the influence of his presence, her anger began to grow.

" No, you are not nervous," she answered, " but you are intensely excited.   I always did say that a person who had strong health and sensitive nerves could command heaven and hell."

" Yes," said Temple, " but it's heaven that I shall command."

Mrs. Ammidown suppressed a groan.   Why does the happiness of youth make an older person groan ?

There was the sound of feet coming hastily from the direction of the school-house, and presently young Dalvecker came in sight under the trees.   He hastened forward, taking off his hat as he did so, his long, sleek hair looking sleeker and yellower than ever in the moonlight.

" I couldn't stay no longer; I couldn't noways stay 'thout you war there, Miss Temple," he said.

His admiration for the girl was so open, so ingenuous, that Mrs. Ammidown smiled with liking at him.   At the same time she inwardly shuddered at thought of this girl's returning the young man's feeling.

Dalvecker had been to school in Asheville one term, and ever since he had been trying not to talk like the mountaineers.   Particularly had he been trying since he had known Temple, now more than a year ago.   He felt that he didn't succeed very well in his attempts at civilized conversation, and he could not help being very glad when Temple herself lapsed into mountain dialect, as she was liable to do at any time, in a degree. At such times the young fellow had wild hopes that his suit might not be hopeless. He knew very well that he himself was not worthy of her; but his station he was quite sure was superior to hers. Did he not live in a "plank house" with real windows to it? And the Dalvecker farm was known to be the very best on Cain Creek. And his father was dead, and his mother adored and obeyed her only son.

When the young man thought over all these advantages he was not dejected; but as soon as he was actually in Temple's presence his confidence flew away, and he could have thrown himself on his knees and begged the girl to have mercy on him, and give him one glimmer of hope.

"That was wrong," said Temple, seriously, "you ought to have stopped to the preaching."

Mrs. Ammidown turned and walked up towards the house, the shining of the hearth fire through the open door beckoning her.

The young man came close up to the bar across Juba's door. The moonlight touched the lower half of Temple's face, revealing the somewhat full lips and the strong chin. The upper half of her face was illuminated by her shining eyes. The moon's radiance is particularly kind to the human countenance—it softens defects, and seems to lend bewitchment even to what might be ugly beneath the sun.

Dalvecker gazed at the girl in silence a moment before he replied. His heart was beating in his throat—even in his finger-ends. A thousand times he had pictured to himself the possibility of being alone with Temple like this. Would such luck ever be his? He had met her on horseback many times; he used to prowl along those paths which opened into magnificent views, for such paths were the places where he was most likely to see ahead of him, or in some twist of the road, a white dog and a white pony.

Sometimes Temple would let him ride by her side a few

miles ; but she was like some wild thing of the woods when she was in the woods with her dog and her horse.

This was different. Still he found it difficult to speak ; it was on account of that throbbing in his throat.

When he could command his voice, all he said was, " But you didn't stay to the preachin' yourself."

The girl seemed to be gazing over his head into the lighted and shadowy spaces behind him.

" That was different," she answered.

" How different ?"

" Why, you see "—she was looking at him now—" you see, Lincoln, I had just got religion, and I had to go out of the house, into the outdoors, or I couldn't bear the—the glory of it."

Dalvecker did not know just what to say ; he was deeply fearful that he should not say the right thing. A strong, hot anxiety was upon him.

Finally he asked :

" Did religion curm to you when you was prayin'? Oh, that was a beautiful prayer ! jest beautiful ! Did it curm then ?"

" Yes," she answered, hesitatingly ; " yes, I think it must have been then."

" What was it like ?"

The young man was impressed that he would do well to continue speaking on this subject, that he might detain his companion here. He feared that she might all at once go back to the preaching.

Temple left the ox and came to the bar where Dalvecker stood. Her face was now all in the moonlight. The man gazed adoringly at that face.

A sharp glint from the diamond on Temple's finger struck his eye, and at the same instant seemed to stab his heart. He did not know where that ring came from, and he had imagined and suffered a great deal about it.

He felt now like snatching the trinket from its place and flinging it down the mountain.

"What was it like?" he asked again. And he added that he had often thought he must get religion somehow; he reckoned that it was a good deal safer when a man came to die.

"I wish you'd try to tell me how it is, an' I 'low I'll make out to get it somehow. Yes," earnestly, "I'll shorely have it, now you've got it—shorely."

Temple put out her hand and laid it upon Dalvecker's sleeve. A tremor came over him, but he stood motionless. If he moved in the slightest degree she might think to take away her hand. He was not so blind that he could not see that the touch was on his arm in an entirely impersonal way.

"It's somehow like a great white light—and like strength —and like a father's love—only I don't know what a father's love is—and like all beautiful things—and as if beauty would not smite you so any more. You know how beauty hurts, Lincoln?"

"Yes—yes," ardently.

It was characteristic of this girl that she did not in the least understand that his answer might refer to something very different from anything that was in her mind. Besides, if she had been asked to consider the subject she would have decided promptly that she was not beautiful. And she was not. But young Dalvecker was of a different opinion. As she stood there leaning on the bar, with that pale effulgence of moonlight upon her, the man shivered with the sense of what seemed an unbearable emotion. He was blindly groping for the cause. He could not understand. He had seen a good many girls—they had red cheeks and sparkling eyes, and, until they were broken down by hard work, there was a kind of beauty about them. He felt that they must be prettier than Temple. Pretty? Why, Temple wasn't pretty at all. She was—here Dalvecker's pulses gave a great, intoxicating beat—she was lovely, lovely—and the look in her eyes— The young man tried not to go down on his knees there in front of the ox shed.

It occurred to Temple that perhaps she might be the instrument of bringing religion to Dalvecker. He had just said he would surely have it, now that she had it.

She looked at him more attentively.

"Why can't you experience right now?" she inquired, earnestly. "Yes," she repeated, "right now. You know that now is the accepted time."

"I know it," he answered. He moved uneasily. "Somehow I don't quite understand how to begin."

She leaned forward eagerly.

"Give your heart to God," she said, in a half-whisper. "He will take it, and cleanse it, and you can live for Him."

"Oh, Temple!" cried Dalvecker. "I want to. You holp me! You tell me how! If you'd only holp me I could do anything."

Her eyes rested on him with a tender interest.

"I'll pray for you night and morning," she said.

The young man caught her hand impetuously. She did not withdraw it, for she thought he was thinking of religion, and not of her.

She was viewing him as a human being to be saved.

"I don't see how I'm ever to go right 'thout you," he said. "You jest marry me, Temple, an' I'll be plumb shore to get religion, an' keep it to er dead certainty. Now, I will! Come, now, you marry me. I wouldn't give an old set of gears for my life if you don't. But you c'n do any earthly thing with me if you're my wife."

VIII

"WE WILL FIGHT TOGETHER"

TEMPLE did not blush in the least. She gazed seriously at her companion. She rather wondered at the great excitement in his face; but she immediately accounted for that by the fact that he was seeking religion. She had been under great excitement herself a short time ago. She recalled Dr. Ammidown's prescription for her.

"Perhaps you need to lean against Juba," she said.

Dalvecker gazed helplessly. She did not look as if she were mocking him, but why should she say such a thing as that?

"Yes," she went on, examining his countenance yet more closely, "I'm sure you need Juba. It's such a lovely way to get calmer. And you know Mrs. Ammidown is a doctor."

Dalvecker's face turned very red.

"I reckon you're making fun of me," he said.

"Oh, no! no!"

"I want you to be my wife." The young man sturdily repeated these words.

Temple seemed to bring herself to a contemplation of the meaning of what he said.

"I ain't much myself," he said humbly, "but I'd be shore 'bout religion; an' I've gurt a plank house, an' I love you."

"Yes," said Temple, "I reckon you wouldn't say so if you didn't."

Dalvecker burst into an oath. Then he tried to control himself so that he could say with tolerable calmness that he hoped she'd forgive him ; but swearin' was sometimes the only way that a man could find words strong enough.

Temple accepted his apology. She had heard too much swearing to be unduly shocked. She said that she reckoned he knew that she wasn't the kind of girl who could love anybody.

If Dalvecker had been less vitally interested he would have been amused. As it was, he was aware that a great confusion was growing upon him.

"You see," said Temple, " I've always been sure that I could only be very friendly—I couldn't be what you call 'in love.' And I wouldn't want to be. I'm cold-blooded. And I'm powerful glad I am. I don't think there's any need of loving a man as the novels tell about. Regard, and respect, you know, and all that. And identity of interest, and—and—and the same religion. You see, my mother married for love, and she was wretched. She left me a letter about it. I've read that letter a great many times."

Poor Dalvecker could not speak directly. He was so bewildered that his under-jaw dropped a little. He was not nimble minded ; and it was a long moment before it occurred to him that her words might in a way be construed as encouragement. She might possibly marry him, even though she was one of that kind of women whose temperaments make a warm affection impossible.

"If you'd marry me jes' because you was my friend," he said at last, " an' then convert me, you know. If I had you with me I sh'd stay converted."

His tone was very beseeching. " Won't you think of hit ? Oh, do think of hit !"

Temple hesitated. Then she glanced up at the young man again. She was thinking that she had had a strong regard for him since they were boy and girl.

"If you like, I'll consider it," she said. " But "—holding up her hand quickly—" you needn't call anything settled in the least. No ! no ! Don't come near me ! I dislike to have people come near me—only Thimble and Yucatan. Now go. I've so much to think of. And I want to pray and give thanks."

Temple suddenly stooped and came out of the shed, and walked quickly up towards the house.

Lincoln Dalvecker stood and watched the slim, rapidly moving figure. Then he also walked away; but he did not go back to the preaching. He made a rapid plunge into the woods. Since he could not be with Temple he was glad to be alone. At first he was greatly depressed. He did not know that it is considered hopeful not to be refused downright. Still he gathered hope, and when he told his mother the next morning what had been said, she instantly assured him that Temple had " jest as good as said yes " ; and she believed her own words. Why, indeed, should not any girl be glad to marry Link ?

She proceeded forthwith to inform this one and that one of her son's engagement. News travels with wonderful quickness even in a wilderness of mountain-side. Every one within fifty miles knew within a week's time that Temple Crawford was going to marry Link Dalvecker, and every one thought she was doing well. She would have a plank house to live in, and Link's farm lay so good near Cain Creek. It was only feared that Link's wife wouldn't be one that would work as women are expected to work. But no doubt she would get " broke in." It was extremely noticeable among these mountains that the women were broken in—they were that if nothing else. It might almost be said that they were that and nothing else.

Mrs. Ammidown, sitting alone by the fire in the log-house, was thinking of the meeting she had just left. She was annoyed that she had been somewhat moved. In her estimation to be moved by any such cause argued some innate weakness.

She had piled on the fat-wood sticks, and the great flames leaped up and made the place from the open door look as if it were on fire.

The Newfoundland walked softly across the floor and stood beside her. She knew that Temple must be coming, and the next moment the girl entered. She leaned against the wall near the fireplace in silence for a time.

The elder woman would not speak. She had put her head back against her chair and was gazing at her companion, whose face was radiantly thoughtful.

Sometimes a louder strain of song could be heard from the school-house, or a wild shout of "Glory! Glory!"

"I'm thinking about marriage."

It was Temple who said this at last.

Mrs. Ammidown sat upright. She had supposed Temple's thoughts to be occupied by conversion and religion.

"I have known young girls to think of marriage," was the response.

But Temple did not seem to hear this remark.

"I should not want to marry," she said, "unless I thought I could do a great deal of good."

Mrs. Ammidown made a slight sound that was not exactly a groan.

"To do good," continued Temple, "of course ought to be the first object in life."

She glanced down at the woman sitting near her, and received an ambiguous smile in response.

"To be the means of saving a human soul must be the greatest good one can do," now remarked Temple.

Mrs. Ammidown remained perfectly still, though in doing so she resisted a great desire to get up, to take the girl's arm, and demand to know what she meant. She was so much interested in Temple that she was moved by what she called her "notions" more than she wished to be. And Temple was constantly taking up notions and being ruled by them, for the time being.

"I thought you said you were considering marriage," now said Mrs. Ammidown, with a gentleness that was suspicious.

"Yes, I am," was the reply.

"Well, I don't quite see the connection. But then I am stupid."

"If you thought you could save a man's soul—save it from endless perdition—by marrying him, wouldn't you do it?"

Temple said "do hit." Her face was quite colorless, her eyes full of brilliance. Mrs. Ammidown had a curious and, for some reason, distressing fancy that the girl's chin seemed to have still more resolution than usual in its contour.

"No, I wouldn't."

Mrs. Ammidown's answer was low but distinct.

"You would let him go to hell?" was the next question, put with intense solemnity.

"Certainly I would—unless I loved him."

Temple placed her hands together in a way she had.

"There's no question of love," she said, "not the least, on my part—as you understand it."

"Oh! . Then there is some particular man who wishes you to save him from hell by marrying him?"

Temple made a slight writhing movement. She did not like to hear the matter put in just that way.

"I suppose he thinks he loves you?" asked Mrs. Ammidown.

"I reckon so."

Temple left her position and went to the table. She took up her violin which lay there. She picked the strings a little, as if it were a banjo. Then she seemed to bethink herself; she put down the instrument quickly.

"You don't understand me," she said. "I think friendship and respect are enough to make a woman marry a man. I think what—well—what you call love is merely something gross and of the flesh. I reckon it's natural for men to feel that, but not for women. It's enough for a woman to have a cordial liking, and affection—and—and so on."

Mrs. Ammidown looked at the speaker in silence. She thought that she had never felt quite so helpless in her life. She wondered what Temple contemplated doing. Whatever it was she wanted to snatch the girl away from it.

"May I ask where you got these ideas?" finally inquired the elder woman.

"You see," said Temple, "I've always had them. To begin with, you know, I'm cold-blooded; I have a cold temperament."

As the girl made this favorite assertion of hers, Mrs. Ammidown said,

"Oh!" and then said nothing more.

"Yes," continued Temple, "and I've thought about these things, and I'm really convinced. My mother must have known. Don't you think my own mother knew, Mrs. Ammidown?"

"How can I tell? You know it is possible that she might have been mistaken."

"Oh no; she was very clear and positive. She wrote a letter for me to read when I was fifteen. I only remember her a very little. She was lovely—she is like a lovely dream to me always. She had such dark, sweet eyes." Here the speaker's voice faltered. But she went on immediately. "Sally knew her. She had Sally for her servant, and so Sally can tell me ever so many things about her. Would you like to see my mother's picture?"

Temple went out of the room and returned with a little case holding an old-fashioned ambrotype of a girl of about Temple's age. The face had that indefinite something which denotes an ardent, tropical, and perhaps undisciplined nature. It had also an equally undefinable resemblance to Temple without tokens of her strength of character.

Mrs. Ammidown looked at the picture in silence a moment before she said,

"She, at least, did not love in a cool, matter-of-fact way."

"That's just it," eagerly exclaimed Temple. "She didn't love in the right way, and she was wretched. She knew where she had made the mistake. And she wanted to keep me from such a mistake. And, besides, my temperament is so different—but why do you smile in that way? What do you mean by that kind of a smile?"

"I mean nothing—absolutely nothing."

"But you do—only you won't tell."

Temple stood holding her mother's picture and looking at it.   Presently she asked,

"Would you like to see that letter ?   I've always wanted to show you that letter because "—she hesitated ; then she knelt down by her friend and leaned her arms upon her lap, looking up into the face above her—"because I am so fond of you.   You've been so kind to me, you know."

Mrs. Ammidown pushed back the thick, short hair on the girl's forehead.

"It's not so very difficult to be kind to you," she said. Then, with a sort of strenuous earnestness, she asked, quickly,

"Will you tell what man's soul you are thinking of saving by becoming his wife ?"

Temple answered, promptly,

"Link Dalvecker.   He says he's sure he can keep religion if I'll marry him."

Again Mrs. Ammidown had that helpless feeling which came to her now and then with reference to Temple.   The girl's simplicity seemed to take every weapon from the hands of the elder woman.

"Are you going to oblige him ?" she asked.

"I told him I'd think about it," was the answer.

"If you told him that he'll be sure you'll accept him."

"I don't see why."

"It's the truth, however.   You'll find out.   Will you let me see your mother's letter ?"

Temple again went to her own room.   She returned with a thick letter carefully wrapped.

"Don't read it here," she said.   "Take it home with you."

She remained standing near her guest, looking down at her with wistful intentness.

"Well, what is it ?" inquired Mrs. Ammidown at last.

"It's about religion," was the quick answer.   The girl

went on hurriedly. "Don't you want the Lord to come into your soul and take possession of it?"

The other seemed to try to answer, but she gave up the attempt. She resolved not to say anything reflecting on Temple's "experience." She did not know how much there might be in it. Who could tell? Her brother believed in such things. She rose quickly and made a motion as if throwing off something oppressive. She walked to the door.

"The preaching is over," she said, with an air of relief. "See the black figures in the moonlight. I'm glad I'm to have a canter of a few miles before I go to bed. I'll meet Richard, and we'll mount at the shed where our horses are. If he doesn't take cold it will be one of the latter-day miracles. Good-bye, dear. May I advise you not to think too favorably about saving a man's soul by becoming his wife?"

The speaker walked out quickly, and the next moment joined her brother, who was coming up the slope.

"Let us hurry," said Mrs. Ammidown, with some authority; "a good gallop is all that will save you. And I have something to tell you."

In a few moments the brother and sister were galloping as swiftly as possible along the rough path that led to the State road. Once in that road they went still faster. As the horses were climbing a hill Mercer said:

"What is it you have to tell me?"

"I will call it a question of ethics," was the answer, "and we'll wait until I have put you into your bed and you are drinking a dose of hot whiskey. If you come to an untimely death from jumping into the French Broad after a drunken man you will have to give up the saving of souls; at least, in this world."

Later, when Mrs. Ammidown was sitting beside his bed, Mercer went back to the subject of ethics.

"Perhaps it isn't ethics at all," was the answer. "It's about that Crawford girl."

She was openly watching her brother. "I suppose she is converted; any way, she thinks she is."

"I hope it's a true conversion, and not merely emotion," responded Mercer, strongly.

"Of course. You'll be interested to know that your convert is going to try to save some one directly."

Mercer was looking full in his sister's face. When she had said "that Crawford girl" he was conscious of a thrill of interest which he resolutely set himself to ignore. He had a tolerably well formed belief that anything spontaneous, involuntary, must perforce be something to be ignored or fought; something of the original devil lurking in us all.

"I suppose a new convert is very eager to convert others," remarked Mrs. Ammidown.

Her judgment told her that she need not be sorry in any way for the man before her. She gazed at him in admiration. Richard always seemed to her like a tempered, keen blade without a scabbard. She leaned against the bed and stroked his hot forehead.

"Did Miss Crawford wish to convert you?" he asked.

"Yes; but what troubles me is that that young fellow with the yellow mustache wishes Temple Crawford to convert him. He thinks he can't save his soul without her help."

Mercer moved his head away from his sister's hand. His face hardened perceptibly.

Mrs. Ammidown went on,

"But a worse feature is that Temple herself wishes to help him save his soul."

"Don't be flippant," said Mercer, severely.

"I don't feel flippant in the least. But I wish you hadn't converted Temple to-night. She's a girl who carries an idea into action at the earliest possible moment."

Mercer's face was now so composed that his burning eyes seemed set in a frozen countenance.

"Does Miss Crawford love this young man?" he asked.

"That is the worst feature of all," was the prompt response. "She doesn't love him."

"And she is considering a marriage with him?"

"Yes; for his good."

Mercer was silent for a few moments. Then he said,

"I think I will get up."

His sister pushed back her chair.

"Not until morning," she said, sharply.

"Now. I have something to do. I want to see Miss Crawford. You said once that she often sat up late. I shall get back there before midnight. If she is up I shall see her; if not I must wait until to-morrow."

Mrs. Ammidown did not waste another word. She rose and left the room. Very soon she heard her brother's door shut. She went to the window and threw up the casement. The moon was in a clear heaven. The night was soft. The mountains, with Pisgah as monarch, stood solemnly against the deep-blue black of the sky.

Horse's hoofs sounded distinctly on the road from the stable. Mercer came into sight, riding swiftly, sitting erect and determined, like one who never failed to do what he resolved to do. His sister knew very well that he would have ridden off just like this if he had known that an old and ugly woman contemplated doing what he thought to be wrong.

Temple Crawford was not an old and ugly woman, and Mrs. Ammidown wondered much concerning the coming interview.

She closed the window and sat down to read the letter Mrs. Crawford had left for her daughter's warning and guidance.

Mercer's horse galloped steadily on. When he was where his rider could see the log-house the animal was suddenly hushed to a walk.

The windows of the house were light, and the door open. When Mercer drew nearer he heard the girl's voice singing,
ing,

> "Oh, my Lawd, don't you forgit me,
> Oh, my Lawd, don't you forgit me,
> Oh, my Lawd, don't you forgit me,
> Down by Bab'lon's stream !"

Another voice joined loudly in "Down by Bab'lon's stream." And then there was a swift clapping of hands, and melodious, guttural exclamations that the man knew could only come from a negro.

Mercer slipped down from his horse. He stood a moment with the bridle in his hand. He lifted his cap and gazed reverently upward for a brief space, asking help from that source of Almighty help which he knew had never failed him.

Then he let go the bridle. His horse would stay near until his master came back.

Temple was standing before the fire. Her hands were clasped above her head, and she was singing fervently, rocking back and forth from her toes to her heels. On the hearth, her knees drawn up and clasped by her hands, was the yellow woman, who, when she did not sing, released her knees and clapped her hands vigorously.

In the instant that Mercer looked before he stepped forward, Temple changed her attitude; she took two or three wild dancing steps across the hearth, singing all the time,

> "Oh, my Lawd, don't you forgit me."

Sally saw the minister first. She sprang to her feet with the agility of a panther.

"Lawd bress us !" with a broad, dramatic gesture. "Hyar's de preacher right yer now, honey ! Look behind yo' !"

Temple turned quickly as Mercer came forward.

"I hope you'll pardon me, Miss Crawford," he said, with cold precision, "for coming at this hour. I shouldn't have intruded if I hadn't been sure you had not retired. I must tell you that I felt it to be my duty to see you as soon as possible.”

Sally’s eyes were on the speaker. There was something peculiar in them. She did not speak again, but walked out of the house and left the two alone—save that Yucatan had come forward to investigate.

Temple sat down and looked up at her visitor, who remained standing, and who also looked at her, but with a veiled gaze that made his glance remote and impersonal. He was standing near a chair, but he did not put his hands upon it as most people would have done. He thrust the fingers of his left hand into his tightly buttoned coat.

“You know a minister is interested in all that concerns his people,” he said. “You are one of my people now.”

“Yes,” said Temple.

“ My sister has just told me of your intentions as regards young Dalvecker.”

“Yes,” said Temple again. “ Though I don’t exactly know what my intentions are yet.”

“Your thoughts, then. May I talk freely with you?”

“Of course.”

The girl continued to gaze up at him. Mercer did not change his attitude, but in spite of himself there was a change in his face. His glance became less impersonal— as if his eyes were something apart from him, something which he could not quite control. Suddenly Temple rose and exclaimed,

“I’m so glad you have come! A minister can advise one. I think I could do a great deal of good if I were Link’s wife. I suppose we are here to do the most good we can.”

Mercer was aware that his mouth was so dry that his tongue seemed to cleave to the roof of it. He was aware of this fact with a deep and angry surprise. This girl was nothing to him, absolutely nothing. He was going to treat her precisely as if she were—well, as if she were any one of those unkempt, dingy-faced women with a wad of snuff under her lip.

"Yes," he said, "but there are some sacrifices that God would not ask us to make."

"Are there? Are you sure? God loves sacrifice, doesn't He?"

"Certainly."

Having pronounced that one word, Mercer did not, for the moment, attempt another.

He had seen this girl in all for so very brief a space that it was absurd that there should be anything in his mind but a general care for her well-being. He tried to reassure himself by thinking, what was the truth, that he should be doing this thing if she had been any other person who was contemplating what he considered a wrong action. But somehow this thought did not reinforce him as it ought.

He could not help thinking of Temple's eyes. Why were they just like that? What was there in them? He had never in his life asked these questions before, and he had never meant to ask them. They also were absurd. He was interested in Temple because she had a soul to be saved. He told this with great emphasis to himself ; but even while he told it he knew that it was a lie ; and a lie is of the devil.

While he was casting about in his mind for some words that should smite with cutting strength, as with a sword, Temple spoke again.

"There's Lincoln Dalvecker's eternal welfare to be considered, you know ; but more than that, there are the mountain people all about. Don't you think I could do them good? Oh !" passionately, "you can't know how I long to do good !"

Mercer had a painful conviction that for the first time in his life he did not understand himself. Worse than that, he was not quite sure that he securely held the reins over his neck. He was like one dazzled. That power of personal presence which others had felt when with this girl, and of which she was totally unconscious, was having its effect now upon this man who had in his heart devoted himself to what he considered God's work. There was a great deal of the spirit of the Middle Ages in Richard Mercer.

He made another attempt to speak, and this time he said,

"You are among the mountain people now."

"Yes; but you see, as Lincoln's wife, I should be identified with them; I could devote my life. I could be a missionary all the time. I could be the means of saving souls."

For the first time since he had chosen his life work the Rev. Richard Mercer was aware that the phrase "saving souls" failed to stir him to enthusiasm.

"Don't you see?" she asked.

"I think I see what you mean," he answered, coldly.

She looked at him in surprise. She was somehow disappointed. She could not understand why he did not urge her to go on. But he did not.

As she looked at him a subtle change came over her mood. She suddenly dropped her eyes.

"I wish you would advise me," she said with some humility. Then, with timid interrogation, "I reckon you're a man of God, ain't you?"

"I try to be."

"Then you'll know what to tell me."

Mercer was struggling with himself that he might be able to advise her without the slightest reference to his own feeling. What was the affair to him personally? Absolutely nothing. When he should have passed a few months working among these people he would go on to another field, and he should never see this girl again.

It was a strange fact that the words "never see this girl again" shook him as if they had been something tangible. Was it possible that he had esteemed himself strong because nothing of consequence had ever tried his strength?

"Yes," he answered, quickly. "I shall know what to tell you. Don't marry that man. Don't do it. Is it that you want a great space—much to do?   Is it?   Answer me. Will your enthusiasm hold out?   Tell me."

Mercer's eyes blazed across the space between him and the girl.   He was fighting against a primitive, furious temptation to go out and throttle that yellow-haired youth, lest this girl might be persuaded to marry him.   He wanted to be in the open air and wrestle alone against this unheard-of emotion.   The very atmosphere here was alive with the presence of Temple.

Mercer wished also to stand there and look at her—to stand there forever and look at her.   He did not understand it at all.   He did not in the least believe in anything like this.   No well-regulated mind ever succumbed to anything of this kind.

His thoughts ran on in such fashion as he stood there meeting the glance of Temple's warm-colored, dark eyes. It was impossible to tell whether eyes of such a hue were really warm, or only had that appearance.   Temple's light hair was rumpled confusedly.   She had rumpled it afresh when she and Sally had been singing by themselves after Miss Drowdy had left them.   There was always much of the unusual in the girl's appearance; perhaps this appearance was intensified now.

"Will it last?"

Mercer repeated his question authoritatively.

"Oh," exclaimed Temple, "I'm sure it will.   Still, how can I tell?   I never experienced religion before.   But Sally has.   Only hers doesn't hold out.   She has the power, you know.   The Holy Ghost gets right hold of her."

Temple said "right holt" with an unconscious but perfect negro intonation.

Mercer inwardly shrank from these phrases.

"It's the helping others—the being of use—it's the service," he began quickly, "that tells whether the thing is real or not."

But Mercer found that he could not go on in that way. He would not make the attempt any more.

" Do you love young Dalvecker ?" he asked, abruptly.

" I like him so much.   And he's very—very respectable."

" Do you love him ?"

Temple drew a little nearer.

" You see," she said, in a confidential tone, " I don't believe in that kind of thing.   I know better than that.   It doesn't amount to anything."

Mercer was confounded.   His sister had hinted at this. But when a man came to stand opposite such a face and have the owner of it speak in this way, the effect was confusion.

Mercer made up his mind.   And he never hesitated after he had decided.

" Since you feel that way," he said, " and since you want to work in the vineyard, marry me.   Join me in this glorious labor.   We will fight together on the Lord's side."

IX

"THE CHAINS, THE SHINING CHAINS"

TEMPLE was silent for so long after this rather peculiar offer of marriage that it became somewhat difficult for Mercer to maintain his impassive attitude. He quite recognized that it was necessary to be impassive. He was so masculine—I had almost said so blindly masculine—that he believed everything she said of herself. It was, indeed, evident that she was sincere; but a sincere person does not always know what the truth is.

Temple put her hand up to her head; she ran her fingers through her hair. She did not blush, as why should she? It was only an offer of partnership to which she had listened.

"Oh, dear!" she exclaimed at last, "I'm so confused. I want to think about what you have proposed."

And then she remembered that she had said something like that not many hours ago to Link Dalvecker.

These two experiences coming in the same evening, when no one had ever spoken in this way to her in all her life before (for with her young Boynton did not count), affected her with an irresistible sense of the ludicrous. She was too much excited to control a semi-hysterical laugh, and it burst forth.

Mercer's face became red. He drew himself up stiffly. He reached for his hat, which he had placed on the table.

"I beg your pardon," he said. "It does not seem to me a matter to excite laughter."

Temple stopped laughing instantly, and became very grave.

"I hope you'll forgive me," she said, humbly. "I don't know what made me laugh. I reckon I must be tired."

There was so much genuine humility in her voice and manner that one must necessarily forgive her directly.

Mercer stood with his hat in his hand.

"I will see you again in a day or two," he said, now able to speak as if in reference to a business arrangement, "and you can give me your answer. In the meantime-let me suggest to you to bear in mind what I have said about the wider field of labor which you would have as my wife. You would go with me—you would help in the meetings; you could work acceptably, I am sure. Good-night."

Temple said "Good-night" in response. She went to the door, and saw the man mount his horse and ride away. She was so tense with the accumulated excitement of the day and evening that she mistook that tenseness for strength. Strong-nerved and full of health as she was, she did not understand that her excitement and her fatigue might now make it impossible for her to think of any subject in just proportion to all phases of it.

She had returned to the fire, and was standing before it, thinking that, after all, she was not tired in the least, and that it was now so late that she need not go to bed that night, when the door leading into the next room opened, and Almina appeared. She had her big blanket-shawl wrapped about her; her bare feet were thrust into her boots, whose heels clicked on the boards as she came forward, with an air of being ready to fly backward on the instant.

"There ain't no man here now, is there?" she asked.

"Oh no."

" And you ain't expectin' no more of 'em?"

"Oh no."

"Then I do wish you'd jest shut that outside door. I ain't hardly seen it shut sence I've been here. 'N' I want to set down by the fire a minute. I can't sleep. I'm jes' 's nervous 's I c'n be. It always did make me nervous to go to a revival meet'n'. But I wouldn't miss one for anything in the world."

Temple closed the door. She came back and wrapped

Miss Drowdy's shawl carefully about the thin, shivering shoulders. The Yankee woman was painfully conscious that she was not yet herself; that she " hadn't got her bearings" since she had come to Carolina.

It was to her like being in another world. Her shrewd sense had not had time to assert itself.

And to live in a house where the outside door was never shut ! And where there was no up-stairs ! She was trying to wait patiently until her senses should come back to her. She had written home to her sister in Hoyt that she appeared to be underwitted since she came to Limestone Township; but then, she had added, "maybe I've always been underwitted, only I hadn't found it out."

It is not soothing to a person's self-consciousness to make such a discovery.

" I thought I saw a man riding down the slope," said Miss Drowdy.

" 'Twas the minister," said the girl.

Almina felt more underwitted than ever. She gazed at Temple to see if she could detect any sign that it was an unusual thing for a minister to make a midnight call on a young lady. But she could see no such sign.

" Ain't it—ain't it ruther late for calls ?"

Almina put the inquiry feebly. She did not know what was the proper point of view.

" I don't know what time it is," replied Temple, carelessly.

" It's goin' on one o'clock," was the solemn response.

" Oh, is it ?" still more carelessly.

" Yes, it is. And it don't seem proper to me, exactly—" began Almina. But she paused, for Temple was not a girl to whom to talk concerning conventions and proprieties.

" I s'pose he come about your soul," finished Almina.

It would certainly be proper to come at any time about one's soul.

Temple was sitting on the hearth opposite her guest. She

had her hands clasped over her head. She was thinking that she was glad Miss Drowdy was with her. She was in the mood to consult her. She particularly liked to get people's ideas, and then do exactly as she pleased. She had a way of asking a person's opinion as if the opinion would have weight with her—and sometimes it did have weight, for a few hours.

"You see, I'm all alone," she began, "for Sally couldn't advise me. Mr. Mercer told me he thought I could do a great deal of good if I married him and helped him in his work. And before that, Link Dalvecker, you know—or don't you know?—thought I could be sure to save his soul if I married him. So you see—"

Up to this point the girl had been deeply serious; but now her sense of humor suddenly came uppermost again, and she began to laugh excitedly.

But Almina did not laugh. She bent forward towards her companion, her shawl wrapped so tightly about her that she looked like a stick.

"Do you love either of them?" she asked, with intense seriousness.

Temple stopped laughing.

"Oh, how odd it is!" she exclaimed. "Why do you and Mrs. Ammidown ask that the first thing? And Mr. Mercer wanted to know if I loved Link. Now, you see," in an elucidating and argumentative manner, "it's rather foolish than otherwise to be in love. Because, you see, if you are, you get over it very soon, and settle right down to friendship; so why not begin with friendship? Then you wouldn't be disappointed or grieved if your husband stopped being in love with you first. It would all be understood and settled at the very beginning."

Almina gradually sank back in her chair as she listened. She was thinking, among other things, of that doctor up at home who had asked her to be his wife, and whom "there was nothing against." That there was nothing against him had been reason enough, apparently, why she should say yes to him. But somehow she couldn't say yes. Had she been wrong? Here was this young girl—

At this point in her thoughts Almina stared yet more intently at the girlish, strong face before her. She supposed the world must be changing, and she herself, not changing with it, was getting so old-fashioned that she could no longer understand. Perhaps young men and women did not in these days fall in love with each other. They arrange a bargain, a partnership, and therefore there was no more any sharp disillusion. Which way was better?

If Almina had been asleep she would have thought she was now dreaming. But a revival meeting, as has been stated, was sure to keep her awake. She rubbed her eyes.

"I guess I ain't very wise," she remarked. "I guess it ain't worth while for you to try to explain anything. It wouldn't pay."

Temple's eyes were so bright, they gleamed so ; her face was so pale, her lips so red, that Almina was tempted to recommend valerian, or something of that sort. But she reflected that the girl had strong reasons for being excited ; had she not just experienced religion, and had not the preacher just offered marriage, not to speak of Dalvecker's proposal ?

Temple clasped her hands over her head again, and walked quickly a few times back and forth along the hearth.

" But, you see, I want to make you understand," she said. "Somebody's got to understand. I shall be wild if I can't talk it over with somebody."

"I should say you were kind of wild now," said the elder woman.

"It seems as if I couldn't have chances enough to do good," said Temple, not noticing her companion's words. "I long to work for the salvation of everybody. I want them to know what it is to have the Holy Ghost descend into their hearts. I believe I could help convert people. And, you see, if I should be a preacher's wife I should have so much more chance. I could work for more people. I almost think I have the gift to rouse. Do you think I have the gift to rouse, Miss Drowdy?"

"Oh, dear! I should certainly think so! If you don't have it I'm sure I can't tell who has," was the answer. Almina added, questioningly, "I s'pose you've about made up your mind to have him, 'ain't you?"

Instead of answering, Temple knelt down and flung her arms across the big chair in front of her. She began to pray aloud. Miss Drowdy shaded her eyes with her hand and listened, and as she listened she thrilled in response to the passionate words of entreaty and adoration and thanks which came pouring from the girl's heart through her lips.

When the words ceased Almina rose quickly; she went and flung her arms about Temple. The woman was sobbing with emotion.

"It seems," she said, brokenly, "as if you had a great work before you."

Temple did not speak; indeed, she could not. She lay with her face pressed down upon the chair.

Yucatan, who had been listening uneasily throughout the entire petition, now ventured to go to the side of his mistress. He sniffed at her hair, then he dropped his head and gently licked one of her hands, which hung down from the chair.

The dog's touch made the girl stir. In a moment she rose.

"I'm going out," she said. "I must go out under God's heaven."

She looked round for her hat. Yucatan, who never failed to understand the phrase "going out," began to wag his tail. He also looked about for the same thing. It was one of his most delightful privileges to bring her hat to his friend, and he always availed himself of an opportunity.

He presently made a dive at a distant corner and returned with the felt in his mouth, wagging his tail violently.

"But is it safe—so late?" anxiously asked Almina.

"Ask Yucatan if it's safe," was the answer.

Temple and the dog left the house. Almina saw them go quickly along the pasture-land farther up the mountain. From that pasture she had already learned could be had a far extended view of the peaks round about. Those peaks were now standing in a glory of moonlight. The valleys were lying, dark and mysterious, between.

Almina, as she stood looking forth from the door, shivered with longing and dread.

She pulled her shawl again about her shrinking shoulders.

"I declare," she said, in a whisper, " there ain't a thing here as 'tis up in Hoyt."

She closed the door, and went to her chair by the fire. She huddled herself down in it, and spread out her hands to the blaze. She would have preferred to go to bed, but she felt it her duty to sit up for Temple. She also felt it to be extremely uncertain when that person would return. She rather admired the girl for going off in that way. Almina remembered that there had been several times in her own life when it would have been a great relief if she could have run away like that. But in Hoyt folks stopped at home, and worked, and talked just the same as usual, no matter what happened.

When, two hours later, Temple came back, her face calm and exalted from her communion with the mountains, a deep, still radiance in her eyes, she found her guest sound asleep in the arm-chair before the coals on the hearth.

Temple did not disturb her. The girl did not think it was worth while to go to her own room. Already on the eastern verge of the world there were coming some faint, pearl hues of morning, but morning would still linger long before really arriving. The girl took a shawl and wrapped it about her. Conventional in nothing, she laid herself down on the warm hearth. The Newfoundland immediately placed his huge bulk beside her. In five minutes the dog and his mistress were asleep.

The sunlight had been warm for two or three hours on the front of the log-house when the yellow woman, a pipe between her teeth and with her hands on her hips, came with long, slow strides from her cabin.

She gently pushed open the door and looked in.

Almina returned the look silently. Then she rose and made her way noiselessly outside. She was trembling with what she called a "complete unstrungness."

"For the land's sake," she whispered, "if you've got any tea, make me a cup as strong as Samson."

The two walked towards the other cabin.

Sally took her pipe from her mouth.

"I'm done shore der ain't no tea," she said. "I war aimin' ter go ter Asheville, an' when I went I aimed ter git tea, fur shore. I'll meek yo' er cup er cawfy 'fore yo' c'n wink, ef yo' say der word."

Sally looked with patronizing pity at her companion. Miss Drowdy could not ride, she couldn't tramp up and down mountains, and she preferred tea to "cawfy." Still, Sally was aware that she liked the "pore little Yankee."

While the coffee was brewing, and while Sally was frying some bacon to go with it, Almina walked about in front of the house. There were still some wreaths of mist floating here and there on the mountain-sides. Miss Drowdy was gazing about her, carefully holding up her skirts as she did so.

As she gazed she heard, very much softened by the distance, the sound of a violin from the direction of the French Broad.

"There's that fiddling feller of Temple's," she said to herself. "I wonder if he's expecting her."

She suddenly forgot her extreme need of nourishment or stimulant. She walked along the path she had once before taken when she had followed Temple down to the river. As she came nearer the music sounded still more clearly, and she was presently aware that the player was also singing. She could not catch the words, but she stopped to listen, and as she listened a smile came to her face. She had so decided a vein of sentiment in her make-up that she was conscious now of a slight pang in regard to this young man. What could a girl who was contemplating life as Temple was now contemplating it do with a young man with a fiddle?

As Miss Drowdy walked on very slowly, the song ceased, and presently there was the sound of footsteps approaching rapidly. The next moment Yale Boynton pushed impatiently through the rhododendron shrubs and came forward.

There was a warm eagerness on his face which instantly gave way to an extremely visible annoyance.

He took off his hat as he exclaimed,

"Oh! I saw a woman's gown among the bushes; I hoped —I thought—I—"

He stopped and looked crossly beyond his companion, as if seeking for some one.

"I guess you're looking for Miss Crawford," remarked Almina.

"Yes. She let me think she would be down to the Broad this morning," was the reply.

Almina indulgently gazed at the handsome, youthful face before her with its frown and the vexed look in the eyes.

"She hadn't waked up when I came out," she said.

"Hadn't waked?" exclaimed Boynton.

He frowned; he ground his heel into the soft, black mould.

"No," said Almina; "she didn't get to sleep very early, and she was mighty tired."

"I didn't get to sleep early, either, and I was tired too," was the response, "but I was out starting from Asheville on time, you may believe. I want to see her. Is she going to sleep all day, do you think?"

The speaker was so pretty, and so disappointed, that Almina did not resent his petulance, and she supposed that he must be very much in love.

As he spoke Boynton was still gazing beyond Miss Drowdy and towards the house. His face changed suddenly; his eyes sparkled. He took a step forward, then waited.

Almina turned, and saw Temple coming towards them. The girl's face was flushed ; one cheek was of a deep crimson ; her eyes still had in them a cloudy, sleepy expression. When within a few yards she stopped and passed her hands over her face, yawning as she did so.

Almina suddenly remembered her breakfast, and hurried towards it.

" I done forgot !" cried Temple.

" That's just like you ; but I didn't forget.   I couldn't. Do you think I shouldn't remember every minute that I was going to meet you this morning, and that you were going to finish learning the ' Kerry Dance' ?   Say, do you think I shouldn't remember ?"

Temple was looking at the young man with a feeling of surprise and self-questioning.

She could not understand now how she had been interested in him at all.   It really must have been pleasant for her to be with him—yes, it must have been.   But it appeared impossible now.

" How odd you look !" he cried.   She made no answer to this, and he added, " Come, let's go down to the boat. My violin's there."

She did not reply to this, either.   She was trying to adjust herself to the fact that he could not excite her interest any more.

" What's the matter ?" he asked, brusquely.   " What makes you look like that ?   Where were you last evening ? Something seems to have come over you.   I say, you don't know what a jolly lunch I've got for you."

He put out his hand as if to lead her down the path.   But she did not apparently see the hand.

She replied to one of his inquiries,

" I was to preaching, down in the school-house," she said.

" To preaching ?"   He laughed.   " Oh, by Jove ! now, I wish I'd been there.   I've always meant to go.   But somehow I never did.   I reckon 'twas a rousing time, wasn't it ?"

" Yes, it was."

Temple spoke so coldly that her companion began to be frightened.   He scowled again.

" I got religion," the girl said.

" The deuce!   Oh, that's too bad !"

" You needn't speak like that."

" That's too infernally bad !   And I can't believe it," persisted the youth.

" You ought to be glad of it."

" It isn't going to last, is it ?"

" I hope so."

" But it doesn't usually, does it ?"

" Oh, I don't know.   I only know it ought."

" Ought ?   Why, Temple Crawford, don't you know it spoils any one ?"

The girl had her hat under her arm.   She now put it on her head, pushed up the brim, and half turned from the young man, her eyes wandering over the mountains.   After the excitement of the previous night she was suffering from a reaction.   But she did not know why she was so depressed and listless.   She had a vague idea that this depression was because of sin.

" I hope it does spoil people for this world," she said, after a pause.

" So you're going to talk that way, are you ?   Well, as long's I'm in this world I don't want to be spoiled for it."

The young man spoke vehemently.   He was aware of a painful stinging in his eyes and a compression upon his throat.   He was looking fixedly at the face near him.   He perceived that it was strangely remote.   Indeed, it hardly seemed like the face of Temple Crawford.

But the attraction of the girl's personality was still as strong as ever over him—stronger, since he began to fear she was removing herself from him.

She did not reply.   She continued to look off at the Twin Brothers, upon whose heads the clouds were settling.

Boynton was furiously conscious that she did not know he was looking at her.

"I hope you're not going to give up the 'Kerry Dancing,' are you?" he asked, speaking as amiably as possible.

"Of course."

"And your violin?"

"I haven't decided that yet. I haven't had time to make up my mind."

"Perhaps the preacher will tell you what to do with your fiddle," sneering. "Who is the preacher?"

"Mr. Richard Mercer."

And here Temple recalled something there had been in Mr. Mercer's face, and she blushed, and then blushed again with irritation.

"Oh, I know about him. He won't let you have your fiddle, you may be sure of that."

"I hope I can give it up, though I do love it a great deal!"

"Are you going to hold on to your horse and dogs?"

Temple put her hands together.

"Oh! Surely there is no need!" she exclaimed. "I—I—it would hurt very much to give them up."

She turned with an involuntary movement towards Yucatan, who had followed her from the house. She looked at him in silence.

"I reckon Mercer's the kind of man that'll advise you to give up a thing you like just because you do like it! I swear there's no sense in the whole business! Can't you look at a fellow, Miss Crawford, as though you knew he was in the same world with you?"

Temple turned her eyes to the clouded face near her.

"I reckon you don't consider it's wicked to eat, do you, even though you've got religion?"

This question recalled to Temple the fact that she was hungry. Her last meal had been not long after noon of the day before. The meals in the Crawford residence occurred at the most irregular intervals. One could not calculate on them in the least.

"I'm hungry, I do believe," said Temple.

Boynton's face brightened.

"Then come down to the boat. I told you I had a jolly lunch. Some of those fat liver pie things—I thought we'd try them—and two bottles of lager. Come."

Boynton turned, and held back some of the branches of the thick-growing shrubs that Temple might pass. The two went down to the old tree trunk which made the landing. The young man hurried as if he feared that his companion might suddenly decide not to accompany him. But Temple did not think of going back. She sprang into the boat moored there. She beckoned to Yucatan, who immediately followed her, and sat down gravely in the bottom of the craft with the air of having to be very careful lest he might overturn the whole thing.

The violin was lying on the stern seat. Temple lifted the instrument and held it tenderly, passing her fingers over the strings, and bringing out a musical clash of sound.

The young man looked at her furtively. He smiled faintly, but was careful that she should not see that he did so.

He opened a bottle of beer, filled a travelling-cup, and gravely handed it to her, saying,

"You look awfully tired. Drink that, while I get the grub out of the basket."

Temple put the violin across her lap, and then drank.

The soft wind blew freshly down the river. The mists upon the heights began to lift again and drift away as the sun grew stronger.

The girl felt that her mood was changing. She was none the less resolved about religion, but religion did not seem to require so much in a certain way.

She still retained the violin as she ate, with keen relish, the rather indiscriminate lunch Boynton had brought.

Her spirits rose higher and higher. But she did not talk much. She smiled at her companion's chatter. The expression of extreme weariness left her face. She was beginning to appreciate the pleasure of this relaxation.

As for Boynton, his heart was bounding again. He was in the habit of telling himself that he knew girls rather well. He had been quite frightened this morning, however. What a hideous arrangement it would be if Temple should take a fancy to keep up that notion about religion ! But she was coming out of it all right.

He was shrewd enough not to return to the topic. He now gazed openly at the girl in the stern. Still he could not please himself with the idea that she was thinking of him.

In fact, she had fallen into one of her states of what might almost be called semi-trance, when mere existence was a joy so intense as to be somewhat oppressive.

There was in her possession the river, the sunlight, the great Appalachian range, and life.

Boynton gently took his fiddle from her knees. He put it under his chin and drew his bow tentatively across the strings, his eyes on the girl.

In a moment he began to play and sing in half-tones, as one might say.

At first Temple did not notice what it was he sang ; she only knew that it was nothing which made any discord with her mood. Indeed, Boynton had too good taste to run any risk in his selection.

But he was so relieved to find that she did not insist on seeming as she had seemed up there among the rhododendrons, that he became a bit more reckless than he had been before.

Hitherto he had tried to have before him the undoubted fact that this girl who lived in the wilderness, and who went riding about in such a dare-devil way, was a girl to flirt with, perhaps, but not to marry.

But now the conviction had come upon him with great force that there was no other woman in the world whom he could possibly think of marrying.

He could not help believing, also, that, if he should confess this state of mind, Temple would agree with him. Still—

The doubt that would obtrude itself made his exceedingly sweet tenor voice even sweeter than ever, and his handsome young face handsomer than ever.

This was what he murmured in his tenor voice at the girl:

> "Oh, blest be he! Oh, blest be he!
> Let him all blessings prove,
> Who made the chains, the shining chains,
> The holy chains of love!"

Boynton sang these lines and then was silent for a moment, making a little interlude on the strings.

He was irritated that he could not in the least tell whether his companion had heard him or not. She did not change her attitude of lounging in the stern, with one arm over the Newfoundland who sat beside her; her face was turned up the river.

Boynton sighed deeply and ostentatiously. Then he began again:

> "Oh, blest be he! Oh, blest be he!"

and sang the words even more insistently.

He made a little clang with his instrument as he finished, and he almost dashed it down beside him.

"I never saw such a girl!" he cried. "You don't seem to have any heart. Can't you look at me? All this scenery is going to be here right along, but I shall have to go away."

Temple turned her eyes towards him.

"Have you heard a word I've been singing?" he asked.

"Oh yes. It was all about the chains, the shining chains, the holy chains."

"Of love," added Boynton, significantly.

"Yes, I think it was of love," responded Temple.

The young man snatched up the fiddle again. And now he did not veil his voice, but sang, sonorously:

> "If you love a lady bright,
> Seek and you shall find a way.
> All that love should say, to say,
> If you watch the occasion right."

Having finished this song, Boynton leaned towards Temple, who did not seem to see that he did so. She glanced at him and laughed a little.

"It's quite funny that so many of your songs should be so very sentimental," she said.

Boynton drew himself up.

"I don't think it's funny at all," he responded. "And let me tell you one thing, Miss Crawford : I've resolved to watch the occasion right."

She laughed again at this remark; she made no other reply. And she did not notice how he flushed and scowled.

She took up the violin. She held it lovingly across her lap, and, still holding it thus, as some women violinists do, she began to play. She sang out strongly and with a note of victory, as befitted the words :

> "Summer is a-coming in,
> Loud sing, cuckoo ;
> Groweth seed and bloometh mead,
> And springeth the wood now.
> Sing, cuckoo, cuckoo."

"You see, one needn't always be sentimental and love-sick. Love is only a small part of life."

She spoke the last words with an ominous seriousness. She extended the instrument.

"Take your fiddle," she said. "It's wicked to fritter away one's days in this way. I want to do some good work for the Lord. I want to help bring souls to the right way. Yale Boynton, you needn't frown. Just tell me if you don't think about saving your soul, and about doing all the good you can ?"

Impossible to resist the manner, the intonation—all the

more impossible because Temple was so unconscious of what her manner and intonation were.

Boynton pushed out his under-lip. He wished he were not in a boat which would wobble so if he threw himself at his companion's feet.

"Yes," he said. "I think about doing good sometimes; but you'll find it's all bosh about experiencing religion and that rot."

"Stop! Don't you know I've experienced? And it's going to make a difference with me, too. You may not think so, but it is. I sha'n't come down here to meet you any more, for one thing. I think it's frivolous, and I sha'n't do it. I'm going back now. You've been mighty kind, Mr. Boynton," relenting somewhat, "to teach me to play, and to bring sandwiches and beer and such. And I'm much obliged. But I'm going to think of other things."

"What things?" asked Boynton.

There was a stubborn look on his face. He extended his hand and took hold of Temple's arm, for she had risen as if to leave immediately.

X

WITH DALVECKER

TEMPLE stood perfectly still. She would not try to go while her arm was held thus. But she resented the touch, and Boynton was discerning enough to see that resentment.

His hand dropped.

"What other things are you going to do?" he repeated. "I should think you might tell me. I'm a human being as well as all the people you are going to convert. Do stay a minute longer. Don't you consider that my soul is worth saving? Because if you don't think so, I do. Now, Temple Crawford, be a little bit kind to me, can't you?"

He was very boyish and very pleading. It suddenly occurred to him to take her at her word.

"What's the matter with me that you can't begin by making me over and helping me to get religion? Don't you call me worth saving, I should like to know?" With insistent repetition.

"Everybody is worth saving," she answered. "God loves everybody."

At first Boynton could hardly believe that she was serious. It seemed incredible to him that this woman, who had seemed to have such a wild flow of animal spirits, should really have taken up this fad. He called the change a fad in the privacy of his own mind.

He gazed at her with a sharp inquiry in his eyes. Certainly there was something in her face that he had never seen before. And whatever that something was, it was accompanied by a good deal of resolution. He considered it a rather curious fact that he felt more drawn to her than ever. The fact that there seemed to be a barrier rising between them had the effect of stimulating into a stronger life what had first appeared to be only a fancy.

Boynton's face partook of what he called the "deadly earnestness" of this new mood.

He longed to take the girl's hand and draw her to him; but he knew he must not do that.

"Please sit down," he said. "You needn't go yet. I want — I wish — Oh, can't you let me join you in this change in your life?"

The young man heard himself speak in some surprise. Still he was sure he was thoroughly in earnest. There was something in the girl's face and presence which had a strange influence over him. He did not mean to let any experience that she might know come between them. And yet he had no consciousness of being in any sense a hypocrite when he became as serious as his companion.

Temple sat down again. She was thinking that perhaps here was work for her to do. And she must not withhold her hand from any labor for the Lord.

As she looked at Boynton she was vaguely struck by the curiously facile features which now expressed nothing but a sort of solemn eagerness. For the first time it came to her that her companion, though he might be impressible, was not profound. She had never been accustomed to analyzing anything or anybody.

But she must do what she could.

"If you're going to be religious," he said, "why, then I'm going to be religious, too."

"But that isn't the right motive," she remonstrated. "That's starting out wrong."

"No matter, if I get into the right path finally. Temple" —the young man's voice changed into a minor key—"you see, I can't get along without you. I can't, and it's no use trying."

Without moving in the least the girl yet seemed to withdraw in some way.

"But you've got to get along without me," she said. "I sha'n't come here again."

She could hardly believe that she had ever cared to come. Between the girl who had found amusement in Yale Boynton's society and her present self there was such a gulf that Temple was bewildered. But, then, having religion made a great difference, naturally.

She looked with serious, anxious intentness into Boynton's eyes.

"You must not talk like that to me any more," she said. "I will not listen to you."

Boynton grew pale.

"Aren't you going to let me see you? Won't you let me come to the house?" he asked. And then, before she could reply, he continued, hurriedly, "You must teach me how to be pious—you can't refuse to do that. You've got to help me be good. I don't see what your religion's good for if it doesn't tell you to help everybody. I say, you can't refuse anything like that."

His face began to flush with his eagerness.

Gradually, as Temple continued looking, an incongruous expression of amusement came into her countenance. She had just recalled what Lincoln Dalvecker had said. It was very odd that these young men—her thoughts could not go any further.

She suddenly covered her face with her hands. She felt sure that she was wicked to feel any inclination to laugh. But certainly there was something very ridiculous in it all.

At first Boynton thought Temple was crying, and this belief gave him a certain satisfaction. But immediately he discovered that she was laughing, and his vanity directly assumed that she was laughing at him.

He turned away with such abruptness that the boat tipped, and Temple nearly lost her balance.

"I didn't know I was so amusing," said Boynton, fiercely.

"'Tisn't that! Oh, 'tisn't that!" exclaimed Temple, now greatly distressed. "Do forgive me! Now I'm going. Good-bye."

Boynton seized her hands and held them fast.

"But what's to become of me?" he reiterated. "Aren't you going to help me? Don't you think I want to be saved? If you think it's best to have religion, why, I'm going to have it, too. Do let me come and talk with you about it!"

"Go to Mr. Mercer. He'll tell you. He knows so much more than I do. Don't you see"—smiling somewhat tremulously—"don't you see, I've been religious such a little bit of a while that I don't know much yet. But I hope to—I hope to. It's such a glorious thing! Oh, you've no idea what a glorious thing it is to feel all at once that the dear Lord loves you—just you, you know, as if there were no one else in the world. It's such a great thing that you want every one to know it, too."

Boynton forgot his anger.

"Can't you try to help me, then?" he asked.

Temple stood hesitatingly.

"I don't know how. I long to help you. I—Mr. Boynton," hesitating again—"I'll pray for you. I reckon you don't know how it is to pray when you really love God, do you?"

"No," said the young man.

Temple turned and knelt down by the stern seat. She did not cover her face, but turned it up towards the sky with her eyes closed.

She began to pray with that fervid outpouring which is so powerful in its effect upon a listener.

Boynton stood a moment gazing steadfastly at the face of the girl. It seemed to him that from a fancy his feeling for her had become a demanding love. He watched her, observing the long, light lashes that were drooped, the strong, vivid contour of her face. Then, all at once, he sank down on his knees beside her, and began to follow the words of her petition. She was very personal. She talked of him and his needs to God as if she were talking to a devoted and all-powerful friend.

When she ceased she rose quickly. She would not be detained. She sprang from the boat and hurried up the hill, brushing the heavy shrubs aside and almost diving through them, her dog close behind her.

Boynton knew that he must not speak to her nor follow her. He sat in his boat and looked after her as long as she was in sight. Then he flung himself forward and leaned his elbows on the side, his hands thrust into his hair as he gazed down into the water.

Temple did not pause until she reached her home. She found the door open and Miss Drowdy sitting by an enormous fire, a plate on her lap, a cup of coffee standing on a chair near her. There was a dog stationed on each side of her.

"I told Sally 'twa'n't no use to set the table jest for me," remarked Almina, "'n' ther was no tellin' when you'd come back. You must be about starved."

"Yas, Miss Temple," said Sally, who was just coming in with a plate of fried chicken, "I tole Miss Drowdy as how yo'd be despit hongry. I tole her as 'ligion was one of der hongriest things on der face of der yarth."

The yellow woman drew up another chair and deposited the plate of chicken upon that, well within reach of Almina.

"I'm dretful hungry myself," Almina said, apologetically, "but I thought 'twas the mountain air; I didn't think of its being religion."

Sally laughed far down in her throat.

"I reckon we kin find 'nough fur yo' t' eat. Now, honey," to Temple, "what 'll ole Sal git fur yo'?"

"Nothing."

The yellow woman gazed solicitously at the girl.

"Dat ain't no way," she remarked. "All dem times I got 'ligion I neber lost one meal."

Temple smiled. She was leaning far back in the chair,

with her feet stretched towards the embers on the hearth. Her face was worn and white.

"I haven't lost a meal," she answered. "I've been down to the river, and Mr. Boynton had brought some lunch."

Sally grinned broadly.

"I heard his fiddle," she said. "You ben fiddlin', Miss Temple?"

"No; that is, not much."

Sally stood contemplatively gazing down at her mistress.

"I never could come to no onderstandin'," she remarked, "as to whether the Lawd liked fiddles or whether de Lawd hated fiddles. Somehow dey don't seem so kind of holy as orgins, now, do dey?"

"Of course it depends upon what you do with violins," replied Temple.

She felt that she was not quite qualified to discuss this subject. But at this moment she had an inclination towards rigidity in regard to everything.

She asked for a cup of coffee, and when Sally brought it she took occasion to inform her mistress that somebody "be'n 'quirin' roun' fur her not so very long after sun-up."

Upon being questioned further, she reluctantly acknowledged that the person thus inquiring was young Dalvecker.

Temple's face clouded. With every moment that had passed since her interview with him she had grown more and more troubled regarding her answer to him.

She now rose. She stood looking irresolutely at Miss Drowdy, who was still pecking away at the leg of a chicken. In response to this look Almina explained that she didn't know as a woman could be so hungry as she had been. She further added that it didn't seem good manners, somehow, to eat almost a whole chicken, besides the amount of corn pone which Sally had brought in.

"I feel like a cannibal," she said, "and the worst of it is, I ain't truly ashamed."

Temple's gaze was rather absent. She walked to the

door, and then paused.   She was not in the habit of telling where she was going, but now, in deference to her guest, she remarked that she reckoned she should ride out Cain Creek way.

When she had gone, Miss Drowdy asked,

"Where is Cain Creek way?" and then was immediately sorry she had put such a question.

Sally was brushing the hearth.   She answered that Cain Creek "war dat kind of ur stream as run so fur one way an' so fur de oder way dat a pusson couldn't tell whar another pusson had gone onless dey knew sumpin' more to de pint than jes' Cain Creek."

Having replied thus, the yellow woman walked out of the house with a waiter of dishes on her head.   She turned thus poised, and saw Temple leading the white pony from his shed.   The pony had on saddle and bridle.   His injury had not been severe and was now practically well, and his enforced idleness made him spring away furiously when Temple had seated herself on his back.   He tore down the path, snorting as he went.   His rider sat calmly. Thimble had rushed along in this way too many times for her to be discomposed.   Her spirits rose as she went. The little white sprite leaped the trees that had been felled across paths to stop travel; he galloped gallantly along clear spaces; he tossed up his neck with its thick hogged mane; he neighed shrilly as if in response to some unheard greeting.   All the time the girl sat him with seeming negligence, swaying as he swayed.

Even at this pace it was more than an hour before Temple drew in her pony and looked down into a valley where a river thundered along a steep bed, going through fields bright with growing grain.   In one of these fields stood a two-story white house, a house without blinds and with narrow windows, but with a long stoop extending across the front.   There were some cows on a slope towards the north.   On a few rods of flat ground a pair of horses were slowly dragging a plough, which was held by a man in a red shirt. His brown trousers were tucked into tall boots heavy with the damp, dark soil.

In another place a woman was dropping corn and a man was covering it.

The mountains stood all about as background. The sky was a pale, warm blue, and crows sailed deliberately across it, cawing hoarsely. But through their cries could be heard the gay, challenging notes of newly mated song birds.

The pony stood perfectly still, its wise face also turned towards the picture below him, as if he also were surveying it with appreciation.

The girl sat quietly in the saddle. Her heart was filled with the beauty of the world. Her eyes looked tense and strained. Her lips were parted. For a moment she forgot why she had come to Cain Creek.

Suddenly a child's voice shouted shrilly down in the valley,

"Somebody's come on ter thur land !"

Then dogs barked, and came racing wildly towards the intruder.

The woman dropping corn stopped, and pushed back her sun-bonnet. The man leaned on his hoe and gazed.

The man who had been holding the plough glanced once ; then he left his horses standing in the furrows, swung off his hat, and ran swiftly up to the horsewoman. As he ran he was aware of the picture made by the white pony and his rider—aware of it with a leaping of pulses and a wild joy that seemed too great, for an instant, to be borne.

His long legs quickly left the space behind him. He leaned up against Thimble, and grasped Temple's ungloved brown hand.

" This is jest mighty good of you, Temple !" he exclaimed. " It was jest like—like—oh, the brightest sunlight in the world when I saw you up here. I was thinking about you— I'm always doin' that. But I was planning how to make the house more convenient 'fore you come. They've got a house to the Junction—John Case's new one, you know; it makes work easier for the women. An' you're goin' to have jest as easy a time as can be when you're here, you know, Temple."

Link Dalvecker's words almost tumbled over each other in his happy eagerness. When he stopped, Temple only said "Don't" in a beseeching tone.

Then there was silence between them for a little time.

But Dalvecker could not be thus rebuffed. He had taken such heart of grace in thinking over his last interview with this girl, and his mother had been so positive that he was accepted, that he also had become positive.

His mother, in the fulness of her knowledge of girls, had also counselled him not to mind any "gal's notions." She assured him that the notions in "gal's heads was beyont anything on the whole yarth." He was to pay absolutely no attention to them. A gal said anything and everything, especially a gal like Temple Crawford, who had been a wild colt all her life.

Nevertheless, Link wished now that Temple had not said "Don't" in that way, though, of course, it did not mean anything — it could not mean anything. She was just a "gal," that was all.

He drew a long breath of relief as he reached this conclusion.

He still leaned against the pony's side, and he still held Temple's hand as he kept his eyes on her face.

He was wondering how he had lived all these years within a few miles of this girl without making himself sure that she would eventually belong to him. Certainly she would belong to him. As if the repetition of this phrase in his mind carried with it a doubt, the young man's face flushed a deep red, even under the tan. His eyes flashed. The hand hanging by his side shut tightly. His temper was not one which could bear much opposition.

But Temple was not noticing him. Her gaze was going, with slow dwelling here and there, over the scene before her. For the moment she had forgotten her newly acquired religion.

"I'm wonderin' what you're thinking," at last said Link, trying to be patient. He was longing for her to look at him, to give him a personal glance. What eyes, he thought, she had! His very heart had gone into their depths. Did any other woman ever have such eyes, or any other man love them so?

Temple moved a little in the saddle. She became conscious that her hand was closely held, and she withdrew it.

Dalvecker sighed audibly; then he repeated his remark, and she made an effort to reply.

"The mountains," she said, "and the sky—the whole world—"

Then she remembered that she had religion. She also sighed. She looked down at her companion.

"I don't see how heaven can be as beautiful as the Carolina mountains, do you, Link?"

But the young man found it an effort to try to think enough to answer. He only said, impetuously,

"I don't want no heaven better'n this—jest to be nigh you, Temple."

And again the girl said "Don't!" and this time more pleadingly than before.

The adoring passion in Dalvecker's eyes became clouded. He felt that he could bear a great deal of everything that did not come between him and Temple, but that he could bear absolutely nothing that did.

"I'm dead sure," he began now, "that I don't know what you're aimin' at. You come down to thur house. Mar's got sumpin' she wants to show you. Mar's awful pleased to think that you—that I—that we—"

The young man paused in his stammering, his face burning, his eyes glowing. He was going to put his arm about Temple as she sat there, but she tried to shrink away. He frowned, and his arm dropped to his side.

Temple, to her great surprise, was finding it more and more difficult to say what she had come to say.

When she had started she had thought that it would not be very hard to tell Link that they would not think any more of what was said right after the preaching.

She was positive that nothing had been settled then. But evidently Link and his mother believed that everything was settled as they wished. The girl was growing bewildered and rebellious.

"Come," he repeated, "mar's got some quilt or sumpin' she wants to show you. An' I want you to tell me whar to put thur pump. I've done made up my mind I'll have a pump. You ain't goin' to draw water."

His voice sank to a tender tone, and he leaned more closely upon Thimble, who maintained his position, ears cocked, and long face seriously turned towards the valley.

"It isn't any matter about the pump!" exclaimed Temple, almost with a savage intonation.

"But I ain't going to have you drawing water like the women round hyar," reasserted Link, "an' you sha'n't follow thur plough. Thur Dalvecker women ain't no call to follow thur plough," with some pride.

Temple sat up straight. She gripped the bridle. Instead of looking at her companion, she gazed in a cowardly manner down at her bridle hand as she began to speak.

"What do you think I came over to Cain Creek for?"

"Oh, Temple, I hoped 'twas to see me."

"Yes, it was."

Now the girl lifted brave eyes and met the intent, masculine gaze, which did not swerve from her face.

"Yes," she said, "it was to see you, and tell you that 'twas all wrong—our thinking of marrying, you know. I can't do hit—oh no, I can't do hit!"

Dalvecker's face darkened. His mouth shut closely, but he stood quiet.

"I didn't say I would," went on Temple, her low voice seeming to her listener like a sharp knife. "You must know

I didn't say I would, and somehow you've understood I did say so. They told me I ought not to say I'd think of hit—that men always thought it was the same as saying yes. I don't see why men should think so, though. But I can't think of hit. I've come to tell you so, Link. Oh, dear, Link, don't look like that! Please don't!"

To the pony's great surprise Temple suddenly flung one arm about Link's neck, while she bent her head down on the top of the young man's felt-hat. Her own felt-hat fell off at the same moment, revealing her short, tumbled, light hair, which looked almost ashen in this strong sunlight.

Dalvecker's mother, who had resumed the dropping of corn in the lot down in the valley, glanced up as Temple's head dropped down on that of her son. She smiled in the cavernous depths of her cape-bonnet, and then she remarked to the man who was following with his hoe,

"That thur gal's what I call in lurv; an' no wonder. She's gurt er good man. My son ain't one of thur dad-burned kind as 'll be rough on a 'oman. She's rid all thur way from Fairview hyar jest to see Link. She's in lurv, she is."

It will be observed that Mrs. Dalvecker, widow, unlike her son, had never been to school in Asheville.

She laughed as she ceased speaking. The man with the hoe had looked up at her first words. He also laughed. And he remarked that Link "allers did hev thur luck."

To this Mrs. Dalvecker responded that she hadn't nawthin' against Temple; but she reckoned as 'twar Temple as was in luck. Jest to think of thur plank house! An' Link war layin' out fur er pump!"

The thought of the pump seemed to incapacitate Mrs. Dalvecker from further speech.

Up on the height young Dalvecker was not thinking that he was in luck.

He stood quite motionless, with Temple's arm about his neck. It seemed a long time before he could speak. Finally he said, in a whisper,

"Don't be so sure you can't lurv me, Temple. I'd try to git along with jest a little lurv at first."

"'Tisn't that."

Temple raised her head, and took her arm from the man's neck.

"It isn't any question of love, anyway. I told you I didn't love you. I only had an affection for you, you know. But I didn't know but I might do more good by marrying you. You said how I could help you—keep you religious, and—"

Dalvecker's face had been growing blacker and blacker. Now he burst out,

"It's that damned young fool from Asheville!" he cried. "The feller with thur fiddle! You lurv him, Temple Crawford! Jim Frady said as how you met urp with him, an' went in his boat, an' fiddled, an' sung, an'—an'— It's him! He sha'n't fiddle no more! I'll kill him 's I would er mad fyst!"

The girl did not try to reply at first to this outbreak. She gazed down at Link. At last she said, solemnly,

"I don't lurv him, Link!"

Dalvecker believed her instantly. His face began to be less distorted.

"But it doesn't make any difference," said Temple— "about us, I mean."

"Why not? It's gurt to make a difference."

"No; I've made up my mind."

"Who is it, then?" fiercely.

"I don't know what you mean, Link."

"What man is it that you do lurv?"

The barbarian beneath Dalvecker's skin began again to come to the surface.

"Nobody."

"Then I'm going to hope."

"No, no; I wish you'd listen to me now, Link."

The man stood still and waited.

Things were growing clearer to the girl, as things will

suddenly grow clearer sometimes in the fire of unusual excitement.

"I want to tell you what my plan of life is."

It was in this moment that Temple's plan of life became defined.

"Tell me. I'll try to bear it."

Dalvecker did hope. He could not help hoping since that assurance that Temple did not love the fiddler. There was positively nobody else. And this talk about not loving any one was unnatural, and he did not believe it. Women talked so strangely sometimes. But they didn't mean much.

Temple was thinking of a power she had felt recently developed in her. She called it a religious power. When she prayed there was in her consciousness a fervid force which she knew moved others as well as herself. She must use this gift for the Lord, who had bestowed it upon her.

Yes, everything was clear to her now. It was God himself who had given her something by which she could bring people into the fold. It was God himself who was opening the way of great usefulness in letting her have the opportunity to be a helpmeet to a man like the preacher.

Couldn't she make Link Dalvecker see this? She saw it so strongly. She had not yet learned that another person cannot occupy our point of view, no matter how strenuously we try to put him there.

The girl's gaze went off to the mountains again. How grand, how glorious life was ! How favored she was in being allowed to serve the Master ! She had all her life felt such longings for she knew not what—of great work. And now this work had come to her hand. All her life she had wanted to fling herself unreservedly into something that should take her and hold her. All her life—and her life seemed long to her. She had a sense that she was very much older than this young man who could not seem to take his eyes from her face.

"I'm waiting for you to tell me," Dalvecker said, at length.

He distrusted every moment of silence during which she looked like that.

Temple glanced at her companion, but for some reason she could not continue to look at him as she said,

"I've been trying to see my way clear, and now I do see it. I shall marry Mr. Mercer, and work with him. You see how—but, Link—"

She stopped suddenly. She had been going to explain her plans, but the words all at once seemed useless, without meaning. She had not known that any one could show such agony as she saw in Link's face.

And, strangest of all, he did not seem to understand. And it came upon her with owerwhelming force that she could never make him understand.

Link was standing up straight, his head flung back, his hot eyes fixed on Temple's eyes.

When she stopped speaking he did not break the silence. It was she who spoke again.

"Dear Link," she said, "it's all so plain to me."

"Do yo' lurv him?" he asked, as he had just asked about "the fiddler."

There was surprise and impatience in her voice as she said,

"It's so odd that everybody asks that. No, I don't love him. Why should I? I can respect and admire him. If I did fancy I was in love I should just have to get over that, and then what better off should I be? Besides, I'm not the kind of girl to be in love."

Dalvecker made a quick movement as if he could bear no more. He raised his clinched hand into the air, crying out,

"No, I reckon you ain't thur kind of gal! If you was you'd stop tormentin' me so! You just put me into hell with your ca'm kind of talk!"

Temple's face quivered with wistful wonder.

"I reckon you think you're in lurv," she said.

"I know I am," with ill-suppressed fury.

"Then it must be awful—awful," she responded, impressively. "I'm glad I'm not that sort of person. There's suffering enough in this world without love—I mean that kind of love."

She gathered up the bridle which she had let fall on the pony's neck. But she continued to look at Dalvecker. She was inclined to be indignant with him. Of course, he could not really feel as he seemed to feel. She could not quite believe in the reality of his emotion. So true it is that what we have never felt we cannot understand.

"I'll be going now," she said.

"No! No!"

The young man seized the bridle so forcibly that the pony turned and nipped at his wrist, leaving a purple mark.

"You can't mean hit! You can't mean hit!"

Dalvecker choked on the words. And yet it seemed to him that he was giving his whole strength to the effort to control himself. Because he did not burst forth into wild oaths, because he did not tear Temple from the saddle, take her to the house yonder and shut her up there, he was under the belief that he was controlling himself.

"We won't talk any more. I'm going," she said, "and I mean it; I mean it all. But I can't tell you how sorry I am. Can't we be just the same friends, Link?"

But Dalvecker could not answer. He nodded vaguely. It was as if he were in the grasp of some malignant monster that was shaking him up and down, and he was dangling helpless in that grasp.

He saw Temple ride away. His eyes seemed to have flames in them.

He could not remember the time when he had not meant to have that girl for his wife. And he had always had what he meant to have.

At the topmost part of the path along which Temple had come she stopped her pony and turned about. The young man saw her wave her hand at him. He heard her cry,

"Good-bye, Link! Good-bye! I want you to come and see me!"

Link took off his hat and waved it. His hand appeared to perform the act without any command from his mind.

When the girl was out of sight Dalvecker had sense enough to know that he must go back to his ploughing, or his mother would come and question him.

He turned himself towards his home. It was only a few moments before that he had been planning how to make the work easier for Temple. There was the house, with the green about it; there was his mother going right on dropping corn, and old Chris Jinks was covering it. Dalvecker could hear the sound of the hoe as it slid under the earth. Jinks's little boy was beneath an apple-tree firing stones at a robin's nest.

Dalvecker's outward sense told him that the farm had never looked so well. And he resented that fact.

He wanted to grip hold of something. There was nothing to grip, however. He thrust his hands into his pockets.

"It's just—oh—" He paused, for there was no word strong enough. "Oh, it's just hell!" he whispered.

Then he walked down to where his horses were calmly standing in the freshly turned earth.

XI

THE MOTHER'S LETTER

MRS. DALVECKER saw her son return to his plough after his interview with his sweetheart.

She set down the basket which held the seed-corn, and went striding over the furrows to him. She wanted to tell him again what a lucky gal Temple Crawford was.

She waited until his horses came back along the line of their work.

Link was tempted to turn and run away; but he came on, ramming the plough furiously down into the earth that rolled richly away from the share. A flock of hens was industriously pecking along behind him.

"Jest stop, will yo'?" commanded the woman.

The young man stopped. He pulled the great flap of his hat far over his face and waited.

"Did yo' tell her 'bout thur pump?" asked the mother.

Link nodded.

"Thur ain't no pump on none of thur mountings."

Having said this with an air of pride, Mrs. Dalvecker spat emphatically, and then drew her hand down over her mouth to remove any too visible traces of expectoration.

"I reckon that Crawford gal ain't none too good to draw water same's her man's dad an' mam hev drawed."

These words were tempered with a good-natured laugh.

"She ain't gwine ter draw water hyar," was the response.

Mrs. Dalvecker pushed her sun-bonnet back quickly.

"Hev you-uns an' her ben quarrillin'?" she asked, sharply. "She mought better luke out. Thur ain't no sech chance 's Link Dalvecker nowhars in Limestone Township. She better luke out fer herself."

There was no response to this. Link stood sullenly gazing at his mother.

"I hope you-uns didn't give in to her in no ways," said Mrs. Dalvecker. "Yo' mus' jest take yer stand an' be boss from thur fust."

Link turned away. He grasped the plough-handles so that his finger-nails showed white with the strain.

"Mar," he said, "yo' shurt urp. I'm gwine ter boss my own business. Mebby me an' Temple sha'n't hitch no ways."

"Wha-at !"

Link felt beside himself.

"Mar," he said again, "will yo' shurt urp ?"

He hurriedly unhooked the horses and sent them off, with the chains dangling against their legs. He walked after them. He would have liked to put a thousand miles between him and every human being who had a right to speak to him. He had a dreadful feeling like hatred towards Temple. "To be friends with her !" she had said.

Mrs. Dalvecker stood in the ploughed field with her sun-bonnet tipped back, watching her boy.

As she watched she mechanically pulled from somewhere in her dress a small paper bag of snuff, poured a little pile into the dingy palm of her hand, and then tossed the pile into her mouth. She tossed so dexterously that she did not lose a grain, but it was all done mechanically. She wanted consolation, and she applied to her snuff-bag without knowing that she did so.

She did not stand long. She turned in the direction of the large barn which was at the top of the field. She walked towards it with those long steps that so often characterized the walk of the mountain women.

"What's urp ?" asked Chris Jinks, glad of an opportunity to rest on his hoe-handle.

"Nawthin'," was the answer. "Yo' go on er plantin'."

Jinks continued to rest his long length on his tool while he watched Mrs. Dalvecker, who disappeared in the dark cavern of the barn. She very soon reappeared, now mounted on a tall roan horse. She cantered off over the field, and was soon out of sight in the way taken by Temple.

"She lied," said Jinks to himself, taking off his hat and passing his hand over his head. "Sumpin' is urp. Him an' her has fought. Durned ef I wanter hev Link Dalvecker turned against me. He's all right ef he has what he wants. But ef he don't hev hit—"

Jinks passed his hand over his head again and neglected to finish his sentence.

The long legs of the roan took him swiftly over the rough way. Mrs. Dalvecker was sitting on a man's saddle, but she maintained her position with a negligent security that was an accomplishment possessed by nearly every woman hereabouts. Her little wad of snuff was safely lodged beneath her lower-lip; her bonnet was pushed back so that the upper part of her yellow forehead and the front of her grizzled hair were visible, but the pasteboard projected so that her mouth and chin were concealed.

This horsewoman paused and deliberated a moment when she had reached the place where Temple had appeared less than an hour ago.

Then Mrs. Dalvecker turned right into the woods. She calmly put her steed over fallen trees and zigzag fences, and the gaunt animal never flinched. He set his bony face forward in a brave way that was habitual with him.

In half an hour the rider came out on a path that wound upward towards the west. She stopped her horse and looked down the path.

"She mought hev gone," she said aloud, "but I reckon she hain't."

She was right in her reckoning, for it was hardly a moment before a white pony, with a girl on his back, came in sight still farther down the mountain.

Temple was riding slowly, Thimble going at his little

amble. The girl had her hat in her hand, and sunlight and shadow were continually flecking her face and figure as she came forward.

Mrs. Dalvecker cantered towards her, and stopped in front of her.

"Howdy," she said, with some sharpness.

Thimble stopped of his own accord, knowing his manners, and his mistress responded,

"Howdy," in some surprise.

"I curm fur yo'," remarked the woman, peremptorily.

"What?"

"I curm fur yo'—I 'low you'll go back right now along of me."

Temple was silent, gazing at Link's mother, who had hitherto been all smiles to her.

"No," said the girl, "I'm not going back."

There was a heat in her face and in her eyes, but she spoke quite calmly. She was asking herself if it were possible that Link had been complaining to his mother.

"You be," was the response. "Thur's Link—he's er ravin' urp an' down thur crick. He's bound ter do his'ef er damage. An' I'm bound ter stop hit. Hyar's you curmin' down ter see him; some gals don't be a cavortin' round arter their fellers in this style. Some gals waits to home fur thur men to curm to see 'um. But you jest run arter my boy, an' then you'll quarril with him, an' he's that mad I shouldn't wonder ef he'd shot his'ef 'fore this. You curm long er me now, right smart. I ain't feared of no upstart gals as runs arter their men. An' he layin' out ter put in er pump!"

It was as if the memory of the pump was too much for Mrs. Dalvecker. She bent forward, and put a yellow, skinny hand on Temple's arm, grasping it tightly.

The girl's eyes dilated, and a flush deepened on her face and neck. After a moment she said,

"I wish you wouldn't touch me. I don't like to be touched."

She glanced down and saw the nails, with their black rims, on her companion's hands. She shuddered. She was trying to remember that she had religion. Surely this was a time when she ought to make use of such a possession.

"Don't like ter be touched!" repeated Mrs. Dalvecker. "I don't know's I care. What you ben doin' to my son— my son, who's better 'n you-uns any day? An' he layin' out fur er pump! I say, you mought drar water! An' yo' runnin' arter him!"

Mrs. Dalvecker was gradually raising her voice. A narrow yellow stream was starting from each corner of her mouth and trickling down.

"You mus'n't touch me," said Temple again. She was aware that a shudder ran over her at the contact of that hand.

Then all at once a flood of pity and longing came into her soul. What did all this matter? What did anything in the world matter when we thought of the Lord who had loved us and died for us?

He had suffered everything, borne everything for our sakes. And should not she, Temple Crawford, gladly bear such discomfort as this?

Mrs. Dalvecker was looking in the girl's face, and she saw the sudden and, to her, mysterious change that came to it.

In her surprise she released the arm, staring as she did so.

It was Temple who now bent forward and touched the woman's shoulder, her fresh young eyes seeking the faded and sunken ones, with a look in them that stirred and strangely moved Mrs. Dalvecker.

She had been like an animal rushing out to protect its young. Link was suffering. This girl had made him suffer. Therefore, she sought this girl that she might make her suffer also, if she would not restore happiness to Link.

But now, as the eyes of the two met, Mrs. Dalvecker's indignation began to subside, she could not tell why.

Temple, in her simplicity, went straight to the thing uppermost in her thoughts.

"You see," she said, "I found the Lord at the preaching the other night."

"Did yo'?"

Mrs. Dalvecker asked the question gently. She had been to preaching many times in her youth, and once she thought she had "experienced." But it did not last. That was years ago. She had given up going to preaching. She would have said that she laid out to have religion before she died. She wanted to "die rejoicing."

"I'm trying to be good," said Temple. "Oh, I am certainly trying! And to live near to good things, you know."

She removed her hand from the woman's shoulder and leaned it on the withers of the tall roan, bending forward from her saddle as she did so, her whole force seeming to pour forth the light of aspiration and intense belief.

"Perhaps you could help me," she said, her voice thrilling along the nerves of her listener, and taking the woman back to those young days when life was full of sensation.

"Help yo'?" said Mrs. Dalvecker. "I can't—I can't. I never gurt no religion as stayed by me—none. Mebbe thur preachers wa'n't thur right kind. Mebbe my heart war like thur nether millstone. 'Tis now, I reckon."

"No; oh no! You have such a kind heart, dear friend. Only it's the natural heart. We must get rid of that, you know, mustn't we? I want you to do something for me to-night. Will you? Will you?"

Impossible to describe the power of moving and winning that there was in Temple's voice and eyes. There was an overflow of sincerest well-wishing, a kind of love going out from her.

"Ter-night?" asked the woman. "Thur ain't nawthin' I kin do ter-night."

"Oh yes, there is. Will you remember? This evening, when the sun gets to the top of the Twin Brothers, will you pray for your soul just as you did when you were young?

And I shall pray for you, too, at that very time. And God will hear us. I know He will. He has promised. And He isn't like us; He never forgets a promise."

Mrs. Dalvecker's gaze was on the illuminated face so near her. She hardly recognized herself. She had been dull for so many years, save where her son was concerned. Now a chill went down her spine, while at the same time a warmth came to her heart.

"I reckon I'll promise," she said, no longer using her loud, strident tones.

"I knew you would," said Temple, ardently, "I knew you would. We shall have a blessing—we surely shall. Good-bye."

Temple sat up straight. The pony started forward, and had gone a few rods when the woman roused herself and called after the girl.

"Thur's Link, yo' know!" she shouted.

Temple turned.

"He'll explain it all," she answered. "Do make him know that I must do my own work. The Lord has called me."

She shook the lines on Thimble's neck. But she turned once more to see the woman motionless on the tall roan.

When Mrs. Dalvecker reached home she was still dazed. There was Chris Jinks, leaning on his hoe as if he had not moved during her absence. She rode into the barn, got off her horse, and pulled saddle and bridle from him. Then she sat down quickly on an upturned half-bushel measure; she covered her face with her hands. It had been years since any tears had come to her eyes, but now they came and overflowed. Inextricably mixed in her mind were the face and the tones of the young girl she had just left, and the thoughts of religion and God and heaven, and a vague, strong longing to be something more than what she was, and different from what she was—the same longings that had been in her heart in her youth, and which in later years she had supposed belonged only to youth.

All her anger against Temple was gone.   She could not be angry with her, she did not know why.

Temple rode directly home.   But she could not rest.   She wanted to be at work for God all the time.

When Bartholomew came slouching forward to take the pony, she asked him if he had been to preaching.   He said, "Naw'm; reckoned he didn't care for hit."

The girl stood watching the youth as he unsaddled Thimble and then took a bunch of hay to rub off the animal. He rubbed slowly, up and down, making a kind of hissing noise as he did so.

"Bart," said the girl, softly.   Bart turned his heavy face, hardly raising his sullen eyes as he did so.

But Temple did not shrink.   She felt as if an inexhaustible fountain of love was in her heart—love that could take in this inert, vicious mass before her.

"Well, 'um," said the boy at last.

Temple came nearer.

"I'm afraid I haven't always kept my temper towards you as I ought," she said.

She was telling herself that she certainly did feel lovingly towards even Bart; and if she could feel lovingly towards him, it must be that she really had religion.

No response to her remark.

"And I want you to forgive me," she said.

No response, save a slight grunt.   The boy took a fresh bunch of hay and rubbed the pony's flank.

"You must forgive me," insisted Temple.   "Can't you?"

"Yes, 'um.   I kin forgive yo' well enough.   I don't care how yo' treat me.   'Tain't nawthin' to me."

The girl was silent.   She was wondering if there were any way to reach Bart.   As she stood, there was a slight noise at the door of the shed; then a little whine.   She looked around.   The Newfoundland was in the doorway. He was standing on three legs; his left front paw was dangling helplessly.   A streak of damp red went down the white hair of his chest.

Temple cried out. Her face grew crimson and then white. She flung herself on the dog, and clasped him in her arms. She had wondered why he had not followed her to Cain Creek.

Yucatan winced and whined, but he licked his mistress's cheek and wagged his tail.

On the floor, with her dog in her arms, Temple lifted a furious face towards Bart, who had dropped his wisps of hay and now leaned against the wall, not looking at anything.

"You did hit!" cried the girl. "Oh!"—bending her head to Yucatan's neck—"my own dog! my own true dog!"

Then, with head up again, and more furiously than before,

"You did hit! You—you villain! Oh, I shall kill you some day!"

"Yes, 'um," said the boy. "Thur critter snapped at me. I flung er sharp rock. 'Twas down in thur bresh, thur! Sally seen me, or I'd er lied 'bout hit."

Temple rose, gently detaching herself from Yucatan. Her hot eyes gazed searchingly about. There was the handle of a rake, broken from the rake itself. She ran towards it, seized it, swung it furiously, and it came cracking down upon Bart's shoulders.

Then it dropped from the girl's hand as if it had been a red-hot iron bar. She stood one instant glaring at the boy; then she covered her face with her hands and moaned, self-contempt stinging her intolerably.

But the boy did not moan. He had shrunk when the blow fell; he tried to dodge it, but, having taken it, he pressed his lips together in silence. He was very ugly to look at as he stood there.

After a moment the girl removed her hands. She gazed at her companion and seemed to try to speak. There was a dreadful fight going on in her soul.

Something was telling her to ask Bart's forgiveness, and something was telling her not to do so.

Yucatan crept nearer to her, and put his head on her foot.

"Bart," said Temple, sharply, "go and tell Sally to come here."

"Yes, 'um," answered Bart, and he moved towards the door. But he stopped before he left the shed. He stopped to say, in his husky voice,

"I'm glad I hain't gurt religion, I am."

Then he went out.

When the yellow woman reached the shed ten minutes later she found Temple lying on the floor and the dog stretched beside her. The pony was standing near, a long, dry blade from a cornstalk depending from his mouth.

But Sally did not see Thimble; she scarcely saw the dog, because of her anxiety about her young mistress. Temple was sobbing heavily and dryly; she was absolutely gasping with the agony she was suffering.

Sally knelt down by Temple; she put her great, muscular hand on the hot forehead.

"Now, don't yer take on so, Miss Temple. Yo' take everything so hard—so dreffle hard. Yo' suffer so, yo' do. Curm now, de dawg 'll be all right. His leg's hurt, dat's 'bout all. We'll hev Mis' Ammidown out hyar, an' put it in two sticks. Laws, Miss Temple, we'll fotch him 'round all right. Don't take on so! Bart am er limb er Satan, shore!"

Sally sat down and lifted Temple into her arms.

"My own dog!" said Temple, brokenly, "my true lurv! My Yucatan, that's always lurved me best of all! And, oh, Sally, I thought I was a Christian! And I did want to kill Bart. I struck him. I tell you, Sally," a fierce flash coming to her eyes, "I just wish I'd struck him harder!"

"Bart ain't no 'count," soothingly answered Sally.

Temple was silent a moment. She was still sobbing. Then she said,

"Perhaps Bart 'll stop my being a Christian and helping to save souls."

"Yo' jes' be reasonable," soothingly, from Sally. "Bart can't. Yo' jes' go right ter Asheville arter Mis' Ammidown ergin. It'll take urp yer mind, won't it, honey? Yo' jes' go."

Without waiting for any answer, Sally put the saddle again on the pony's back. She bridled him ; then, with her arm thrust through the bridle, she stooped over her mistress, who was now sitting on the floor with her hand on Yucatan's head.

The yellow woman smoothed the girl's hair, picked up her hat, and put it on.

"We jes' gurt to hev Mis' Ammidown," she said.

Temple made no response. She rose and got into the saddle. She looked down at the dog, who had risen piteously to his three legs, and who was whining to accompany his mistress.

Temple's lip quivered.

"You take care of him, Sally," she said.

It seemed to Mrs. Ammidown and to most of the guests at Battery Park Hotel that it was still rather early in the day when Miss Crawford's pony, with Miss Crawford on his back, came galloping towards the side entrance.

The girl came towards the side because she saw her friend strolling along a path with a book in her hand. Mrs. Ammidown usually had a book in her hand.

"There's that Crawford girl," said a lady who was sitting on a bench a few yards away. "I don't know what there is that seems so interesting—"

"I know," said Mrs. Ammidown, calmly interrupting ; "it's because she is so suggestive, and she makes your blood go as it used to go when you were twenty years old. And anybody who can do that for us—"

The speaker smiled instead of finishing her sentence. She walked out quickly towards Temple, who was slowly walking her horse.

This was the first time the girl had come to Asheville without previously changing her shabby short dress and old velvet coat for the one decent, ordinary suit that she owned.

"It's Yucatan this time," said Temple, without any preliminary salutation. "And Bart did it again. I want you to come quick and fix his leg."

There were times when Mrs. Ammidown acted with the leisurely appearing promptness of the physician. She did so now. She ordered her horse saddled, and then she took Temple to her own room while she made herself ready.

"I should advise you to send Bartholomew away," she remarked, as she stood before the glass braiding her hair tightly for the ride.

"I do; I have. But he comes back," was the answer. "He hasn't any place to stay. I'm sorry for him, and I keep him."

The girl would not sit. She was standing with her back against the wall. Her hat was on the floor beside her; her hands were clasped tightly, and hanging in front of her.

"I think," said Temple, in a low voice that yet was intensely piercing—"I think that he will be the means of my going to hell."

Mrs. Ammidown turned quickly. The braid slipped from her fingers.

"Worse than that," went on Temple, in the same tone, "he will stop me from being a good woman and serving God."

Mrs. Ammidown went to the girl and lifted her clasped hands in her own warm grasp.

"How can he do that?"

She put the question tenderly. She hardly dared to show how much she was moved. Always when she was with Temple she was surprised at the girl's power to move her.

"Because he makes me hate him; he makes me want to kill him. I struck him just now. And when I struck him I should have been glad to see him fall down dead. Oh, how wicked I am!"

She did not raise her voice. She fixed her eyes on the face before her, and Mrs. Ammidown felt her own face yielding and trembling.

But she pulled herself quickly together and smiled.

"Oh yes; we're all wicked. But don't let us dwell on the fact. And let us remember that God takes account of our provocations; and God knows just the kind of creature Bartholomew is."

She went back to the mirror.

"You think He will forgive me?" with painful earnestness.

"I know He will."

Neither spoke for a few moments. At last Temple asked, timidly,

"Do you think that Mr. Mercer would still consider that he—that I—"

Here the speaker paused, and blushed deeply.

Mrs. Ammidown dropped the brush she held. She gazed silently at her companion, and as she gazed she became more and more convinced that Temple was not now referring to religion.

"That Mr. Mercer would consider?" she repeated, interrogatively, and with unconscious sternness. She was asking herself if her brother could possibly—

"I was wondering if he would think I was still worthy to help him in his work," replied Temple now, with no blush and no girlish consciousness. Indeed, she did not understand why she had blushed.

"To help him?"

"Yes; be his wife, you know, and share his work."

"What did you say?"

There came a gleam into the woman's eyes.

Temple was now becoming calmer.

"Yes," she said, "he asked me. I'm to give him my answer in a day or two."

"He asked you?"

"Yes. I know I'm inexperienced and — and — but I hope I could learn—"

"You are going to say yes, then?"

The gleam was still in Mrs. Ammidown's eyes, and there was now an incisiveness coming to her voice in place of the mere surprise.

"Yes," answered Temple.

"Did he tell you he loved you?"

"Oh no. It's not a question of love."

"Only of marriage, then?"

"You know," said Temple, "that I should have to marry him so that I might go with him and work with him, and—"

"Will you stop talking like that?" sharply.

"Oh, Mrs. Ammidown, don't you think I'm right?"

"I know you are not right."

Temple gazed straight before her without speaking.

Mrs. Ammidown stooped and picked up the hair-brush from the floor. She glanced at the girl, but did not break the silence. She saw the peculiar expression of resolution coming to Temple's mouth, and what seemed a certain squaring of the chin.

"I am convinced that I'm right," said the girl, "and when I'm convinced of a thing I have to do it. If I were that kind of a girl who thinks of love—" She hesitated, and the other finished the sentence for her.

"But since you have a cold temperament and cannot love—"

"Yes, Mrs. Ammidown," advancing quickly towards that lady, "that's just it. Have you read my mother's letter?"

"I have read it twice—three times."

"Well, I'm going to do as my mother counsels."

That afternoon, when Mrs. Ammidown was back again from her surgical work for Yucatan, she sat down with Mrs. Crawford's letter in her hand for one more perusal before she returned it to its owner.

This is the letter which this mother had left to influence her daughter. The words were written in slender, unimpressive characters, strangely at variance with their meaning:

13

"My precious little girl, as you are all I have that is precious, it is for you that I have the strongest desire that is left to me. And I have always had strong desires—strong — deep — burning. That's why I have been so unhappy. I ought only to have cared a little — loved a little, or not any, hoped a little, then I could have been placid and comfortable. Instead, I have been agitated and uncomfortable. I have flung away the comfort of years for the rapture of moments. And the moments have been very few.

"It is love that brings rapture. It is love that brings misery. Therefore, never love. Mind, I am not saying never marry. If some good, upright man wants you for his wife, I tell you to say yes to him—say yes. Then you will never know happiness, but you will never know misery. And love has days of wretchedness for every second of bliss. And after a little while—oh, such a very little while—there is no happiness at all. He — your possible lover and husband—will get tired of you long before you have ceased to think of him with pulses growing fast. You will not believe it now, but he'll make you believe it. Then you will begin to eat your heart. It is not well for a woman to spend her best years eating her heart. That's what I did. And I am going to die of it sooner than you would. You are a great deal stronger than I ever was.

"Your father was what they call in love with me. When I see how cold his eyes are when they rest upon me now, I think how much better it would have been if he had never had more than a friendship for me, and I for him; then I should not have had this love to remember and to long for. That is the way it is. The woman remembers and longs; the man grows tired and wants a new love. Anyway, he doesn't want the old love.

"And there is that disgusting revulsion that is liable to come when disillusion comes. When the glamour is gone it is not that you see more correctly; it is that the face you did love is not half as attractive as it really is. At first it was more beautiful than reality, then it is more ugly than reality.

"I do not suppose that your father is a bad man. All men are like him in this particular. Once he could not live unless I smiled upon him. Now he does not know whether I smile or not.

"He knew how to make love. No human being ever knew how better than he.

"I was seventeen when he came down to my father's house. That was in Louisiana, you know. At seventeen a Louisiana girl is as old as a Northern woman of half a dozen more years.

"He wakened my heart. I hope and pray you will never know what it means to have your heart awakened. Oh, I could tell you in words of fire all he was to me then! He is sitting here in the room with me now as I write. Sometimes he glances at me, and it is as if he looked at a chair or a log. The curse is that I remember what there can be in his eyes. I am only able to write a few lines before I must rest. I cough so, and then I am so tired. But I shall finish this before I die. And you, my little girl, will have my dying words. You know the vision of the dying is very clear. I see into the future, and I tell you to fly from love as from death. You will not read this until you are old enough to understand it.

"I am not beautiful any more, and if I were I should not now be novel. After all, it is novelty more than beauty or charm that attracts men. There isn't any such thing as constancy, remember that, not in the male heart—

"It is three weeks since I wrote the last lines. I have just been reading them over. They are not half strong enough. And I thought I could write such words as would be like a hot iron to burn into you that it is misery to love, save coolly, reasonably, and love is never cool or reasonable. But there are no such words, or if there are I am too weak and sick to find them.

"Sometimes when my cousin Rosalind comes up from the other plantation, I see your father go out and take her off her horse, and I catch in his eyes that look which used to be there for me. Not that I care now. He has that way with him, and women like it. I'm almost sure he left some one up North who loved him and believed in him. And then he fell in love with me.

"Never let a man look at you in that way—never.

"I wish I could find those words that would mean enough and be strong enough. When I am coughing and lying awake nights I am trying all the time to find those strong words. There must be some such words that would make you remember.

"Bear in mind that I am speaking to you from my grave. If you bear that thought with you, you may remember not to love, not to go one step in the way with love. He is a shining angel at first. But turn from him. Perhaps you will have a cold temperament, one of those which know nothing keenly and warmly. Constantly, before you were born, I prayed that you might be cold. And God sometimes answers prayer.

"Now I am so tired that I will wait until to-morrow before I finish this—

"It is to-morrow, and I am sure it is the last. Dear little daughter, your cool hands might have helped my hot heart. But no ; the grave is cool. And, after all, I could not find words strong enough to tell you not to love."

Mrs. Ammidown dropped the sheets in her lap.

"What a letter to leave!" she said to herself. "How morbid!"

As she sat there thinking of it and what its effect must be on a girl like Temple, she heard footsteps in the hall, then a knock on her door.

"May I come in?" asked her brother.

XII

"MUTUAL REGARD"

WHEN Mercer entered his sister's room he did not at first speak. He glanced at the written sheets in Laura's lap; then he sat down opposite her, his head thrown back against the chair. Though his features were as remotely cold and calm as usual, there was yet on his face something that made it different. There was some extraordinary force working in him.

This Mrs. Ammidown felt rather than saw. But she was still thinking of Mrs. Crawford's letter.

"I call it a crime for a dead woman to leave commands on the living."

She spoke with a bitter emphasis. She folded the letter. When she had spoken she looked again at her brother, and perceived that he had not noticed in the least what she had said. After a moment she asked, "Well, what is it now?"

There was not very much sympathy in her voice. She was thinking of what Temple had told her.

Mercer leaned forward towards his sister. She noticed that his hands were not quite steady. She remembered him from his boyhood, and she knew that his ordinary appearance was not indicative of his temperament; that it was only a veneering he had built about himself—and an excellent veneering it was.

"You heard that girl pray?" he inquired.

This was so entirely unexpected that Mrs. Ammidown could not at first reply. But she rallied and made the satirical remark that she supposed that Temple was what is called "gifted in prayer."

"Gifted ? Yes, God has given her this wonderful power that she might use it for Him. She would melt the hardest heart."

"Has she melted your heart ?" Mercer did not reply.

He left his seat suddenly. He walked the length of the room, and when he came back he paused just behind his sister so that she could not see him.

" Laura," he said, " don't jeer at me."

There was that in his voice that made the woman turn quickly. She stretched out her hand and seized his ; his cold fingers closed tightly over hers. She pulled him down to the footstool close to her. She was five years older than he, and was liable at any moment to return in her attitude of mind to that time when, as an older sister, she had been his tender friend and confidante. At thirty even an iron-willed man has moments when he is not quite all iron, particularly with a beloved sister.

" Is it possible ?"

This exclamation from Mrs. Ammidown could not have reference to anything that had been put into words.

With a movement of abandon that was infinitely touching in such a man, Mercer put his head down in his sister's lap.

" But you don't know her." She almost whispered this remark.

She was stroking his hair. Her eyes had suddenly filled. And there was a faint resentment against Temple in her heart.

" You are not in the least what is called acquainted with her," she went on.

" No matter. It is written that I must love her. God has willed it. I'm convinced of that. I can't fight against that. From the moment I saw her, met her glance, heard her speak, felt that strange sweetness of her presence, I knew I could make no fight against this. Everything else I could fight, but not this—oh, not this !"

Mercer had suddenly gone back to himself as he had

been as a boy and youth.   His nature, his temperament
arbitrarily asserted themselves in this great moment, in
spite of all the bonds of years.

He was now gazing into his sister's face.   And she, with
a curious mingling of fear and admiration, was responding
to his gaze.   And she was trying to banish that unreason-
able emotion of anger towards Temple.

" And she ?"

She did not just then dare to say any more, lest he
should suspect the existence of this anger.

" I don't know what she thinks or feels," was the answer.
"Only I'm quite sure she does not love me.   Why should
she ?   How could she, and in this little time, too ?   There
is nothing about me to draw her to me as she draws me to
her; nothing.   And I'm afraid to hope—"

He paused, his words showing the humility of the true
lover.

His blazing eyes, his tremulous mouth, the strange, trans-
figuring effulgence on his face made his sister's heart ache
more and more.

Even she had been deceived by the armor he had worn,
the repression he had put upon himself in the last half-
dozen years.

The fiery enthusiasm of his nature had found expression
in his work, and this was one of the secrets of his marvellous success in moving others.

" You afraid to hope !"

Mrs. Ammidown made this exclamation with pride.   She
bent over and kissed her brother's forehead.   It seemed to
her that she had gone back more than a dozen years—to
those days when Richard had let her see what he feared,
and longed for, and felt.

" She ought to be grateful for the love of such a man as
you are," she said.

Mercer smiled a little.

" I haven't looked at this as a matter for gratitude on
her part," he responded.

"Did you tell her about this sudden love?"

As Mrs. Ammidown put this question she was thinking of Temple's manner when she had spoken of sharing Mercer's work.

"No. She would have been shocked, repelled, I'm afraid. I tried to be calm and cold, and I asked her to marry me and share my labors. I think I told her how wonderfully she was gifted. Anyway, I meant to tell her that. Mostly my mind was occupied in the effort to seem calm."

"You are just like a man!" exclaimed Mrs. Ammidown.

"And why shouldn't I be like a man? What do you mean?"

"I mean that you would have a woman marry you whether she loves you or doesn't love you."

"Yes; but I would prefer that she should love me."

"She isn't likely to be the first to proclaim that love. How utterly blind men are!"

Mercer looked intently at his sister. His face grew paler as he looked.

"You think I ought to tell her?" he asked. "Remember, Laura, I don't know women at all. They are strangers to me; they seem not to belong to the human race as men do—only these rough mountain women, who are another species. I have always thought I never should love, and it seemed greatly best that I should not."

"If you know a person loves you, that fact inclines you to love that person. There is nothing new in that assertion, and, like other trite things, it is very true."

"But it is so very soon."

"Oh, I am not advising you."

The woman spoke more lightly than she felt. She added, with serious emphasis,

"Temple Crawford is rather a mystery to me. She actually thinks she has a cold temperament."

Here the speaker did not restrain a slight laugh.

"And what do you think?"

"I? Oh, I know better; it's not a matter of opinion with me. She is as warm as the tropics, but she has a dash of something, I know not what, in her. Still, firmly to believe yourself cold may be just as good, or bad, as to be so. There's something in her make-up which enables her to contemplate marrying a man whom she does not love if her judgment seems to approve. And that makes a puzzle of her, because she seems superlatively sensitive and innately refined. Why not approve of the man you love, and not marry the man of whom you simply approve, and whom you don't love? She's got a lot of stuff in her head, but perhaps life will teach her better, only she'll have to suffer first. She has an indefinable and powerful personal charm. Perhaps it's magnetism. Don't think I don't feel it, simply because I'm another woman. That would be too common and too stupid.

"Her father was an attractive, selfish scamp. He could hardly help making love if a woman were just passable. She doesn't respect him, but perhaps it is natural for her to judge men by him in some ways. And this letter— Richard, I'm going to let you read this letter. You will see what an influence it would have. Perhaps she thinks she has a cold temperament because her mother prayed that she should have it. And the child has come up in the oddest way—exactly as she pleased."

Mercer took the letter. He rose, and stood a moment with it in his hand.

Finally he spoke, his voice deepening with his resolution,

"I shall marry her if she'll consent, whether she loves me or not."

"Oh, Richard, you are blind—blind!"

Laura gazed up at him as she spoke. She added,

"I think she will say yes. She wants to be an evangelist."

A flash of light came over the man's face.

He left the room with Mrs. Crawford's letter in his hand.

Mrs. Ammidown was telling herself that he ought to read it.

The door opened again directly, and Mercer came back. He laid the letter on a table, saying,

" I can't read it; she has not asked me to read it."

" But I am sure she would be willing.   And it would explain so much, perhaps.   But, then," Mrs. Ammidown hesitated, "nothing can be explained."

She moved quickly towards her brother and put an arm over his neck, as she had done when they were children.

" Dear little Dick," she exclaimed, "can't I make you see what you are doing ?   I'm sure she doesn't love you. Don't trust your life with her !"

But Mercer only smiled as he kissed his sister and left the room.

Mrs. Ammidown sat down as one who gives up.   Then she rose and hurried into the corridor.   She called her brother back.

"I've told you, but I want to say it again : tell that girl how you love her   Do you think coldness will win her ? Richard, be reasonable, be human.   Let your heart speak. Remember, I know what I am talking about."

She pushed him away from her and was left alone.

"Now, if I were like Temple I should pray," she said, aloud.

But she did not pray.   She presently went to the window and threw up the sash.   She leaned out, inhaling the fresh, sweet air, and looking off towards the mountains.   But just now there were no mountains.   As if in a freak, they had veiled themselves in a thick mist.   The great peaks were obliterated.

But as she looked a portion of the cloud lifted, as if it were upheld by some gigantic hand, and the woman saw the top of Busbee and the sort of rift which from this distance hinted at the lower elevations where were the farms among which she had often ridden, and where the Crawford house was. She knew just where the Swanannoa went on beneath its graceful trees and by its high-banked curves. Just for one moment; then the mist was let down again, and there was only a level of cloud to be seen.

Mercer rode out of Asheville an hour later. He took the road to the junction, but he turned off and went up through the woods to visit a man who had begged him to come and see "his 'oman." She was tied down to her bed with rheumatism, but she longed to see "thur new preacher" and have him pray with her.

And Mercer prayed with her, and sat by her bed an hour, telling her of the Lord's love and of the promises of the Gospel.

He sat there because he made himself do it, although it seemed as if his will could hardly keep his body from flying off towards that log-house which he believed held his destiny.

A man often has the belief, at one time or another in his life, that some woman has in her hand the very threads of his existence. And generally a man lives to smile at that epoch in his journey through the world, and to be convinced that if it had not been that woman it would have been another; that it was a phase of his life that was ruling him more than that particular feminine individuality.

Mercer stayed in the mountain hut until the wretched rheumatic seemed comforted. He promised to come again the next day, and he went away. leaving a substantial as well as a spiritual token of his presence.

The husband walked along by his horse, thanking him fervently in the midst of his complaints about the hard luck it was to have his 'oman sick and planting time going on ; and he didn't know how he should make "er crap noways, on'y young Dalvecker wor comin' over ter give him a lift."

"Link reckons as how he's gurt thur luck in his 'oman," said the man, grinning and showing his yellow teeth.

"I thought Dalvecker wasn't married," remarked Mercer, trying to be interested.

"Oh, he hain't yit ; but he an' Miss Temple's gwine to

make er match. Miss Temple, she's as splendid er gal 's ever I viewed anywhars, but I d' know how she'll be fur craps, an' thur plough, an' sech. She's kind of er wild filly, she is. But she's er picter on that thur pony ; jest to see her er flyin' down by thur branch thur—"

The man paused as if contemplating the picture in his mind.

Mercer turned a steady face towards him.

"That's the gossip, I suppose," he remarked, as if incidentally.

"It's jest straight from Link's mar. I seen her on'y day 'fore yisterdy. She said as 'twas fixed. I hope you'll get hout hyar right soon ergin ter see my ole' oman, Mr. Mercer."

The preacher promised, and the two separated.

Mercer's horse was damp from his gallop and he was breathing heavily when he had brought his rider within sight of the Crawford house—and this rider was usually very careful of his horse. But Mercer himself was apparently perfectly cool and composed.

It was Miss Drowdy who met him just in front of the house.

"I came to see Miss Crawford," said the man, after the greeting was over.

"She's in there," was the answer, as the speaker glanced towards the open door. "She's takin' care of her dorg. She seems to love dorgs more'n most folks."

There was an unmistakable air about Miss Drowdy that showed that she would like a little conversation with some one. But Mercer did not stop for conversation. He had dismounted, and he walked directly to the door and entered, hat in hand.

There were only two in the room, the girl and the dog, and they were both on the floor.

Yucatan's shaggy white head was lying on Temple's lap. His leg, closely bandaged, stuck out straight ; he was rolling his eyes up at his mistress and then at this intruder. He immediately began to thump his tail on the floor, and he tried to rise, but he was held down by the girl's arm.

Temple had a Testament and Psalms in her hand.

"I'm keeping Yucatan from hurting his leg," she said; "you know he's got to be kept from hurting his leg now until it is well again."

Mercer said yes, he supposed so, and he stood looking down at the girl.

"I've just been told that you are going to marry young Dalvecker," he said, without any preliminary. "In that case, of course, you cannot consider my proposition."

His voice was so very calm, as if he were speaking of the sale of some land, that Temple did not blush or look confused as she answered, concisely,

"No, I am not going to marry Link, and I have told him so."

It was in this moment of relief that something peculiar came into the preacher's eyes. He still fought, however, for that self-control which he meant always to maintain. The only outlet to the warmth and intensity of his nature was the outlet he allowed it when he was conducting religious meetings. It was for the work of God that he must use the strength and the vitality that God had given him.

"You did not break a promise to him?" he asked, not knowing how stern his voice sounded, anxious only that it should not weaken in a tremor of gratitude and joy. It was in vain that he tried to call that joy senseless.

Temple was looking up at him like a child who is being catechised.

"Oh no," she answered; "I would not promise. I said I would think about it, and I have thought, and I've seen him; he knows how I've made up my mind."

Mercer walked forward and deposited his hat on the table with great care. Then he put his hands behind him and clasped them tightly as he gazed down at the girl.

Her face was still upturned towards him, and so it happened that he gazed directly into her eyes.

The gaze lasted but an instant.   The man's hands grew cold and his eyes burned; his temples beat heavily.

He recalled his sister's counsel.   Should he tell this girl that he loved her?

He had a strong fear that to speak thus would shock and repel her.   If he did not know women, he thought that he knew human nature.   And he dared not—no, virtually, he dared not mention his love.

It seemed to him that there was not a hint of any such emotion in the girl's face.   Certainly his sister must be wrong; it would be better in this instance to wait.

He sat down and looked into the fire.   As soon as he could bring his voice into proper subjection, he asked,

"Have you sufficiently considered the proposition I made to you?"

Temple's eyes were fixed on her dog as she answered,

"I think I have."

"And will you be my wife and share in my work?"

"Yes."

Mercer drew a long breath.   He straightened himself in his chair.   He tried to speak, but his lips were dry.   He tried again, and said,

"It seems to me you are greatly, wonderfully gifted.   I believe our marriage will be blessed.   I believe that together we can do a great work."

"I hope so," responded Temple, in a low voice.   Then she said that she felt that a marriage where there was mutual respect and regard—here she hesitated, and finally continued, "I suppose this respect is mutual—as I was saying, only such a marriage seems fitting for reflecting human beings. Feeling counts for nothing in the long-run.   We have minds and judgment to use."

She spoke with great deliberation, and paused often in the selection of her words.   She had not long ago begun to try to discard the terms she had been in the habit of employing, and if she took a great deal of time she was more likely to succeed in this attempt.

As Mercer heard her he inwardly thanked Heaven that he had been wise, and had refrained from speaking of love. And still there sounded in his ears his sister's exclamation,

"You are blind—blind!"

But his sister was emotional, and her judgment could not be as good as his. Besides, she was prejudiced in his favor. She could not judge.

"That being the case," he said, "it seems to me that it is not necessary that we should delay. Do you agree with me?"

Temple smoothed Yucatan's head. She was gazing down at the dog, and suddenly, and it seemed to her unaccountably, tears filled her eyes and blinded her.

"I don't know as I have any sensible reason for delay," she answered, in a moment. "Perhaps you'll think it's foolish, Mr. Mercer"—here she lifted her eyelids for an instant, and her companion saw the drops on the thick lashes. And still he combated his inclination, and held himself quietly in his chair, his pulses beating in his throat and in his eyes, while some irresistible wave seemed rising, rising within him.

But he held it a mark of superiority to be able to govern a natural impulse, even though the impulse were entirely innocent. And had not Temple just talked of judgment and reason? She would shrink from anything else.

She had paused, but now she began again. She repeated her last words.

"Perhaps you'll think it's foolish, Mr. Mercer, but I couldn't think of—of leaving here until Yucatan's leg was nearly well. And—and—oh, I don't see how I could ever part from him, or from Thimble!"

She caught her breath sharply.

Mercer glanced at her, and then looked away immediately as he answered,

"You need not part from them; surely not."

"Oh, that is so good of you! You see, I didn't know what your plans might be, and I would not do anything to hinder your work. I would not put a straw in your way. I want to help you all I can."

She was so guileless, so humble, so utterly sincere that it grew harder and harder for her lover to keep up the proper self-restraint. There was one thought, however, which helped him greatly. That was the conviction that it was not to himself that she deferred, but to his work.

As he sat there his attitude partook of his mental effort; it stiffened with more and more rigidity.

He did not know what else to say. He did not feel that he could now ask Temple to set the time of their marriage.

As he looked at her it came to him forcibly how little he knew her. Indeed, how could he know her at all? But a few days before he had not been aware of her existence. Like all genuine lovers, however, he believed in that mysterious intuition in regard to the beloved.

But what if, in his real ignorance, he should wound her in any way?

He would study her; he would watch her as love may watch. And some day in the future there might come a time when he would tell her something of what was in his heart now. All of it could never be told.

Under the sweetness of this thought he found it impossible to sit quietly. He rose and walked to the door. He vaguely saw Sally coming up towards the house with a large basket of something poised on her head. He watched her as if she had been an inanimate object.

"Fo' Gawd's sake, what's happened to de preacher?" Sally said to Almina, whom she met wandering rather aimlessly about, looking at the scenery.

She was constantly in an exalted state as to nerves and spirit. "It was the air, she supposed. It really seemed as if she could be taken up for intoxication just breathin' this air; but since she was here she guessed she'd got to breathe this air or nothing." Therefore she continued to breathe it.

"The preacher?" she repeated, in an indefinite manner;

"oh, I d' know. He seems to be made of cast-iron, except when he's preachin', 'n' then he's fire 'n' flame 'n'—'n' blazes. I 'ain't no idea what to make of him. Is he here still?"

Almina had already fallen into the habit of talking intimately with the yellow woman.

Sally did not nod her head because she could not, but she said yes with her eyelids. Then she remarked that she "jes' seen de preacher standin' like er stone figger in de do'way."

Having said this, Sally went into her own cabin.

Miss Drowdy continued to walk about and to talk to herself. She was remarking that she had never in her life before been where there wasn't a thing for her to do. There wasn't even a mantel-shelf to dust. Since the Lord had let her come, she s'posed she must have come for some good purpose.

Then she fell to thinking of the letter which had made her leave her home. Roger ought to have known what kind of a person his daughter was. She didn't need any one. She—

Here her thoughts were interrupted by hearing Temple's voice calling her name.

Almina hurried towards the house. She saw Mr. Mercer riding away.

Temple was standing in the middle of the room. She had her hands put together tightly, and her eyes were very bright. When Almina entered she took a quick step forward, and, to that woman's unspeakable surprise, she flung an arm over her neck as she exclaimed,

"Oh, I'm so glad you're here! I must speak to somebody. And Sally isn't the one now."

Miss Drowdy felt as if this were a kind of answer from Providence to her thoughts.

She put her arms tenderly about the girl as she asked,

"What is it? I hope there ain't anything troublin' you."

But Temple did not reply.   She sobbed a little with her head on her companion's shoulder.   Almina waited for her to speak.   She did not like to question her any more.

After what seemed a long time the girl spoke, without lifting her head.

" I reckon I love the mountains too well.   I reckon I've got 'em in my heart."

Here a shuddering sigh, but no more sobs.

The woman patted the girl's shoulder gently.

" Keep 'em in your heart, then," she said, " and you 'ain't got to part with um."

" Oh, you don't know !   But I sh'll take Thimble an' Yucatan.   I kin do that."

" Mercy sake !   Where you goin', anyway ?"

Temple raised her head.   Her eyes were inflamed, but they were dry ; her face was pale.

" Not anywhere at present," she answered.   " Mr. Mercer said his work would be among these mountains for many months, and then among the States about here."

" Mr. Mercer ?"

" Yes , and it's among such people that I can work, you see."   The speaker's eyes began to flash.

" Are you going to marry him ?"

" Yes, in a few weeks.   He thinks it will be losing time to wait, and I think so, too."

" But you don't know each other," said Miss Drowdy.

" Our work is the same ; that's the main thing," was the answer.   " And, as Mr. Mercer says, we shall be united in that.   Sometimes I can't wait to begin.   I shall do what I can all the time now."

Miss Drowdy walked across the room and sat down. She said afterwards that under the circumstances she didn't think it was strange that she hadn't the strength to stand up.

" So it's all settled ?" she asked, after a moment.   " And you haven't any doubts ?"

" Why should I have ?" in surprise.

"Oh, I—I—oh, of course I don't know anything about it. I think Mr. Mercer is a real good man."

Having said this, Almina gazed in uncontrollable interest and wonder at the girl before her.

At last she remarked,

"I should like to ask you one question, Temple."

"Well, what is it?"

"I s'pose you 'ain't never thought you was in love with any one, have you?"

"Oh no; no, indeed."

"I was sure you hadn't."

"Of course not. I'm not that kind of a girl."

"I declare there's one thing I must say," exclaimed Almina, with a great deal of emphasis, "and that is that you look exactly like that kind of a girl!"

Temple laughed slightly. The woman who heard this laugh could not imagine why there seemed something pathetic in it. But perhaps the pathos was in her own heart.

Mercer, riding down towards the State road, found it difficult to think coherently. And he was one of those who wished always to be able to order his thoughts as a commander orders his troops to defile before him.

The man was exultant; and yet his judgment told him that he had not sufficient cause for that exultation. He was man-like enough to think that he would be able to win Temple's love; and, as his wife, all other men would be debarred from trying to win her.

Cantering around a curve, Mercer came suddenly upon another horseman who was coming at much greater speed. It was Link Dalvecker, and the two men pulled in their horses suddenly and looked at each other.

It was strange to see a face so fair of skin and beard look so black as did Dalvecker's face as he sat there on his horse gazing at the man opposite him.

"I made shore I'd meet urp with yo' along hyar," he said, presently. "I couldn't make urp my mind ter shoot yo'. But you've gurt ter fight. So off with yo'!"

He dismounted and seized Mercer's bridle.

Mercer was on his feet instantly. Dalvecker leaped at him with that furious movement which makes a human being so terribly like a wild beast.

This was one of the occasions when the preacher's self-discipline served him well. He only defended himself. Through the next ten minutes he did not make an aggressive motion.

At the end of that time he had Dalvecker by the throat, and was saying to him,

"Now I'm going to let you go. And you've got to clear out of my sight. I won't fight you. Remember that I mean I won't even defend myself again. If you've got any honor you won't try to strike. You're a fool to fight. I know why you've done it, and I tell you you're a fool. Every woman does as she pleases. All the fighting in the world can't change that. Now I'm going to let you go."

Dalvecker, released, staggered back.

He glared an instant; then he mounted his horse and rode away, Mercer standing and watching him.

The next week it was rumored on the mountain that Dalvecker had gone down into South Carolina. Nobody knew exactly why he had gone nor how long he would stay. He had left his mother to "make the craps" as she could.

Time seemed to gallop to Temple Crawford.

In the first month of the fall she and the preacher were married.

They remained at the Crawford home, following their joint labor, and Miss Drowdy did not go back to Hoyt until the next spring.

One of the first things her sister said to Almina on her return was that "it was just like Roger Crawford to have got Alminy down there, and then have things turn out like that."

XIII

NOT BUDDHISM

"THEY say the dog always comes."

" Does it?"

"Yes; and he sits beside her, and he and she make a lovely group—so they say."

" Do they?"

" Yes ; I couldn't help hoping that he was an animal of a phlegmatic sort of temperament, you know, so that he wouldn't get to barking and howling when the people begin to shout and pray."

" I should hope so, too."

" Altogether, there's something quite different from the common about these evangelists. I meant to hear them the moment they came to Boston."

"Did you? But they've had three meetings here before this, I understand."

"I know it, but, then, I was waiting for you to come."

As she said this the girl glanced up at her friend, who was a young man with a small, pointed beard, and a little mustache curled up and out at the ends. He was dressed with extreme care. He was standing at the end of a crowded pew in a church in Boston, and when the girl glanced up at him he glanced down at her impressively. His name was Yale Boynton, and he had just come home from a university abroad where he had been supposed to be completing some kind of studies. It was not generally known exactly to what kind of studies Boynton had been giving his attention, and he had not yet been able to decide what profession he would enter. But there was always time enough, he thought, for a man under thirty. He did not wish to make a mistake, and his inclinations towards a calling were so different at different times that he was waiting, as he said, for the needle to stop wavering and settle in one direction.

Meantime, before he had gone to his university, where he only remained a year, he had engaged himself to a Boston young lady of good family.

He had come home the day before, and Miss Wallis had asked him to take her to this meeting.

Amy Wallis was a girl with a thin, spiritual face and ardent eyes. She considered Mr. Boynton to be in possession of more talent than had ever before belonged to any one man. There were times when Boynton felt that he agreed with her in this estimate. Nevertheless, Boynton's appreciation of himself was not in the least disagreeable, and only tended to give him an ease which usually insured to him the use of all his powers, for nothing was lost through diffidence.

People continued to pour into the church. The seats were now all taken, and the new-comers ranged themselves, several deep, against the wall. Men began to bring in camp-chairs from some adjoining room, and at last the folding-doors of this room were thrown open and the crowd gradually flowed in there, keeping itself well towards the main auditorium.

Boynton maintained his place in the aisle next to the wall, and close to Miss Wallis. They were not many yards from the pulpit, where the leaders were to place themselves. There was a table and several chairs on this platform, where the pulpit was, but no organ, as was usually the case in meetings of this kind.

"I'm so glad you could come with me," now said Miss Wallis, looking up at her escort, "because I want to know what you think of this kind of thing. Several of my friends have been, and they say it's really wonderful. But I want to know what you think"—here their eyes met for an instant, and the speaker blushed slightly. "There really must be something in it, you know." She went on, "And who knows but that it may be religion. Religion is so mysterious."

"It may be great personal magnetism," remarked Boynton, and Miss Wallis had a feeling that her betrothed could even explain magnetism if he cared to do so.

"That's what I told Lily Baintry," she answered, quickly—"that it must be that. But to have such a power over people, here in Boston, you know! If it were somewhere in the South, or where the audience was more emotional—"

"And Boston isn't emotional, then?" interrupted Boynton, with another smile.

He was not much interested in these evangelists, but he was greatly interested to be anywhere with Miss Wallis.

"Well, you know, Boston, I suppose, is just a trifle more given to analysis and questioning than—than some other places, don't you think?" modestly

"Oh, I dare say it is. Anyway, it wishes the world to think so, which amounts to much the same thing," was the reply.

The young man looked at his watch. "How the crowd comes in! If these evangelists, if that's what they call themselves, only charged an admission fee, they would be in good paying business."

"But they say," responded Miss Wallis, eagerly, "that they never take a penny more than just for bare expenses. They have enough to live on, and they refuse to be paid. That makes me respect them. The Gospel ought to be free. I never believed in having to pay money for your pew in church. It isn't right. Do you think it's right, Yale?"

It seemed quite necessary for Miss Wallis to know what Mr. Boynton thought upon all subjects that came up. He gave her his ideas upon this topic fervently and agreeably, thinking all the time that the man must be an idiot who could not be in some degree eloquent with such eyes gazing up at him.

"There's another queer thing about these people," Miss Wallis said, after a moment's watching of the men and women who were coming in; "they don't have an organ. The woman plays a violin sometimes when she sings."

"Does she?"

Some slight change came over Boynton's face, but Miss Wallis was looking at the door and did not notice it.

"Just think!" she exclaimed, with a little laugh; "a fiddle and a dog! Isn't it odd?"

"Very," said Boynton. "But you haven't told me their name yet."

In truth he had not been sufficiently interested to think whether they had a name or not.

The girl did not answer his remark. She exclaimed,

"There they are! That must be they!"

Boynton, standing, could see the man and woman very plainly as they entered.

"The name is Mercer," he said to himself. And he tried not to let his face show the startled interest that was in his heart.

He had been called away from Asheville on the very day following that last visit of Temple's to his boat; and his life had been full of other thoughts and had been passed a great way from that North Carolina city. And nearly three years had passed since then.

Mercer came in first. Although Boynton had heard of him and his work among the inhabitants of the mountains near Asheville, he had never seen him before, and he was surprised at the keenness with which he scanned the erect, agile figure, the thin, pale, ascetic face, with its deep, powerful eyes. He was conscious of a slight shrinking, as if he dreaded to look at the woman following Mercer. But he did look, and he was surprised that he should still be moved in any degree by the memory of that foolish time when he had gone almost every day up the French Broad in his boat, and when Temple Crawford had joined him. It was true that during that time he had thought of nothing else. But life had opened so since! So many other things had happened!

There was Temple again. She did not look any older, Boynton thought at first. She looked just the same, he fancied, and that was, as it had always been, entirely different from any one else. And her presence was never like the presence of any one else.

Boynton made a slight movement of impatience with himself. He knew that Miss Wallace glanced at him, but he continued to look at Temple.

She carried a green baize bag in her hand. Behind her walked an immense white Newfoundland dog. This dog had one black ear. He went up on the platform with Temple, and sat down so close to her that he leaned against her.

His mistress put her hand on the dog's head, but she did not appear to notice him as she did so.

Mercer came forward immediately to the pulpit. He stood an instant glancing over the congregation. Then he said,

"Let us all unite for a moment in silent prayer."

Nearly all the people bowed their heads, but Boynton did not. He continued to look at the group on the platform. He thought it was curious that the sight even of the dog should affect him perceptibly.

While the people were apparently praying, and he was gazing straight in front of him, for an instant he ceased to see what was before him, but only saw a broad river, with mountain peaks in every direction; a boat, and in the boat an eager youth, with expectant eyes fixed on the rhododendron shrubs through which a girl was sure to come. There even flashed through his mind the fact that on that last day there had been pâtés and lager.

Yes, it was the same woman who was sitting there now, with her head bent to her hand. But Temple's hair was no longer short, save about her face, where it was thick and fluffy, as it had been ; but it was coiled up at the back, and took from her head that particularly youthful and what Boynton just now called "the North Carolina look."

Even this self-satisfied young man could not please himself by thinking that Temple had ever been in love with him ; and he was obliged to own mentally that he had very much wished that this had been the case.

He continued staring intently at the top of her head as it rested on her hand. He remembered the prayer she had made that day in the boat. He was quite sure he should always remember that and its effect upon him.

She had been very much in earnest at the time. And she had married the preacher !

Here the preacher opened his eyes and raised his head. There was a slight rustle of expectation, and people glanced at each other. Mercer read in a very quiet way the whole of the "Sermon on the Mount." But though he was quiet, he was impressive, and he did not try to improve what he was reading by any comments of his own.

Amy Wallis, listening, was saying to herself that, beautiful as she had thought that chapter from the New Testament to be, she had never before known how beautiful it was, nor how strongly it bore upon daily life.

Boynton was thinking, "He's too clever to try the shouting business here, I imagine. Boston is a different sort of a place."

Meanwhile, behind the speaker's tall figure the woman and the dog sat quietly, both of them looking calmly about over the people. It seemed to Boynton now that Temple's face appeared to be somewhat older, because it was so calm. There was some change in it, he thought, as he contemplated it uninterruptedly. But he could not find an adjective quite suitable to apply to that change even in his own mind.

When Mercer had finished reading he asked if some brother or sister would start a hymn.

In the slight pause that followed this request Miss Wallis turned towards Boynton, and he bent down to hear her say,

"You see they are different, don't you?"

The young man nodded. It was true that, though the meeting was opened precisely as others would have opened it, yet these people "were different."

Boynton himself suddenly began to sing—

"Come, thou fount of every blessing,"

and the crowd joined in lustily, the sound rolling out at the open doors and seeming almost to shake the walls.

Mercer stood motionless behind the pulpit. He did not sing, because he could not. And Temple was not yet singing either. There was something like an absent expression on her face.

When the first verse was done there was an instant's hesitation. Boynton could not think of the lines immediately following, so he began on the last verse—

"Oh, to grace how great a debtor."

Temple reached down and took her violin from its bag. She laid it across her lap without trying its strings, and she did not touch it when she began to sing at the line—

"Prone to wander, Lord, I feel it."

It was a curious thing that happened then. Almost every one else stopped singing as the new voice commenced, and its volume of melody filled the large room—

"Prone to leave the God I love ;
Here's my heart, oh, take and seal it ;
Seal it for thy courts above."

Temple had risen immediately, and had come forward to her husband's side. She had clasped her hands lightly about the instrument, and thus held it to her. Her voice, as has

been said, was a contralto, and it had the sympathetic qual-
ity so largely developed that it was as if she sang out of her
very heart—as if, indeed, the rich blood of a rich nature
were flowing through her tones into the hearts of those who
heard her. Boynton told himself that it was a kind of trans-
fusion, not of blood, but of spirit.

Those hearts suddenly leaped with an emotion that took
on the guise of religious enthusiasm.

Some of the sensitive spirits present were fired with an
intense longing for a kind of self-abnegation, some giving up
that should make the world at once a better place.

Amy Wallis interlaced her fingers under her mantle and
pressed them tightly together. She shivered with what she
called a " justified delight."

She had heard a great many singers, famous singers, who
played with notes and tossed them about as a juggler tosses
balls—the old trite comparison coming directly to her mind.
She was amazed, and a trifle afraid of herself. She glanced
up at Boynton, but again he did not notice her, for he was
gazing at Temple, who had laid her violin on a chair and
who now said,

" I am going to pray."

And she began praying ; not kneeling, but standing there
with her head back, her magnetic personality already beginning to have its effect upon those present.

It has often, and truly, been said that women are too personal ; that they are not likely to judge broadly or to work
broadly.

But sometimes, for that very reason, their power concen-
trates and moves almost miraculously. That arrow which is
shot only at the horizon often hits only the horizon, as it
goes over the heads of humanity.

As once before, Boynton had felt that Temple was praying
for him, for his individual soul, so now he felt it again ; and
he fought against the effect of her prayer. He did not believe
in the slightest in " experiencing religion."

There was hardly a person present who did not feel in

varying degree that the woman standing there was praying for him, for her.

She was singularly frank; she alluded to weaknesses and shortcomings, to hopes and fears, and to all with the confidence of a child speaking to its father, who will presently greatly comfort it.

Her fervent nature vitalized the old phrases which are but husks on ordinary lips.

After the first few sentences Amy Wallis leaned her head forward on the seat in front of her. Tears gathered in her eyes and fell, but she hardly knew it. She was conscious of a deep longing to be a better woman; to live higher; to help more; to be far, far truer to her ideals.

And then there came to her a distinct and well-defined wish to be nearer that woman who was praying, to touch her hand, and partake of her strength and her exaltation.

Here and there among the people there was a groan, or a sob, or a swiftly uttered ejaculation of entreaty or gratitude.

Even to Boynton, who, as travelled man of the world, might be supposed to be a judge, even to him these exclamations did not seem like the usual exclamations in an ordinary revival meeting. He decided that the difference, the vast difference, was caused by the fact that the two leaders brought not only extraordinary power, but absolute sincerity, to their work. This impress of sincerity made itself felt from the first, and made any thought of charlatanry impossible.

Temple did not pray lengthily. When she ceased, Boynton noted how pale she had grown during her pleading, how spent she seemed. At least he thought he noticed this, but to others she was only white, and perhaps a little fatigued.

When she sat down, a woman's voice immediately began to sing "Jerusalem the Golden," and the great concourse joined her. But Temple did not sing. She was leaning back in her chair, and the white dog was couched at her feet.

If any one had thought it an affectation, which might help

to notoriety, that the dog was permitted to be present, there was probably no one now who thought so. It was thoroughly evident that there was no affectation in this man and woman.

Mercer presently began to speak. His sentences were terse and forcible, sometimes cutting, but generally the entreating note prevailed.

He said that it was the fashion in these days to call religion a mere matter of emotion — something for the weak-minded man and the hysterical woman.

Yes, it was for them; for the weak and the unfortunate of every kind, and for the innocent and the guilty. And it was a thing for the emotions and for the reason; it was something that fed and sustained the natural and innocent in everybody; but it did more: it opened to us a life for which every one longed, to which every one looked forward. It stimulated, it urged, it soothed, it satisfied. That man was a fool who called religion mere emotion. Mere emotion!

Mercer stood perfectly still, save that occasionally he lifted his left hand and flung it out with a restrained, forcible gesture. His face showed more and more, as he went on, the fire and force of the spirit within him.

"And yet," he said, "it is emotion that rules the world. It is love that is conqueror. Because I love you I seek to do you a service, and my love makes that service a delight to me; and your love, if you have it, makes that same rendered service a happiness to you too. Not that emotion which spends itself in sighs and tears and longing, but that which incites to good deeds—the fire which warms the world, which starts the machinery of life and keeps it going.

"Do you scoff at emotion? It is life, warmth—the lack of it is death. Life should be feeling and reason—the flame of being and the hand that guides the flame."

Mercer spoke a few moments in this strain; then he asked his hearers to see to it that they had the religion that should shape their lives for them, the fire that should melt and mould their hearts.

And here he became inexpressibly touching as he appealed to the people before him.

But when Boynton tried to analyze afterwards, and to find out why the man had such power, he could make no progress at all. He only knew that he did have it. He only knew that he made him long for that new life—long for it, and almost resolve to have it in some way.

Once the speaker stretched out his hands as he exclaimed,

"The new life! The new life for us who believe in God and Christ and in ourselves! Will you not have it? Will you not?"

He bent over the table and repeated the words, "Will you not?" in a cadence so beseeching that a thrill went through the audience.

Instantly a man arose and began tremulously to tell how he was trying to break away from the love of drink; how it seemed to him now that he should conquer; he had never felt this assurance so strongly before; he asked his friends to pray for him.

As he sat down some one began to pray. When that prayer ceased the fine, long drawn notes of a violin sounded in the stillness.

Boynton's pulses were hurrying with excited interest, even though he was telling himself, with an attempt at scorn, that these people were using the same old revival methods really; that the only difference was that they could manage these methods more skilfully. Would they ask those who wanted to be better, who wanted to love Christ, to come forward or rise? He had not known he was so weak as to be moved in this way. Was it merely because it was Temple Crawford there behind the pulpit? But others were moved also; were they all weak-minded—all mistaken?

A jumble of questions was in Boynton's mind, and a rising emotion was beginning to rule him.

The violin prelude was ended, and Temple began to sing with her instrument—

> " We may not climb the heavenly steeps
> To bring the Lord Christ down ;
> In vain we search the lowest deeps,
> For Him no depths can drown.
>
> " But warm, sweet, tender, even yet
> A present help is He :
> And faith has yet its Olivet,
> And love its Galilee."

The singer and the instrument paused an instant here. Then Temple, who had been sitting, rose with her violin under her chin, and moved forward to the front of the platform. She did not seem to see the eager faces turned towards her. She drew her bow over the quivering strings and sang again the words—

> " And faith has yet its Olivet,
> And love its Galilee."

And as she sang her voice laid hold on the hearts of her hearers and wrung them with an ecstatic longing.

She went on, with head uplifted and impassioned eyes that saw—ah, what did they see ?—

> " The healing of the seamless dress
> Is by our beds of pain ;
> We touch Him in life's throng and press,
> And we are whole again.
>
> " Oh, Lord and Master of us all,
> Whate'er our name or sign,
> We own Thy sway, we hear Thy call,
> We test our lives by Thine !"

The tones rose firm and strong, and it was as if there were a palpitation in them, as of a heart beating through the simplicity of the tune, beating in strenuous sympathy with other hearts.

Amy Wallis hardly knew whether any one else spoke or prayed after that. She was not even so vividly conscious that Boynton was standing close by her. But she did hear Mercer say after a little that he would like to have those who were interested, and who would like to talk with him, remain after the benediction.

Boynton stood back against the wall while the people crowded by him. So many, apparently, were going to wait that the audience seemed not to be dismissed.

At last the young man was able to reach Miss Wallis again. She was standing with her hands resting on the back of the seat in front of her. She was looking at the platform to which men and women were pressing.

"I must see her," she whispered ; "I must speak to her. I want to touch her hand."

Boynton's face showed a slight annoyance. He wished now that he had mentioned, the moment the Mercers arrived, that he had known Mrs. Mercer before she married. But he had reasoned that Miss Wallis would never know her, and there was no need to give the information. And he himself shrank from meeting her ; he could hardly tell why he felt so strongly that he would better not meet her. And here was Amy taking this notion that she must speak to Temple.

"You mean Mrs. Mercer?" he asked, quite coolly.

"Of course ; there is no one else," was the answer.

"Very well. I'll sit here and wait. It may require time to effect a meeting, as so many seem to be of your mind. What are you going to say to her?"

Boynton was not aware how sarcastic an intonation was in his voice until Miss Wallis gave him an imploring look.

"I know you think I'm weak," she said, "but I can't help it. And perhaps I'm not weak," courageously, "and the Mercers may be right and we may be wrong. What then?"

Boynton smiled indulgently and admiringly as he answered,

"Oh, I'll risk your going far wrong, Amy. Go ahead and shake hands with Mrs. Mercer."

At this point Boynton suddenly decided that it might pre-

15

vent still greater embarrassment in the future if he added, "But this wonderful woman is not an entire stranger to me, Amy."

The girl turned quickly towards him.

"What!" she exclaimed, "you know her? It's odd you didn't mention it directly."

Then she was sorry she had spoken the last sentence.

"We haven't had much opportunity for conversation this evening," he answered, easily. "I used to meet her when I was in Asheville, two or three years ago."

With a show of unbiassed judgment he continued: "She struck me at the time as being in some way different from the ordinary girl. I thought she might develop into something. But she seemed more like a child then. She rode about in an old velvet coat of her father's, and she had this same dog. She was excessively, unnaturally fond of her dog and her pony. I wonder if she takes her pony about with her as well as her dog."

The young man spoke with a great appearance of frankness. His companion had withdrawn her eyes from him, and she kept them withdrawn, as she said,

"Perhaps you will go up and renew your acquaintance?"

"Not now, at any rate. It would strike a wrong note; and she might not remember; and I hate to explain in that way."

"I think she would remember you," said Miss Wallis, quietly. She was thinking that the wrong note had already been struck. Then she quickly put away from her any unpleasant feeling. What if Yale had known that woman? He had not then known her, Amy Wallis; and she was quite ridiculous, anyway.

By the time she had taken her place in the press beside the leaders, Miss Wallis had stopped thinking of what her lover had just said. She was really a fair-minded girl, and she knew when she was unjust.

She waited patiently, watching Mrs. Mercer when she could see her, as that lady shook hands with the different people and listened to what they said. It did not seem to Miss Wallis that Mrs. Mercer said very much, but there was so much feeling in her face, so much warmth in her smiles, such a sincerity of well-wishing in her whole aspect, that no one came near her without being comforted in some degree. There were incalculable sweetness and strength in herself; and she gave of herself, gave unstintedly.

At last Amy drew near.

"I wanted to shake hands with you," she said; "I wanted—" Here the hands of the two women met, and Miss Wallis held the hand closely, with that touch which partakes of the nature of a caress.

Temple looked into the girl's eyes. What is that mysterious something which sometimes streams from one pair of eyes to another, and which at once and authoritatively declares kinship?

A different and more personal smile came to Temple's face.

"What is it you wanted?" she asked. "Can I help you? I have been helped so much, and that makes me wish to help others. But you look happy."

"Yes, I am happy," was the reply. "Still I want to see you to tell you everything, and to have you tell me about religion. Religion is a kind of rite, isn't it? Will you let me see you? Have you time? May I come?"

Miss Wallis had not known in the least that she was going to ask this, but, as she told Boynton later, the moment she was near Mrs. Mercer she had to ask if she might visit her.

"Yes, come," was the answer. "We are at No. — Ashburton Place. Come between two and six in the afternoon."

People were waiting; Miss Wallis could not linger. Another hand was extended, and Mrs. Mercer grasped it, nodding and smiling good-bye to Amy, who turned away and rejoined Boynton.

The two walked out into the street. The young man gave

himself a slight shake, as if to dispel the influence of the last hour.

"There's something theatrical about it all," he said.

"I don't think so," was the positive response. "This was genuine!"

"Perhaps I ought to have said dramatic," he amended.

"Perhaps you ought," said Miss Wallis; "but I shouldn't choose that term, even. It was moving, stirring, awakening."

"But what does it all amount to? The age of revivals, so called, is rather gone by. Reasoning beings don't look to such means now. We are theosophists and Buddhists and Pagans and scientists nowadays. We know what nerves in the body are set vibrating by this influence and that influence, and we have ceased to ascribe anything to the spirit of God working in our souls."

"Why not say that we don't even know if we have souls?" said Amy.

"Precisely. But we know we have nerves in our bodies and gray matter in our skulls; we know this because the wise men have dissected a lot of us and proved thus much."

"How grateful we ought to be to the wise men!" exclaimed Amy.

She began to walk still faster. She would not own to herself that her lover jarred upon her mood. It was her theory that the man whom you love and whom you intend to marry should never be capable of jarring upon your mood. Not that she blamed him. Of course, it was her own fault —she should not be in such a frame of mind.

Boynton glanced down at her. They had now turned into one of the walks on the Common, and the young man wished that they need not hurry so.

"You don't really wish to run, do you?" he asked; "because if you do, I'll try and keep along with you."

She laughed, and slackened her pace.

"I was thinking," she remarked. And after that she did not speak for a long time, and apparently kept up her thinking.

Suddenly she exclaimed,

"There must be something in it! And why isn't it just as likely as that all this kind of talk that does not comfort, and that leads nowhere, should have something in it? You see, you can't prove anything."

"Exactly," responded Boynton, "so we. can take our choice ; only we must take what seems most reasonable to us."

"I find I care less and less about Buddha, and reincarnation, and such things," said Miss Wallis, who was now walking slowly. "These people must be nearer right than any one else. To love, to serve ; to serve, because one loves. That's the whole, isn't it? Oh," with a sudden access of fervor, "I should think that man and woman might be the means of converting people! They made me feel about what we call revivals as I never felt before."

"That's just it," said Boynton, with the comfortable superiority of a young man who has passed a year in a German university, and who is not yet old enough to know how much he does not know, "that's just it: they make you feel. It isn't feeling we want. We are emotional enough already. It's science, logic, that we need."

The girl did not answer. Again she felt that Yale ought to have been affected differently by that man and woman whom they had just heard. He might differ from them, of course, but there must be a lack in any one who did not perceive that there was something true in what had just been said of the grand secret of life and work.

"Are you really going to call on these Mercers?"

Boynton put this question after rather a prolonged silence.

"Certainly. Why, I just told you so," smiling at him.

"I know it; but I didn't know but that it was only an impulse that would pass off directly. I wonder if you'll take them up."

"I don't imagine they would let themselves be taken up by me ; and I shouldn't think of trying to do such a thing."

Miss Wallis spoke gravely.

Boynton made an effort, and said that he had been an exile for so long that he was afraid he was selfish, and he did not like to think that Amy could be occupied with anything but his own worthless self. Could she pardon him?

Then their eyes met for an instant, and the shadow between them departed as suddenly as it had come.

Nevertheless, on his way to his hotel, a couple of hours later, Boynton began again to think about the Mercers. But he did not think so much of Amy's contemplated visit as of the way Temple had looked and sung and prayed.

"I wonder if she has been at this kind of thing ever since she married," he said, aloud, as he sat smoking in his room. "And I wonder—"

Here he paused. Then he flicked the ashes from his cigar and laughed.

He was thinking of that time when he had taught a girl how to play "The Kerry Dance" on the violin. And somehow the glamour of that time and that presence and the mountains and the river—all was so sweet in his memory that it seemed quite necessary, under the circumstances, to stop remembering.

XIV

BREAKING DOWN

MISS WALLIS went the very next day to Ashburton Place. She was shown into a room where were three or four women besides their hostess. But as all these women save one were standing, it seemed as if they were going.

Mrs. Mercer was not talking with them; she was listening. She smiled at Amy as she entered.

Amy was telling herself that she ought to have thought that it was likely there would be others here, but the truth was she was unreasonably disappointed in not finding Mrs. Mercer alone.

She wondered afterwards if she showed this disappointment very plainly, for the lady sitting in a lounging attitude on a couch rose when the others had gone, and drew her wrap about her.

" Are you going ?" asked Temple.

" Yes, I am," was the answer. " I suppose you have another meeting to-night. I hope you'll take your malt, and not forget the extract of beef; and between whiles I wish you'd drink a raw egg or two. If you won't rest, you must crowd down the nourishment. The whole thing is outrageous, and I don't care who knows it."

Here the speaker laughed slightly and glanced at Miss Wallis, who had taken the chair Temple had moved towards her.

" Why, it's Miss Wallis !" exclaimed the woman. She advanced and held out her hand.

" Don't you remember Mrs. Ammidown ?"

The two greeted each other cordially.

"I thought there was something familiar about you," responded Amy, "but you were before the window and I couldn't see."

"Since you know my caller, introduce us, Laura," said Temple.

Mrs. Ammidown complied, and the three chatted a moment. Every time Temple spoke Miss Wallis was conscious of a desire to turn and look at her, not with the superficial attention one often gives, but with a feeling very different.

Temple's voice was of that kind which penetrates and stirs, even when speaking commonplaces. But Miss Wallis, though she tried to describe it afterwards, could find no word for its peculiar timbre. She felt an excitement from merely listening to it—an excitement and an attraction which were made stronger by the fact that Temple's eyes had the same power as her voice.

It was the indefinable something with which some people are born, which cannot by any possibility be acquired. Sometimes the term "magnetism of presence" is applied, and then the user of that term may think he has defined the thing. But the thing remains just as mysterious as ever.

Temple undoubtedly did possess personal magnetism, but added to that was an inextinguishable good-will and well-wishing and sympathy which it was impossible for the most stupid not to feel, though they might not be able to analyze it.

But she looked worn and thin, and older now in this room than Miss Wallis had thought her to be the night before.

Under the beautiful golden-black eyes were purple marks, but the eyes, as well as the lips, smiled cordially at Amy when the two sat down by themselves after Mrs. Ammidown had gone.

"Now I have come I feel wicked," began Miss Wallis directly. "You are tired; you are seeing people all the time. I ought to have spared you."

"Then I should have missed a pleasure," said Temple.

It was what a conventional society woman might have said, but the tone made it genuine. Miss Wallis could not imagine the woman before her as saying anything she did not mean. She said kind things ; therefore, she must feel kindly.

"I was so interested last night," began Amy. "I wanted to ask you if your religion always satisfies, if it really fills your heart, if—oh, Mrs. Mercer, don't you know that, even in your very happiest moment, there is something?—I mean, isn't there ?"

Mrs. Mercer did not reply immediately. She sat with her hands loosely clasped in her lap, her eyes lowered. The girl, looking at her, could not but notice what she mentally called a "disciplined appearance" of the whole face. And she noticed, too, how thick the light-hued eyelashes were, how strongly marked and heavy the brows, of a color not much darker than the abundant, pale hair. Miss Wallis could not compare this woman with the mountain girl of three years before ; if she could have done so she would have been startled at the change. And yet the mountain girl was there, and something more : a rich-natured woman, holding in herself seemingly inexhaustible emotional powers. But the girl had possessed all that. What was it, then, that the years had brought ?

Miss Wallis leaned nearer.

"Dear Mrs. Mercer," she said, "you don't think me impertinent, do you ?"

Temple raised her eyes.

"Impertinent?" she exclaimed. "Why should I think so ? Are you not asking the same question that every heart is continually asking of itself, of the world, and of God ?"

"Then you are like me, like the rest of us," returned Miss Wallis. "You have not found that something which satisfies longing ?"

"No," said Temple, "I have not found it."

She spoke in a low tone, and she fixed her eyes on her companion, who returned the intent glance.

"We seem each to be made of two creatures," went on Temple, as if she were talking to herself, "of something finite and something infinite. There are moments when the finite in us may be fed until it is satisfied, and no longer cries out. But the infinite is always hungry—always asking and yearning and longing."

Temple had put the palms of her hands together in her old way as she bent forward.

Miss Wallis was thinking that had Mrs. Mercer not been absolutely sincere, she would not, revivalist as she was, have replied exactly in this way.

Amy hesitated a moment before she said,

"I thought that Mr. Mercer told us that the religion he preached does satisfy?"

"Yes, he believes that. He believes that it is possible for one to be so filled with the very spirit of God that all this undefinable yearning is satisfied—at least, it is no longer a pain."

The two women sat near each other in silence for a few moments.

Mrs. Mercer leaned back in her chair. Miss Wallis noted how thin and veined the temples were, how far too delicate the contour of the whole face.

"You are wearing yourself out," she suddenly said; "it isn't right. If I had any authority, I should forbid you to work in this way."

Temple roused herself and smiled.

"Work is the best thing in the world," she said, with marked emphasis. She went on quickly, "I don't want you to think that I am not sincere in my belief in our religion. I am. I do not tell people it satisfies and always makes happy. Do you think it is happiness that should be our goal? It is to do right, to be in the right path, that I urge upon people when I do speak."

"I believe that we have a right to demand happiness, our share of it, in this world," returned Miss Wallis, with conviction. "It is part of our heritage as human beings. We are capable of it, we long for it—yes, it is our heritage, and we are defrauded when we do not get it."

The girl's face flushed as she spoke.

" And yet you acknowledge that there is always the something lacking?" said Temple.

"Yes," trying to speak more lightly, "but I am heir to happiness all the same; still I may never come into my inheritance."

Temple's eyes seemed to be fixed on something invisible.

"Sometimes," she said at last, "I used to think I was perfectly happy, down there among the mountains, living among them; knowing when I went to bed at night that they would be there when I waked—always there. But I know, too, that there was always at the very bottom of my heart a dull ache, because I could not really take in all that beauty. I was suffering because of my limitations. I used to long to be able, just for one moment, to absorb that grand loveliness so that I should be saturated with it, and not feel somewhere in me that something, after all, escaped me. I desired that nothing beautiful should escape me. I suppose that is the way with our human nature. And as for happiness—I've thought and thought about it, until at last I have almost decided that it is a mere matter of temperament, of health. It may not be within our grasp. But to be right on all important occasions—that comes with being right each day, upon having the true attitude of mind, upon not struggling. Don't you think we often help one another when we confess our own aims and shortcomings?"

Here Temple's eyes dwelt on the girl's face in interrogation.

Miss Wallis made a gesture of assent. For some reason she found it impossible to speak at that moment.

"As for me," went on Temple, in the same quiet, thrilling voice, "I find myself so often struggling not to struggle. We don't give up enough. I want to yield—yield. Some people think that the having religion means that you are constantly resigned, even if you are not all the time happy.

It doesn't seem so to me. But I have seasons when I do stop trying to yield, and do really lean upon God."

Miss Wallis could not help thinking that it was Mrs. Mercer, more than herself, who was in a manner making confession. Perhaps the same idea came into Temple's mind, for she ceased speaking, smiled, and pût her head back again upon her chair, showing, in spite of herself, unmistakable signs of great weariness.

Miss Wallis knew that she ought to go directly, but she did not go. Instead, she exclaimed,

"You are too generous!"

Temple raised her eyebrows in surprise and incredulity.

"Yes," went on the girl, hurriedly; "don't you think I can see how you give of yourself to all these people who ask of you? Oh, I know very well that I am one of them. But I'm going in a moment. It seems to me that you are an old friend. So let me tell you that you must stop giving us sympathy. You ought to know that the wise and selfish people have decided that we must no longer sympathize with others. It's only 'going into the bog with them;' it hurts us, and does them no good. I'm sure I can't tell what there is about you—you are one of those people who have healing in their very presence. Something lovely and strong emanates from you; I feel it as I sit here. And I can feel my conscience smiting me, too, for sitting here."

Miss Wallis rose, and her hostess rose also, making some deprecatory explanation.

There was a scratching at the door, and, as Temple went to open it, she said,

"Stay one moment, and let me present a friend of mine to you."

She swung the door back, and Yucatan walked in and up to Amy, snuffed at her skirts with great gravity, then sat down by his mistress and gazed at the visitor.

"Here is some one who gives of himself, and who holds nothing back," said Temple, with her hand on the dog's head.

Miss Wallis stood hesitating. It was as if she wished to say something. But all she said was,

"Please let me come again. Please don't think of me as a stranger."

"No, no, indeed," was the cordial reply; "I could not think of you as of so many who come to me—I want them to come, you know, if they fancy I can help them—but it is different, the seeing you."

"I am so glad of that. And may I bring a friend with me?"

"Certainly."

"It's—it's the man I expect to marry—" Miss Wallis could not make up her mind to go without saying this, and she could not tell why she wanted to say it. "And he says he used to know you."

"Yes," said Temple, calmly; "I saw him in the audience with you last night. Yale Boynton?"

"Yes. I had no idea he knew you."

Temple laughed, and as she did so half a dozen years seemed to be taken from her aspect.

"It was he who gave me my first violin lessons," she said. "Does he play any of late?"

"I hardly know. He has been abroad for some time."

"How hungry we were in those days!" went on Temple, "and what good lunches he used to bring from Asheville!"

She spoke as if her hearer must know these details.

"It all came back to me when I saw Mr. Boynton last night."

"Anyway, she never cared for him," thought Amy. "But he must have been blind if he did not care for her—blind!"

Then she said good-bye, and went her ways.

All that day and all the next she could not put the thought of Mrs. Mercer from her mind. Even the presence of her lover could not quite banish this remembrance. But she did not mention this subject of her thoughts until Boynton made an apparently careless inquiry,

"Oh, did you call on Mrs. Mercer?"

The tone piqued the girl, and she only said,
" Certainly."

The young man would not glance at her, and yet he was
longing to know what Amy knew.   A stinging self-consciousness, of which he could not rid himself, made it impossible for him to ask questions.

And yet it would be odd if he did not.

" Well," he said, " were you disillusioned ?"

" Not in the least."

" Charming, isn't she ?" he inquired.

" I shouldn't choose that word.   She is more ; she has a
strong attraction.   She draws and holds one's interest."

" Ah !   It strikes me, Amy, that I don't seem to be able
to select terms to please you in these days," he said.

" It strikes me you wilfully put yourself out of accord
with me," she answered.

She was very cheerful.   She could not imagine why there
should be a certain something in Boynton's manner.   He
had no idea that she perceived this something.   He could
not entirely banish the remembrance of the effect this sudden seeing of Temple Crawford had had upon him the other night.

He was quite astonished at himself.

In the silence which came the lovers were vaguely following out disagreeable trains of thought, and feeling quite
apart from each other.

" She remembers you," said Amy.   " She noticed you
that evening."

" That was more than I expected," responded Boynton,
afraid that he did not sufficiently conceal his interest.

" She says you first taught her to play the violin," went
on Amy.

" Yes ; so I did.   The child took to playing wonderfully."

" She could hardly have been a child three years ago,"
said Amy.

" That's true enough.   But a girl in a velvet coat and a

little faded short skirt and a big felt hat dashing over the country on horseback doesn't have the effect of a grown woman, somehow. She was, in fact, though, twenty three or four, I suppose."

The girl did not speak directly.

"You don't seem to approve of me," remarked Boynton.

Amy looked at him.

"Your manner is a little peculiar," she said. "It need not be," with a good deal of firmness. "Even if you were in love with Mrs. Mercer before her marriage, I should have nothing to say to that."

Boynton wished that he could explain that it was the way he was thinking of Mrs. Mercer now that gave any peculiarity to his manner. But he could not explain that. And he did not say that he had been to the meeting the evening following the night when he had gone with Amy. He had kept carefully behind backs in the crowd, and he was quite sure that Temple had not noticed him. But he had gazed at her and listened to her. The sound of her voice had gone into his soul.

He could not tell all that to this girl who was now looking at him with frank interrogation in her eyes.

Presently the two began talking upon another subject, for Amy did not seem inclined to give any more particulars about her call upon Mrs. Mercer.

When Boynton left her he went straight to Ashburton Place. Having reached the house, he paused irresolutely, went back to the corner, returned, rang the bell, and sent in his card to Mrs. Mercer.

He was admitted instantly. The Newfoundland was the only occupant of the room when he entered, and he rose from before the grate and came solemnly forward, his tail sweeping slowly from side to side.

"Don't you know me, old fellow?" exclaimed Boynton, unreasonably glad to meet the dog. "Give me a paw, Yucatan?"

The rush of remembrance and emotion which the young

man had been battling against for several days seemed for an instant unendurable, when a voice at the door said,

"Yucatan hasn't forgotten the sandwiches in the boat on the French Broad, Mr. Boynton."

Temple stood with the drapery of the doorway in her hand, and smiled at her guest. He advanced hurriedly to her.

"It is delightful to see you again!" he exclaimed, quite taken off his guard by this reference to the past.

"It is kind of you to think so," she answered.

"Kind!" he repeated.

He was still holding the hand she had given him in greeting, holding it and looking at her, not at all aware of how much he was revealing in his face.

He had never been one to think much of self-denial in any way. He had a habit of considering himself as one who was so refined and delicate in his habits and tastes as to be in no special need of self-denial.

Of course there were gross natures whose impulses needed restraint. But he was not one of that kind. He did not go about to do evil, he would have said.

Temple withdrew her hand and sat down, as one sits who is too weary to stand.

Boynton placed himself opposite her, his eyes still upon her face.

"Really," he began, with a long breath, "I did not know I had missed you so much; but now I realize how thirsty I have been for a sight of you."

He spoke in that tone of half-banter which is so difficult to resent.

Temple was lying back in her chair. She could not conceal the effort she had to make to speak at all.

"You haven't forgotten your old trick of exaggeration," she said.

"Does it please you to call it exaggeration?" he responded. "I'm not conscious of being guilty in that direction. But I'm not so presuming as to think you remember that time among the mountains as I do."

"I remember the mountains," she answered, in a low voice.

Boynton sat silent an instant. His gaze seemed to envelop the woman and the dog beside her. He had a curious, baffling perception that he had been a blind idiot to fancy for a moment that he was in love with Amy Wallis. He had also a conviction that he ought to make much of the affection he did feel for Amy. Why, there was a delight in sitting here in the room with Temple that was a different thing altogether from anything—

Here he tried to break away from a certain power that was holding him.

"You are ill, Mrs. Mercer," he said, at last.

"I am very tired," was the answer.

"More than that," said Boynton, with some vehemence. "These people will kill you; all these souls clamoring for help from you—"

"It's not that," interrupted Temple, starting up from her recumbent attitude, her aspect changing; "it is because I can help so little that I am worn out. I long to give what they want, but I cannot—I cannot."

There was something tense in her whole appearance, in the very fingers that she tried to make lie quiescent in her lap. Boynton pitied her. And he was genuinely alarmed, too. What was Mercer thinking about to let her go on in this way? he asked himself, savagely. Were not her health and life worth anything as weighed against the demands of the rabble? The young man fiercely called the people rabble.

"Since you cannot," he said, sharply, "why not, at least, give rest to yourself? Do pardon me, but I don't think you quite know how used up you look. When I see you at the meetings you are different, somehow."

"I am then the horse that is spurred," she answered—"spurred by my desire to be of some use. Why should I live if I cannot be of use to other souls who are seeking as I am seeking?"

She paused, and made an effort to be calm. She did not know why it was, but for a long time now it seemed to her that she was all the time trying to be calm—trying and failing. There was continually within her frame a tingling riot of nerves. Often she succeeded in concealing all tokens of that riot, but it was only concealed, not appeased.

This was one of the days when her efforts met with little success. She wished that her visitor would go. At the first moment she had been glad to see him. Now the memories the sight of him awakened were intolerable—memories of the mountains, and of wild, free days.

And to remember all this seemed wicked. She could not reason out why it was wicked. She could not reason out anything any more. And she longed to be able to stop making the attempt to do so.

Boynton, at the end of a quarter of an hour, rose to go. He had been the principal talker, and she seemed to listen. He begged to be allowed to come again.

When he had gone, Temple quickly summoned the girl who attended the door, and instructed her that she was to admit no one else during the day—not even in the usual hours.

"You be lookin' sick, sure," said the girl, kindly. "And I've seen it ever since you come."

Temple made no reply. She returned to the middle of the room. She stood there with one hand pressed to the back of her head.

"It's only because I'm so tired," she said, aloud, "and I used to be so strong. How long ago is it since I used to be strong? A hundred years? Seeing Mr. Boynton makes me think of those days."

She looked at the dog, who was lying on the mat in front of the fire.

Suddenly, with a movement of abandon, she laid herself down beside Yucatan. She took his head in her arms, and pressed it closely to her.

"Oh, my dog! My own, own dog!" she cried, in a sharp

whisper. "My true love, what should I do without you? Tell me, dear heart, tell me! When I look in your eyes I know you love me. How foolish you are to love me! Oh, how foolish to love—to love!"

The voice changed from a whisper to a cry.

Temple's head dropped on the dog's side, and she began to sob in a fury of excitement and weakness. Her tears came as rain comes in a tempest. The dog's hair became wet with them.

The words in her mind were: "It's just because I'm tired and nervous—tired and nervous."

As she lay there weeping the door opened, though she did not hear it, and Mercer entered.

He stopped instantly, just within the room. His face contracted. Then he made a quick step forward, as though he would lift his wife in his arms. But he did not touch her.

She heard the step, and sprang up. She put a hand each side of her head as she looked at Mercer. Her effort to become calm was so visibly painful that Mercer's face again underwent that spasm.

"You must let me help you, if possible," he said, his words not quite distinct. "You are worn out. I have seen it for some time."

"Yes, yes," she said, eagerly, "that is it: I am worn out. I was just hugging Yucatan and crying because I am tired. You know women cry because of — of anything and everything. You mustn't be troubled about me, Richard."

Mercer turned and went into the next room. He came back almost immediately with a glass in his hand.

"It is wine and liquid food," he said.

She took the glass and swallowed its contents.

"Thank you," she responded, just glancing at him. "I am really ashamed of myself. I'm afraid I have never had enough sympathy for hysterical women."

"You are not an hysterical woman," was the reply.

Mercer arranged the pillows on the couch near. He

took Temple's hand and led her to the couch, then covered her carefully after she was lying upon it. He stood looking down at her. She was gazing into the fire.

"I hope you will give up going to the meeting to-night," he said, at last.

His manner was full of gentleness and kindness.

"I must go," she answered.

He drew up a chair and sat down. He had never laid any command upon her. He was tempted to do so now.

"It is not wise," he remarked.

He had himself well in hand by this time. His face showed only sympathetic consideration.

"Perhaps it isn't wise in one sense," she responded; "but there are a few who will expect me, and I might be able to help them. Richard, I must go to-night."

And she did go. Her singing and her prayers were never so full of their own peculiar appealing power. The people thronged up to speak to her.

But when she went with Mercer to the carriage which awaited them she suddenly clung closely to his arm, and he heard her whisper,

"This time I am really too tired."

She sank back unconscious upon the seat.

He took her home. It seemed hours to him before he had brought his sister to her bedside. The physician in Mrs. Ammidown always came uppermost at call, and her brother had in times past had many evidences of her skill and judgment.

As she bent over the bed on which Temple had been placed, Mercer stood beside her, his gaze fixed on his wife's face, which was white and set, the eyes half closed. He had asked if he should get another doctor, and Mrs. Ammidown had answered that it was not necessary at present; that Temple would revive directly.

And her prediction proved true a few moments later, for Temple's breath came long and shudderingly; then she opened her eyes.

"I'm sorry I've been so much trouble," she said, feebly, "but you see I am so very weary. Richard was right; I ought not to have gone."

"Why do you try to talk?" asked Mrs. Ammidown, with asperity. "Of course Richard was right; but he would have been right still more if he had locked you up in your room. I shall forbid you attempting to save souls for one six months, I can tell you."

Mrs. Ammidown sometimes allowed herself considerable latitude in speaking of saving souls.

"Am I so badly off as that?" questioned Temple.

"Just as bad as that," was the prompt response. "You have lived on your nerves as long as they will permit the imposition; and now you may take your choice between a long rest and becoming a wreck. I'd like to make you understand that you are to let other people's souls alone for months, if not for all the rest of your life."

"Oh, Laura!" murmured Temple.

"I mean it all," continued Mrs. Ammidown, "and much more that I don't say."

"You need not fear to frighten me," said Temple; "I'm not afraid of death—I don't dread it."

Here Mercer turned suddenly away. He walked into the adjoining room. He leaned his back against the wall and stared straight before him. His hands hung tightly shut by his side. There was a strange, glassy look in his eyes.

By his wife's bed Mrs. Ammidown responded,

"No, you may not dread death, but I'm sure you dread years of inefficiency, when you'll feel as if you were one tangle of nerves untuned and clashing helplessly, and you a plaything in the hands of these demons, anticipating everything evil, dreading your own shadow."

"Laura!"

Mrs. Ammidown now smiled reassuringly. She sat down by the bed and took her patient's hand in hers.

"Don't talk to Richard like that!" exclaimed Temple. "He will be so worried. He is so kind, so considerate, and he has been begging me for a long time not to go to the meetings."

As she spoke thus, Temple felt her companion's eyes fixed upon her in such a penetrating way that, without knowing why she did so, she blushed with the painful intensity of weakness.

"I meant to frighten you," went on Mrs. Ammidown. "Fright was a bitter dose I wanted you to take. Of course you haven't been sleeping well?"

"Oh no," wearily.

"And I know you don't care to eat."

"No."

Mrs. Ammidown sat holding the hot hand that, while it seemed to be perfectly quiet, yet had a kind of flutter within it. She was contemplating the face before her, and thinking with keen pain of the difference between it and the face of the healthy girl who had ridden among the mountains—who had saved her life. On Temple's finger was still the diamond ring she had given her.

Mrs. Ammidown rose.

"I'm going to give you something soothing now, but afterwards I shall not order medicine for you. Nobody but a doctor knows in how many cases medicine is powerless. I'm going home to think about you. Meantime, lie here until to-morrow."

The speaker moved away from the bed, but Temple called her back.

"I want to tell you something," she whispered. "I think you're deceived about something."

"Well," with an incredulous smile, "you won't make me believe that you are a very deceitful person."

"No; but—" here a pause. "It's about—well," another pause; then hurriedly, and with an access of color, "saving souls, you know. I've been sincere—I long to help—yes, I long to help, but I confess that of late—for a time—I've craved the excitement that came with the knowledge of the power I seemed to have. I've lived on it, somehow.

You see how wicked I am. I don't know what Richard would do if he suspected such a thing. He is sincere. I thought I was. Now I'm sure that I've loved the excitement. What do you think of me? Oh, Laura, what do you think of me?"

Temple caught at Mrs. Ammidown's skirt in a way that was so unlike her old self that the woman hearing her could have cried out in sorrow.

The man in the next room heard the words and the tone. He started. Then he restrained himself, and put his hands over his face, standing still.

"Think of you?" returned Laura, cheerfully. "Why, that your nerves are all worn to an edge, and that they give you impressions that are not to be trusted ; therefore, you draw wrong conclusions."

"Do you think it's that?" piteously. "Do you really think it's that. And that I needn't worry for fear I've been deceitful? And that Richard would not think I'd been insincere? I would not have him think that. Richard is honor—truth itself."

Mrs. Ammidown was going to reply when her brother suddenly entered the room, walking swiftly and softly up to the bed.

He bent over Temple. He took her hand and held it closely for an instant, his face melting into a look of ineffable tenderness and pride.

Then suddenly, as if remembering, he gently put down the hand.

XV

THE RELAXING WOMAN

Mrs. Ammidown turned to leave the room. She had never been able to think quietly and resignedly of this marriage, and just now she was more rebellious than ever concerning it. She was saying to herself that it was really astonishing what idiots sensible people would make of themselves.

Mercer continued to stand by his wife's bed. He was paler than usual, and his mouth was less firm, try as hard as he might to control its expression.

After one swift glance at him Temple turned her eyes away.

"I'm afraid this will interrupt your work," she said, anxiously.

"I'm not thinking of my work," he answered. He found that he was obliged to make an effort to speak with the calmness of courtesy. And he was always very gentle and courteous and considerate with Temple. "I am thinking of you. I feel as if I had been a criminal because I did not absolutely prevent your taking part lately in these meetings. I shall never forgive myself. I cannot bear to have you suffer in any way."

There was a vibration in his voice that made Temple glance at him again with that look which dives, but does not linger an instant.

"I shall be able to join you in a few days again," she said, and her tone sounded cold in contrast with his. "Laura exaggerates. I'm a little worn just now, that is all."

There was that in her manner which made Mercer draw himself up with a visible effort.

He thrust his hand into the breast of his tightly buttoned coat as he stood there erect. There was something antique, something strangely heroic in the severe outline of face and figure.

"I shall certainly see to it that you have every opportunity to rest," he responded.

Then he left the room. He did not even glance at his sister as he strode through the sitting-room where she sat. He did not seem to be aware of her presence in any way. When he had reached his own sleeping-room he shut the door noiselessly behind him and drew the bolt.

He advanced to the middle of the floor. He stumbled against a chair. He took close hold of the back and straightened himself again. It was always his instinct to throw back his head and meet a foe front to front.

"I can bear it," he said, in a just audible voice. "God knows I can bear everything He sends."

He stood a moment thus before he knelt by the chair, hiding his face in his hands on the cushion. He prayed, a fire of longing, an ice of despair in his petition.

"Even though I can never make her love me, oh, God, let her live in this same world with me!"

Over and over these words rushed through his brain. He tried to form other words, but he could not.

At last he rose and sat down in a chair by the table which held his Bible. Mechanically he took up the Bible. He had intended to read something in reference to the meeting for the evening, but he found that he could not take in the meaning of a single sentence. But he held himself, as if bound with cords, in this place until at last his thoughts obeyed his will.

The next day Temple was languidly sitting up, and the next she seemed so much better that she announced her intention of seeing the people who called.

"No," said Mrs. Ammidown, who had just come in, "you

will do no such thing. I have had your case on my mind, and I've decided what you must do. First of all, I am going to put you under the relaxing woman."

Temple looked up with a faint smile, but not much show of interest.

"You are becoming a tyrant, Laura. Who is the relaxing woman?"

"Oh, she doesn't call herself that, but that's what she is. She has a mission, and her mission is to teach people to bear their whole weight."

"Oh!"

"Yes, when they sit down or lie down."

"Is that all?"

"All? I assure you that is a great deal. You have no idea how much it involves. The safety of the race depends upon the power of each individual to bear his weight—then he rests. I don't suppose you have really rested since you took up this fad of saving souls."

"Laura!"

"It is a fad," was the calm response, "but I don't mean that it shall kill you. And you sympathize, and give of yourself to all these creatures."

"They are my brothers and sisters," was the reply.

Temple's face kindled as she went on. "Why shouldn't I help them? What is the use of living if it is not for service to God and man—if it is not to help, to spend your very self?"

"You are going to stop spending yourself," said Mrs. Ammidown, still calmly. "The relaxing woman will attend to that. She doesn't allow her pupils to sympathize, or emotionalize, or do any of those things. If there is any power left in you it is to be conserved for your own use. You are not to give any more of it out for any reason whatever. Store it up."

"As a miser stores his money," said Temple, scornfully.

"Exactly. Then you'll have it to draw upon. And you are not going to feel anything more, only as you are permitted."

"You are speaking of a great life, full of human possibilities," remarked Temple, with still more scorn.

Mrs. Ammidown smiled indulgently.

"She does it for three dollars an hour," she said. "She combines an eye to what is called the main chance with great good to nervous women."

Temple clasped her hands suddenly and forcibly.

"But I'm not a nervous woman!" she cried.

"Aren't you?"

"No, no! Why, don't you remember, Laura, how strong I always was down there in Carolina, and how I didn't even know what nerves were—save that my happiness was too great sometimes? Don't you remember?"

The speaker's eyes dilated painfully and then filled with tears.

"Yes," replied the other, "I know; but you have changed all that. You have made such calls on your strength; you seemed to think that it was limitless. And then, pardon me, Temple"—here the woman bent forward and took the clasped hands—"you have not been happy."

"Oh, don't! don't!" murmured Temple.

"No, no. But a little harshness is sometimes strengthening. I am not going to say anything more than this: you acted upon a theory you had about marrying on a basis of respect and regard merely. You thought you could improve upon nature. You thought going against the natural impulses of the human heart was a fine thing to do. Well, you can't do that and come off victor. You're vanquished. Your being gives up the unequal battle.

"When a sensitive and refined woman acts out the theory of a marriage for anything else than love she certainly deserves to lose her self-respect, and generally does lose it.

"Do you remember that writer who says: 'No woman marries a man without loving him but has her moral sense obscured?'"

Temple's eyes had been fixed upon the speaker.

"Laura, I wish I could tell you some things—I wish—"

Having said so much, Temple withdrew her hands and twisted them together.   She smiled piteously.

"But no; I really have nothing to say.   It is weak to talk about one's self and to pity one's self.   And I wanted to do good, and to help people.   Now if I'm going to be a nervous woman—"   Here her lips quivered and the tears dropped from her eyes.

"Oh," said Mrs. Ammidown, easily, "because you have worn yourself down like this, it by no means follows that you are going to keep on being a nervous woman."

"I suppose I shall be well again in a few weeks," said Temple, pleadingly.

"No; let us look the thing in the face.   You must rest for months, perhaps for a year.   Here is the programme: First, you go to Miss MacCallum for treatment.   Her treatment is good for people who live too fast, because she tries to teach them not to live at all.   And that is exactly what you need now.   You are to be taught simply to rest.   If you can rest long enough you will be well again, for there is no organic trouble.   Then I want you, as soon as it gets mild, to go into the country; stay all the summer with Yucatan; have Thimble; ride, stroll, vegetate.   If you feel as if you were going to sympathize with somebody, stop where you are.   You need not help a creature.   Would you like to be back in Limestone township when spring is really here?"

A shade came over Temple's expressive face.   She hesitated, but at last said,

"No; let me go to some new place, and I will send for Thimble.   Oh," with a sudden brightening, "I will write to Miss Drowdy.   She lives here in Massachusetts.   Perhaps she will let me stay with her."

"Miss Drowdy let it be, then," was the answer.   "Only to-morrow we will call on Miss MacCallum."

Mrs. Ammidown walked towards the door.   She knew that she had been a little harsh in her manner, but it had been purposely.   Now she paused and looked back.

"It seems to me," she said, "that your dear old mountains ought to be able to heal and strengthen you. Are you sure it is wise to go somewhere else?"

There was something in the face of the younger woman as she heard these words that made Mrs. Ammidown's heart suddenly contract with the keenness of her sympathy. Yielding to a strong impulse, she crossed the room and knelt down by Temple's chair, putting her arms about her and drawing the slight form to her.

Temple's head dropped upon her companion's shoulder, but she did not sob nor weep; she was very still.

"You are morbid and supersensitive," said Mrs. Ammidown, after a silence. Then, with a slight laugh, "You see, it's hyperesthesia, and that kind of thing. Everything will be different after you are rested and nourished. Flesh and blood and nerves resent certain things, and then we think it's our souls or our spirits which are diseased. But bless me! here I am sympathizing with you! How ridiculous of me!"

Mrs. Ammidown rose. She announced, in the most practical manner, that she would call at three to take Temple to Miss MacCallum.

When she had reached the hall she hesitated a moment. The seeming result of her hesitation was that she took a card from her case, wrote a line upon it, rang the bell, and asked the servant to take the card to Mr. Mercer immediately.

When Mercer read what his sister had written, "Call upon me within the hour," he put his overcoat on his arm, and with his hat in his hand he entered the sitting-room.

He had one glimpse of Temple's colorless face as it was leaned upon her chair before she was aware of his entrance. That glance was like a knife-thrust in his heart. Instantly she had assumed a look of some animation, and her lips put on a smile.

"I only came to say that I was going out for a short time," said Mercer, advancing into the room. "I wish I could get you something — to amuse you, to entertain you in some way."

He took her hand and held it a moment, lightly, in a sort of distant manner, then laid it gently down.

"Thank you, Richard, I can't think of anything," she began. And then, "If you'd bring some kind of fruit, I should be glad. And if you would try to rest a little yourself—"

"Oh, I'm well—well and strong," he answered. "Don't think otherwise."

He hurried away. He was quite conscious that he was childishly grateful that she had mentioned something he might get for her, even though he suspected that she had spoken thus chiefly to gratify him.

Mrs. Ammidown was waiting for him at her rooms. He walked straight up to her and took hold of her arm in a way that made her wince.

"Now, tell me the exact truth," he said, harshly, "is she going to live?"

"Yes," was the instant reply.

Mercer released her arm. He suddenly began to tremble. The tremor shook his whole frame.

His sister pushed a chair towards him, and he sat down in it. He gazed at her vaguely. He vaguely felt her hand on his forehead and heard her say,

"Poor fellow!"

He roused himself to murmur, apologetically,

"It's been a strain."

Laura was the only person in the world to whom he could allow himself to show weakness.

She did not reply. She only continued to caress his forehead.

"She must go down to Carolina," he went on as soon as he could. "She will get well among her own mountains. And I will stay here. Laura, you arrange it; you go with her."

"It was the mountains that I thought of first," was the reply. "But she doesn't want to go."

Mercer started forward in his chair.

"It is because she was happy there," he exclaimed, "and she cannot bear to go back! Yes, she was happy there. Good God! Laura, do you know what I've made her suffer?"

The woman did not reply. She could not. She stood there with her eyes fixed on her brother.

At first there was a stirring of resentment against the woman who was making him so unhappy. But he did not mention his own unhappiness. He was thinking of his wife.

She felt that what she had to say was becoming more and more difficult. But she must say it. She began bravely.

"I asked you to come to me because I wanted to advise the very thing you mention." Here she stopped abruptly. He did not speak, only gazed at her.

"It's a hard thing to say," she went on; "but when a person is in a nervous state, on the verge of prostration, we must make allowances—"

Again she paused. She moved quickly still closer to her brother, leaning over him, as she went on, but not glancing at his face.

"I wanted to tell you that I think it would be better if you did not go into the country with Temple; better if she should come to me now while she is under this new treatment which I advise for her. She needs a complete change, and if she does not see you she will not be reminded of her work—your work. Don't misunderstand me."

"No, I don't. I understand you thoroughly."

Mercer rose as he spoke. He girded himself up. "I could not by any possibility fail to understand you. And it is what I have been thinking. More than that, when once Temple goes away from me I am convinced that it will not be advisable for me to join her again. But let that come about naturally. That is in the future. I may be obliged to go abroad, or to the West—a hundred things may be arranged. I will not shadow her life any longer. My presence represses her. I seem to stand between her and the sun."

The man gazed about him in a blind way, as if there were a veil before his eyes.

Suddenly he added,

"Did she love any one down there?"

"She did not believe in love," said Mrs. Ammidown, bitterly. "She called herself one of the cold-blooded women who have affection, but no love. She had her mother's letter and her own notions, and she built up a beautiful little code. There is no mistake so fatal as the mistake which makes a woman ignore the possibilities of her own nature."

"Are you sure?" asked Mercer again.

"Sure about what?"

"That she did not love any one down there?"

The man seemed so little like himself to his sister as he repeated this question that she could not help wincing visibly.

"One can never be positive on such a subject," was the answer, "but I'm sure enough to satisfy my own mind."

"That young man—that Boynton," went on Mercer. He checked himself. "I know that I am no longer clear, no longer just, in my conclusions. But to be so hopeless as I am, to be so far from her while I seem to be so near her— sometimes I am ready to believe that she has some memory which stands between her and me. Be sure, Laura," with a flash of the eyes, "that I am not reflecting upon her honor, her entire high-mindedness."

"Oh, I know that. Do I not know her?" replied Mrs. Ammidown. "You may be sure she never loved Boynton; she had no fancy even for him, or for any one."

The speaker refrained from saying, "I told you so," but that phrase was in her mind. She was asking herself indignantly what right any one had to suppose that such a marriage would turn out happily.

There was but little more talk. Mercer agreed to everything his sister could suggest in his wife's behalf. He was like a man who stands by and sees himself shorn of this hope and that expectation. It was, however, but the open acknowledgment of the despair he had long felt.

When Mrs. Ammidown called that afternoon she found a great bunch of hot-house roses on the table near Temple, and a basket of the most extravagant, out-of-season fruit.

"You have an admirer who does not stint in his offerings," remarked the lady, somewhat coldly.

Temple smiled. There was a slight flush on her face as she took up a card and extended it towards her guest.

"Here is his name," she said; "this was among the flowers."

The name was Richard Mercer.

Mrs. Ammidown looked narrowly at the woman in the lounging-chair. But Temple did not seem conscious of this inspection. She languidly selected a Marshal Niel and put her face down to its petals; then she held it off from her and contemplated its beauty.

She did not seem much interested in going to Miss Mac-Callum's rooms.

Miss MacCallum was established in a good street at the south end. Everything betokened prosperity; but Temple took no notice of her surroundings as she sat down in an easy-chair to wait. Miss MacCallum had not yet arrived. For some reason she was late. An assistant had taken her place.

Three or four women were waiting. One was a young girl who was fidgeting about the room, apparently unable to keep still. She was thin and white, with large eyes, whose pupils were continually contracting and expanding.

At last she came and sat down by Temple.

"Do pardon me," she said, in a fluttering manner, "but I'm so glad to see you; I've just longed to speak to you since I heard you sing and pray at one of your meetings. I should have gone up and spoken to you then, only mamma wouldn't let me. She said 'twould make me nervous. She always says everything 'll make me nervous. Are you coming to Miss MacCallum?"

Temple said she thought of coming.

"Then I s'pose you've got nervous exhaustion, or St. Vitus, or something," was the girl's response. "Perhaps you've been emotionalizing too much. Have you?"

"I don't know," answered Temple.

"Oh, I've no doubt you have," went on the girl, "and you haven't been normal; you may think you have been, but you haven't, and she'll find it out. She's after the abnormal like a cat after a mouse. It pays, too. You see, she keeps a kind of factory where she takes abnormal women and turns them out normal."

Here the girl gave a slight laugh. Temple smiled, and said that of course, then, Miss MacCallum would naturally prefer to have women abnormal at first.

Whereat the girl laughed again, and responded,

"Of course, then, there'd be all the more to turn into the factory. She's just awfully clever, though. You wait, and you'll see. It's the Delsarte system—at least, some of it is. And she wants to do for the nerves what ordinary exercise does for the muscles. She's got it all down horribly fine. Mamma adores her. She says if Miss Mac—I call her Miss Mac—doesn't take the kinks out of my nerves nobody can. There's a lot of women whom the doctors don't know what to do with; medicine's no good. Then they make a great parade of sending them to Miss Mac, as if it were their prescription, you see; and it's all good for the relaxing woman."

The girl fixed her eyes upon Temple in silence for an instant. Then she said,

"You are not relaxed. You're not sitting so that you rest. You're kind of tense, though you look so quiet. That never 'll do. Miss Mac 'll fix all that. There, I think she's coming now. I'm going to relax. Watch and see me do it."

The girl flung herself in a chair with the utmost abandon and half closed her eyes, rolling her head slightly.

Mrs. Ammidown, who had been reading a magazine at the end of the room, looked up as some one entered; then she rose, and the two greeted each other with a slight appearance of effusion on Miss MacCallum's part. The newcomer was tall and well knit; she had sleepy blue eyes which yet probably perceived things. Perhaps they were not really sleepy, but only had that appearance, because their owner so deprecated alertness and vividness of life in others. To be alert and vivid and intense is a drain on the nerves; and all drain should be avoided.

In a few moments Temple was sitting alone with Miss MacCallum, and the latter was asking her some questions.

Her first remark had been to inform Temple that Dr. Ammidown—the speaker was very particular in applying titles—had given her no information other than to say that Mrs. Mercer was in danger of a general break-down of the nerves.

" And that is evident," said Miss MacCallum.

Temple made no reply to this.

. " You must pardon me," went on the other, " if I say that you have the appearance of being much exhausted by sham emotions. I shall have to beg you to avoid all such experiences."

Temple was looking full at the speaker.

" I don't know what you mean," she answered.

" You know," was the response, " that there are real things, and that the real things almost always have imitations. It is the imitation which exhausts."

" Doesn't the real emotion exhaust?"

" Only for the time; there must be reaction, and then comes invigoration, like that attendant upon healthy exercise. Generally speaking, however, emotion should be avoided."

Miss MacCallum went on with a skilful and extremely well-put dissertation on the depleting power of the emotions in general. Starting from the standpoint that the highest state of the human being would be that of a sort of animal, without any particular sensation or feeling, but with some intellect, her argument was utterly convincing.

"I don't always talk as much as this," she said, in conclusion, "but I saw that you would wish to know the theory as well as the practice."

Temple was silent. She had been conscious of a rising indignation which she had tried to smother.

Finally she said,

"I can understand perfectly that many limitations might be necessary for one out of health. One must do, or refrain from doing, much which would be legitimate in health. But this is, in a great measure, your theory of life?"

"Yes. We are reasonable beings. We should live more in the clear light of reason, and emotion is, after all, so largely a matter of diseased nerves. We think we feel; it is nerves. We think we love; it is nerves. In other words, it is sham emotion. The American woman is getting to be but a bundle of unstrung nerves; but she thinks she is full of feeling; she prides herself on that belief. What we want is to be practical."

"To think of facts?" said Temple, with a stiff kind of smile.

"Yes; and to relax. To stop struggling; to give up."

"I should like to give up," said Temple. "I've tried a great deal to give up."

"Let us stop trying. Something is making you unhappy, Mrs. Mercer; but perhaps, after all, it will be nothing when you are well."

"You would call it a sham unhappiness, perhaps?"

"Very likely."

Temple sat up suddenly.

"I don't believe one particle in your theory of life," she said, warmly; "and you have a cold nature or you would never have embraced such a theory. To your temperament such a life may be possible, admirable. Could you but know the possibilities open to a different nature you would never talk thus. You think you know, but you don't. Your very attitude of mind proves your ignorance. To do as you suggest would be like following out that old Eastern saying:

'It is better to sit than to stand; it is better to lie down than to sit; it is better to be dead than alive.' Miss MacCallum, we were given powers of exquisite and intense life —some of us have been given such powers—are we to stifle those powers and try to be as if we did not possess them? Are we to be simply reasonable beings? Why, then, are we made so marvellously sentient? And may I ask if it be in your power to decide what is sham and what is genuine? I may be so made that I feel an emotion which it would be impossible for you to feel from a like cause—are you, then, to set down my emotion as sham, as abnormal? Oh, don't interupt me, and don't think me rude. I used to believe that I was of a cold temperament. That was a girlish notion of mine, and I thought it would be a fine thing if it were true. But it isn't true. No; it isn't true."

As she finished speaking, Temple rose from her chair and stood before her companion, who smiled and said,

"I needed no such assurance."

"I know that. I know," went on Temple, more and more earnestly, "that I'm in a wretched condition now. I want you to give me treatment. I long to be able to rest—in fact, I must rest. Somehow, I must rest."

There was something extremely touching in the slight figure, which seemed to palpitate with a too insistent life.

"I am sure I can help you, dear," said Miss MacCallum.

Temple frowned.

"Don't call me dear," she said. "I hate those terms when they mean nothing. Such use takes all significance from words."

Miss MacCallum did not lose her temper. She smiled as if she were used to any and every kind of remark, and was saying to herself, "Oh, it is only a nervous woman."

Temple caught that smile, and was still more irritated, but she compelled herself to apologize. She hardly knew herself when she was irritable; she had always believed she possessed an amiable temper.

After a few more sentences in regard to terms and hours, Temple went back into the waiting-room. The same girl came forward to meet her.

"What do you think now?" she asked, in a half-whisper. "Are you going to fall in love with her?"

A negative shake of the head was the response.

"I shouldn't, either," went on the girl, rapidly, "but my doctor said the girls were always falling in love with Miss Mac, but that she just stopped it. You know it's awfully abnormal to fall in love with a woman—for a woman, I mean. It's just the abnormalest thing you can do. Miss Mac is death on it. She thinks it is quite hellish. Don't be shocked because I say hellish. I often can't find words strong enough to express what I mean. I fancy that's why men swear. And don't ever tell mamma I said that."

The girl was standing close beside Temple, looking at her in a somewhat beseeching way.

"It would be just as easy as breathing to fall in love with you," she said, "but I know better than to do it. Miss Mac would be down on me like a stone house. She knows a good many things, still there are a few things she doesn't know. But the devilish part of it is that she thinks she knows it all. Did she tell you what to do when you are wretched about anything?"

"No," answered Temple, who was waiting for Mrs. Ammidown to return from a call she had started to make during the interview with Miss MacCallum.

"When you are unhappy you must think how heavy your legs are; and presently you'll find you are happy again. I've tried it."

"Well?" questioned Temple, smiling.

"It didn't work in my case, because I couldn't seem to make my legs seem heavy; the more I tried to make them heavy the lighter they grew. But, then, I'm hopelessly abnormal, anyway."

The girl stopped to laugh, and Temple was rather surprised at herself to find that she joined heartily in with her.

There was something shrewd and penetrating in the girl's face and in her words, in spite of her seeming frivolity. She was dressed with a dainty and exquisite plainness, and there was about her an air of refinement, notwithstanding her use of some startling words.

"I suppose she called you 'Dear,'" she now remarked.

"Yes."

"Of course. She's sweet as honey in the comb. Maybe that's why some of the girls fall in love with her. I'm going to blow my trumpet for her because she certainly does help a person to rest. You see, when you've sat on the floor a few minutes and melted like an ice-cream in a warm day, you do feel like sleep—you can't help sleeping. And when she has you roll like an elephant—well, you'll see—your nerves do have to give in and subside. But you've got to be faithful and go through the movements at home, and if you have movements and walking, and watching yourself to see that you don't emotionalize, why, you don't have any time left. I'm going to ask her to give me a list of shams and genuines — emotions, you know—so that I needn't make any mistake. I declare, what with bacteria for your body and shams for your feelings, you do feel as if life were hardly worth living. I'm going in now to melt. If you come here I shall see you again. Won't you shake hands with me?"

Temple gave her hand, and a warm pressure with it.

XVI

OLD MAID DROWDY'S

ALMINA DROWDY was standing in her door-yard. She had put on her dish-brimmed shade hat for the first time this spring. She knew that it was too early to wear that hat, but she said that somehow it seemed to bring the warm days nearer if she brought the old thing down from under the eaves. It made her feel as if the violets were actually coming.

In Hoyt, Mass., it often seemed to the impatient resident that spring never would actually arrive.

Mr. Wilson had ploughed up a patch of land on a south slope for early pease. That ploughing was an encouragement to Almina. She decided that if Brother Wilson could plough she could leave off her white cloud and resume her hat.

She was expecting Mr. Wilson now. He was going to bring Freddy to spend the day with his aunt. He would necessarily bring him early, for he would be on his way to the next town with eggs and milk.

Freddy had grown in the three years that had elapsed since Almina had gone to North Carolina. She had left him making perilous, tottering journeys across the kitchen floor, and occasionally swallowing shoe-buttons.

Freddy had set up a dog—a young bull-dog that squinted and that made charges at people's ankles in the most ferocious way, but who would not have bitten any one upon any provocation. Only the people upon whom he charged did not always know this; and this ignorance caused a great deal of unpleasantness in the hearts of some of Freddy's acquaintance. Indeed, that acquaintance threatened to narrow down to those who would submit to having their ankles mumbled by the puppy. Those who would not submit, Freddy unhesitatingly called "darn fools."

Freddy's mother thought that a person must be extremely mean who was irritated when a cunning little boy like Freddy called him a "darn fool." And as for being afraid of a bull-dog puppy—

Here Mrs. Wilson would toss her head and leave the sentence unfinished.

Almina once told her sister that the world seemed to be divided into two classes—those who were friends with Freddy's puppy and those who were not; and Olivia judged everybody with reference to their standing with Jefferson, for the dog's name was Jefferson, usually called "Jeff."

Almina, as she stood in the yard on this April morning, was conscious of a decided wish that Jefferson would not come—not that she was afraid of him, but that it was usually impossible to watch him closely enough to prevent his chewing some valuable article.

The last time Jefferson visited her, accompanied by his young master, he had chewed and swallowed the whole vamp of one of her best boots.

She had not expected the boy to be sorry, but she had been tried when the boy's mother's only remark in the case had been,

"I want to know! Wall, Jeff is dretful fond of leather."

A pair of bluebirds circled down into the yard as Almina stood there. They called to her—or was it to each other?—and the woman's heart swelled joyfully.

The frogs were peeping in the meadows.

Almina turned her face upward. She spoke aloud.

"There certainly is a look in the sky—there certainly is a look," she said.

She went into the house and brought out a shawl. This she wrapped about her, and began walking briskly back and forth in the yard, for it was chilly, in spite of the soft sky.

Almina poked the toe of her "rubber" into the black mould around the peony root. A red tip would soon show itself. She had found saxifrage among the rocks at the south of the house the day before.

When her eyes swept over the country, however, the hills and valleys—they were hills and valleys in smallest miniature — were still bare and brown and desolate. But she knew a bit of swamp-land where skunk-cabbage was already green and flourishing.

As her eyes, in their cursory glance, rested upon a cart-path that wound over the pasture in front of the house, she made a quick step forward, then paused, gazing with distrustful air, as if she could not believe what her eyes told her.

"Merciful sakes!" she exclaimed, "I d' know but I'm gittin' so old I can't see straight."

There was a note of strong excitement in her voice. She ran across the road and to the bars of the fence; these she let down with trembling hands; then she stood still in the opening.

A white pony was coming at a leisurely amble along the rough way. He did not seem to mind that it was rough, but came as one used to uneven roads.

His intelligent face, with its ears at full cock, was towards her.

On the animal's back was a tall, stalwart woman of a dusky countenance. This woman began to smile broadly, her white teeth shining. She threw up her hand.

"I reckon it's you, miss!" she called out. "Howdy, Miss Drowdy?"

Instead of responding to this greeting Almina said, helplessly,

"Oh, good land! I can't b'lieve my senses!"

By this time the pony had brought Sally nearly up to the bars; and now he stopped his amble and walked forward, his slender legs looking just as much like "injy rubber" as they had always looked to this Yankee woman.

Sally continued to grin.

"We've done brought roun' hyar," she remarked.

"What!" cried Almina, "you 'ain't come up from North Carliny on that pony, have you?"

Sally laughed. The rich, throaty sound seemed quite out of place opposite that strictly New England house, and in the hearing of that strictly New England woman.

"Bress yo' heart, honey," she answered, "of co'se I ain't. I'se jest curm urp fum de deepo-house. We uns curm in de kyars, we uns did. Thimble's awful scraped 'n' rubbed on his laigs. But he kep' urp er good heart all de way, he did. 'Fore de Lawd, I reckon de pony knew he war comin' ter Miss Temple. He knew all de same's I knew. Dem kyars is jest a hell upon yarth; but I'd come all trew hell ter git ter Miss Temple. Reckon by your s'prise, Miss Drowdy, as Miss Temple 'ain't got yere yet?"

"No," said Almina. She still stood directly in the way, and the pony's white face was within a yard of her own face.

"Of co'se," said Sally, "dey must of wrote."

"I 'ain't got no letter," was the response.

Then Almina tried to rouse herself.

She stepped back, and the pony put himself over the dropped bars with a little jump, plainly assuming that a jump was the easiest way to get over, and showing in every slightest movement that he was not in the least like any Northern horse.

"Won't you walk in?" said Almina.

She instantly corrected herself.

"I mean, come right over to the house. I'm real glad to see ye, though I'm so 'stonished I can't collect my wits. 'N' we'll put the pony in the barn, 'n' fodder him. He looks kinder used up, 'n' that's a fact."

As she talked, Almina was gathering her senses, which seemed far afield.

She turned and retraced her steps across the road.

She was surprised that she should feel so decided a pleasure at sight of this yellow woman. ·

To see Sally was like having back again a bit of that strange life in the Carolina mountains.

Almina had been glad to get home, but a hundred times since her return she had suddenly caught herself wishing for one day among those mountains—one day of the strange, unconventional life.

And she had longed to see Temple. She could not tell why she so desired to see that girl. Of course, a proper amount of longing would be strictly the right thing, but sometimes she had felt like crying out for a glimpse of that young, strong face, with its signs of superabundant life and emotion.

On one occasion, in an expansive mood, after a cup of tea with Mrs. Wilson, she had confided to her sister this feeling she had about that girl.

"I d' know how 'tis," said Almina, "but she ain't a grain like common girls. I have spells of bein' actually hungry and thirsty for a sight of her. She was like sunshine 'n' fresh air; 'n' then, again, she was like some nights when there ain't no moon, 'n' the stars shine, 'n' the air is jest as full of sweet smells—"

"Alminy," her sister had interrupted her, sharply, "I guess you'd better stop talkin'. I'm glad there ain't no one but me to hear such talk. I know what folks would say. Jest to think of a human bein' that was like a night when there ain't no moon, 'n' all that stuff! I declare you do put me out of patience, Alminy! But you always was odd. 'Member that time when you wouldn't marry the doctor? I wish you'd pass me the sugar."

Almina passed the sugar and smiled to herself as she did so. She was thinking that Freddy's mother, even though she had Freddy, yet lacked some resources which she, the old maid, possessed, and of which no one could deprive her.

"What made you come by that cart-path?"

Almina put this trivial question as she stopped at the barn door and took the padlock from the staple, preparatory to rolling the door back.

Sally was pulling her foot from the stirrup. She replied that she done couldn't tell why, "'less 'twas 'cos a man told her de path war er short curt to old maid Drowdy's."

Here she rolled her eyes towards Almina, who laughed slightly. She had hardly heard the answer, for she was wondering how it happened that she was so pleased to hear that negro voice and that mixture of dialect which Sally used. Almina could not remember that she had particularly cared for it when she was in Carolina.

The two women went into the barn. Sally's fingers attacked the buckles and straps of the saddle.

The pony reached his head up towards the hayloft, from which dangled a few spears of hay.

"Mr. Wilson gits in my grass," remarked Almina. "Sence I got home from Caroliny I 'ain't kep' a cow; but I've got meal 'n' shorts I have for my hens 'n' pig."

"Where is Temple now?"

"Laws! how 'd I know? I done thought I'd find her hyar. She ben preachin' 'n' prayin' trew de land fur de Lawd. She ben up Norf hyar."

"Has she?"

"Yas 'm."

"Is her work blessed?"

"Powerful," with unction, "so dey say. De Lawd sends His Sperrit right down."

The yellow woman flung the saddle on the floor. She pulled Thimble's bridle over his ears and dropped that on the saddle.

Then she suddenly sat herself flat on the floor and began to sob loudly, and rock herself to and fro.

Almina, inexpressively distressed, gazed blankly at her. She was running over in her mind all the restoratives she had in the house.

Naturally she thought of red lavender, but for some reason this remedy did not seem appropriate for a tall yellow woman who was swaying like that.

"Oh, Lawd Gawd Almighty!" cried Sally, "I jes' want

Miss Temple! I jes' want my Miss Temple! She mus' be daid! She mus' shorely be daid!"

Almina took hold of Sally's arm and shook it.

"Stop!" she said, sharply.

But Sally did not stop. She went on worse and worse. Her voice sounded out from the barn and along the road.

Sally was tired and hungry and bewildered. She was also much disappointed to find that Temple was not there. She had fully expected to find her. And she was deathly homesick. The more homesick she felt the louder she shouted her calls upon "Gawd Almighty." And she slapped the palms of her hands together almost as if she had "the power" upon her.

Almina was at her wit's end. She caught up a barrel cover and tried to fan Sally. She dropped the cover and began to pound her on the back as if she were choking.

Meantime, the pony was sauntering about as well as he could in the small space, occasionally finding a grain of corn or oats among the chaff on the floor.

In the midst of this a sharp, high voice cried out,

"Par! par! Jes' come here 'n' see what auntie's got! Jes' come! Par! I say!"

A small figure in a gray suit, with a cap on the back of its head, and with a good deal of red, knitted scarf about its neck, was standing in the doorway. This boy held a chain in one hand, and there was a bull-dog at the other end of the chain.

The dog now lurched forward and tugged at his chain towards Sally, who minded this arrival not a whit, and who continued to call upon God, and to assert that her Miss Temple "mus' be daid."

Little Freddy jumped up and down in his enjoyment of this unexpected entertainment.

"St', boy!" he cried, and let go the chain.

Thus released, at the moment of his utmost strain, Jefferson landed with some force in Sally's lap.

Sally stopped shouting instantly. She took Jefferson by

the loose skin on his neck and flung him back towards his master, who was still jumping up and down and crying on his "par" to "come 'n' see what auntie'd got."

Almina advanced towards her nephew and boxed his ears with great firmness. That was one thing she could do—she could box Freddy's ears.

The action restored her somewhat to herself. She began to have a glimmering perception that Sally had been going on in that manner simply because it was her way to do so if she happened to feel so inclined.

"I guess," she said, dryly, to Sally, "that if you jes' as lieves stop hollering, we'll go into the house 'n' I'll git you something to eat."

Sally rose and shook herself. She was in no way abashed, as why should she be?

Almina turned towards the house. She met her brother-in-law driving into the yard. He had gone on a few rods, but had then decided that the noise he heard was not all made by his son, and that it would be a satisfaction to learn what it was that did make it.

"Wall, Alminy," he said, "what kind of a circus have ye got here?"

He nodded towards Sally, who stood up, tall and straight, not showing now the least symptoms of her late excitement.

"She come from Caroliny," was the answer.

"I thought she didn't look much like a Massachusetts person," was the response, with some pride in the fact.

Mr. Wilson had grown rather stout within the last few years. He did not like to climb in and out of his wagon unless this act seemed strictly necessary.

But he carefully placed the lines about the dashboard, and laboriously went through the process of leaving his wagon and reaching the ground.

He came forward with his eyes fixed on Sally, who now stood just behind Almina.

Sally had a red handkerchief twisted turbanwise about her head, and an old straw hat on top of that. She wore a blue shawl, crossed in front of her broad chest, with the ends tied behind. Her skirt was short, revealing her heavy boots, which still retained upon them a goodly quantity of the yellow mud from the "State road" of North Carolina.

As Mr. Wilson gazed at her a feeling of admiration for this magnificent physique stirred and grew within him.

"By George!" he said to his wife later, "I ain't never seen no such critter 's that before. Somehow she made me think of something, I can't remember what, that I'd read about some time or other."

"She's jest up from Caroliny," said Almina, not recalling that she had already made that statement.

Here Sally went through a kind of motion which consisted of bending of the knees and bobbing of the head.

"How de do?" said Mr. Wilson, favorably.

Here another individual joined the group.

It was Thimble, who, having exhausted the small area of the barn, now came forward, followed with extreme closeness by Freddy, who in turn was followed by Jefferson.

Mr. Wilson eyed this procession intently. He was thinking that he did not wonder that Freddy had called upon him to come back and see what aunty 'd got.

Mr. Wilson thought he knew about horses, but he had never seen one like this; never one with a head and face so intelligent, nor with a form so peculiar.

The pony paused and regarded this man, who was thinking, as Almina had thought, that the animal seemed made of "injy rubber." His legs had to the last degree an appearance of suppleness. Now, as he stood, his front feet were close together, and his hind-legs, from the hocks down, slanted out somewhat, his whole appearance favoring the conclusion that he could double himself up, and could leap as well as run.

Freddy ran up alongside and put his hand on the pony's chest.

"Par," he cried out, "I want this little horse! You git this little horse for me! You swap your'n for him, par!"

"By George!" cried Mr. Wilson.

Then he turned to Sally.

"D' you come up from Caroliny on that critter, Miss—Miss—"

"We call her jest Sally," interposed Almina, who did not know why it seemed so entirely incongruous to apply such a title to the yellow woman. She felt a sense of shame for her brother-in-law's ignorance.

"I curm in de kyars," answered Sally, with a grave aspect of deep respect.

"Par," said Freddy, "you swap your'n for him! Swap your'n, I tell ye!"

Mr. Wilson made no reply to this command of his son. He walked up to Thimble and punched his ribs. In instant response the pony drew up one hind-leg as if with ferocious intent to kick; then he slowly lowered the leg, turned his head, and nipped at the man's hand.

"Curious critter!" exclaimed Mr. Wilson. "What you harness him into?"

"Dere ain't no gears ever touched him," said Sally, proudly. "He's jes' fur my Miss Temple ter ride."

Mr. Wilson had now opened the pony's mouth and was gazing into it.

"'Bout ten," he remarked.

Freddy jumped up and down.

"Swap your'n, par!" he cried.

"I guess, Sally," said Almina, "we'll go right in. The teakittle's boilin'. 'Twon't take no time to git ye a lunch."

Sally followed her hostess into the house, leaving father and son and pony and dog in the yard.

Sally sat down in the first chair, and leaned her elbows on her knees. Almina, for the first time, noticed how haggard she looked.

"I jes' carn't git over hit—'bout Miss Temple not bein' hyar," she said. "I done reckon she's sick. She's be'n convertin' too powerful. She carn't stan' such powerful lot er de Lawd's power."

18

Almina, going hurriedly into the buttery, heard these words.   She wanted to ask after Mr. Mercer, but she would not.

Mr. Mercer, being a minister, would naturally do what was right. If Temple was overworked he would see that she rested.

While Sally was eating, which she insisted upon doing in the chair where she was, and not at the table, holding her bread in one hand and her cold meat in the other, Mr. Wilson came in.

There entered with him Freddy and Freddy's dog. But the boy, unable to remain away from the pony, immediately returned to him.

Mr. Wilson declined a chair offered him by his sister-in-law.

" I guess I better not stop," he said. " I just found a letter in this pocket, Alminy.   It's for you.   I rec'lect now I got it last week, when I went to the village.   I ain't had on this coat sense."

He tossed the envelope on the table as if it were of no consequence, but as if he had now unburdened himself of that errand.

Almina took the letter eagerly, her face flushing.

" I done tole yo' so," said the yellow woman.

Mr. Wilson stood a few moments longer, his interest in this new-comer evidently holding him as with cords.

When he had gone Almina opened the envelope.

She had heard twice from Temple since she had left Carolina, but not within a year, and she had not expected ever to hear again.

All this phase of Almina's experience seemed entirely to have dropped out of her life.   And here it was suddenly and vividly recalled, and she was asked to take up the threads again.

This was not Temple's writing.   Almina's hand trembled a little as she turned the sheet.   The name signed was Laura Ammidown.

"MY DEAR MISS DROWDY,—I know you will remember Temple Crawford, and that she married my brother. The two went on a crusade to save souls. Temple is now suffering from a break-down of nerves in consequence of too much strain put upon them.

"She desires strongly to go to you, to stay for a while in your home in quiet. She liked you. I have promised to ask if she may come. I don't know how you are situated, but I cannot put it to you strongly enough that you must take her if you can. She depends upon spending this coming summer with you. She refuses to go back to the mountains; she will not go abroad. I will send Sally to you; she will work, and will take care of Temple.

"It is necessary that this arrangement be made almost immediately. If I don't hear from you by the 10th inst. I shall consider that you consent. Temple will be glad to pay you well for the trouble she will cause you. She insists, however, upon my saying to you that she knows you would be willing to take her without pay, if you can take her at all.

"She has this wish to go to you so much at heart that I dare not think of her disappointment if you find it impossible to have her with you. Sincerely yours,

"LAURA AMMIDOWN."

Almina's glasses had fallen two or three times during the reading of this note. She was becoming more and more excited. She was aware that she had not before been excited since she had come home from Carolina.

She found it impossible to think of Temple as otherwise than strong and active, full of a life that was life-giving to others. As she said to herself, she "couldn't sense it."

She was well aware that her sister would oppose her; but then her sister Wilson usually acted upon the general grounds that "Alminy hadn't got common-sense."

Almina leaned her shaking hand on the table. She did not know that Sally was watching her over the top of the teacup out of which she was drinking.

"I d' know nothin' 'bout how I shall git ready for her," said Almina. "I sh'll give her the south front room—the sun lays in there—'n' of course she c'n have the run of the house. I always did take to Temple. I do wish I had something cooked up."

"Oh, laws! Miss Drowdy, yo' jes' lemme put my hand to thur plough."

Sally rose, set down her empty cup, and stretched out her great hand.

"What 'm I hyar fur?" she asked.

Just then a shrill shriek from the yard startled Almina. She sprang to the window.

She beheld Freddy lying on his stomach upon the damp ground. His arms were spread out, and his dear little feet were kicking into the sod as fast as they could go, as scream after scream broke from him.

Mr. Wilson had mounted into his wagon, and was gazing with distressed face at his prostrate son. The man was thinking of climbing out again, but it was easier to think of doing this than it was for a person of his size to perform the act.

Almina ran out-of-doors. The pony had found a tuft of dried grass which seemed to his taste, and was nibbling upon that.

"Is it a fit?" she cried.

She bent and tried to lift her little nephew; but her little nephew stiffened himself and would not be lifted.

"Swap him, par!" he shouted.

"I guess 'tain't no fit," said Mr. Wilson.

Freddy's feet went faster.

"I want the pony! Mar 'd git me the pony!" he now proclaimed. "Mar 'd git it!"

"He wants me to swap my hoss for that pony," explained Mr. Wilson with some pride in his manner, as if not many boys would have been bright enough to make this demand.

Freddy again ordered the swap to be made, but his voice was now interrupted by a croupy cough, which stimulated Almina to try once more to raise the child from his recumbent position.

"Yo' jes' step back, miss," said Sally, gently pushing Almina one side.

The yellow woman stooped and took the boy in her arms.

She walked with him to his father's wagon, Freddy keeping himself all the time quite rigid, his only movement being a surreptitious attempt to pinch Sally's arm.

He was deposited on the floor of the vehicle.

The instant he touched that floor he became as limber as a boy can be, which we all know is limber enough. He scrambled over on to the seat by his father.

"Darned old fool!" he said, breathlessly, looking at Sally, who laughed broadly at him.

This laugh but infuriated Freddy still more. He stood up and violently kicked out his small foot incased in its small rubber.

Then he began to cough more croupily than before.

At this point his father grappled with him. He flung the horse-blanket about him, having a keen fear that Freddy might be capable of developing an attack of the croup on the spot.

With one hand holding his son pinioned in the blanket, Mr. Wilson shook the reins in his other hand, and the horse began to walk out of the yard.

Jefferson, accidentally shut in the house, now yapped peremptorily to be let loose. Being released, he flew furiously after his master.

Almina said she felt "jest like cryin'. She knew her sister 'd blame it all on her. 'N' if Freddy should have the croup 'n' die, Freddy's mother 'd never forgive her."

"Laws, honey!" remarked Sally, "dat boy ain't de kind as dies. He'll live, he will; he'll grow up to be a man an' he'll hab a wife, an' he'll torment her to def."

And the yellow woman laughed again.

Almina tried to be cheered. She promised herself that she would go over to her sister's before she went to bed, and see how Freddy had borne the storm and stress of that half-hour after he had seen the pony.

The two women went back into the house. Almina stopped at the door to advise Sally to put Thimble in the barn, but Sally replied that the pony was used to being loose, and that he would "take care of his'ef." Nevertheless, she fed him.

Then Almina went into the "south room" and began to take everything out of it, so that she might give the whole apartment what she called a "good goin' over."

As she did not know when to expect Temple, she ran to the window every time she heard the sound of wheels, and she was soon, as she acknowledged, "as nervous as a witch."

Sally, cheered and invigorated by food and drink, now thought that it was highly probable that "Miss Temple wasn't daid at all." She helped Almina. She carried out a roll of carpet on her head, a thing that was never before done in Hoyt.

Unfortunately she was seen in the act by Mrs. Newton, from the other neighborhood, who was at that moment driving by in the Goddard buggy which had belonged to the Newtons for as long a time as Goddard buggies had been made.

Mrs. Newton's horse was walking, because it always walked when it was not standing still or trying to roll over in the pasture.

Mrs. Newton was very thin and long-waisted, so that when she tried to lean out of her buggy to see what was going on she could lean out a great ways, and consequently could see a great deal.

She now saw Sally appear with the carpet on her head, and fling her burden on the ground in the front yard.

The sight was one as astounding as if "an earthquake had swallowed her up," as Mrs. Newton said the next day in every house within reach of a walking horse.

Almina, who was wiping off the south-room looking-glass, heard a voice say,

"Whoa!"

As she knew the voice, her heart sank; but she was aware that it would in no wise serve her to delay. Therefore, she appeared immediately at the open front door, with the looking-glass in her hand.

"How de do, Mis' Newton? Do come in 'n' se' down a spell," she said ; and felt like a false villain, because in her secret soul she wished to tell that woman in the buggy to go along and mind her own business.

XVII

"A MAN MAY BE A FOOL ONCE IN HIS LIFE"

"No, I guess I can't git out," said Mrs. Newton, with her eyes fixed on Sally, who was shaking the carpet in great billows. "Was goin' by, 'n' I thought I'd jest haul up. Ain't you begun to clean house ruther early? The flies ain't hardly come yet. I tell um if I git my house cleaned fore fly-time it's early enough."

"I thought I'd clean up the south room," remarked Almina in a dignified way, as if she reserved the right to clean house when she pleased.

"It's jest 's anybody's a mind to, of course," was the tolerant reply. "But I tell um if I git it done 'fore fly-time it's early enough."

Mrs. Newton was so occupied in gazing at Sally that she was not aware that she had repeated her former remark.

Almina said nothing. She employed herself by carefully rubbing the cloth in her hand back and forth over the mirror.

She was glancing at Mrs. Newton, and she saw that lady's eyes bulge still more. She immediately discovered that the cause was the appearance of Thimble, who had strolled round to the front of the house, and now stood with his ears cocked towards the horse in the buggy-shafts.

"Be'n buyin' a hoss, Alminy?" Mrs. Newton tried to put this question in a casual manner, but her face could not have looked much more startled if her interrogation had referred to an ostrich.

"No," said Almina, "I ain't be'n buyin' no hoss."

Mrs. Newton reached forth a long arm, which ended in a

hand with a brown cotton glove on it. This hand was directed towards Thimble.

"'Ain't that some kind of a hoss?" she inquired.

Sally shook the carpet in greater billows than ever, and clouds of dust flew up from it.

"That's a saddle pony," answered Almina. "Don't you think you better come in 'n' se' down?"

Mrs. Newton ignored this second invitation.

"Where'd it come from?" she inquired.

She was so carried along by the intensity of her curiosity that she was unable to try to arrive at these questions gradually.

"North Caroliny," was the answer.

"Oh!"

Mrs. Newton's hand sank to her lap; but her tall figure still remained leaned out of the buggy, as if she had been a marionette put in that position.

"Ain't you kinder old 'n' stiff to begin ridin' horseback, Alminy Drowdy?"

"I ain't goin' to."

"Oh!"

A short silence.

"When d' you conclood to set up nigger help, Alminy?"

"I ain't goin' to."

"Oh!"

The tension on the marionette relaxed sufficiently to enable the figure to sink back on its seat.

"Cluck! G'long! Huddup, I say!"

The Newton horse moved slowly away, dragging the Newton Goddard buggy behind him.

The occupant of the carriage turned and peered from the narrow slit of a window at the back.

"I declare! I do declare!" she exclaimed, aloud. "I'm a good mineter call on the Selectmen; I'm a good mineter, 's ever I had to eat. Somebody ought to do something. 'Tain't safe to let Alminy go to her own head."

But as Mrs. Newton drove on she gradually changed her

mind about going to the Selectmen.   She did not know precisely what to say to these guardians of the town, so she decided definitely to let Almina go to her own head.

Miss Drowdy, when the Newton equipage was out of sight, told Sally, rather sharply, to take the carpet around to the back of the house and finish shaking it, and to tie up Thimble in the barn.

The two women worked all the forenoon.   By two o'clock not only the south room, but all the lower rooms, had been through a regular house-cleaning.

Almina was tremulous with fatigue and expectation.   She said half a dozen times that she did wish she knew when Temple was coming, for if there was anything that wore on her it was uncertainty.   She made a pot of strong tea, and she and Sally drank it.

As the hours of the afternoon crept on, Almina was continually going to the window to look down the road in the direction of the station, some miles away.

She told Sally that she hadn't been so worked up since that time she started to Carolina, three years before.

Sally herself partook of the excitement, but her expression of the emotion was very different.   She went about singing hymns in a loud, deep voice; sometimes she struck her hands together and shouted,

"Come down, Lawd!   Come down dis yer minute!"

Her dark face shone; there was a smouldering fire in her eyes.

Almina was constantly fearing that, if she gave way, she should herself begin to shout, and she had a New England Congregationalist shrinking from loudly asking the Lord to come down.

The faint, apple-green twilight sky was deepening in shade after the long spring day when Almina, sitting at the kitchen window, saw a large dog come loping along the road.   He was white, and, as he came nearer, she perceived that he had one black ear.

All the light from the west seemed concentrated on the

animal, who now stood still in the middle of the highway and looked back, as if waiting.

Almina rose, pushing her chair violently from her.

"It's Yucatan!" she said, in a high voice. "She's comin'! Sally, she's comin'!"

But Sally dashed out of the door first. She ran down to the end of the yard, and just then a carry-all, drawn by two horses, came rapidly along and turned up towards the house.

Some one in the carry-all uttered an exclamation and leaned forward.

The two women saw a pale face, brilliant with emotion.

Somehow Sally reached forward and took her young mistress in her arms. The yellow woman turned away, still holding the slight figure. She carried it towards the house. She was saying, in a sobbing voice,

"Honey! Lamb! Bress her! Bress her!"

The large dog walked close beside them, and sat down on the floor near the lounge in the south room, where Sally put her charge.

The yellow woman knelt down and began unfastening the furs Temple wore. She was crying audibly.

Notwithstanding that she had been told that Temple was ill, she had not expected this change. The thin, pale face was transparent, and, though now held quiet, it had upon it a suggestion of intense excitement.

But Temple usually carried herself so quietly as to deceive some people into exclaiming, "You don't tell me that woman is nervous!"

Sally threw back the fur cloak. Then Temple reached forward and took the large, brawny, dark hand. She clasped both her own about it. She smiled up into the dusky, tropical eyes gazing down at her.

"Don't yo'! Don't yo'!" cried Sally.

"Don't what?"

"Smile at me! I tell yo' I carn't abear it! I carn't!"

"But I'm so glad to see you, Sally."

Sally's face worked. She choked on the word she tried to speak. Then she burst out in the beginning of a prayer.

" Stop !" said Temple.

" I war gwine ter pray fur yo'," answered the yellow woman.

" I know it. I don't want you to pray for me."

Sally gazed in surprise at the face before her. The face had hardened a little.

Temple tried to speak in a different tone.

" I'm tired, you know, and—and—" She paused; she knew that she must not say what was in her mind.

Then the two were silent. Temple continued to hold Sally's hand in both her own. She closed her eyes, but she could feel the lids quiver and burn over the eyeballs. Still she kept them closed.

The dog thrust his nose into Sally's lap and whined.

Outside, Almina was standing by the carriage which had driven up close to the door.

Mercer had occupied the seat with his wife. When Sally had taken Temple away he had descended quickly. He took Almina's hand, standing for a moment bareheaded before her.

He greeted her with a calm cordiality. It seemed that he in no wise partook of excitement of any kind.

Miss Drowdy noted that he also was haggard and worn; but when she inquired concerning his health he answered that he was perfectly well.

He turned and busied himself with the wraps and satchels in the carriage. Every motion he made was controlled and effective.

When the luggage was deposited just within the kitchen door, Mercer turned to Almina, whom he had not allowed to help him, and asked if he might see her for a moment. He was going away that evening, and—

Here Almina could not help interrupting with the exclamation,

" Going so soon ?"

"My engagements are made," was the reply, "and I must keep them, if possible. The driver here will wait an hour, when he will take me back to the station in time to catch the return train to Boston. I shall get there before midnight."

Mercer drew out his watch and looked at it. His face did not show that he could not tell the time, though his eyes dwelt on the dial.

Almina led the way into the kitchen. She hurriedly placed a chair for the minister, and then sat down and gazed at him.

Mercer also sat down ; but he rose instantly. He thrust one hand into the closely buttoned coat. The other hand held tightly the rim of his hat.

The woman gazing at him thought she had never seen any one look so calm and cool. She respected Mercer greatly ; but just now she thought she did not much like him.

"After all," he began, in a clear voice, "I don't know that I have much to say. I know you will do all you can for Mrs. Mercer. She is wretched. It will require a long time for her to recover. Don't spare money in the slightest degree. I shall forward you a certain sum per month. Please don't demur at that. I know you are hospitable, but you haven't much money."

Here the dry, even voice paused a moment. Almina wondered why she felt such a growing excitement. She had never seen any one quite so calm as this man was.

"I shall be only too glad to do all I can for Temple," she said.

"Yes, I know; I'm sure of that," with a slight movement of the hand and hat. "I'm going to ask you to write to me every Monday ; you will tell me how Mrs. Mercer is every Monday? You understand ?"

The tone rasped a little.   -

"I understand."

"And you promise ?"

"Yes."

"I thank you. I can rely upon you. I am necessarily leaving her for an indefinite time."

Here Mercer drew his hand from the breast of his coat and passed it slowly over his forehead.

"You will come to see her sometimes?"

Almina pronounced this sentence in a positive manner.

It was a perceptible space of time before the man replied,

"Everything is extremely uncertain. Duty will keep me much of the time at a distance."

"But she is your wife!" This exclamation broke from the woman involuntarily.

Then she blushed at her temerity.

Her eyes were fixed on the severe, masculine face above her. She saw it grow gray, like ashes. But Mercer's voice was just the same as he said,

"I shall be anxious; but this is one of the trials to which I must submit. I have brought Mrs. Mercer here because she and I believed that here she would be most likely to recover rapidly. She has longed to come here to you. She has often spoken of you."

It seemed, for some reason, necessary for Mercer to pause frequently. And after each time he paused his voice was more dry and cold.

"One thing more," he went on again; "I shall keep you informed of my whereabouts, so that you will know where to send to me; and if any change, no matter how slight, for the worse takes place, you will telegraph to me instantly. And you will not, I think, find it necessary to tell Mrs. Mercer of this arrangement. She will write to me, and it might worry her to know that I had thought it necessary to ask this favor of you."

By this time Mercer was talking as nearly like an automaton as a human being may be able to do. And by this time Almina was thinking with great surprise that she could very soon hate a man like this, even though he were a minister of the Gospel.

"That is all, I believe," he now said.

And again he took out his watch and studied the face of it, not seeing the position of the hands.

"I will now see Mrs. Mercer for a few moments."

Almina rose. She felt as if her mind were gradually stiffening in some mysterious way, and that her body was involved in the process.

She opened the door into the south room.

Mercer looked into the room. He thought his eyes were balls of fire that were scorching his brain. As in a flame, an instantaneous picture of the group came to his vision.

He saw his wife on the lounge with her face turned towards Sally. The yellow woman was kneeling over her. The great dog was sitting on his haunches, his heavy, plumy tail spread out straight on the floor behind him, while his head was resting on the lounge, thrust up close to his mistress's neck.

Mercer cleared his throat as he advanced into the room.

Sally rose instantly. As she turned towards him he saw how moved her face was, and that the cloudy eyes swam in tears.

"Thank de Lawd fur a sight ob Miss Temple!" she said, fervently. She passed by the man, and joined Almina in the kitchen.

Yucatan had risen also, and he came towards his master, slowly swaying his tail.

Mercer stopped the dog. He put one hand under the lower jaw and the other hand on top of Yucatan's head. Thus he gazed down at him, seeing with an aching vividness the magnificent lion face, the loyal eyes full of tenderness and strength.

The words in the man's mind were : "Oh, my God ! My God !"

In a moment he drew a chair to the couch. He spoke pleasantly, as if he were going away for a week or two.

"I'm glad you'll have Yucatan. When you get strong enough to walk about the country here I shall know you'll be well protected."

"Oh yes," said Temple. She had glanced up as Mercer sat down by her. Now her eyelids were lowered. Mercer looked at the thick, light lashes.

He sat back firmly in his chair. By what might be called " main force " he took his eyes from Temple's face. But direct them where he would, they only saw that face, that head, with its plentiful light hair, with its lovely contour.

" I'm sorry you did not arrange to stop longer here, Richard," said Temple.

" Are you ?" quickly.

" Certainly. And you are so tired."

" I shall take every opportunity to rest. Don't think of me as being tired."

" Where shall you go now ?"

" To North Carolina, within the week."

" Ah !"

Temple raised herself on her elbow. A flash of interest passed over her.

Within the last few weeks she had not cared to know any plans for work; she could not think of meetings. And what had terrified her much, what she had not confided to any one, she found that she could not pray. Worse than that, she had no wish to pray.

She used to spend hours thinking of that evening among the Carolina mountains when she had " experienced religion."

A thousand times she asked herself if she had not, after all, experienced. Was not that precious gift hers ? Had she been deceived ?

" To North Carolina ?" she now said.

" Yes. Temple, do you want to go there ?"

The flush of interest on her face made Mercer suddenly ask this.

" No, oh no ! No ! I could not possibly bear the mountains now."

" But you love them ?"

" Yes. That is why I could not bear to see them. Still,

I am so different now.   I wonder why, now that I really am so different, I could not change about the mountains.   I wonder why, Richard?"

Mercer tried to answer.   But all he could say was,

"You are not well; your nerves are weak."

Temple smiled.

"Don't mention my nerves, please.   I've heard enough from Miss MacCallum about my nerves to last me a long life."

The man was silent.   Again, in spite of himself, his gaze dwelt on Temple's eyelashes.

He was thinking that he had noticed these lashes on that first time when he had seen her—noticed them with that curious thrill of tender admiration which he felt now.

He tried to get himself in hand.   He had tried to do that every day, it seemed to him every moment of his life, since he had known this woman.   And he had never succeeded.

It was true that he had succeeded in appearing to have full control of himself.   But he struck deeper than that.   It was the feeling that he wished to command.   A man ought to be king of everything within him, or how should he be a man?

Mercer tried to speak.   He had thought that he had something special to say to his wife, now that he was leaving her.   But he could not say anything.

He was leaving her.   He leaned his head forward and put his hand over his brow, looking down at her.

Could he ever stop looking at her?   The three years since his marriage had been horrible years.

But there had been one thread of golden light running through them—she had been near him.   He knew that she had not been happy, but she had been near him.   It was something to be able to turn and glance at her, though she was never expecting his glance and never returned it.   Indeed, outwardly it was but a casual, friendly eyebeam.

She had been his comrade and his sympathetic fellow-worker, never anything more.   And he knew that now had come the end even of this comradeship. But she did not know it. How much would she care if she did know it? She had always been so friendly and so kind, he was sure she would care somewhat. And she had worked so hard. She had thrown herself without reserve into their labor. She had used without stint her magnificent strength. How she had poured herself out!

At last Mercer made a greater effort and said, "When the weather grows warmer you must be out-of-doors all day long. I shall think of you as on Thimble's back, almost from sunup to sundown."

How dry as dust his voice sounded to the man! And he thought cloudily that the words were strange things; they did not amount to anything; they were dead. Could not he find some simple, living word to use now that his heart was breaking, his life going out of him?

Then he bethought himself that even if there were such words he must not employ them. He must go away from Temple as calmly as he had lived with her.

She was so tender-hearted that she might grieve in a superficial, brief way.

"It was so kind of you to send Thimble and Sally here," said Temple. She raised her eyes towards him. "But, then, when were you not kind? I shall miss you so much."

Mercer wished that she would not talk in that way. And he wished that she would not lift her eyes.

How long would it be before she ceased to miss him, even in her way? She could not help thinking of him for a while, they had been so intimately associated.

"I find all my remarks narrowing down to these words," he began: "you must take the best kind of care of yourself."

His voice sank to a husky whisper at the last word.

"Oh, there's no fear but that I shall take care of myself," Temple answered; "and you'll write to me often, Richard?"

"Certainly."

"You will be among the mountains when the rhododendrons come?"

"Yes."

Temple drew a long breath.

"And you will see Busbee in April?"

"Yes."

Another long breath.

Temple smiled wistfully.

"I know Busbee isn't much of a mountain among the rest of them there, but it's my own."

"I shall think of that when I see it."

The man's tone was so very rasping that his wife wondered at it.

"Do you suppose that old fallen tree still makes a kind of landing on the Broad near my home?"

"I will find out, and I'll write to you about it."

"Oh, thank you! It was on the Broad, you know, that I learned to play the fiddle. Richard, you do look so tired!"

Temple raised herself again on her elbow as she fixed earnest eyes on her companion's face.

"I'm all right," more brusquely than he usually spoke.

He rose.

"I think I'll go now. I'm so glad I leave you in good care. I have great faith in Miss Drowdy and Sally."

"And when shall you come to see how I am getting on?"

"I can't tell now, really. But you must keep me advised of your welfare. God bless you, Temple!"

He took both her hands. His own were steady and cold, not at all like live human flesh.

"Good-bye."

He kissed her hands in the lightest manner. In the same way his lips touched her forehead.

He left the room. In the kitchen he shook hands with Miss Drowdy and Sally.

The next moment he was out in the yard.

Temple had risen from the couch and gone to the window.

But Mercer did not once glance towards the house.

He entered the carriage and was driven away.

When Almina came into the room a few moments later her guest was still standing at the window, leaning against the casing, gazing out as if she saw something beside the chill trees and fields.

"What is it?"

Almina, alarmed, she knew not why, hurried to Temple's side. But Temple turned immediately to her and said, gently,

"It's nothing. I was wondering how soon the new oak leaves would push off the old ones. The new always pushes away the old, doesn't it?"

Temple did not resume her place on the lounge. She asked if she might go to her room. She said she did not want Sally; she only wanted Yucatan.

Being informed that she was then in her sitting-room, and that the bed was in the little adjoining room, she asked if she might be left alone with Yucatan. She tried to explain that she could rest better so.

"Laws!" interrupted Sally, "don't yo' go an' try to s'plain nothin'."

Being thus left alone, Temple sat down on the floor by the chair in front of the couch, the chair Mercer had occupied. She leaned an arm across it. She beckoned to the dog, who came to her. But he went back to the window, put his paws on the shelf, raised himself and looked out, whining under his breath as he did so.

Temple gazed at him with widened eyes, not speaking.

In a moment he came to her side and stretched himself out beside her.

The two remained quiet for a long time. The sunlight grew warm in the low room.

The house was strangely still. Its other occupants were hoping that Temple was asleep.

But she was not sleeping. Her eyes were open, but vague and unseeing. She was listening to the sound of the wind as it rushed round the corner of the house. She heard the oaks thrash about. She remembered how a peach-tree used to rub its branches on the roof of the Carolina log-house. That was when she was somebody else.

After a while the door of the kitchen opened, and Almina, picking over beans, looked up to see Temple standing there with the Newfoundland close behind her.

" I wanted to speak to some one," she said.

" Bless me ! I thought you were asleep, 'n' I've been just holdin' my breath for fear I should wake ye. Come right in.   I've got some milk-toast ready 'ginst you should want something, and I'll make some tea or coffee."

" A woman with nerves doesn't drink tea or coffee," was the response. "Give me a glass of milk. And don't 'make company ' of me, please."

Temple sat down by the table in the kitchen. She tried to seem hungry as she forced down the food.

Almina went on with her work. The beans dropped from her hands into the tin pan in her lap. But she was not thinking of what she was doing, and she knew very well that these beans would have to be picked over again.

She explained that Sally had gone to the barn to feed the pony ; that she had been gone more than an hour.

" She has dropped asleep," said Temple.   " I know her ways.   When she is tired she will fall asleep anywhere."

As she spoke, Temple wondered at her success in controlling her wish to see her pony.   And she hoped that she was losing that power to feel intensely, since in this world that power must inevitably bring more suffering than happiness.

Then she thought of Miss MacCallum, and smiled derisively. Miss MacCallum knew all about emotions ; she had them tabulated, she prescribed some and proscribed others. Some were to be cherished as strengthening to the feminine human being—such as love for a man, for a child, and so on.   Others, such as a too ardent love for a friend of the same sex, too deep a feeling for beauty in nature or in humanity, were to be nipped in the bud. You were not to " emotionalize "— that was her word for all feeling which a lack in her own temperament made it impossible for her to understand.

Almina could not help gazing somewhat markedly at her guest. Temple, holding her glass of milk, and sipping it occasionally, glanced up and caught this look.

" What are you thinking," she asked, with the quick suspicion of an invalid.

" Nothing to speak of."

" Tell me," with a touch of her old manner.

The elder woman colored and hesitated. Finally she said,

" I was wonderin' if you had any of your old temper. You seem so changed."

Temple pushed back from the table.

" Am I so changed?" she exclaimed, a sharp note in her voice. "God knows I have tried to change myself—I've tried to make myself all over."

" Were you dretful bad, then?"

" I don't know—yes, of course, I was. Aren't we all dreadful bad? Our original, carnal natures, you know, Miss Drowdy."

Almina lifted a handful of beans and let them fall contemplatively.

" I d' know," she said, slowly; " I've been thinkin' a good deal myself."

Here the speaker smiled and turned more fully towards her companion. "Fact is," she continued, " I ain't never seen nothin' very bad in you, 'cept your temper. I was wonderin' if you'd get the better of that. 'N' what's become of Bartholomew?"

The quick-coming, quick-going flush came to Temple's face.

" Bart's gone to the bad—I always think I might have done more for him."

" Mebby. But you had him when there wouldn't nobody else have him 'round. Why don't you think of that, 's well's of what you didn't do for him?"

Temple started up from her chair with another touch of her old self.

"How comforting you are!" she cried. "But I haven't been looking at things in that way. I've been thinking of sins and shortcomings, and scourging myself on. And you know—oh, I can't bear to think of it, but you know I struck Bart. Perhaps if I hadn't struck him—"

"Oh, how foolish you be!" interrupted the other woman. "You jest go out-doors 'n' git a breath of air. It'll do you more good than thinkin' such stuff."

Temple came close to Almina's chair. She paused there for a moment. Then she said,

"I was sure I wanted to come to you, and I was right."

Having said this, she walked quickly from the room.

Almina held a handful of beans with unconscious closeness, gazing at them with dim eyes. She had a feeling as if she had been caressed, though Temple had not touched her.

As for Temple herself, she felt a hint of coming rest as she stepped off the old flat stone from the kitchen door into the sunny coolness of the spring day. The simplicity of Almina's goodness was a refreshment. There did not seem to Temple to be anything complex in Almina's nature. She lived without that continual questioning and analysis.

Temple turned her face up towards the sky.

"Oh yes," she whispered, "I must have been right when I longed to come here."

She hurried to the barn. A shrill neigh greeted her entrance.

She ran into the stall and clasped the pony's neck. She kissed his soft nose ; she stroked the broad, intelligent forehead ; she held the sharp ears in her hands ; she laid her face down on Thimble's shoulder ; and all the time the tears were falling from her eyes.

"How could I let two hours go without coming here to see you?" she kept saying. "I did long to come, dear ; you know I longed to come. But I wanted to try to wait. I wanted to see if I could wait."

Sally was not there. Temple looked about for the saddle and bridle. She put them on, her hands trembling piteously, the perspiration starting from her face.

She threw open the barn door. Then she got into the saddle.

The pony walked out into the yard; the air blew over Temple. She shook the lines. Thimble broke into his little amble, tossing up his head, his ragged, neglected mane falling in rough locks on both sides of his neck.

A window in the house was flung up sharply.

"Be you sure you're able?" cried Almina.

For answer Temple waved her hand and smiled radiantly.

But Almina did not quite trust to that manner.

She went up-stairs and watched the horsewoman going down the long road, the pony at his slow amble.

Temple suddenly knew that her strength was ebbing. A tremor came to her hands; a faintness took possession of her. She turned the pony back.

Almina rushed down to the door. She put her arm about Temple as she dropped from the saddle.

"You see," said Temple, just above a whisper, "I wasn't able. Perhaps I never shall be."

"Land of love!" was the brisk response, "you'll be cantering all over the country 'fore you know it."

While Temple was thus returning, Mercer was riding towards Boston.

He was sitting by himself in the train, apparently watching every object to be seen from the window.

Ten, twenty miles from Hoyt. Twenty miles from Hoyt.

When the conductor came in after the last stopping-place, Mercer touched his arm.

"How far to the next town?"

"Six miles."

"Does this train stop there?" The conductor nodded, and hurried on.

Presently Mercer stood on the platform at the next station.

What he was saying to himself was what he had been saying for the last hour:

"A man may be a fool once in his life.   A man may be a fool once in his life."

He went into the station and inquired for the nearest livery-stable.   It was rather a large town, and he had no difficulty in getting a saddle-horse.   He asked the way to Hoyt, and then he galloped out over the road in that direction.

XVIII

RETURNING STRENGTH

THE spring sunlight was warm. The robins were making excursions here and there as if selecting building spots. Among the trees there could be heard the resounding taps of the woodpecker, and one might see the bird briskly running up a tree-trunk.

But Mercer did not hear nor see any of the country sounds or sights. He was riding swiftly over roads mostly solitary. He had more than twenty miles to go. It would be evening long before he reached Hoyt. He had no definite plan as to what he should do when he should arrive. All that he knew was that he must see his wife once more. Just once more.

Sometimes, as he rode, he childishly repeated these last words aloud. Then he would draw himself up as he would have drawn up a fractious horse.

"There's just about so much of the idiot in every human being," he said, "and the time always comes when the idiot acts. That time is come for me. I thought I had will. reason, common-sense. Well, just now I haven't either."

He urged his horse to go yet faster through the now slanting beams of the sun. The earthy, spring smells came out more strongly as night approached.

"What shall I say to her when I see her?"

But he had no reply to that question.

'Perhaps it was the subtle influence of the spring; perhaps the reaction from the strain of leaving Temple ; but true it was that Mercer had never found it so difficult to combat the natural impulses of his heart, never so hard to fight against nature.

As he rode on, thinking of Temple at the end of the journey, the thrill of love and longing for the beloved quite overmastered him.

But only for the moment, he told himself. His purpose remained just the same. His purpose had been formed by reason and long deliberation. Therefore it was right. The thing that reason sanctioned must be right.

He had prayed much; he had laid this matter many times before God; had passionately pleaded for light and guidance.

But Mercer had never been absolutely sure as to the answer. God, for some mysterious reason, did not vouchsafe His aid. That meant, of course, that Mercer was to do what he could with his own mind to direct him.

There had been times, often repeated, when, as Mercer prayed in public at his special meetings, he found himself pleading with an abandon of fervor that his wife might love him.

Not that his words were to that effect; not that the people listening guessed what was in his heart. He did not know how it was that he could pour out hot words of entreaty for the men and women before him, when his soul was only crying out for the love of his wife.

Often he asked himself what she felt at such times.

There she was on the platform near him.

Week by week, day by day, Mercer had seen that Temple had less strength, less vitality.

The robust mountain girl, whose physical power was great enough to bear the thrill and vibration of a sensitive, æsthetic nature, was changing all the time into the delicate woman who quivered and shook with what people so curiously call "nerves," and who was prostrate after any intense feeling.

Miss MacCallum said it was "emotion." Miss MacCallum proposed to eliminate emotion from Temple's life, not merely now that she was an invalid, but after lack of emotion should have restored her to health.

All this went through Mercer's mind as he rode on, and

the sun went down below the horizon. The man owned to himself that he was groping blindly.

He did not know but that human nature principally needed suppression in this world. He had believed that it did.

It required an effort on his part for him to make the necessary inquiries as to the direction in which he should ride. He could hardly detach his mind from the thoughts that filled it, and he had what he knew was an unnatural feeling that he ought to be aware by intuition as to the way to go.

The clock at Hoyt Centre had struck eight when he came within sight of Miss Drowdy's home. The little brown house looked black in the moonlight.

Mercer had a fear that he should disturb some one.

It was as still as if a great peace had descended on the world.

He dismounted, and led his horse slowly into the yard. As he did so he heard Thimble's shrill whinny from the barn. Then Yucatan's deep voice came from the house.

A light in the kitchen moved and came towards the outer door, which opened softly.

Mercer saw Almina peer out. Then the woman went back, set her lamp on the table, and again came to the door, the moonlight covering her figure and glorifying it.

"It's just as pleasant as it can be," said Almina to herself.

Then she started, uttering a little cry.

Mercer advanced, still leading his horse.

He held up his hand.

"What's happened?" she whispered.

"Nothing. Only I came back."

Almina looked narrowly at the man before her.

She thought that perhaps the moonlight gave him that ghastly appearance. And she had never seen such eyes "on any mortal being."

"You came back?" she repeated. "Then there ain't no accident?"

"No."

" Hadn't you better come in ?"

" Thank you.   I'll hitch my horse to this tree."

" Ain't you goin' to stop ?"

" Oh no.   I shall go right away."

The woman stood in silence while Mercer fastened the bridle about the limb of the oak.

" I thought I might see Mrs. Mercer for half an hour."

Mercer said this when the two stood in the kitchen.

Almina was thinking that this man looked even more strange by the lamplight than he had looked by moonlight.

" Yes," said Almina, mechanically.

" Where is she ?"

" She has gone to bed.   I just peeped in at her, and she was fast asleep—sleepin' like a baby."

" That is good.   It has been so difficult for her to sleep."

Mercer stood in silence after having spoken thus.   Then he asked again,

" Where is she ?"

" In there."

He opened the door indicated, and noiselessly closed it after him.

The Newfoundland was lying by the bed in a broad bar of moonlight, which also fell across the bed and on the face of the woman lying there.

Yucatan came forward slowly.   He thrust his cold nose into Mercer's hand.   Then, as Mercer remained standing motionless, the dog went back and resumed his position.

Do men look at the face of their dead as Mercer now looked at the face of his wife ?

Remote and white and still she was.

Fatigue from the journey, the sudden sense of peace, the relaxation from an unguessed strain—all had made Temple sleep, as she had not slept for months, profoundly.

She had longed to come out into the country to Miss Drowdy, whose simple nature she remembered with a sense of rest.   She had come, and now she had fallen asleep and was dreaming of riding her pony over the mountain to the

Dalvecker farm. But that was before Chris had been "in lurv" with her.

She moved, and said some indistinct word.

Mercer stood there.

"Since she is asleep, that is a sign that I must not speak; that I may only look at her."

That was what he was thinking.

That precious, that inestimable sleep must not be disturbed.

Now he knew what he must do. He must go away without hearing her voice again.

He could fancy she spoke. He almost thought she said "Richard."

But his mere presence might waken her. And if, indeed, she spoke his name, it was only from habit, the iron habit which fetters, whether it be with happiness or with misery.

As Mercer stood there he tried to put himself in the place of some one else, and to ask if there were any other path but the path which led away from Temple. Useless questioning!

She had married him in the midst of the religious exaltation of an "experience." She had longed to be a missionary.

He had offered her this work, and she had accepted it; the acceptance had entailed the necessity of becoming his wife.

Now she was worn out with the work; and in the bottom of his heart Mercer was convinced that her present condition was caused still more by the bondage in which he had placed her. She had put on the harness bravely, and worn it heroically. But it was a bondage; it was a harness that galled her whole nature.

Gradually, like some subtle poison diffusing itself in the system, this conviction had fastened itself upon Mercer.

It was killing Temple to live in this way. Therefore, her life must be ordered otherwise.

And he would see to it that it was otherwise ordered. He

would see to it, without any regard to his own wishes or hopes.

What was life in this world at the highest? Merely a probation, a time of trial. He would get through it as best he could. In the life to come it might be that God would bless him in full measure. But in the life to come he could not expect Temple's love. When he would reach this point Mercer would fight against the wild rush of the conviction that he would be willing to exchange all the blessing of the future existence for the rapture of possessing his wife's love here on earth.

He turned away dumbly from the bed where she lay. Yes, doubtless God had ordered this also—that he was not to have this one word with her. It was best. Oh yes, it was best. There could not be the slightest question as to that. If he could have spoken it was not in the least likely that he would have said the right thing.

So the man left the room. In the kitchen Almina was sitting by the lamp on the table. She had some knitting in her hands. On the floor near the stove Sally was lying fast asleep, her head resting on a folded shawl which her hostess had insisted upon placing for her.

Almina wondered what the neighbors would think. She laughed a little as she wondered.

But at this moment she was thinking of Mr. Mercer's sudden appearance. She looked up anxiously as he now entered.

"It seemed too bad to waken her," he said, in a low voice.

"You c'n see her to-morrow," responded Almina.

"No."

Mercer said no more. He was standing in his usual upright way, his tall figure looking very tall in the low room.

He was trying to make up his mind to ask this woman not to mention his sudden visit. But he could not quite decide to do that.

After a moment he advanced and held out his hand.

To himself he seemed like some foreign individuality, and he could not adjust his mind.

But he said good-bye again in his ordinary tone, and he left the room and mounted his horse.

Directly after he had gone Almina threw a shawl over her head and hurried into the yard. She went to the road and gazed at the horseman, who was riding fast.

When he was out of sight she returned to the house.

"It jest beats me," she remarked to herself. "He hadn't no errand. Yes, it certainly beats me."

As she stood there with the shawl still on her head the door of the bedroom opened softly, and Temple said,

"Miss Drowdy."

Almina hastened forward.

She put her arm about Temple, and hurried her to the bed and covered her. Then she sat down by her.

Temple gazed at her companion intently.

"I've been dreaming," she said, at last. Then she sat up quickly in bed. She caught hold of Almina's arm.

"The dream was so real that—that—but then it can't be true. I thought Richard had come back for some reason—that he was here in this room but a moment ago. And I tried to speak to him. It seemed necessary—a question of life or death—that I should speak."

Having said this, Temple tried to be more calm. She still kept her eyes fixed upon Almina, who moved uneasily, and who finally said,

"Dreams do sometimes seem jest as real."

She shrank from speaking of Mercer's visit, fearing that a knowledge of it might prevent Temple from sleeping.

"I know they seem real," was the response. "In this one I heard the sound of horse's feet. They were galloping, always galloping; and Richard's back was towards me; he was riding away from me. Miss Drowdy—"

Temple sat up in bed. She looked so weary, and so full of a quick, painful life, that the elder woman's heart ached.

"He has been here!" cried Temple.

" Yes."

" Why did he come ?" in a high voice.

" He said to see you again."

" But he rode away," still in that voice.

" I know it. He said your sleep must not be disturbed."

" Did he come in here ?"

" Yes."

" It was real! It was real, then !" Temple sank back on the bed again.

Yucatan, who had come to the bedside when his mistress had raised her voice, now nuzzled his nose against her hand. She glanced down at him.

" You saw him, old dog; he spoke to you, I'm sure," she said.

Yucatan wagged his tail for answer.

" He left no word ?"

" No. I guess he jest come back 'cause—well, 'cause he thought he would," said Almina, rather ineffectively. " Now you lay right down 'n' try to go to sleep again."

Temple drew the clothes up about her. She promised to try to go to sleep. She said she was so thankful to be in Hoyt with Miss Drowdy. She thought in a few days she should be able to ride her pony.

Almina rose. She suggested that she should bring some skull-cap tea for the purpose of soothing her guest. But her guest answered that she would try to pass the night without skull-cap.

When she was left alone Temple called Yucatan to her. She leaned out and clasped the dog's head between her thin, nervous-looking hands.

" What did he say to you, dear ?" she asked. " Sweetheart, what did he say to you ? I know he noticed you. He is kind to everything."

Again the dog gave his inarticulate response. Temple bent farther forward and kissed Yucatan's face between his eyes.

Sinking back on her pillow, once more she closed her

eyes.   She began to fancy she heard that horse galloping again.   It began to gallop to a strange rhythm that grew more and more indefinite until she was asleep.

"I guess," said Freddy's mother the next morning to Freddy's father, as all three sat at breakfast—"I guess you better harness up, 'n' I'll go over to Alminy's 'n' spend the day.   I d' know what she will git up to next.   What with a nigger woman, 'n' that old pony, 'n' that gal of Roger Crawford's that married the evangelist, I ain't no idea what she'll come to."

"Whatever she comes to, you can't stop 'er," said Mr. Wilson, in a momentary interval between one slapjack and another.

"I c'n try, anyway," was the response; "'n' if 'tain't Alminy's sister's duty to try, I'm sure I d' know whose duty 'tis."

Freddy began to kick his short legs violently back and forth under the table.   He shook his spoon at his mother.

"Mar," he announced, "you've got ter take me! I wanter see the pony!   Make auntie lemme ride the pony!   Make auntie lemme ride it, I say!"

"But, Freddie, 'tain't auntie's pony," said his mother, with ingratiating explanation and deprecation in her voice.

"Make auntie lemme!" was the peremptory response, the legs going faster than before.

"Mummer 'll try," now said Mrs. Wilson; and to her husband, "I guess you better harness soon's you git through eatin'."

Mr. Wilson nodded.   He did not like to talk much while laying in his stores of food.

His wife rose from the table, and left her husband still breakfasting.   She moved back Freddy's high-chair and led that young man to the sink, took an end of a towel, dipped it in water, then rubbed it on the cake of yellow soap, then tipped back her son's head, and applied the towel to his face with relentless thoroughness.

Freddy kicked the sink, which was already much battered

from the same cause. He writhed, but he could not escape from the maternal grasp.

In less than an hour mother and son were sitting in the open wagon, and were driving towards Almina's. Freddy insisted upon driving, thereby keeping his guardian in a dreadful state of nervous tension and watchfulness, for she was constantly obliged to snatch the reins, for the horse stumbled and had a way of shying when there was nothing whatever visible to the human eye that should make him shy.

Therefore, by the time Mrs. Wilson came in sight of her sister's home she was in an irritated frame of mind not calculated to make her judgment lenient.

She would not let Freddy clamber from the wagon by himself, but got out first, and then lifted him and set him down emphatically. He instantly started to run towards the barn.

His mother took the horse severely by the bridle and walked in the direction taken by her son. But she went in rather a zigzag fashion, for her eyes were fastened on the house, as if she were a detective, and were determined to discover in the very shingles some sign of her sister's strange doings.

But she saw nothing unusual.

It was a clear, cool morning. The smoke, as it came from the chimney, rose in a straight line up towards the blue sky.

Some doves flew down on the roof, and strutted back and forth. They were Almina's pigeons, and it was just like her to keep them, her sister thought, and let them eat as much corn as twice as many hens would have eaten.

The woman leading the horse pressed her lips yet more closely together.

As a married woman, and the feminine head of a family, she knew that she was in a position to rebuke Almina, who was only an old maid.

At this stage in her reflections she rolled open the barn

door, and at the same moment Almina appeared in the yard. She had just seen her sister, and now came running out, with her long apron flung over her head and held tightly under her chin.

"I thought I heard wheels, 'n' then I thought I didn't," she remarked. "Lemme help you take the horse right out. I s'pose you've come to spend the day, 'ain't ye?"

"Yes," was the reply; "I guess I sh'll stay till towards night, anyway. You jest unhook that tug, your side, will ye?"

One woman stood at one side of the horse and one at the other, and he was soon led out of the shafts.

"I thought I seen Freddy," said Almina.

She knew that her manner was not quite as cordial as it ought to be. The firm belief that her sister had come from curiosity, and that she would reprove her, made genuine hospitality for the moment impossible.

"Yes, Freddy come," was the answer. "I guess he's gone right in to see that pony. He's crazy 'bout him. 'N' I must say it does seem ruther strange 'bout that pony."

Almina restrained herself from making any reply to this remark. In silence she pulled off the saddle and crupper from the horse.

Mrs. Wilson was busy with the rope that took the place of a buckle on the throatlash.

"I don't s'pose for one minute," she said, "that if you'd married the doctor you'd be'n havin' a nigger woman, 'n' a pony, 'n' a sick person comin' to live with you."

"No," said Almina, "I don't s'pose I should."

"No, I guess not," with emphasis. "'N' there wa'n't nothin' aginst the doctor. You can't say there was."

"No, I can't say there was, 'n' I never did say so."

"I don't wonder you're touchy."

"I ain't touchy."

"Oh, ain't you? Where is that colored woman? Why ain't she out here helpin' us? My husband said he thought she was taller'n he was. He was all struck up 'bout her."

Almina waited a little before she replied. She had made up her mind to keep her temper; also to do as she pleased. It seemed to her that, though she was an old maid, possibly even somewhat because of that fact, she had a right to her own individuality, and her own way of living.

Before she was quite ready to reply there came a sound from the other side of the partition that separated the front part of the barn from the back where the horse and cattle stalls were.

It was a sound like the sudden and violent hitting of something hard against planks, and it was repeated with great rapidity two or three times.

Almina ran to the scene, followed by her sister. She was first to arrive, and she found Freddy with a long stick in his hand, standing behind Thimble.

She caught the boy by the arm.

"I 'ain't whipped him !" he cried, "I was only just touchin' his hind-legs with the end of this to see what he'd do. I 'ain't whipped him a natom."

"You'd better not," said Almina, sharply. "He's as good-natured 's he can be, but he won't stand no whip, now, I tell ye."

Freddy began to pull and strain at his aunt's hand.

"Lemme git on him ! Lemme git on him !" he shouted.

"He ain't mine," replied his aunt.

"But you c'n lemme git on him ! You know you can !"

"I sha'n't," answered Almina.

"Here, Freddy, come to your mummer, now," interposed Mrs. Wilson. "Auntie's got other things to think of now besides little Freddy. If she don't want you to git on that nasty pony, why, you can't git on him—that's all there is about that."

Almina turned to her sister. She found it quite difficult to hold to her resolve to keep her temper.

"Now, I do wish you'd be reasonable," she said. "'Tain't my pony, 'n' I 'ain't no right to let Freddy do anything with him. You know jest 's well 's I do, that I'd give my eye-teeth to Freddy if he wanted 'em—if I'd still got 'em in my head," she added, with a laugh.

The mother was mollified at this mention of sacrifice to her boy. She knew very well that her boy was living in this world that he might have sacrifices offered to him by his relatives, particularly by his female relatives. She also laughed and said she " guessed Freddy could git along without his auntie's eye-teeth, even if she'd had any.

Then the two women put the horse in the stall next Thimble, and Thimble kicked violently against the dividing planks, and danced as much as he could, tied by the halter as he was.

In the midst of this Sally appeared.

She had on a dark wool dress, with no wrap over her, and a red cotton handkerchief tied, turban-wise, about her head.

" Laws, Miss Drowdy," she said, striding forward and laying her arm over the neck of the Wilson horse, and pulling up his halter, which was not yet in place, "dis yere kind of work 's Sally's work. Yo' ain't gwine to do dis yere labor while Sally's hyar. Yo' ladies go 'long to de house."

Almina and her sister left the barn together, but Freddy refused to go with them. He had secret hopes that he might induce this strange colored woman to put him on Thimble. More than that, he wanted to be where he could watch Sally. He had never seen anything in the least like her before. She was as strange to him as if she had been a striped zebra from one of his picture-books appearing to him bodily in his father's dooryard.

Mrs. Wilson continued to be mollified as she walked beside her sister towards the house.

" So that's Sally, is it ?" she asked. " She ain't like nobody that's ever be'n in Hoyt, is she? She looks big 'n' strong 'nough to do every bit of your work, Alminy. But mebby she'll eat you out of house 'n' home, so 'twon't be no savin' to ye. I d' know what you're goin' to do, for my part."

" Oh, I sh'll git 'long well enough," responded Almina, delighted that her sister was becoming more amiable.

"My husband said there was a dorg, too," said Mrs. Wilson; "'n' so I wouldn't let Freddy bring his along for fear there'd be a fight, or something, and Freddy was so took up thinkin' of the pony that he give up real easy 'bout bringin' of his dorg."

Evidently Mrs. Wilson could find something to ameliorate the asperities of life with her son, since he had known that there was a pony at his auntie's.

As Almina placed her hand on the latch of her back door her sister inquired,

"Is she real feeble?"

She put this question in a loud whisper, as if Temple were within hearing, and would find a whisper more agreeable to listen to than the ordinary voice.

"Is she up 'round?" supplemented Mrs. Wilson, in the same whisper.

"Oh yes," replied Almina, aloud. "I think she'll be better as soon as she can git rested."

"But what's been tirin' of her?"

"She's been helpin' to hold meetin's, you know."

"So I've understood; but I don't know 's I see what there is 'bout holdin' meetin's that should tire anybody, though 'tain't woman's place. If she'd been to work, now, I could see why she should be tired. Likely's not 'tain't nothin' but nerves, after all."

By this time the two were in the kitchen.

"I believe they do call it nervous prostration, or something like that," Almina answered, inwardly wishing, as she had wished hundreds of times in her life, that her sister was a little different in some ways.

"But folks were just as they were made."

That was Almina's charitable conclusion always.

"Does she look like her father any?"

This was the next question, as Mrs. Wilson began to unpin her shawl and unroll her cloud. She had made this inquiry repeatedly after her sister had returned from Carolina, and had invariably received the same reply,

" I don't see 's she does, a grain."

" I always did think Roger Crawford was a real good-lookin' man."

As Mrs. Wilson said this the door of the south room opened, and Mrs. Wilson directly began to bring her face into what she would have called her " company look " if she had been called upon to describe it.

But though the door had opened, no one at first appeared save a large white dog, who came gravely forward, went to the outer door and put his paw on it, looking at Almina as he did so.

Almina let him out-of-doors.

Yucatan had been drilled much in the attainment of circumspect manners since he had travelled in many places with the Mercers, and he had responded intelligently to this education. He had cheerfully given up his mountains, and his free, out-of-door life, but he loved that life just as much as ever.

Now Mrs. Wilson hurried to the window and looked out. She felt an inextinguishable curiosity in regard to everything concerning these new-comers.

She deprecated their coming to herself, and would take that stand about them to every one ; but at the same time she was conscious of a certain reflected importance, as being the sister of the woman who had these unusual beings in her house.

" That's the dorg, ain't it ?" she now inquired.

" Yes."

" He'll eat a lot. Not that I should begretch the victuals of any live critter."

" You wouldn't have to begretch the victuals of a dead critter," responded Almina, with a rather sarcastic laugh.

" Ain't it funny that they not only brought a pony, but a dorg, too ?" now remarked Mrs. Wilson.

But before any reply could be made to this interrogation there sounded in the yard a shrill cry that might be of terror or of intense delight.

Both women uttered an exclamation, and at the same time the door of the south room opened again and Temple herself appeared, coming quickly forward, startled by the cry.

Mrs. Wilson, fearing that every sound came from her son, made a darting movement towards the door. She was used to making these movements many times a day. Little Freddy had grown beyond the stage of swallowing shoe-buttons, but his progress had brought no relief to his long-suffering parent.

Temple turned towards her and caught her hand. She laughed as she said,

"You needn't be alarmed. That's your boy, isn't it? Don't you think he is having a good time?"

There now appeared in sight the head of the white pony, followed by his whole body. On his bare back sat Frederick Wilson, and by him walked Sally. The yellow woman was holding Freddy firmly by one leg.

The boy saw the faces at the window. He grinned, and screamed, and waved his hands, but he could not fall off because of that grasp on his leg.

When this exciting pageant had passed on to the other side of the house, Mrs. Wilson, now in a very amiable frame of mind, on account of Freddy's happiness, turned to examine her sister's guest.

"Why," she thought, in the extremest astonishment, "I do believe I'm going to like her!"

Temple had sat down quietly. She was in the blue-covered rocker, and the morning pallor of her face was emphasized by that color. The thin face, the darkness under the eyes, the painfully sensitive lips, the still, firm-looking chin, made a combination that Mrs. Wilson could not understand.

"You don't look a bit like your father!" she exclaimed.

"I forgot that you knew him," was the languid response.

Mrs. Wilson noted that she betrayed no interest in her father, and drew her shrewd conclusions in consequence.

"You're goin' to pick right up here," she began, heartily. "You can't help it. Hoyt's called one of the healthiest towns in the State of Massachusetts. If you want to keep sick 'tain't no kind of a place to be in. Alminy," turning to her sister, "cream 'll be real good for Mis' Mercer. I c'n send some over every other day jest 's well 's not."

Temple's gaze rested upon the woman.

"That's so good of you; and I particularly like cream," she said.

Mrs. Wilson's heart glowed. There was an unusual throb to her commonplace pulses. She had a glimmering perception that this was not the kind of woman she was used to seeing.

It was curious to watch the people who came in during the next few weeks; and Miss Drowdy had not had so many callers in all her life as in the month following Temple's arrival.

These people came as to a menagerie. They came, pitying Almina Drowdy.

Temple said very little to them. They talked to her. Almost immediately those who had special troubles—and who has not?—told Temple those troubles, and she listened, her eyes dwelling with soft pity and sympathy on their faces.

It was an utterly genuine pity and sympathy, but it was a trained pity and sympathy as well. The last three years of Temple's life had done the training.

When these people left her they could not remember a word she had said, and yet they had missed nothing in her presence; and missed nothing in remembering the interview.

Meantime, as the April days grew balmier, Temple could tell herself that she was better. Oh yes, thank God! she was better.

Who but one who has been an invalid can understand the rapture of such a knowledge?

Every morning Sally brought the pony, saddled, to the back door, and Temple mounted him, Yucatan loping back and forth in the yard in impatience to be gone.

Temple scoured the country farther and farther afield, choosing, when she could, the solitary cart-paths through woods and pastures.

It seemed to her now that a weight was lifting from her soul. She could see far into the spring blue of the sky.

She began to think she would unpack her violin.

It was on the day when she was thinking of her violin that, turning her pony into a path that led through a chestnut wood, she saw a man coming along the path.

The man waved his stick and whistled cheerily to Yucatan, calling the dog by name.

In a moment Temple recognized Yale Boynton.

XIX

"A LITTLE PLEASURE"

BOYNTON hurried forward. The glow on his face made Temple think of old days in her old home.

"This is almost as good as Carolina!" he exclaimed, with some eagerness, as, hat in hand, he came to her side. "Here is the pony, here is the dog, and here am I. Ah, Mrs. Mercer, can't we fancy that Pisgah is holding up a majestic head somewhere beyond those trees, and that the French Broad is down there?"

Temple breathed a long breath. Her eyes sparkled.

"Oh, to think of it! Oh, to dream of it!" she answered.

"Fills my heart—" went on Boynton with the quotation.

Then he stopped suddenly. It seemed as if, in spite of himself, there had come too much feeling into his voice.

He put his hand on Thimble's neck and stroked the sleek hair. He almost expected to see his hand tremble, and he watched it intently lest it should do so.

He had come down from Boston that he might call on Mrs. Mercer, and he had arranged in his mind his precise manner during the interview. But just now, meeting her thus, he feared lest this prearranged manner might slip away from him.

He was thinking that he was senselessly glad, and he was also cynically asking himself why it was that when a man was senselessly glad there was a thrill in that joy that a reasonable pleasure rarely brought. And he was also thinking that this fact must be because of the devil in us all.

He wished that he might feel like this when he saw Amy Wallis.

Amy Wallis was the nicest kind of a girl, but the sight of this woman on the white pony had sent his blood along its channels at a rate that Amy Wallis must never know about.

And what a delicious thing it is to feel the blood start in that way!

That writer spoke the truth who said that we are likely to "choose in life that which brings us most thrill."

Certainly many of us weakly do that.

Boynton looked up at his companion when he had made sure that his hand was steady and that his voice would also be firm.

"How grateful I am to see that you are better!" he said, earnestly.

"Not half as grateful as I am to feel better," was the reply. Then Temple added, in her old way, "If you had a horse we could gallop down this wood road."

In his own mind Boynton immediately flung away all other plans in the resolve to stay somewhere in the vicinity and ride with Temple.

"You know there's nothing in the world I'd like better," he answered, with that air of exaggeration which he used to cover his meaning sometimes. "Perhaps you'll let me come to-morrow on the best steed I can find?"

"That 'll be so pleasant!" Temple smiled down at the man beside her. Her spirits were rising as our spirits will rise at anything which seems to take us back to a time when life was light and careless.

"But where are you?" she now asked, in sudden wonder as to why he had appeared thus. "And is Miss Wallis with you?"

Boynton was gazing up at her. "I am here," he said, "and it is Mrs. Mercer who is with me."

He was careful not to have too much feeling in his voice.

Perhaps no man knew better than Boynton how to approach near, but not too near, to a woman.

Temple felt that agreeable glow which comes to us when we are made to feel that we are giving pleasure.

"But where is Miss Wallis?"

"In Boston."

"Is she coming into the country?"

"Perhaps; but not until later."

"I liked her," said Temple, with that frankness which made her so unconventional at times. "I wanted to know her. But I was so ill then!"

Here the speaker shuddered slightly but uncontrollably. Her eyes clouded. She looked off down the path.

Boynton stood away a short distance. He tried not to see his companion's face; it moved him so in its pallor and its unconscious appeal.

He swore inwardly at Mercer. He called him a damned idiot to have brought this woman to this state. Letting her pray and sing for the rabble!

"Yes, damn him!"

Boynton set his teeth against his oaths that they might not be heard.

"But you are getting well," he said, gently; "anybody can see that."

"Do you think so? Do you really think so?" turning quickly and bending slightly towards him. "You can't imagine how I like to have any one tell me that I seem to be getting well. Of course I know I am gaining. But it's so slow. And I have times of such depression, and I feel as if I couldn't be of any use to—to Richard, you know; and then I have seasons when I fear about my belief and faith. But, of course, that is because of my ill-health. You see, a person's state of health accounts for a great deal of what is called mental trouble; don't you think so, Mr. Boynton?"

"I know it does."

Temple began to say more. Then she hesitated. She laughed slightly, but there was something wistful in her voice as she spoke again,

"I'm going to be as well as ever in a few weeks, Mr. Boynton. In the fall I can join Mr. Mercer in his work—

that is, I can if I keep my faith. I want to keep my faith."

Boynton did not find himself able to speak immediately.

He was feeling strongly that if this woman had tried to find some means by which to make herself more attractive to him she could not have chosen better than to have appeared in the guise of an invalid. But Boynton knew very well that Mrs. Mercer was not thinking of herself in relation to him.

"We all want to keep our faith," the man said, at last.

"It's curious, but I'm tempted to ask these people whom I meet here if they really have faith," went on Temple, still with a far-away look. "Of course, it is one phase of my illness — it must be. I suppose Miss MacCallum would say that I didn't relax enough." Here Temple brought her glance down to her companion, and smiled again. "Mr. Boynton, did you ever lie on the floor and roll your head around?"

"No; but I will if you think I ought. Does the process make one have more faith?"

"Indirectly, I suppose. And it tends to reduce abnormality. I could tell you a few things that are almost specifics against anything abnormal. But perhaps your tendencies are not in that direction, are they? If you could find it within the bounds of truth to answer 'yes,' you've no idea what a comfort that answer would be."

"Yes," was the prompt reply.

"Oh, thank you so much! You know we poor mortals are made so that if we have small-pox it is a great comfort to us to find that some one else has it also."

Temple's face was gradually clearing while she spoke, until, as she finished, she broke into a laugh which sounded out in the woods as Boynton remembered her laugh to have sounded in the little boat on the Broad.

What infernal chance had made her think she had experienced religion, and then that she must marry the preacher?

These questions flashed through Boynton's mind as he joined in her laugh.

Then he seized the leading part in the talk, and kept it persistently upon the old time when the two had known each other.   He called it the "old time" with a slight tenderness in his voice, although hardly four years had elapsed since his first acquaintance with her.

He saw her grow brighter and brighter.   He had never exerted himself more to be entertaining, and never felt more keenly the stimulating certainty of success in the effort.

His spirits rose intoxicatingly as he walked through the wood by the pony's side.

With every moment that passed Temple seemed more and more like the girl whom he had taught to play the violin.

When they emerged from the path into the public highway he said that he dared not keep Mrs. Mercer at a footpace any longer.   He begged that she would allow him to ride over from the next town where he was stopping, and join her.   Would she let him come to-morrow?

"Yes."

"Thanks—a thousand thanks."   He lifted his hat.   She noted vaguely the happy gleam in his eyes.

She cantered on towards Miss Drowdy's.

Boynton walked down the road.   A keen sense of life, the inebriating fulness of life, made him step like a king.

As for Temple, she set her pony into a swift gallop; she whistled to Yucatan.   The two animals seemed to be running away as they fled down the lonesome road.

No one saw them but the birds and the chipmunks.

A half-hour later, when Temple rode into Miss Drowdy's yard, Sally ran out and lifted her off the saddle.

"Bress the Lawd!" she cried, ferveutly, "Yo' done got yer ole look on!"

But Temple sank down on Sally's arm, her strength all taken, apparently, by her ride.

A half-hour's rest and a cup of milk restored Temple so that she rose from her bed and went to her trunk, which set against the wall. She opened it and flung out the things until she came to her violin case.

She set this on her lap and held it there for some moments, her eyes fixed on the window opposite her.

She was recalling the last time she had played it, and how the people had been moved by the hymn she sung.

And she had prayed then. Well, she had not prayed since. But she should do so some time. She must. Richard did not know that she did not pray any more. She had finally told Mrs. Ammidown, told her painfully, as if making a confession of great sin, and Mrs. Ammidown had laughed gently, and replied that it was only a matter of healthy nerves and body generally.

That was just like a physician. Physicians ascribed everything to the body.

Temple took her fiddle from its place and tuned it. Presently she put it up to her shoulder and began walking about the room, playing, singing with the music she made:

> "A little bird in the air
> Is singing of Thyri the Fair,
>   The sister of Svend the Dane ;
> And the song of the garrulous bird
> In the streets of the town is heard,
>   And repeated again and again."

Temple sang this twice over. Then she quickly laid down the bow and violin. She walked to the window like one who suddenly discovers that he is imprisoned, and who is wild to escape.

She threw up the sash and put her head out.

A mild air blew upon her. In the distance a chickadee sang cheerfully.

She let down the sash. She stood in the middle of the room. Then she flung herself down on the bed and began to weep as stormily as if she were only ten years old.

Presently there was a whine and a scratch outside the door, which was hesitatingly opened to let the Newfoundland walk in.

Temple raised her head. She beckoned to Yucatan, who trod solemnly up to her and put his big muzzle to her face, solicitously licking it. She pressed the shaggy head to her bosom, moaning as she did so.

Outside, Almina heard the sound of sobbing, and did not know whether she ought to intrude or remain where she was.

But Sally, coming in from the barn with the odor of hay and out-of-doors strong upon her, did not hesitate. She strode up to the closed door and flung it open, her feet shaking the little house as she went across the floor.

Temple was lying face down upon the bed, with Yucatan's nose pressed up to her neck. Her hands were flung out and shut tightly.

The yellow woman bent over and lifted her mistress in her arms. Temple was so pitiably thin that her weight was not much, and Sally put Temple's head down on her shoulder after she had gathered her closely. She walked about the room with her burden, saying,

"Sh! Honey! Sh! Sh! De Lawd's gwine fur to take care of yo'. Fur shore, de Lawd's gwine to do it. Yo' needn't worry more ; no, yo' needn't.   ' N' hyar's ole Sally. Hyar's ole Sally, who jes' pintedly gives her worthless life up ter yo', honey. Sh! Sh!"

The husky voice was sweet and tender with sympathy.

Temple began to listen to it. It was a voice she had heard ever since she could remember. It began to comfort her, but she was in a paroxysm of self-pity, and was feeling that curious and unwholesome enjoyment that sometimes comes from such a cause.

"My mother would be sorry for me," she whispered as she lay on Sally's shoulder. "I don't believe my mother ever suffered as I suffer."

"'Tain't no matter whuther she did or not, Miss Temple," answered the yellow woman, with a gleam of common-sense. "You's jes' sufferin' 'cause you's sick, honey. But you's gittin' well jes' as farst—yo' be."

Temple was silent. She was beginning to be ashamed of herself.

She lifted her head.

"Put me down, Sally," she said in a moment, somewhat sharply. "I'm not going to be a baby any more."

Sally placed her burden in a chair, and stood gazing down at her, her big, strong face working.

Temple pressed her hand to the back of her head. Her features were settling into something of their natural appearance.

She smiled whimsically.

"I reckon 'twas my violin," she remarked, as if making an explanation to herself. "And you, Sally, you've done very wrong to sympathize. Miss MacCallum doesn't approve of sympathy."

Sally grinned. She did not know precisely what her mistress meant, but she knew enough to respond,

"Reckon, den, yo' done better shoot Yucatan hyar."

Temple sent Sally out of the room. She went to the glass and brushed her hair, her movements revealing a resolution and calmness which they had not shown of late.

There was a lustre in her eyes unlike the weak, feverish gleam which had been there for months past.

As she stood before the mirror she thrust out her hand and looked at it, then glanced at the reflection of her face.

"My soul shall be as steady as my hand," she was thinking. "I am not going to be hysterical any more."

But even as she thought this a weakness came over her, the bodily weakness of muscles and sinews long out of training.

She sat down quickly. She leaned her forehead on the table in front of her. She was trembling, but her face did not relax into a tremor.

All at once she became aware that her forehead was not

resting on the table itself, but on an envelope. It was the envelope containing Mercer's last letter.

She raised herself and took the letter, opening the sheet slowly. It had come nearly a week ago, on a Monday. She had not failed to hear from him on each Monday since he had brought her there.

She knew every word of this letter, but she read it again.

It was a very friendly epistle. All of Mercer's letters to his wife were extremely friendly ; and they related everything the writer thought she would like to know ; they told of the minutest trifle that had reference to Temple's old home among the mountains.

Perhaps she did not think that Mercer must have been at great pains to find out everything about that mountain-side.

Now she read again a few lines that made her flush with renewed interest.

" You remember you wondered if the old tree made a little landing for boats on the Broad as it used to do when you played the fiddle in young Boynton's boat. I was there the other day. I went down from Asheville in a boat. The tree trunk has rotted away and fallen into the river—only a bit of it is left. I was sorry when I saw it. I knew how you loved it. I pulled in my oars and looked up the slope. I saw the smoke coming from the chimney of your log-house.

" I landed and gathered some arbutus. It is almost gone now. The rhododendron thicket by the old tree trunk has been cut away. Your tenant is putting in corn in that field.

" I stood and looked off at Pisgah and the Twin Brothers. I wished you were with me. I was comforted by the knowledge that you are getting well."

And so on.

Temple's eyes took in the whole ; then they went back to the line, " I wished you were with me," and they rested there until the words seemed to lose their meaning, as words will.

She suddenly lifted her hand and threw the paper from her.

" I have read it enough," she said, aloud.

She sat back in her chair and tried to shut her eyes, but the lids burned so that she allowed them to spring open again.

She reached forward to the table and pulled towards her a book which had been in her trunk—a volume she had once borrowed of Laura Ammidown and had not returned.

The book opened of itself at a page where Temple had often read in the last few months. Now she pronounced aloud the familiar words,

"That which is not allotted the hand cannot reach, and what is allotted will find you wherever you may be."

"What I've got to do," said Temple, her will helping to make the face firm, "is to accept my fate. I'm not going to be happy. Happiness is not allotted to me. I'm not going to pray for it any more. Perhaps I never ought to have been so selfish as to pray for my own happiness. What does it matter—happiness or misery?"

Some swift change came to the face of the woman. It lost all its ascetic stoicism, and took on a look of soft brilliance, which made it like the face of that mountain girl who had welcomed Almina Drowdy to her home, and who had proclaimed that she was of a cold nature.

Temple rose and took her violin again. She laid it across her knee. She half closed her eyes and began to play "Dissembling Love," the strains seeming to melt into the still air of the room.

In the kitchen Almina heard, and stopped picking over the rice for her pudding. Her elderly heart gave a leap, and then went on beating at an unusual rate.

There seemed to be, all at once, an air of romance about everything. Before the eyes of the old maid there came a picture of her youth, with all its intoxicating hopes and thrilling joys. For an instant Roger Crawford and she were young again, and he was true.

Almina put her hard-worked, faithful hands over her face. She could actually fancy that the middle-aged, commonplace face was radiant and beautiful.

And all because a young woman in the next room was fiddling "Dissembling Love." Almina was glad that her sister was not there. She had a feeling that "Sister Wilson" would have thought there was something immoral in a woman playing the violin like that.

In a few moments the strains stopped.

Almina was trying to resume her work, mechanically scanning a handful of rice, when Temple entered.

"Oh, how much better you do look!" cried the elder woman.

"Thank you," said Temple. She advanced to Almina's side. She was smiling in a confident sort of way.

"I wanted to ask you, Miss Drowdy," she said, "if a person who isn't going to be happy has a right to taste a little pleasure?"

"What?"

Almina looked up in a dazed way, and Temple carefully repeated her question.

She sat down as she did so, and took up some grains of rice, examining them with bright, undiscriminating eyes.

"I s'pose you call happiness and pleasure two different kinds of things," remarked Almina, at last.

"Oh, of course."

"Then I tell you what 'tis," began the other, after a short pause, "I'd jes' stick to happiness, even if I was miserable. I'd let pleasure slide."

Here Almina took Temple's thin hand in her own. Then she laughed nervously.

"But I guess I 'ain't much idea what you mean, Temple. But, somehow, you kinder scare me! I d' know why, I'm sure. You look jest 's you used to among the mountains— only not jest so, either."

"So you'd let pleasure slide, would you?"

Temple laughed as she spoke. She looked at her companion, and then she leaned nearer and kissed her.

"You needn't be scared, dear friend," she said, in a low voice. "If it's meant for me to be happy, I shall be.

Don't you know, 'that which is not allotted the hand cannot reach'?"

Having said this, Temple walked away to the window and gazed out of it. But she was not seeing the stretch of rolling pasture, with its distant frame of pine-trees. She did not even notice Thimble, who had been let out, now caracoling up and down that pasture.

What the woman saw was a different landscape: peak rising beyond peak in a vivid moonlight; fringes of black trees on some summits; on the side of one of the mountains a log-hut, used sometimes as a school-house; a crowd of people in the hut; a blazing fire of fatwood on the hearth, and before the fire the commanding figure of Mercer.

Temple was seeing all this, and recalling the preacher's voice and words, the power of his presence over the assembly.

She had felt that power many times since, but this particular evening was the turning-point of her life. It was then that she had believed that the spirit of the Lord had come to her and sanctified her; had given her a new heart. She had experienced religion.

And the months and days and hours of the three years that had followed!

Had she not worked faithfully—nay, ardently?

And why, since her strength had failed, had this sacred work assumed a different aspect?

The sacredness and value of the work must be just the same.

It was she, then, who had changed. But she could not allow her convictions to be made different by a state of the body. The body, even the mysterious nerves, could not alter the relations between man and God. The soul must be saved. A man's heart must be given to God.

Almina went on with her preparations for her pudding.

She took the rice to the sink and began to wash it. But she was thinking of her companion, and asking herself many questions which she could not answer.

Suddenly Temple spoke, but she did not turn her face from the window.

"I met an old friend to-day," she said.

"That so?" responded the other woman, who would not betray her curiosity.

Temple now turned, and came and stood by her friend's side at the sink.

"You remember the French Broad, Miss Drowdy?" she asked.

"Oh yes!" with animation.

"And how worried you were about my going out in a boat with that young man from Asheville?"

"Yes."

"And how you waited for me so long on the bank among the rhododendrons?"

Here Temple laughed and Almina grew red.

"I guess I do remember," said the elder woman, "'n' I guess you don't know how queer things all seemed to me down there. But what made you think of that time now?"

"Because of the old friend I met this morning."

Almina gave a little start. She could not understand why such a sense of fear came upon her. She glanced quickly up at the face near her.

"You mean you've seen that young man?" she asked.

"Yes. I met him. He was coming over to see me."

"Yale Boynton in these parts?"

"He's living in Boston. I saw him this spring. I saw the girl he is going to marry."

Temple did not know why she so particularly wished to mention Miss Wallis.

"Oh, did you?"

"Yes; and I liked her so much."

Almina seemed to have no remark to make, though Temple waited for some response.

"Mr. Boynton is coming over to-morrow to ride with me," she said.

She was conscious of a rising feeling of irritation, and was surprised at the fact.

"I s'pose you've been lonesome," now remarked Almina.

"No, not in the least," Temple answered, quickly. "I'm never lonesome with my horse and my dog."

No response whatever. But what response was Temple looking for?

She went and sat down by the cook-stove. She was silent, trying to overcome her annoyance.

"I s'pose seein' Mr. Boynton made you think of your fiddle," at last remarked Almina.

"I suppose so. But I've been thinking of my fiddle ever since I began to feel better."

At this point the conversation ceased entirely, and was not resumed that day.

In the afternoon Temple rode out again. Indeed, she now spent more than half of her waking hours in the saddle.

The neighbors for a dozen miles in all directions were becoming accustomed to the sight of the white pony going by, sometimes as if he were running away, sometimes at a gentle amble, with the woman on his back, the Newfoundland loping somewhere near.

"Somehow, I can't make such a sight seem kinder Christian-like," said Aunt Hitty Blake, peering over her glasses as the pony flew by her one morning while she was at the woodpile for chips. "I do feel as if we needed a missionary, or something."

This last remark she made to her husband when she was putting the chips into the stove a few moments later.

"I understand," replied Mr. Blake, in his slow, judicial way, "that that there woman is a missionary herself. She's an evangelist. But I ain't accustomed to evangelists with ponies 'n' dorgs 'n' fiddles, 'n' them kind of eyes. I guess I'll make an arrand over to old maid Drowdy's 'fore long."

And he made his "arrand," together with nearly everybody in the neighborhood, as has been stated.

The next morning by ten o'clock Boynton cantered into the yard.

He dismounted, and came in to greet Miss Drowdy. He was in high spirits.

Almina watched the two ride away. She knew very well what Aunt Hitty Blake would say if she saw the riders— what Mrs. Newton and all the neighbors would say.

But she made up her mind not to care for what they said. What she really cared for was the look which had been on Temple's face when she had come in the day before, after she had met Boynton.

It was the day for Almina to write her weekly letter to Mercer. She always wrote it between ten and eleven in the forenoon.

Just before she signed her name she paused, trying to decide whether she should mention Boynton.

For some reason she decided not to do so.

It was perhaps a week later that Sally was coming back from an errand to the village. She was walking along that path through the pasture that she and the pony had taken on their first arrival.

Somebody called suddenly,

"Sally!" in a sharp, imperative tone.

The woman stopped short and looked about her.

A man advanced from among some pine-trees.

The yellow woman's face expressed overwhelming surprise.

"Goramighty!" she cried, "it's Mister Dalvecker!"

And it was Link—Link, in an ill-fitting suit of ready-made clothes that made him look like something quite different from his old self.

He apparently had no intention of wasting any words on Sally.

"Miss Temple!" he said, quickly, nodding his head in the direction of the house. "Yo' ask her to come out hyar— right now."

Sally turned to go.

Link began to walk back and forth.

"Tell her I 'ain't no time ter waste. Tell her I must see her."

Sally went on.

The young man kept up his walk in the short space under the birches. He was watching the path where Sally had disappeared. As he watched his tanned face became as pale as it was possible for it to be. His lips, under the yellow mustache, kept twitching nervously.

Suddenly a deep flush rose to his forehead. He started forward, taking off his hat as he did so.

There was Temple coming along the path. She had not lingered a moment. She came eagerly, with both hands outstretched.

Dalvecker, holding her hands and staring at her, exclaimed,

"Oh, Temple, how you've changed! You ain't happy! I war powerful feared you wa'n't happy!"

"Link! Don't! I've been ill, you know."

"Temple, yo' carn't look me in the face, yo' carn't, an' say yo're happy."

He did not wait for her to reply. He went on hurriedly, still holding her hands,

"I took it into my head as I'd gurt to see yo'. I'd jest gurt to see yo' 'fore I done one thing."

"What thing?" asked Temple, who was more moved at sight of her old friend than she wished to show. He was a part of her young life—of that time when, as she phrased it, she was somebody else.

This emotion was something very different from anything evoked by a meeting with Boynton.

"Come to the house with me, Link," she said.

"No, no. I'm gwine to stay right hyar fur ten minutes. I don't wanter see anybody else. I curm to see you. I'm gwine to be married, Temple. Don't speak. I don't lurv her. But mar, she's set her heart. An' it don't make no difference to me. I wanted to see yo' and tell yo' myself that

I didn't lurv her. But I mean ter make a good man to her."

Here Link paused.

He did not stop gazing at his companion, and Temple found it difficult to think what to say to him.

Her confused thoughts would not clarify so that she could speak.

" I hope you'll—"

" Now stop," he cried, " yo' needn't talk that-a-way. I do wish, Temple, that you'd been happy! God! I d' know who should be happy ef 'tain't you !"

The young man's voice vibrated strangely. He was afraid to try to express the tumultuous sorrow that Temple's appearance caused him.

He had been continually telling himself that, of course, she would be changed. But to be like this—

" I'm getting well," said Temple, quietly.

He made no answer. He continued to look at her.

" I jest had to come an' tell yo'," he said, at last. " I couldn't a-bear to have yo' think I'd be'n an' fell in lurv with anybody. She's a good gal, though. But I don't lay out to put no pump in. I wanted to tell yo', Temple." He looked at her wistfully. She met his eyes with that warm kindness that was part of her nature.

" It was good of you to tell me," she answered. " And I'm sure you'll be happy, Link. Oh, I hope so !"

" Now I'll go."

He would not stay. He gripped her hands hard and said good-bye.

She watched him go. She remained a long time among the birches. And when she came back to the house Almina was sure she had been crying.

" PROOF ARMOR "

" I suppose you don't read Cherbuliez, Mrs. Mercer?"

Boynton made this remark one day in June. He had been riding all of a long and delightful morning with Temple. They had been silent a great part of the time. He had discovered that it was quite delicious to be silent with Mrs. Mercer. He had not tried to find anything to say. Occasionally he had glanced at his companion, but it had not happened that she had glanced at him. When she did look at him it was with a full, serious, sometimes a troubled gaze.

Boynton had been with Temple a great deal in the last two months.

He knew very well that he was what he called in love with her. He thought of her almost every waking moment, and he often dreamed of her.

There was a subtle and thrilling delight in the very knowledge that he was in the same world with her. He did not trouble himself much about the existence of Mercer. He was, as he would have said, " realizing his present."

And it is a great gift to be able to do that.

Of course Temple had never loved Mercer, a cast-iron fanatic who hadn't a thought above saving souls.

But sometimes Boynton had a strong desire to discover what Temple thought of her husband. He used to discourse occasionally on the subject of love and marriage, in an impersonal way.

At such times Temple would listen, but she did not often express any opinion.

She was recalling her old conviction that it was a great
mistake to marry for love, because love did not always last.
Of late she had caught herself quoting those old lines from
somewhere :

> " Pray, how comes love ?
> It comes unsought, unsent:
> Pray, how goes love ?
> It was not love that went."

Now she turned and looked at Boynton as he put his
question concerning the French author.

They had been talking of marriage in general ; or, rather,
he had been talking, as he often did.

The two riders sat on their horses at the end of a wood
road that opened suddenly into a high pasture.   They were
alone together save for the presence of the dog, who was sitting soberly on his haunches by the pony's side.

"No," said Temple, " I don't read Cherbuliez. It doesn't
seem to me that I read anything. I think I never cared extremely for reading. Human beings, dogs, horses, life—all
seem more interesting to me than books."

"Life? Oh yes," exclaimed Boynton, meeting her eyes,
"life is enchanting! Until this summer I never knew how
enchanting."

He spoke hurriedly, and then he was afraid he had expressed too much.

He looked away, and spoke more calmly.

" I was going to remind you of a paragraph : ' That there
are two kinds of poetry, that which is born and that which
is made ; that the first is good, that the second is not worth
a rap ; and it is the same with marriages.' "

"I don't agree with your author," responded Temple,
coldly.

Then she said she thought it was time to go home. She
should be late to dinner now.

Boynton pressed his lips tightly together. A flush of irritation rose to his face. He wanted to lash his whip out into
the air and hit something.

But he only silently acquiesced in her suggestion, and turned his horse's head.

Their homeward route lay past the Wilson home. They were going at a foot's pace as they came opposite the house. The front door opened suddenly, and Mrs. Wilson appeared. She beckoned. The two drew in their horses.

"I jest want er speak to you, Mis' Mercer, a minute," she said.

There was such an air of resolution in manner and voice that Temple involuntarily was conscious of a slight inward opposition.

But she nodded assent, and Boynton, lifting his hat markedly to Mrs. Wilson, rode away.

Thimble walked up the path to Mrs. Wilson's very door, coming safely between flower-beds because he was a pony.

His rider slipped off on to the step.

"You seem to be 'bout well now, don't ye?" asked the woman, as she led the way into the parlor, and pulled up one curtain a little way.

"I'm much better," answered Temple, feeling a sense of battle in the air, and bracing herself.

When the two women sat down opposite each other Mrs. Wilson's heart began to sink.

She had been saying to her husband that she would certainly speak to Temple, and her husband had invariably responded by telling her she would be a fool if she did.

"It's gittin' to be real pleasant ou' doors, ain't it?" she now said, feebly.

Yes, Temple thought it was lovely. She no longer had any inclination to say "lurvly."

"I s'pose your husband 'll be a-sendin' for you 'fore long, won't he?"

"I don't know. I came to stay all summer with Miss Drowdy."

Having said this, Temple's face suddenly changed. She smiled and asked,

"Are you thinking it is time for me to go? Is your sister

tired of me? I thought Sally was doing very well in her help with the work."

"'Tain't that," burst out Mrs. Wilson, explosively. "Don't ye know folks are talkin' dretfully?"

Temple grew pale as she gazed at her companion.

"Talking?" she said, vaguely. She had never in all her life thought whether people "talked" or not.

"Yes," said Mrs. Wilson, who was rolling up the hem of her apron and unrolling it with great rapidity. "'Bout you, you know. I told Mr. Wilson I was bound to speak to you. I knew you wa'n't thinkin' no evil."

"Thinking evil?"

Temple felt the pulses in her throat swelling.

"Yes, I knew it. I tried to make Alminy say something to you, but she said there was one thing she wouldn't do, and that was speak to you 'bout folks talkin'."

"What do they say?"

Mrs. Wilson hesitated. Temple repeated her question.

"They say"—here the speaker summoned all her courage—"they say that you 'n' that young man seem too intimate. Why, old Mr. Blake told my husband only yisterdy that if you'd got a husband anywhere he'd better be sent for. 'N' he said that if you had got one he guessed he didn't care much what did happen to you. 'N' Mrs. Lemuel Lane said day before yisterdy that Alminy ought to know what kind of a woman she was a-harborin'."

Mrs. Wilson paused to take breath.

She had not intended to speak just like this, but after she had begun she was conscious of a strong desire to justify herself for mentioning the subject at all. Besides, as she now remarked, she was only telling the simple truth, and not half the truth, either.

"They say," she went on, recklessly, "that that young man's got a girl down to Bawston somewhere. All I c'n say, if he has, I'm mighty sorry for her. He round here a takin' off his hat, 'n' a smilin', 'n' a scrapin', 's if we could be swallered whole!"

Mrs. Wilson was quite carried away by the interest her subject excited in her now she was fairly launched upon it.

Temple had risen.   She now turned towards the door.

"Where you goin'?" quickly asked Mrs. Wilson.

"I'm going back to Miss Drowdy's," was the answer.

Mrs. Wilson hurried round in front of her guest.

"You mad with me?" she asked.

Hardly knowing that she did so, she took Temple's hand, which was cold through her glove.

Temple looked at her in silence.   She exerted herself to bring her mind to answer the question.

"Oh no," she said.   "I am—I am greatly surprised.   I wonder if people are right when they talk like that about me?"

"No! no!   Of course they ain't right!" was the violent reply.

"I'm going to ask Miss Drowdy," said Temple.·

Mrs. Wilson clutched at her companion again.

"No, no, don't ask her!" she exclaimed.   "If you do she never 'll git over my speakin' to you.   She thinks such a lot of you!"

"I shall have to ask her," repeated Temple.

Mrs. Wilson sat suddenly down in the nearest chair.

"You mustn't tell her I've said anything, then."

Temple paused an instant.

"No," she replied, "I won't tell her."

She opened the door and walked out of the room.   But she returned immediately, standing just within the door, and looking at the woman sitting there.

"I want to say," began Temple, hesitatingly, "that I can't believe you think I've been doing anything wrong—that is, anything very wrong."   The pronouncing these words was a penance that Temple was resolved to perform.

"Course I don't," was the eager reply.   "I tell um you're jest kinder thoughtless, 'n' don't mean nothin'."

"No," said Temple, still intent upon the penance, " I'm not thoughtless ; and I meant to have some kind of amusement or pleasure."

22

Mrs. Wilson's jaw fell as she looked at Temple standing there.

"You meant to?" she gasped, rather indefinitely.

"Yes.   Now I'm going."

Temple hurried away.   She scrambled up into the saddle, and Mrs. Wilson saw her gallop down the road.

Mr. Wilson turned from a closet where he was trying to find a paper of late beans for planting.   He glanced at his wife.

"What in thunder you be'n up to now?" he asked, "'n' where be them yeller-eyed beans, anyway?"

Mrs. Wilson answered the last question first.

"They're on the top shelf to your left hand, marked Y. E."

"The devil!   I've be'n to that paper bag half a dozen times, 'n' I thought 'twas Young Eagle tomatuses."

"You ain't very bright," was the response.   "Beans don't feel much like tomato seed.   Wall, I've been and spoke to her, jes' 's I said I would."

Mr. Wilson stepped down from the chair on which he had been standing.

As he did so the paper bag he held in his hand burst open, and the yellow eyes scattered on the floor.

"You was more of a darn fool than common, then," he remarked, with husbandly frankness.

Then his curiosity got the better, and he asked,

"What d' she say?"

"She said she hadn't done it thoughtlessly, but on purpose."

"Done what?" with masculine obtuseness.

"Do be as bright as you can, Mr. Wilson," returned his wife.   Then her temper triumphed, and she snapped,

"Done nothin', you great gump you!"

And she flounced out of the room.

Thereupon Mr. Wilson went clumsily down on his knees to gather up the yellow-eyed beans.

Temple, riding swiftly along in the beautiful solitude of

the country road, seemed to herself not to be thinking of anything definitely.

It appeared to her, not that Mrs. Wilson's words had effected anything, but that the time had come for a crisis.

As she turned into Almina's yard she heard, through an open window, Almina's thin, piercing treble singing :

> " So noble a Lord
>   None serves in vain ;
> For the pay of my love
>   Is my love's sweet pain.
>
> " In the place of caresses
>   Thou givest me woes;
> I kiss thy hands
>   When I feel their blows."

Temple stopped her pony and leaned forward to his neck, listening for the rest of the words. She knew them well ; it was she who had taught the old Sequidilla to Miss Drowdy, whose imaginative, pious mind had absorbed the lines and their meaning immediately.

The singer cleared her voice, and then went on, at a higher pitch than before :

> " I die with longing
>   Thy face to see ;
> And sweet is the anguish
>   Of death to me.
>
> " For because Thou lovest me,
>   Lover of mine,
> Death can but make me
>   Utterly Thine !"

The mingling of what seemed like human passion with sacred longing gave a strange power to these old verses, a power not dependent upon the skill with which they might be sung.

As Almina ceased singing she came forward to the open door.

"That you?" she asked, blushing at having been heard. "I've been keepin' the lamb-stew hot for you."

Sally stepped out of the woodshed, walked up to her mistress, and took her from the pony.

"He's been a-waitin' fur yo', honey," she said, in a whisper.

Temple shrank as she asked, "Who is waiting?"

"Mr. Boynton, ob co'se. He say I needn't tell Miss Drowdy. He's under de pine."

Temple stood hesitating an instant.

The pine-tree was on a knoll at the back of the house. She had sat there several times with Boynton.

After a moment she walked there now.

Boynton rose from the bench at the tree trunk.

"I forgot to ask you to set the hour for our ride to-morrow," he said, as she approached. "I—" Here he paused suddenly, not finishing his sentence.

"What has happened?" he asked, quickly.

A color was rising to his face. He clasped his riding-stick with both hands, fearing that his hands might tremble.

There was something in the aspect of the woman before him which made her more intoxicatingly attractive than she had ever been. And these weeks of companionship with her had gradually undermined his resisting power.

Besides, he was not a man who intended to resist forever. There is to many fastidious natures almost as much enjoyment in a certain sort of combat as in the yielding. And there is always before these natures the thought of the hour of surrender.

Directly now as he looked at Temple, Boynton knew that he could not help the coming of some words he had thus far rigidly held back.

As Temple did not immediately reply, Boynton repeated his inquiry; but before she could speak he advanced a step and said, almost in a whisper,

"Do sit down."

Temple obeyed.

Yucatan had come with her, and now placed himself beside her.

She glanced at him, and suddenly started to her feet.

"I don't want him to be here now!" she exclaimed. "I cannot have my dog with me now!" Then, seeing her companion's uncontrollable look of surprise, if not alarm, she resumed her seat, smiled constrainedly, and said,

"You know one cannot account for the whims of a nervous woman."

Boynton, who had also seated himself, now rose.

"You are tired, Mrs. Mercer. Perhaps I ought to go? Only," with a change of voice, "it is very hard to go."

She looked up at him as she responded,

"You may stay—a moment."

She turned to the dog again.

"Yucatan," she said, "go—go back to the house!"

As the dog slowly rose his mistress bent down to him with a quick, ardent movement, and pressed his head between her hands in a way she had when caressing him.

Yucatan gazed up wistfully at her.

Then he walked deliberately towards the house, and disappeared through the open door.

Temple gazed after him with an intenseness for which Boynton could not account.

Then she turned towards the man near her, and seemed to be waiting for him to speak.

He did not at first find it possible to say a word.

For some indescribable reason to him their attitude towards each other seemed now full of a sweet significance. And yet nothing had happened, apparently.

Was it merely that the hour had struck?

This was what Boynton asked himself. And he longed to know what, just now, this woman was asking herself.

And why had she sent away the dog?

The excitement upon him was growing so intensely penetrating that he felt that he could not much longer keep up any semblance of calmness.

He leaned forward with his elbows on his knees, his hands still grasping his stick.

"Somehow I didn't feel as if I could speak to any one—not even Miss Drowdy," he said, "so I rode up that cart-path, and left my horse hitched down there while I waited. Sally said she would tell you."

He was conscious of a feeling of triumph in the appearance of intimacy at which these words hinted. And he watched Temple to see if she resented this intimacy. But her face told him nothing. It was downcast; the thick, light lashes seemed to veil more than her eyes.

Still he allowed himself to fancy something to suit his own wishes.

She had never snubbed him. She had had plenty of opportunity to do so. Therefore—here his vanity rose confident.

"I've made a mistake—a horrible mistake," he suddenly exclaimed, with some violence, rushing pell-mell into a subject which he had been longing to mention to Temple.

She now turned slightly towards him, but she did not raise her eyes as she said,

"We are always making mistakes, I think."

"Yes, I know. But this is a very bad one."

He put his hand into the inner pocket of his coat and drew out a letter. He extended it towards her, saying,

"This note came to me two days ago. Mrs. Mercer, will you read it?"

Temple just glanced at the writing on the envelope. She drew back a little, and made a sign of negation.

"Then I will tell you," hurriedly—"I must tell you, Mrs. Mercer. Miss Wallis wrote this note. There are not many words in it. She says she is convinced that it will be better to discontinue our engagement."

"Oh!"

Temple's voice uttered the exclamation sharply. She threw back her head, and her eyes flashed over her companion. But they seemed to flash in dew.

"She loves you," she said. Her voice trembled.

Boynton's head drooped. He knew very well that Amy Wallis loved him ; but how could that be helped? Still, it was unfortunate. But, however unfortunate, a man never grieves too much because some woman loves him, even when he cannot return that love.

"And I," began Boynton—"I thought I loved her. I have a sincere affection for her. Mrs. Mercer—" Here a pause that was full of meaning. He went on now quickly, like a horse who breaks from a hesitating trot into a full gallop :

"Mrs. Mercer, perhaps I'm going to offend you. I can't help it. I can't see you another hour just as a mere friend. I tell you "—in a more intense tone—"I tell you, it is beyond human endurance to go on in this way. I thought I could bear it ; I thought I could not live without it—the seeing you, you know. Only to have the right to meet you just as all others meet you. I was sure I could endure that, and be thankful for that. Well—"

Here Boynton arose and stood in front of Temple, gazing down at her, his eyes emphasizing his words dangerously.

He was silent an instant, the silence enveloping the two in that wonderful way which is so much more powerful and insinuating than words can be.

Boynton looked at Temple's hands lying clasped in her lap. He did not quite dare to take possession of them. He had, possibly, already dared too much.

He had long prided himself upon not having Puritanic ideas about anything. He did not have Puritanic ideas concerning marriage. And, moreover, he was sure that there was no love between Richard Mercer and his wife. He did not think there ever had been. He understood their marriage well enough. It must have turned out a horrible mistake for the wife.

This belief and these thoughts were confusedly in the man's mind now as he stood there in front of Temple.

And he was growing more and more bewildered.

He was not so unsophisticated as to think that a woman's silence always means assent. He knew very well that it may mean revulsion and repulsion.

"You know I loved you when we used to meet on the French Broad," he said. "I've loved you ever since I knew you. And I cannot help it. There are some things that are stronger—that overcome us, Temple!"

He bent down towards her, and put out a hand to touch her.

She did not shrink away, but she looked up at him, and his hand dropped to his side.

"Oh, I love you!" he exclaimed. "You must have known it all this time! You must! And you are not going to be cruel to me now?"

Again he came nearer to her. This time he put his hand on her clasped fingers.

"Please don't touch me," she said.

He drew back. His face became almost purple as he gazed down at her. He raised his head, that his breath might come more easily. But he could not find the power to withdraw his eyes from her face.

"It's all my fault," she said, at last.

"It's your fault that I love you," he said, eagerly, "because you are what you are. But you can't help that."

"Yes, it is my fault," Temple repeated.

She unclasped her hands and put one of them to the back of her head, pressing it there.

"I wanted to try to find something to amuse me," she said.

"What?"

The blood left the man's face. His nostrils dilated.

"What did you say?"

"I wanted to be amused," she repeated, "and I thought that was your wish also. Other women seem to find amusement this way."

"But you?" harshly.

"Oh, don't make me say it!" piteously, still with her hand to her head.

She was now looking full into Boynton's eyes.

He could not for the life of him have found a word to describe what he saw in those eyes.

He was tingling with the raging of mortified vanity, and with what he called a love repulsed. He was beside himself with the intensity of his anger and humiliation. And in the midst of it all he still felt the same attraction to this woman—the charm which one personality sometimes has for another.

"Yes," he said, " say it. Don't mind my feelings."

He laughed. He wanted to laugh ferociously. "Did you find it entertaining, Mrs. Mercer?"

"No," she answered, still in the same piteous way.

"Dull, perhaps?" with suppressed fury, and that self-scorn which a vain man finds the very worst thing to endure.

"Yes," she replied, "very dull."

"And I wasn't even amusing?"

Temple looked about her as if seeking something she did not find.

"Other women, they say, like to have admirers," she went on. "I hoped the seeing you would take up my mind — turn it in another channel. They've told me I must turn my mind in another channel. Miss MacCallum insisted upon that. She thought I was morbid, abnormal. I was so different from her, you see, that I must be abnormal."

"Your playing with me proves you to be strictly womanly and normal."

Boynton spoke bitterly enough, but he was getting himself a little in hand.

"Playing with you?" She looked at him beseechingly. "Oh no, I didn't do that."

"Didn't you?"

"No."

Boynton turned away. He went a short distance down the slope of the knoll. He had never been so bewildered in his life. And he thought he had never suffered so much.

He came back again.

"I seem to be a failure in every particular," he said. "I didn't even furnish you with amusement."

Temple did not reply.

"Why did you send Yucatan away?"

Boynton put this question suddenly.

"Because"—Temple blushed painfully—"because he is so loyal and noble. I was ashamed before him."

"And you are not loyal?"

"Oh no. I—I hardly know what I am. But in my heart I am loyal."

"If you ever love," began Boynton, "you will then know what suffering is."

"Shall I?"

"Yes—a thousand times, yes."

"Oh, that is what I always said," exclaimed Temple, distressfully. "My mother was wretched because she loved my father. She told me true! She told me true!"

"What did she tell you?"

Boynton could not help asking this question. And he waited for the answer with absorbing interest.

"That I must never marry for love."

"Ah!"

The man's eyes flashed.

"And you obeyed her?"

Temple tried to recover her self-control.

She glanced towards the house, hoping to see Sally or Miss Drowdy approaching.

She asked herself in dismay where was her old spirit, her old, fiery independence. Was that girl who rode among the mountains gone forever?

"You haven't any right to ask me such a question," she said, at last.

"No; not the least right in the world," said Boynton, savagely, "but I ask it all the same."

Silence on Temple's part. She leaned heavily against the tree trunk.

"What sort of a woman are you?" he cried.

" A cold-blooded being, who means to take life easily," was the reply, in a mechanical voice.

" That is false.   No one can believe that," Boynton broke out.   " You can love.   Nature never gave those eyes to a woman who could not love.   And I have heard you sing, I have heard you play the violin.   Oh, Temple " — his voice breaking with emotion — "do you remember those days ?"

Temple's head was thrown back against the trunk of the pine ; her lips were parted ; her eyes upon Boynton.

And yet, somehow, there was a remoteness in her aspect that chilled the man.

He was not one who readily believed appearances that were adverse to him.

" I remember them," she said.

" And can you be hard to me ?   You have been playing with me ?   Oh, that is incredible !"

Temple said nothing.   She was very pale.   Her lips seemed to be growing stiff.

" I love you so !" Boynton suddenly murmured, in a beseeching way.   Then, with a bitter after-thought, " And I have not even amused you !"

Temple put her hand on the arm of the bench and helped herself to rise to her feet.

" I think I will go into the house," she said.

Boynton stepped forward coldly.   " Let me help you," he said.

But she shook her head.

She walked slowly forward.   Boynton stood watching her. When she had nearly reached the door she turned and looked at him.   Her lips moved.   He thought she said, " Forgive me."

He hurried down the slope, mounted his horse, and rode away.

" What a blind fool I have been !   What a blind fool I have been !"

He shouted these words aloud to the solitude.   He had a

wish to torture himself physically that he might forget his wounded vanity.

She had tried to amuse herself, but she had not succeeded even in that attempt.

He had never for one instant suspected the truth. He would have suspected any one in the wide world sooner than this woman—even Amy.

As the thought of Amy came to him, it was as if a cool and comforting hand were laid on a burning wound.

Of course he did not deserve to be comforted, but he longed for comfort as strongly as if he deserved it, for that is the way of poor human beings.

Before nightfall Boynton was entering Boston. He had taken the first train to that city.

In the first part of the journey he was thinking that he would tell Amy everything; in the latter part he decided that it was quite unnecessary. He would go back to his betrothed with such eagerness that she would understand that she was dearest of all the world to him. She would certainly understand that after a while.

His self-love would soon be rehabilitated in the atmosphere of her loving admiration. And he was right in his calculation.

Temple, when she reached the door of the kitchen, paused and leaned against it.

Miss Drowdy was standing by the stove stirring something in a kettle.

She glanced up and dropped the spoon.

"Why, Temple!" she exclaimed.

She ran forward and put her arm about her guest. She led her to the bedroom and saw her lie down.

"You mustn't git so faint!" exclaimed Almina. "Here, 'tis two hours after your dinner-time. I'll bring you a beat-up egg."

But Temple clung to her friend's hand.

"Wait," she said.

"No, I sha'n't wait."

“ But I want to say something to you.”

Almina was at the door.   She paused to answer.

“ You may say it when I come back.”

A few minutes later, when Temple had drank a glass of milk and egg, she sat up in bed and again seized her companion’s hand, her pallid face and strained eyes hinting at her emotion.

“ I think something is going to happen to me,” she said.

“ You’re just nervous,” was the soothing reply.   “ You go to sleep ’n’ rest you.”

“ I should like to rest,” was the answer.

A pause.   But the hold on Almina’s hand did not relax.

“ I’m going to be ill,” said Temple.   “ Never mind contradicting me.   I want to tell you something first.   I want to say it while I have my mind clear.

“ Richard has been very busy—too busy to come here, of course.   And he knows I’ve been improving.   I told him that Mr. Boynton was here, and he wrote that he hoped my old friend would make the time pass more pleasantly for me. I hoped so, too.   But I wasn’t going to talk about that.   It was something else I wanted to say.   And you must understand.   Will you understand?   Surely?   Surely?”

“To be sure I will ; yes, indeed,” Almina hastened to say, conscious of a growing anxiety, but trying to speak calmly.

“ If I’m not ill, or if I get well, you are to keep what I tell you a solemn secret as long as you live ?”

Temple’s serious, intense eyes were fixed on Almina.

“ Yes.”

“ Is it a promise ?”

“ Yes.”

Temple withdrew her hand and pressed it upon her bosom.

“ If I don’t get well, tell Richard I love him—not loved him ; for I shall keep on loving him whether I’m living or dead.   I love him !   Oh, make him know it !   Not affection, not liking ; but love—love !   I know why he married me— to help him in his work.   I know why he thinks I married him—and I remember all my mistaken thoughts at the time. But no matter about all that. I must be quick. Are you listening? I love him! And it's killing me. I thought I was really better. But I don't think I want to be better. What is the use? Dear Richard! Dearest! Dearest! Oh, I love you!"

Temple sank down on the bed. Her eyes closed. But she seemed conscious, for she was smiling.

Suddenly she opened her eyes again. They did not look quite the same.

"Laura, you know I have not the 'ecstatic temperament,'" she said, in an unnatural voice. "That is why I cannot love, perhaps. You need not laugh at me, Laura. It's like being protected by proof armor—to have a cold temperament."

" EMOTIONALIZING "

"I SEEN the colored woman riding by on that pony, 'n' the pony was goin' like possessed; 'n' I thought something was up; 'n' I told my husband to go right over to Alminy's 'n' borrer a nutmeg. 'N' he went; 'n' he come back, 'n' he said Mis' Mercer was took real sick, 'n' Sally'd gone for the doctor; 'n' that was when I seen her go by."

Mrs. Hitty Blake was relating this tale to three neighbors who stood in her yard that afternoon towards sunset. One had come to swap a dozen Plymouth Rock eggs for a dozen of what she called "Braymy" eggs; another to get a "receipt" for making gingerbread that should be soft, and yet not too soft; and the third to complain that the rose-bush that Mrs. Blake had given her had refused to live, and was now as "dead as a nit."

But all three of them forgot their errands in the interest of the news.

"So she's really sick?" asked the rose-bush woman. "She's got something besides nerves now, 'ain't she? I 'ain't no patience with nervous women, for my part. My husband says if I ever show any signs of nerves he'll clear out for good 'n' all."

"Where's that feller she's be'n ridin' round with constant?"

"I guess Alminy 'll have her hands full," remarked the seeker for a soft gingerbread recipe. "But you can't do nothin' with Alminy. She kinder appears 's if she was goin' to yield, but she ain't goin' to, all the same. I guess I'll go over 'n' offer to watch."

"I've be'n over myself," now said Mrs. Blake, "'n' they said they was goin' to try to git 'long 's long 's they could themselves."

"Miss Mercer's really got something the matter of her now, 'ain't she?" was the renewed inquiry.

"Oh yes. There ain't no doubt of it. Some kind of a fever, the doctor said; he couldn't for certain tell what kind, yet."

"I hope 'tain't ketchin'."

"I guess not. My husband said he heard down to the village that that feller who's be'n ridin' with Mrs. Mercer had gone off, bag 'n' baggage."

She who was in search of "Braymy" eggs now shook her head and averred that she believed that folks didn't know what 'd be'n goin' on, and she thought, for her part, that if that young woman had really got a husband he'd better be round himself.

Here Mrs. Blake took occasion to state that she had always kinder pitied Mrs. Mercer; she couldn't help it. There was something in Mrs. Mercer's face that, somehow or other—

At this point she was interrupted by the rose-bush woman, who proclaimed that she had felt jest so, exactly. "She s'posed Mrs. Mercer couldn't be expected to be jest like Hoyt folks; but, then, everybody couldn't be Hoyt folks."

The neighbors were hardly done with talking of Temple's seizure, when it became known that a woman doctor had come all the way from Carolina to take care of that young woman who was sick at old maid Drowdy's.

Some asserted that this new-comer could not be a real doctor, being female; that she was probably one of "them new kind of nusses."

This latter doubt has never been absolutely laid at rest in the town of Hoyt.

There are people there now who maintain that Mrs. Ammidown was only a nuss; others believe that she was just as much a doctor as any man doctor that ever was in the world.

Meantime Mrs. Ammidown took the responsibility of the care of Temple. She skilfully guided the old-fashioned doctor who had nominal charge of the case, so that while she respectfully deferred to him, she really brought him round to what she thought was the best method of treatment.

As she sat hour after hour by Temple's bedside, none could know better than she that the treatment could not be much more than judicious nursing. She was physician enough to be aware that in most cases it was the nursing, and not the medicine, that assisted nature.

She had not paused a moment after she had received Almina's telegram. In an hour she was in the train speeding northward. At the railroad station, before she started from Asheville, she had telegraphed to her brother, who was in California, called there by unexpected business.

Almina had also telegraphed to Mercer, who had never failed to keep her informed of his address.

But California was a great distance away. It had never seemed so far away to Mrs. Ammidown as it did now while she watched by Temple.

But what was the good of Richard's coming? If his wife lived, it would be but the old life again.

And that old life, Mrs. Ammidown, with all her keen insight, had never been able to understand. She thought many things, but she was sure of none.

Temple talked a great deal in her delirium, but her words were mostly of her work with her husband—of her longing to help him.

Sometimes she sang hymns before the crowd of people. Sometimes she was playing her violin. Then she was talking with those who came to her about their eternal salvation.

Painfully restless she was. Sally would lift her in her arms and carry her about the house wrapped in a blanket.

The Newfoundland stalked after the yellow woman and her burden, his head and tail drooping.

When at last Sally put her mistress down on the bed again, Yucatan laid himself on the floor close to the bed.

23

He would gaze mournfully and intently into Mrs. Ammidown's face until that woman would murmur,

"Oh, don't, Yucatan! We'll do all—all that we can do."

Sometimes the dog would lift himself, place his front paws on the bed, and reach forward to lick the face on the pillow.

This almost always made Temple put out her hands and cry,

"Oh, why have you taken my own dog from me? My true love! My loyal one! He loves me! I tell you there is one who loves me!"

Yucatan would whine a little. He kept very quiet in the sick-room, and he would not be driven from it.

Mrs. Ammidown, sitting by the bed, thought at such moments that she noted a revealing emphasis in that phrase,

"There is one who loves me."

But she knew her thoughts might be baseless. She was really sure of nothing but that Temple had been changed by her marriage from a happy, natural, wild-spirited girl to— alas! what was she now?

Even in this illness Temple's darkened and perturbed mind held to its resolution to conceal her secret.

She had spoken once, just once, and she could trust Almina. Oh yes, she could surely trust her.

In that strange, confused space of time after that last interview with Boynton, Temple had thought hurriedly that it could be but natural and reasonable that she should wish Richard to know, after she was dead, that she had loved him.

She had tried with all her strength to think clearly in that half-hour. He must not know the truth while she lived. The knowledge would but be a burden to him. How nobly and strongly he would try to respond to that love! And how unhappy he would be because he could not!

Such a knowledge would hinder him in his work ; and he loved his work.

But to know the truth after she was gone. It was not possible there could be any harm in that.

She was sentimental and morbid, very likely.

But, really, she could not help telling Almina. And she could trust Almina.

It would be such a good thing for her to die now.

Then, perhaps, she could forget the evil impulse that had made her renew her acquaintance in that way with Boynton.

But the wish to take up her mind had been so strong, and she was sometimes reckless. And Richard had not cared to come back once to see how she was getting on. But Richard was right. She had written him that she was gaining every day. Of course, there was no need for him to leave his work and come.

Certainly, Richard was right, as usual.

And the only way out of it all was to die.

She wondered how women could possibly be amused by any kind of a flirtation. She had tried it faithfully, and there was not the least bit of amusement in it.

Perhaps it would do her good to sing. Yes, she would sing. There would be nothing in a hymn that would betray her secret.

While she lived it must be a secret, for the knowledge would trouble Richard. She didn't wish to trouble him.

It had been a strange happiness to tell of her love, to say aloud to some one that she loved him. To call him " Dearest." That was what he was: Dearest—oh, thousands of times dearest.

But even if she were crazed, in her illness, she should not tell that.

And perhaps illness and death would wash out that foolish sin of kindness to Boynton.

Yes, she would sing.

But instead of singing she began to recite, she knew not why. She spoke in that hollow but piercing and insistent voice which is so dreadful to hear from the sick.

She fixed her eyes immovably upon Mrs. Ammidown's face.

> " ' He turned his charger as he spake,
>   Beside the river shore ;
> He gave his bridle-rein a shake,
> With adieu for evermore,
>   My dear !
> Adieu for evermore !' "

Without taking her gaze from her companion, Temple laughed slightly as she remarked,

"Isn't it singular that people seem to regard those lines as sad ? Why, there's nothing so cheerful in the world ! If I die, Laura—and I shall die if it's a possible thing—I want you to have a little slab, just a bit of a slab of marble, at my feet—mind you put it at my feet, to keep them down so that they need not follow Richard—and you may put on it,

> " ' Adieu for evermore,
>   My dear !
> Adieu for evermore !'

"That will be such a good joke. Richard will laugh—if he has time. And now, Laura Ammidown, you are the woman who believes in love and who married for love. That's a good joke too. That's the best joke of all—to marry for love. But there are people who do it. My mother did it. But I wasn't such a fool. Dear friends, I will pray."

Then Temple prayed, passionately believing God was her listener, and that He heard her beseech Him in public and in private.

But after a little the voice wavered, then started on again with :

> " ' He turned his charger as he spake
>   Beside the river shore—' "

Here the voice ceased, and Temple was as silent for hours following as if she could not speak.

Mrs. Ammidown nerved herself to hear and see Temple thus.

She sat by the bedside, or she lay on a couch near, while

Sally and Miss Drowdy waited upon her, bringing everything, doing everything, she ordered. She and the Newfoundland watched, hardly knowing day from night.

And nothing was heard from Mercer.

His sister telegraphed again, saying, as she had done in the first message, "Reply."

This time an answer came from the town where she had addressed him in California. It was from the office, and said,

"Mercer gone to Red Cañon. Expected back daily. Left no address."

Mrs. Ammidown stood by the bedside holding the bit of paper in her hand.

It had been Temple's worst day.

She lay now with her eyes shut. She bore very little resemblance to herself. She was not merely haggard; the hand of illness had moulded her face into something terribly different—some horrible mask seemed to hide the real face.

She was no longer so restless. Her hands lay outspread on the white bed-cover.

The form of the skull was plainly discernible on forehead and temples.

Mrs. Ammidown thrust the paper into her pocket.

There was nothing more to be done—absolutely nothing.

She would wait. She did not yet despair, for she had great faith in her patient's youth and strong constitution.

She wished her brother were not so far away. It seemed as if Red Cañon might as well be out of the world. And if he knew— Mrs. Ammidown counted up the days that it would take for him to come in the very fastest manner.

"By that time," she thought, "she will be recovering, or—"

The woman compressed her lips.

She heard Temple say, in a half-whisper,

"They've hidden my violin."

It was three days later that the unwearied watcher knew that her charge was going to live.

In the morning of the third day Temple's face, worn and wasted as it was, had ceased to look like a mask.

Then she began to gain ; in two days more she began to gain rapidly.

She wanted Yucatan to sit close to the bedside, and put his head down on her extended hand. Thus the two would look at each other. Sometimes she would kiss his head. The tears would drop from her eyes.

"You needn't think I am crying," she said once, glancing up and seeing Mrs. Ammidown looking at her.

"It is very evident that you are not crying," was the response.

"They are tears that wash away evil," said Temple. "I don't think my soul is so oppressed."

"Because your body is not so oppressed," explained the other.

"Have it just as you please. I'm going to call it my soul."

Temple's hollow face and great eyes showed the ecstasy of returning life. She felt this ecstasy, notwithstanding that she was telling herself that she did not understand it, and she had no right to feel it.

"I'm going down to my mountains," she said, "though the world is beautiful everywhere."

She was gazing out through the open window. It was June.

"It is a curious thing," remarked Mrs. Ammidown that afternoon, as she sat and contemplated Temple, who lay on the bed propped high with pillows—"a curious thing that you seem to be a frank sort of person ; you don't seem to be concealing anything ; and of course I'm sure that I have penetration ; and yet there is one thing about which I have never been able to decide in my own mind."

"And what is that ?"

Mrs. Ammidown hesitated an instant, then she answered, "It is whether you love Richard, or don't love him."

Temple's eyes had been full upon her sister's when these

unexpected words were spoken. The eyes did not lower or blench, but an obscuring expression, almost like a shadow, came over them.

She gave no answer whatever, and directly Mrs. Ammidown made some casual remark.

After a little time Temple said that she hoped that Richard had not been sent for on account of her illness. It would be too bad to interrupt his work.

"Most certainly he has been sent for," was the prompt reply.

Temple's eyelids suddenly fell as if they were too heavy. She shut her mouth tightly.

"You were so ill that I did not dare not to send," responded the other woman.

"He has not been here?" in a stiff voice.

Then Mrs. Ammidown explained.

A moment later the silence which had followed was broken by Temple. She leaned forward and touched her companion with a cold hand.

"Do you think he can be ill?" she asked.

Mrs. Ammidown shook her head.

"If he were he would surely send to me," she answered.

"Not to me?" said Temple.

In spite of herself a tremor went over the woman at hearing Temple's voice saying "Not to me?"

"He knows you are ill," she said, hurriedly—"at least, he must know by this time."

Temple said nothing for a long while. Then she spoke to ask if Laura would not telegraph immediately to Richard —tell him there was no need for him to come. He might get the message in time to prevent his starting.

"I insist," she said, harshly.

So the message was written, and Sally was sent on the pony to the station, where it could be despatched.

Meantime, seeing her patient adverse to sleep, Mrs. Ammidown began to try to amuse her by speaking of various things.

"You remember Link Dalvecker?" she asked, at last.

"Yes," was the answer, without much apparent interest.

"And you know there's a family of six girls up at the head of Cain Creek—named Pace?"

"I know them.   Girls with bright eyes and red cheeks?"

"Who will soon be faded-eyed and flabby-cheeked," added Mrs. Ammidown.   "Well, Link is going to marry the oldest one; I heard this before I came North to take care of you; and Link's mother tells everybody that her son couldn't really make urp his mind ter marry thur Crawford gal, though thur Crawford gal use ter curm over to court him."

Temple smiled languidly.

"That's maternal devotion," she remarked.   After a moment's silence, she added, "I hope Link will be happy.   I was always fond of Link."

She said no more.

The day was wearing on towards sunset, and Temple had been helped to a chair by the window.   She sat there with many pillows behind her.

The red sunshine was on her figure and streaming across the room.   It fell also upon the dog, who was lying soundly sleeping close beside her.

The dog had grown gaunt and thin in the past ten days.

Suddenly he sat upon his haunches, his head raised and ears cocked.

There was so much of excitement in his whole appearance that Temple became excited also.   She tried to sit upright, but she could not.   She sank back again on her pillows.

"What is it, old fellow?" she asked.   "Don't go on like that.   He isn't near."

As she spoke the last word she was aware that some one was crossing the next room.

Yucatan leaped forward, barking sharply.

Mercer thrust aside the dog with a strong sweep of his arm.

He knelt down by his wife's chair.

For the first time Temple could not keep from her face the feeling in her heart.   And Mercer saw that look.

He rose quickly.   He gathered the slight form up in his arms.   He did not know what words burst from him.   He felt that he could never find phrases of love strong enough.

He sat down, holding Temple closely.   His face was wet with tears, and his tremulous lips but half obeyed him in his attempts to speak.

"Oh, my love !   Oh, my love !"

This was the first that Temple could distinguish as she lay with her face pressed against his breast.

She lifted her head.

"Why, you love me, Richard ?"   She whispered this, withdrawing herself a little that she might look at him.

It seemed to the two as if this were the first time their eyes had ever met.

When he could speak, Mercer said,

" I have loved you ever since I saw you."

After a while Temple, still in her husband's arms, made a movement yet nearer to him.

" I feel as if I should be able to pray again," she said. " Oh, how much one ought to help others when one is happy."

Just before it was dark Mrs. Ammidown came to the door.

" Really," she said, gayly, though her voice was not quite steady, " I am afraid you two are emotionalizing."

THE END

www.ingramcontent.com/pod-product-compliance
Lightning Source LLC
Chambersburg PA
CBHW021723110726
47902CB00005B/1322